ROAD TO ISABELLE

J.C. Bourg

ISBN: 099100762X
ISBN 13: 9780991007622

For Manya

Author's Note

*R*oad to Isabelle is a historical novel. I've attempted to portray an accurate but fictional account of the multicultural players who emerged in the aftermath of the Second World War. My imaginary story lines were drawn from events that did occur or possibly might have. The cast is fictitious. Any resemblance to persons, living or dead, is coincidental.

My honor is loyalty.
—Motto of the Waffen-SS

CHAPTER ONE

It was a sweltering Saigon late Friday afternoon in the summer of 1954. A stern sun hung high in the cloudless sky. Punishing rays sparkled off the French colonial architecture dominating the skyline. Sputtering scooters and bicycles wove through the sluggish flow of belching traffic. Locals migrated on congested sidewalks. Buddhist monks in saffron robes added color to the drifting Vietnamese masses. A warm breeze served a foul, fragrant cocktail of pungent street cuisine, fetid inhabitants, and diesel fumes.

Max Kohl, a broad-shouldered German in a white linen suit, strode confidently down the crowded concrete path. His bleach-blond locks fluttered. The Aryan's deep-blue eyes carefully scanned the surrounding buzz of commerce. Beside the twenty-eight-year-old German, Moua Loc kept pace. The short, wiry Loc was Hmong, a tribesman from the isolated mountains of Laos. In an oversized business suit, Loc's attempt at Western fashion, he resembled a boy playing dress-up. Mimicking his German partner, Loc diligently surveyed their advance. Passing a baker, the duo enjoyed the comforting aroma of fresh bread. In the alley past the bakery, ominous silhouettes danced. Max subtly reached into his suit coat. A callused hand gripped the consoling power of a concealed pistol. The handgun was Soviet made, a rugged and durable TT-30 Tokarev. A captured Russian Tokarev sidearm was considered a prize by the Germans during the Second World War. Max had acquired his weapon off a dead communist in Indochina. Gun in hand, he nodded at Loc. The tribesman accelerated. Within the pedestrian herd, they separated. Passing the potential ambush venue, the tribesman casually waved off the threat.

Reflecting on the Corsican bounty on his head, Max grinned. *It is not the first time I've been stalked by death,* he reflected. *I need to find and kill the Corsican,* he realized. *In a city of motivated cutthroats and thieves, it's just a matter of time before some street punk gets lucky and collects the reward.* Standing beside Loc, Max gazed down the alleyway. Squatting on their haunches, a gaggle of soiled children rummaged through moist garbage. Penetrating sunlight cast skinny orphans' shadows high on a redbrick wall of the narrow passage. Releasing the grip on his shoulder-holstered weapon, Max muttered, "Before returning north, we need to terminate the gangster."

Loc responded with a childish grin common among the hill tribes.

The vigilant trek resumed. Beads of sweat glistened on the German's tan forehead. Moisture flowed beneath the uncomfortable flapping sport coat. Ahead, the Imperial Hotel secured the street corner. Constructed in the 1920s, the Imperial's glory days had expired long ago. Intense sunlight emphasized the fatigue across the hotel's tired French architectural facade. Cracked plaster scars marred the building's face. Rusty and hastily repaired wrought-iron balustrades shielded second-story balconies. Dying plants in mismatching pots skirted the establishment's ground level. Raucous barroom clamor flowed out of the double-wide open door entrance of the weather-beaten hotel carcass.

Standing in front of the Imperial, Loc asked, "Is this the place where we find the American?"

Max nodded. Adjusting the lapels of his wrinkled jacket, he took a deep breath. Boisterous laughter punctuated the cocktail prattle. Max grinned. "Sounds like a gathering of cocky Americans."

"Why are they always so loud?" Loc questioned, squinting into the crowded festivities.

Max chuckled. "Because they won the war."

"The big war?"

"Yah," Max mumbled, stepping into the saloon.

Alcohol-induced dialogues softened. Investigative stares greeted the new arrivals. Max scanned the barroom occupied by segregated racial cliques. Stoic French columns supported a raised ceiling. Rusted base plates secured two long-stem industrial ceiling fans. One worked. Its slowly rotating blades churned a massive cloud of cigarette smoke. A chubby Asian bartender in a white tuxedo jacket stood attentively behind a heavily lacquered wood counter. Perched on a stool, a sleepy Vietnamese hostess in a blue satin dress smiled. A table of slouching local businessmen in dark suits and loose ties caught the

German's eye. The cadre of Asian accountants examined Loc's presence with disdain. Max bristled. *Loc fought communism for these ungrateful, bigoted bastards. I probably should be sympathetic for their ignorance,* he surmised. *Hell, I bathed in the racial poison of the Third Reich.* A soft smirk surfaced. Max placed a protective hand on the tribesman's shoulder. Focused on the table of cultural hate, he calculated a shooting sequence. The mask of death appeared. A businessman gasped. His associates sheepishly retreated into the sanctuary of their cocktails and soft conversation.

Five casually dressed Americans, surrounding a round table laden with beer bottles, flexed. The Yanks' gruff squints challenged the German's demon persona. *Now I know who the warriors in the room are,* Max concluded, softening his scowl. Showing submissive palms, he approached the white patrons.

"*Excusez-moi, messieurs,*" Max offered. "I'm looking for Roche."

"I'm Roche," replied a clean-cut, chiseled Yank in a bright floral shirt and baggy chinos. His close-cropped flat-top salt-and-pepper hair and rigid features clashed with the casual attire. Flicking his head, he asked, "What can I do for you?"

"I am Max Kohl. My associate is Moua Loc. We would like to propose an anticommunist opportunity."

"I know who you are," Roche revealed, pushing back from the table in a squealing chair. "I recognize both of you from my last business trip to Laos." Glancing around at his drinking companions, he snickered. "*Excusez-moi, messieurs.*" Slowly rising, he conceded, "OK, Max, let's grab a quiet table for your presentation."

Max and Loc migrated to the back of the cantina. Roche, heading toward the bar, flashed three fingers. The barkeep nodded and slammed three perspiring bottles of 33 *Biere* on the glossy countertop. The German and tribesman hovered around a vacant corner table while the American scooped up the cold amber bottles.

"Do you mind if we sit facing the door?" Max inquired.

"No problem." Roche nodded. "If I had a Corsican bounty on my head, I would drink with my back to the wall."

Max squinted, taking the coveted seating option. "How do you know about the Corsican contract?"

Roche grinned as he sat down and slid two frothing bottles across the scarred tabletop. "I'm in the information business," he informed them. "It's my job to know." He took a quick glance over his shoulder at the double-wide open entrance. "The Corsicans are formidable adversaries." Focused on the German, he confessed, "Frankly, I'm surprised to see you in Saigon."

Max chuckled. "At Dien Bien Phu, forty-thousand Viet Minh attempted to punch my ticket. Callused by that encounter, I don't consider a Corsican pimp's vendetta a significant threat."

Roche grabbed a cold brew. Leaning back, he nudged, "OK, Fritz, I'm all ears."

Max took a composing breath; his spine stiffened. "I have a friend…a brother…a Composite Airborne Commando—"

"Is he German?" Roche interrupted.

"No," Max responded, shaking his head. "The brother Loc and I owe our lives to is a French Jew." While the American pondered the revelation, Max continued, "Several years ago, Sergent-chef Jean Guillian parachuted into the highlands to organize a guerrilla army. Today, he commands a partisan unit of six hundred battle-tested warriors. Guillian is defying the French order for his withdrawal. He will not abandon his troops." Max squinted hard at Roche. "I'm seeking a patron to finance his tribe's anticommunist struggle."

Roche swallowed.

"Loc and I will assist with the logistics required for a monthly airborne supply drop…"

Roche extended a flexed hand, terminating the presentation. "Max, let me cut you off there. I'm sorry, but the answer is no. The United States has no interest in establishing a resistance movement based on the French model. It is a political no." He took a healthy swig off the cold bottle to dilute the bitter taste of his rejection. "As a veteran," he confessed, "I feel for the idealistic French commando forsaken by his government."

Max's shoulders drooped. Slowly nodding, he muttered, "Thank you for your time." Looking at Loc, he shrugged. Grabbing the cold bottle of pilsner, he toasted, "Thanks for the beer, Yank."

"You're welcome, Fritz." Roche grinned. "Now to salvage your noble and risky quest in Saigon, let me put some feelers out about the location of the Corsican pimp who placed a price on your head."

Max flinched. He shot a curious glance at Loc. Refocused on the American, he questioned, "Why would you do that?"

Roche chuckled. "The Corsicans oppose the American presence in Saigon. The disclosure of the hit man Petru Rossi's whereabouts falls in the category of 'enemy of my enemy is my friend.'"

"Danke." Max nodded.

Roche slowly stood, offering, "Sit back. Enjoy your beers. Let me make a few calls. Hopefully this won't take too long."

Slouching into the German, Loc whispered, "Can we trust the American's information?"

Pondering a response, Max gazed through the smoky barroom haze at the Yank. Leaning against the glossy counter, Roche commandeered a jet-black rotary telephone. "I don't see why not," Max muttered. "We still bear the risk of terminating the gangster. If we succeed, Roche has one less adversary; he spelled it out with enemy of my enemy is my friend."

"That's what I don't understand," Loc confessed, tapping out a Chesterfield from a full pack. "The Americans destroyed your village, killing your family. Are they now friends?"

Slowly nodding, Max conceded, "It's complex, partner." Leaning back, he propped his chair against the back wall. *What is your story?* he pondered, scrutinizing the confident American. From an inside coat pocket, Max produced a long, fat cigar. Delicately, he bit off the tip and shoved nearly half the tobacco log into his mouth. A tarnished Zippo lighter ignited the beast. Tilting his head back, he released an impressive smoke ring into the cracked and stained plaster ceiling. Focused on the dissipating misting circle, he reflected on the war that defined him.

CHAPTER TWO

It was a pleasantly cool, crisp morning in the summer of 1944. The fresh smell of fertile and succulent pastures lingered across the French countryside. Small villages and clusters of tall trees peppered the gently undulating landscape. Livestock grazed in rich green grass. A scraggly strand of tall weeds lined the banks of a meandering creek. Trickling water emitted a melodious tinkle. In the middle of this tranquil setting, a unit of the 12th SS Panzer division scrambled in preparation for battle. A convoy of transport vehicles shrouded in foliage flanked a shallow stone wall. Drivers checked engines. Supplies and equipment were hastily loaded. Troops nervously milled around designated departure points.

Baby-faced seventeen-year-old Max Kohl cinched tight the belt of his pea-and-dot camouflaged tunic. From the coat's pocket, he retrieved a one-inch-diameter shooting-proficiency badge. Swelling with pride, he admired the award in a moist palm. The pin displayed crossed rifles over a target. In the center, a diamond in white and black accented a black swastika. *My time has come*, he realized, pinning the good-luck charm under his collar. A rabble of butterflies fluttered in his belly. Swallowing back surfacing emotion, he reflected on the terror bombing of the homeland that had claimed his parents. Just last night, he awoke to the drone of the enemy bombers en route to deliver their deadly payloads over the fatherland. *My naive parents never realized that Germany and the National Socialists are one in the same*, he regretted. *My father was no more than a gruff bricklayer; Mutti's devotion to the Catholic Church blinded her from the reality of Aryan racial superiority. If there is a god, he certainly wouldn't have a Jewish son. I lectured my parents on the folly of their beliefs*, he sadly recalled, *and now they are no more.* Remorse tugged on his heavy heart as he slung a 98K carbine over a shoulder. *I will make my Furher proud,* he vowed, flexing a thin frame. *We'll drive the invading Tommies back into the sea by week's end.*

A faint hum of aircraft floated out of the cloudless blue sky. Instinctively, Max collapsed and rolled under a transport. His brothers-in-arms clamored, seeking cover. In seconds, all was still. Wisps of dust danced across the staging area. The overhead roar intensified. Out of the rising sun, a squad of Me-109s labeled with the Balkan cross appeared. Skimming treetops, the low-flying German fighter planes' shadows magically drifted across the rolling terrain. Enthusiastically, the boy soldiers emerged, shouting and waving their arms. A trailing Messerschmitt rocked its wings in appreciation. Sporting a wide grin, Max admired the departing specks in the morning sky. *Victory is ours for the taking,* he confidently surmised. Large callused hands latched onto his shoulders. He jumped.

"Are you ready, Maximilian?" Sergeant Franz's gravelly voice questioned. "This is not a drill. The invasion has begun."

"Yes, Sergeant," Max replied, hitting an embarrassing high note. Coughing, he turned to face his mentor.

Battle-hardened thirty-year-old Sergeant Franz was an Afrika Korps veteran. The broad, compact Bavarian's complexion was leather. Deep creases framed focused brown eyes. A scraggly scar traversed his forehead. When it came to Max, the chiseled Franz had a soft spot. Was it because Max hailed from the state of Bavaria? Or was it that he admired the boy's amazing marksman talent? During the expedited six-week basic training in Belgium, he informed Max that his parents had perished. The boy accepted the news like a disciplined soldier. It really didn't matter. Franz just liked the kid. "Just remember my sharpshooting *kamerad*," Franz informed his protégé. "Unlike the cardboard targets you trained on, Tommy shoots back."

Max cleared his throat of any lingering high-octave notes. In an exaggeratedly deep voice, he responded, "Tommy doesn't stand a chance."

Grinning, the sergeant patted the boy's shoulder.

"Mount up," an officer barked, swirling a finger over his head.

Teenage warriors climbed into transports. Engines coughed to life. Exhaust fumes polluted the country air. On a dusty road, a caravan of fanatic youths rolled toward the coast. Helmeted heads bobbed in the jostling journey toward the unknown. The young troops sat in silence. Tension was thick. Beside Max, the acne-infested Hocker leaned forward and fired an impressive stream of vomit on the truck bed. Sour faces acknowledged the regurgitated stench. Max placed a consoling hand on his comrade's arched back as Hocker spewed the last of his breakfast.

The winds of war had shifted on the Third Reich. Colossal military defeats had drained Germany of its military manpower. Desperate, Germany initiated a new recruitment policy. The fatherland sought volunteers from the ranks of the Hitler Youth. Dedicated to the National Socialist cause, seventeen- and eighteen-year-old boys enlisted in what would become the 12th SS Panzer *Hitlerjugend*. To add combat expertise to the untested boy soldiers, the division was seasoned with battle-tested veterans.

It was hot, muggy. Dust tormented all but the lead vehicle. The apprehensive young cargo scanned the cloudless sky for enemy aircraft. Nodding, Max concluded the Luftwaffe had cleansed the royal-blue heavens of those bastard Brits. Drifting past an apple orchard, he spotted a French farmer, waving at the parade of mechanized bushes. Envisioning biting into a succulent, ripe red sphere, he swallowed. *How much longer?* he wondered, checking his watch for the umpteenth time. The journey was closing in on the four-hour mark. Max fidgeted on the uncomfortable wooden bench with a full bladder. Scanning the young faces under steel helmets, he spotted the puckered gaze of other comrades seeking relief. *Misery loves company.* He sighed. *At least I'm not the only one longing for a healthy piss.*

The transport's wheels locked. Squealing tires skidded to an abrupt termination. A cloud of hot dust blasted the jolted human cargo. Jerking heads surveyed the rural surroundings. At the crossroads of the back-road highway, the caravan yielded to traffic. A massive convoy of German might rumbled through the intersection. The boys cheered at the endless line of rambling armored personnel carriers, antitank guns, radio trucks, command vehicles, and troop transports. Motorcycle dispatch riders buzzed in and out of the growling procession.

A grating crunch freed the transport's tailgate. Looking up at the soiled teenage faces, Sergeant Franz informed the troops, "We may be here for a while. This would be a good time to stretch your legs and take a piss." In unison, combat boots thumped the truck bed. The boy soldiers leaped to their feet. "Stay close to the vehicle!" Franz shouted at the exiting stampede.

In an orderly line beside the camouflaged vehicle, the juvenile warriors showered the dusty road with a steady torrent of urine. Franz joined the boys. Securing his drained manhood, the sergeant, looking down the line, barked, "If you shake it more than three times, you're playing with it."

The focused formation responded with raucous laughter. Distant man-made thunder silenced the levity. Looking up from the roadside urinal, the boys glared at the horizon. Like an approaching storm, the rumble intensified. Barely visible puffs of black smoke appeared above the outlying tree line. Max buttoned his trousers. Retrieving the bolt-action rifle he'd slung over his shoulder, he loaded it with a five-cartridge stripper clip. The click of weapons resonated down the line. Flowing out of the summer sky, a squad of enemy fighter bombers appeared. Beneath the stalking predators, massive chunks of earth erupted. The ground shook. A farmhouse exploded. Random slabs of dismembered livestock hurled into the blue sky. After plowing the fields, the aerial assault swooped down over the idle caravan. A salvo of penetrating rounds tore into the traffic jam. A provisional transport detonated. The truck burst into flames. A fireball rolled skyward. Tracking a low-flying assailant, Max opened fire, his carbine spitting out calculated concentrated rounds. Unscathed, the howling aircraft joined the departing attacking flock flying into the blinding sun. The pop of small-arms fire faded. The flames of the ignited truck crackled. A soft breeze teased the smoldering charred remains of the carcass and body parts encircling the vehicle. Max snorted at the aroma of singed death. Sucking hot air through an open mouth, he felt his heart sink. Sweat flowed out of every pore. Lightheaded, he took a knee. *I missed*, he lamented. *I never miss*. Shocked expressions of disbelief and doubt surrounded him. *We all missed*, Max realized. *Tommy slapped us hard and flew away laughing*. Hyperventilating, he stood defiantly. *My enemy is a formidable opponent*, he concluded, gazing north. *I will not underestimate them again*.

CHAPTER THREE

Rumors of a great war filtered into the Laotian highlands. Mountain ranges and deep ravines blanketed in dense growth dominated the harsh landscape. Towering limestone buttes stood watch over the sharp terrain. In the depths of a narrow gorge, five armed tribesmen in black pajamas, a Hmong boy, and two mountain ponies trekked briskly down a jungle trail. Sunlight sparked above the concealing canopy. Agile sandaled feet treaded lightly. The surefooted horses' hooves clopped on rock shale. The pack animals were a unique breed, short in stature, no more than ten hands high. Their thick manes were cropped short to form a crest. The bay pony was saddled with water flasks and provisions. The sorrel horse was burdened with two large wicker baskets of unrefined black-tar opium balls.

In a black smock and baggy trousers, Moua Teeb, of the Moua clan, led the small trading expedition. Teeb was a short, middle-aged Hmong and wiry thin. A tribal cap encased dark, ratty bird's-nest hair. Proudly, he flaunted a heavy silver torque-ringed necklace. His right hand stabilized the flintlock rifle casually balanced on a shoulder. The long gun barrel swayed back and forth. As a comforting breeze flowed up the trail, he broke into song. Behind him, his brother Kaub and four sons, Leej, Che, Riam, and Loc, joined in the cheerful tune. Glancing over his shoulder, he smiled at his youngest son, Loc. Beaming, the boy bellowed out the familiar song. Loc was the youngest of ten children. His age was unknown, as the hill tribe did not track birthdays. Unlike his father and brothers, his hair was dark brown and he had a pale-yellow almost white complexion.

Loc has a gift for languages and a nose for business, Teeb reflected, refocused on the trail ahead. *I know a few words and phrases of the Fackee (French), but my youngest son can actually converse in their tongue. The boy can read people*, he proudly surmised.

His talents will assist us in negotiating with the lowland inhabitants. Visualizing the city-dwelling Laotians and Chinese merchants, he spat in disgust. *They are all cheats and thieves.*

The forest thinned. A shale overhang provided a scenic view of the valley below. Teeb leaped over a deep rock fissure to gaze at the fertile basin. A patchwork of rich green fields surrounded a frontier town and French garrison. Strings of smoke rose from the rural community. Teeb took a deep breath. Leaving the sanctuary of his mountains always produced angst within him. *The French troops I scouted for have long since departed,* he realized, *the heroics of my youth forgotten. I am just another savage to be exploited by the locals. What surprises await us?* he wondered, resuming the trek.

The grade softened as the mountain path intersected with a rural dirt road. A blistering sun hung high in the deep blue sky. A warm breeze jostled the tall weeds marking the trail. On encompassing undulating hillsides, rice paddies sparkled under nurturing sunlight. In ankle-deep water, a farmer toiled behind a water buffalo. The fatigued Hmong, catching a glimpse of their destination, accelerated. Wood shanties appeared. Teeb squinted at the strange white and red flag fluttering over the French garrison. It appeared to be a red sun dot centering symmetric rays. *Has the great war reached the mountain slopes?* he questioned. *Is a new master ruling the flatlands?* Teeb led the trading party into the frontier town. Pitched thatch-roofed storefronts lined the thoroughfare. A stone communal well anchored the village square. A dust devil swirled down the deserted street. Curious Chinese merchants peered out of shop windows. It was eerily quiet.

Teeb squinted at his younger brother and mumbled, "Where are the *Fackee?*"

The round-faced, flat-nosed Kaub shrugged.

A cloud of moaning dust burst out of the fortified French garrison onto the main drag. Yielding to the oncoming traffic, the Hmong trading party migrated to the side of the road. A dozen khaki-uniformed Asian soldiers, brandishing bolt-action rifles spiked with long bayonets, escorted a parade of twenty battered French soldiers and civilians. The captives' hands were bound behind their backs, their noses impaled with large fish hooks attached to twin tethers. The guards delighted in tugging on the line. Fresh blood glistened around pierced snouts. Desperation, fear, and pain radiated from the bruised and leaking white faces, their tattered clothing speckled with fresh blood. The Hmong traders bowed submissively. The Japanese soldiers disregarded the tribesmen's presence. The procession of misery staggered past the communal well and exited the trading post.

Teeb's stomach churned. *The new masters have cruel hearts.*

"Should we leave?" Kaub questioned.

"We need salt," Teeb mumbled, shaking his head. "Loc!" he called out to his youngest son.

"Yes, *Txiv*," Loc responded, standing before Teeb.

Teeb placed a reassuring hand on his son's shoulder. "Your uncle and I will tend to the horses while you barter." He instructed. "Do the best you can, but conclude quickly. We need to leave this evil place."

Loc nodded.

With a ball of opium in hand, Loc entered a provisioner. His big brothers carried the wicker baskets teaming with the bountiful harvest. Planked flooring creaked. The stagnant air was thick, the shop cluttered. Burlap sacks of rice and salt infested the limited floor space. A startled cat darted for cover. Pots and pans of all sizes hung from the rafters. Under the low cookware ceiling, a confusion of pickaxes, spades, hoes, and sickles lined a wall. Towering stacked bolts of cloth and canvas dominated a corner. Perched on a stool behind a glass counter, the Chinese proprietor sucked on a long, thin-stemmed bamboo pipe. Tobacco smoldered in the pipe's tiny cupped brass bowl. The merchant was old. His long, thinning silver hair was combed back. Out of flared nostrils, smoke flowed down a scraggly mustache into a snow-white beard. Behind the merchant, a Laotian teen stood high on a short ladder. Balanced on the balls of his feet, the young clerk took inventory of the brand liquor lining the top shelf.

"Monsieur," Loc stated, extending his arm with a grapefruit-sized black ball of opium currency.

The shopkeeper removed the pipe from the corner of his mouth and grunted. His young subordinate hopped off the ladder. The expressionless teen walked past Loc and plucked a random tar ball from the basket. After handing the sample to his employer, he began unloading the unrefined opium spheres into the large weight pan of a balancing scale. Leej, Che, and Raim stoically stood watch, cradling long-barrel muskets.

Loc focused on the shopkeeper. The Chinaman clawed at the rough ball with an obnoxiously long fingernail. Peeling off a small sample, he rubbed it between thumb and forefinger into the size of a pea. After an inquisitive sniff, he rubbed it on his tongue. The bitter taste puckered his face. A raised brow confirmed high morphine content. Loc grinned. Retrieving an abacus from under the counter, the Chinaman glared impatiently at his assistant, toying with smaller balancing weights. The scale's teetering beam stabilized. After receiving the results, the opium broker frantically flipped black beads on the manual wood-framed calculator. The clinking beads went silent. The merchant scribbled two numbers on butcher paper. Spinning the page, he presented the offer to the Hmong boy.

Tapping the first number with the freakishly long fingernail, the broker declared in pidgin French, "This is the store credit I'm offering." Identifying the second number, he informed him, "This is the market tax I deducted." Leaning back, he secured the long pipe in the corner of his mouth. After a few long draws, a feather of smoke drifted out of the pipe's brass bowl.

"Pardon, monsieur," Loc inquired. "Is that a French market tax?"

The Chinaman, scowling down at the savage, growled, "Tax is tax."

Loc looked over at his older brothers and shrugged. *Father wants a hasty settlement*, he realized. *But I won't allow this city dweller to cheat us. I saw this thief's delight with our product.* Grabbing the opium ball from atop the pyramid in the weight pan, he tossed it into their wicker basket.

"What are you doing?" inquired the merchant.

"Leaving," Loc snapped, loading up the basket.

"Pourquoi?" the merchant asked.

"No French, no French tax," the boy replied.

Conceding, the Chinaman cleared his abacus and began flipping beads.

Stacked neatly on the rough wooden deck in front of the provisioner were the results of a successful opium harvest. Teeb delightfully admired the pots, pans, bolts of cloth, axes, saws, and precious canvas sacks of salt needed for meat preservation. Playfully, he shook his youngest son's shoulder. *The bartered merchandise far exceeded my expectations*, he realized. Loc beamed. Tugging on the bay horse's lead, Leej positioned him for loading. His brothers began strapping merchandise to the wooden pack saddle.

Cinching a bulging, wet water flask on the sorrel pony, Kaub caught Teeb's eye. Raising a brow, he nodded in the direction of the empty saloon across the street.

Teeb grinned. Scanning the deserted city, he pondered celebrating the successful trade. A distant volley of gunfire terminated the notion. "In the sanctuary of our mountains, we will drink to our good fortune," he declared.

Kaub nodded as a second volley resonated.

A warm breeze stirred dust across the town square. The soiled mist drifted down the deserted main street. Leej slapped the ass of a heavily laden pony. The beast of burden lunged forward. The cadre from the Moua clan was heading home. Teeb paused. His party followed his lead. Out of the dusty haze, laughter approached. A dozen Japanese soldiers casually strolled into town, the wind rustling the neck flaps of their military caps. The setting sun reflected off bayonet-spiked rifles. The Hmong bowed their heads. Gazing down, Teeb focused on the long shadows spilling across the dirt road. The silhouettes approached. A pair of boots stood before him. Spirally wound cloth protected the intruder's ankles and shins. Teeb raised his head. At eye level, he looked into the thick spectacled lenses of a Japanese soldier. The round-framed eyeglasses distorted the Asian's face. The inquisitive soldier smiled. Crooked yellow teeth appeared as he spoke pleasantly and pointed at Teeb's long rifle. Teeb surrendered the weapon. Nodding his appreciation, the soldier examined the flintlock with childish enthusiasm. A uniformed audience peered over his shoulder at the antique. Raising the musket into a firing position, the soldier targeted the end of the road. Glancing at the tribesman, he sought permission. Teeb nodded. The soldier cocked the weapon's hammer and squeezed the trigger. Flint sparked. The antique rifle, snorting sulfur, barked. A sledgehammer recoil staggered the shooter. The Japanese audience burst out laughing. Returning the weapon, the soldier bowed. Teeb nodded. Snickering like children, the troops patted the shooter's back and resumed their leisurely stroll.

Teeb glanced at his docile companions. His sons and brother subtly disengaged anxious trigger fingers. "Let's go home," Teeb announced.

The successful Hmong traders walked out of town into the setting sun. The blinding light radiated just above the mountainous horizon. Dusk approached. On a hillside, laborers toiled in the rich soils with spades. Squinting, Teeb could make out five emaciated whites digging. It was odd to see Fackee shoveling. He stopped. The French were digging graves. Littering the hillside in various poses of death, the white inhabitants of the garrison awaited interment. Bullet holes riddled the corpses. Flies buzzed about. The impaled noses and leashes that led them to slaughter were still in place. Two Japanese soldiers, enjoying cigarettes, supervised the task. The Hmong resumed their trek. Teeb glanced at his brother. Kaub nodded. They knew what they had to do.

A footpath intersected with the rural dirt road. Teeb stopped at the cross-roads. The jungle path parted dense growth and ascended up the foothills into the mountains and home. Teeb placed the butt of his rifle on the ground and poured black powder down the muzzle. A patch and lead ball followed. "Leej," he mumbled.

"Yes, Father," Leej replied, flexing.

Ramming the charge down the muzzle-loading weapon, Teeb informed his eldest son, "I want you and your brothers to take the horses up to the shale rock cliff overlooking the valley and wait for your uncle and me. If we do not get back by dawn's first light, continue on home."

Leej took a deep breath and nodded.

"Loc," Teeb mumbled, securing the ramrod. "Get me my knife."

Loc scurried to a packhorse and retrieved the leather-sheathed blade. Presenting the knife, he admired his father's stoic, confident features. Loc's heart pounded. *Please don't go.*

Teeb drew the wide-bellied blade from its cover and inspected the razor-sharp hand-forged Hmong knife—the perfect tool for cutting, skinning, and close-quarters combat. Securing the weapon, he glanced at his brother. Kaub nodded.

Night came quickly. The jungle trail faded into darkness. Leej yanked on the leash of the lead packhorse. The stubborn animal resisted the steep grade. Frantic hoofs sparked rock shale. A calming whistle soothed the beast. In apprehensive silence, the sons of Moua Teeb trekked. Heavy breathing pierced the night air. Loc glanced over his shoulder. Thoughts of his father tugged on a heavy heart. The embracing forest stirred. A low shadow darted across the path. The blanketing canopy thinned. Overhead, stars sparkled across a black canvas. Moonlight illuminated the rock cliff overlooking the valley. Leej tethered the ponies and grabbed a corked bottle of water from a saddlebag. He leaped over a fissure onto the stone ledge. His brothers followed. Standing in an arc, they peered into the black basin. A soft glow identified the garrison and trading post.

Leej took a refreshing swig of warm water and passed the bottle. "They are coming back," he mumbled to reassure himself and, he hoped, his younger brothers. After the bottle made the rounds, he instructed Che, "Stand watch over the trail."

Che nodded and departed into darkness.

"And don't fall asleep," Leej added over his shoulder. "Riam, it's your turn to tend to the horses," he reminded him.

Begrudgingly, Riam shuffled toward the task.

Leej meandered beside Loc. A good fifteen years separated the brothers. Leej placed a comforting hand on the family's youngest sibling. "You did very well today, little one," he mumbled. "How did you know the merchant would change his offer?"

Focused on the valley below, Loc questioned, "Father is coming back?"

"He always returns from a hunt," Leej reassured him. "Now explain your business magic."

"The Chinaman raised his brow," Loc revealed. "He tried to conceal his delight by toking on the pipe. The flatlanders are not like us. They pride themselves on cheating and deception. When we hunt, we search for tracks and other signs to find our prey. In negotiating with the merchant, I look for tracks and other signs to determine his intentions." With a shrug, he conceded, "Dishonest men are easy to read."

Riam joined his brothers and handed them a strip of dried venison. The three siblings sat cross-legged on the shale overhang. In silence, they gnawed on the tough slabs of meat. Overhead, a crescent moon meandered across the sparkling sky. Random pockets of cold air drifted by. Nocturnal creatures rustled the surrounding brush. Anticipation and anxiety hindered the passage of time.

The horses stirred. The boys leaped to their feet. Out of the depths of the rain forest, Che declared, "They're back!" Jogging up the trail with a heavy load, Che appeared. Across his shoulders dangled the lifeless body of a Japanese soldier. Looking up from beneath the burdensome freight, he gladly informed them, "Father and Uncle are coming." At the edge of the deep fissure, he stopped. Bowing forward, he released the dead weight. The carcass rolled over Che's head into the crevice. A fading, careening thumping tracked the descending cadaver's journey down the narrow shaft.

Uncle Kaub, with a musket slung across his back, plodded into the clearing. "Thanks, Che," he mumbled, extending an arm in the direction of the water bottle. Leej obliged the request. After taking a refreshing gulp, he wiped his lips with a backhand. "Loc, we are going to need more water, and get the dried venison." Glancing down the silent path, he informed his nephews, "Guests will be arriving soon."

Heading toward the packhorses, Loc stopped. His father appeared with another dead man on his back. Plodding past the boy, Teeb headed for the fissure. At the edge of the chasm, he deposited his load. Placing his hands on the small of his back, he stretched. "Missing soldiers don't point fingers," he informed his sons.

"Water, Father?" Loc inquired.

Teeb looked at Kaub. The warriors exchanged solemn expressions of accomplishment. Victorious grins emerged. "Whisky, Loc," Teeb muttered. "It was a successful hunt."

Loc raced to fulfill the drink order. Running back from the pack animals with a wicker-encased bottle of moonshine, he skidded to a stop in front of his father. Teeb winked at his youngest son and snatched the firewater with a bloodstained hand. Securing the cork stopper with his back teeth, he opened the container with a jerking hand. After spitting out the plug, he took a mean gulp.

All eyes turned as a French soldier, lugging a commandeered bolt-action rifle, tumbled to the rocky ground at their feet. Rolling onto his back, he gulped down cool mountain air. His skinny chest rose and deflated with each precious breath. Sweat, dirt, and clotted blood covered his face. A mutilated nose marred his youthful features. Three other young soldiers with shredded snouts staggered into the campsite and fell to the ground beside their hyperventilating companion. Squatting among the fallen, Loc assisted in hydrating the depleted Fackee. A soft chorus of "Merci" resonated from the fallen.

"Leej! Riam!" Teeb called out to his sons. "Go back down the trail and find the last Fackee."

Before they could respond, a silver-haired Frenchman in a white linen suit and baggy pleated slacks strolled out of the jungle. He was middle-aged, tall, and stocky, his bulbous nose ripped open. Straightening out the lapels of his blood-splattered jacket, he said with a dry, raspy throat, "Excusez-moi, messieurs?" Pointing to his mouth, he added, "Eau?"

Loc rose and handed the strange man the water jug.

"Merci beaucoup, garcon," he said, accepting the bottle. Admiring the precious fluid, he took a deep anticipatory breath. Tilting his head back, he poured the water down his dusty throat. "Ah!" he sighed. On jelly legs, he walked to a knee-high flat bolder. With great effort, he held his head high. Victoriously, he took a seat. Raising a bent leg, he removed a black leather shoe. After freeing his other foot, he closed his eyes and smiled.

"What an odd fellow," Teeb muttered, taking a swig of whisky. "Loc, see if this peculiar man would like a drink," he asked, handing his son the communal whisky bottle.

Loc approached the silver-haired chieftain, rubbing blistered, bright-white feet. "Monsieur?" Loc inquired, displaying the bottle.

A quick sniff produced a wide grin on the Frenchman's face. "Don't mind if I do," he said, partaking. "I prefer a fine wine," he commented. "But given the circumstances, this is exquisite." Nodding his gratitude at Teeb, he asked rhetorically, "Pourquoi?"

Teeb understood the question. He looked at his youngest son to translate. Focused on the white man, he responded, "The Fackee Henri of the clan DeSonier is why I risked all to save you."

Teeb spoke in pulsed sentences. Loc translated. The soldiers on the ground stirred. A focused French audience listened.

"Henri was a Legionnaire," Teeb stated. "We fought the Black Flags. We became friends. He took me into Fackee taverns. We ate and drank as brothers." Grinning, he commented, "Henri always paid. It was a sad day when he departed back to his village in France." Glancing over at the scraggly graveyard chasm, he concluded, "There are lots of fissures in my mountains to plant those who herd members of Henri's tribe to their deaths, hooked through their nose like water buffalos."

CHAPTER FOUR

It was eerily quiet. A three o'clock sun floated in a summer sky. A warm breeze flowed aimlessly down the bombed-out remains of a northern French hamlet. The soft wind carried dust, smoke, and the stench of death. The temperature leaned uncomfortable. In the shade of a windowless shell of a two-story inn, the remnants of a 12th Panzer infantry gun patrol reclined on rubble. Sergeant Franz snored through an open mouth. Around the napping Afrika Korps veteran, twenty boy soldiers reclined in various poses of exhaustion. The pimple-faced Hockler, choking back tears, pinched his sniffling nose. Lost in the depths of reflection, detached expressions dominated the faces of the youths. They had witnessed the harsh penalty for desertion and the execution of Canadian prisoners of war and suffered the loss of *kameraden*. Fanaticism can distort perspective, but truth is a constant. The reality for the survivors of the 12th Panzer unit was that they were outnumbered, outgunned, and outmaneuvered by the Allied forces. Defeat was inevitable. The mission had changed from repelling invaders to hindering the Allied advance.

Propped up by the hotel's used brick facade, Max took a swig of warm water. The image of his first kill surfaced. The shock and surprise on the Canadian's face had haunted him for weeks. After committing that mortal sin, the faces of the invaders he terminated were just a blur. Concluding all soldiers, including himself, were just targets, he took another hydrating gulp. After quenching his thirst, his body presented a petition of grievances. Sleep, hunger, and the need to defecate topped the list. Slowly rising, he felt his fatigued muscles groan. "I need to shit," he mumbled to no one in particular. The somber patrol did not react. Stepping over bricks and mortar chunks violating the cobblestone thoroughfare, he passed an overturned cart harnessed to a bloated horse carcass. Flies buzzed around the expired nag. Ignoring the wafting aroma of decay, Max enjoyed his moment of solitude. It was quiet, and he was alone. Red checkerboard drapes fluttered out of café's shattered storefront. He peered into the fractured window. Chairs, tables, and broken dishes blanketed the floor. A single table stood defiant. On its dusty surface, a half dozen baguettes beckoned. Secreting saliva signaled his delight. Swallowing, he high-stepped through the window frame. Glass crunched. Grasping a long, lean loaf with a soiled hand, he playfully banged the tabletop with the rock-hard bread. Dust erupted. Gnawing on the impenetrable crust proved futile. With a sigh, he leaned his 98K carbine against the cracked plaster wall and plopped his steel bonnet on the table. Scanning the debris, he salvaged a tin pot and tablespoon. After taking a deep breath, he cleansed the utensil and pan with a puckered exhale. Over the metal serving tin, blackened hands crumbled the stubborn loaf into gravel chunks. After a splash of canteen water, Max slowly stirred the pathetic meal. Dropping the spoon, he mumbled, "I failed...I failed my Führer." A lump swelled in his throat. His eyes watered. Wiping back tears with a tattered sleeve, he realized death was near, if not today, perhaps tomorrow.

"Are you all right, Maximilian?" Sergeant Franz inquired, framed by the jagged glass and flapping red checkerboard curtains. Max's mentor stood tall. Franz's leather face was covered in soot. Confidence burned in his brown eyes. A hint of compassion resided in his curious squint.

Slowly nodding, Max boldly inquired, "Were the executions necessary?"

"I'm afraid so, my sharpshooting *kamerad*," Franz replied, stepping through the window. Placing his helmet beside Max's, he ran a large, callused hand over the sweaty dew of his bristled scalp. Dipping a shoulder, he released his pack and informed him, "Cowardice is not tolerated in the Wehrmacht, regardless of the deserters' ages."

"I was referring to the execution of the three Canadian prisoners," Max clarified.

Slowly shaking his head, Franz concurred, "That was a crime. In the Afrika Korps, Field Marshall Rommel forbade any reprisals against civilians and prisoners of war. In combat, the temptation for retribution always exists. An English scouting party lashed a captured German officer to the front of their vehicle as a human shield. In response, three Canadian prisoners were shot." Franz shrugged. "Atrocities are committed by criminals on both sides of the front. But, Max, we are soldiers in the finest fighting force to march across the face of this planet, not murderers. We fight for Germany not the fanatic Nazi regime. When we meet our maker, we do it with pride."

Max squinted, questioning Franz's labeling the Fuhrer a fanatic. His empty belly churned. Lightheaded, he needed clarification. *How...what...should he ask?*

Overhead, exposed roof beams exhaled. A sprinkling of dust floated down. The sound of crackling wood escalated. Max and Franz cast investigating stares into the ceiling. A ripple rolled down the brick walls. Franz shoved Max under the table as the two-story structure imploded.

All was black. Max inhaled dust with shallow breaths. Delicately, he attempted to move. There was no pain. Raising his head, he felt his forehead kiss wood. Concluding it was the underside of the table six inches away, he lay back down. Massive weight restrained his legs, but he could wiggle his toes. His left arm was pinned against his side; his right hand lay across his chest. Probing fingers investigated the tomb. Bricks, chunks of plaster, and splintered wood encompassed a shallow-angled tabletop ceiling. *Don't panic*, he counseled as his heart raced violently. "Franz!" he hollered into the coffin lid. Taking a deep breath, he conjured all his strength. Growling, "Aaaahh!" he attempted to rise and soiled himself. He lay quiet. The pounding thump of his pulsing heart escalated. Taking a calming breath, he ignored the panic of suffocation and dehydration tormenting his thoughts. *Franz is probably summoning help*, he hoped. *If not, my comrades will be investigating the building collapse. Will I be dug out before the air expires?* entered the debate. His pulse accelerated. Patting his chest with his free hand, he decided not to just lie there in his own shit. Reaching into the darkness, he clawed at a brick in the constraining rubble. It took considerable effort before the stubborn brick jiggled free. The sound of trickling sand followed. Placing the prize on his stomach, he used his fingers to scratch out chunks of mortar. Movement was awkward. His fingers, arm, and shoulder cried out in distorted agony. Sweat migrated across his forehead. Raw fingertips pulled out another brick. A rush of seeping grit followed. A ray of light appeared. Panting like a dog, Max found hope in eliminating lack of oxygen as a cause of death. Faint illumination flowed into the crypt. Among the crippled wood, shattered bricks, and crumbled concrete rested the lifeless arm of Sergeant Franz. Realizing his mentor had sacrificed his existence to save him, Max's heart sank. Conceding to the hopelessness of his predicament, he started to weep. Sleep followed.

Sporadic distant small-arms fire woke Max. His mouth was dry. Dormant muscles groaned. Gunfire crackled. "Help!" he shouted with a scratchy throat. The sound of the skirmish faded. All was quiet once again in the tomb. Nodding off in the darkness, he returned to the comforting embrace of sleep. In his dreams, he once again escaped the café grave.

CHAPTER FIVE

It was Friday morning, September 15, 1944. The sky was clear, the vast encompassing Pacific Ocean royal blue. A battleship gray armada churned peaceful waters. A shroud of billowing black smoke hovered over an obscure six-mile-long, two-mile-wide mass of limestone coral. Spiting fire, the warships pounded the tiny island. A swarm of carrier-based Hellcat fighter planes tormented the smoldering isle with fifty-caliber tracer rounds. A singed aroma laced with diesel and sulfur hung in the static, sweltering atmosphere. Man-made thunder rumbled. Beneath a blazing sun, the morning temperature crept past 105 degrees Fahrenheit on its way to a 115-degree high.

Lieutenant Tom Roche leaned against the gunwale of an amphibious amtrac. The twenty-three-year-old Roche hailed from New Orleans. As a high school football star, he lacked the size and speed to play college ball. With a Louisiana State University degree in political science, he dropped out of law school to become a marine. Packed in with two dozen other leathernecks in the transport, Roche swayed in the choppy sea. Over the vehicle's coughing engines, a battle raged in the distance. Within the confines of the landing craft, the passengers did not have a visual of their destination. "Get off the beach," Roche mumbled under his breath. *I can do this*, he rationalized. *Following my training increases my odds.* Swallowing with a dry mouth, he realized the odds of survival were still long. Like a leaky faucet, sweat dripped off his nose. Taking a deep breath, he flexed. The taxing weight of his gear taunted apprehensive muscles. *I'm in the best shape of my life*, he proudly reflected, adjusting the web belt around his waist. The canvas strap was burdened with clips of ammo, a first-aid pouch, a sheathed knife, a holstered pistol, and two large canteens of water. *There is no water on Peleliu*, he contemplated, feeling the weight of a half gallon of H_2O tugging on his belt. *I'm already parched*, he realized.

PFC Doyle vomited. The bug-eyed, wiry, thin youth from upstate New York appeared much younger than his eighteen years. A quick glance confirmed regurgitated steak and eggs. Roche reflected on the First Marines traditional prebattle meal. *Coffee and toast was all I could muster out of the delicacy.*

"Smoke, Lieutenant?" Gunnery Sergeant Duke offered, flashing a cigarette out of a virgin pack of Chesterfields.

Roche gazed into the stoic features of the old-breed marine. The creases in the tan leather face told tales of hardship, loss, and triumph. The resolve burning in the depths of the battle-hardened sergeant's dark eyes provided reassurance. *The Japs don't stand a chance,* Roche realized. *I thought the Duke despised my rank and education,* Roche reflected, *but not today.* "No thanks, Gunny," Roche confidently replied. "I don't smoke."

Gunny nonchalantly shrugged, placing the exposed Chesterfield in the corner of his mouth. The skilled flick of a Zippo lighter ignited the tobacco. "You will," Gunny predicted, exhaling.

Roche enjoyed a brief whiff of cigarette smoke. An enemy artillery shell erupted in the water beside the transport. Roche's guts clenched. A geyser of seawater shot into the sky. The saltwater fountain drenched the passengers as the amtrac stumbled drunkenly forward. The clamor of war intensified. Japanese firepower escalated. Shell fragments buzzed overhead. Erratic misses tossed buckets of the Pacific into the landing craft.

Captain "Tex" Slaughter wove through the tight compilation of seasoned veterans and new men. Water careened off his camouflaged covered helmet. The US Marine Corps strategy molded combat experience and new recruits into a disciplined fighting force. Slaughter was soft spoken but direct. His slight drawl diluted harsh orders. The lanky Texan had served with distinction on Guadalcanal. Approaching Roche, he squeezed the green lieutenant's shoulder. Making eye contact, he gave Roche a reassuring nod.

"Thanks, skipper," Roche muttered as the Texan departed to inspire other novice warriors.

"The show is about to start!" Gunny hollered, flashing a half-pint bottle of Dewar's. After taking a hearty swig, he offered, "Anyone want a nip?" A few combat veterans responded with nervous laughter.

PFC Doyle lowered his head. Twitching hands attempted to buckle his helmet's chin strap. Rocking softly, he lamented, "Hail Mary full of grace, the Lord is with thee…"

Accepting the rotating libation, Roche questioned, "No ice?" He took a polite sip and passed the whisky. The swallow of scotch stung rolling down his throat before loosening the knots in his empty belly.

The order, "Stand by," jolted the passengers.

PFC Doyle accelerated his repeated plea to the Virgin Mary.

"You can talk to your girlfriend later!" Gunny hollered as the amtrac rolled out of the water and up a soft sand incline. The transport terminated with a hard jolt. The rear ramp fell open into shallow water. Marines poured out the back exit.

Stumbling, Roche got his first up-close glimpse of war. Amtracs smoldered on the reef. Streams of black smoke ascended into the blue sky. Motor shells and heavy artillery fire rained down across the bay. Waterspouts rose and fell. In the choppy surf, lifeless bodies drifted aimlessly. Plumes of blood meandered across the surface, the blue waters stained a pinkish hue.

On jelly knees, Roche turned inland. Seeking traction in the grasping sand, he fell. His face kissed the moist beach. Red water lapped at his lower extremities. "Mother of God, have mercy," he prayed, hugging the polluted water's edge. Machine gunfire sprayed the shoreline. White-hot tracer rounds kicked up sand, sparked off beached landing crafts, and tore into the amphibious task force. Crimson spray erupted out of advancing and idle marines. *The remnants of the first wave*, Roche tried to comprehend, squinting at the wrecked vehicles, burning transports, and bodies, lots of bodies. The dead remained motionless, the wounded writhing in pain. Braving the Japanese blizzard, corpsmen administered aid. *This can't be real*, Roche rationalized. *Where am I? What is happening?* The storm intensified as his amtrac spun around and plunged back into hostile waters.

"Get off the beach!" Gunny hollered, crawling up the white, sandy slope.

Roche slithered forward. *How long did I lay there?* he wondered. *Was it seconds or hours?* He tried to focus. *Just do what you were trained to do*, he conceded, sliding past terminated life.

Hidden machine guns blanked the advance with interlacing fields of fire. The deadly spray rolled over the prone invaders, shredding Captain "Tex" Slaughter's legs. Blood quickly saturated the skipper's tattered dungarees and embraced white sand.

"Son of a bitch," Slaughter growled.

"Corpsman!" Roche hollered, scurrying beside the Texan. "Over here!"

"It's your show now, Stonewall," Slaughter informed Roche through gritted teeth. "Make us southerners proud."

Roche fumbled with his first-aid kit as the skipper's color faded.

"Keep moving," Slaughter whispered, closing his eyes.

Following orders, Roche dug his elbows into the soft sand. Clawing forward, surfacing rage eliminated his fears. *I'm going to die*, he rationalized. *But not before I get off this beach*, he vowed. A wicked grin appeared on his sweat-glistening features. *Since the Virgin Mary is not going to intervene, I might as well raise some hell before my exit.*

Roche scrambled to his feet. Crouched down, he ran. "Don't bunch up!" he ordered, passing sluggish marines. "Stay low and keep moving." Bullets buzzed about. Small-arms fire crackled. Blackened snarly brush marked the end of the beach. Roche sprinted through the grasping thicket. Taking cover, he leaned against a decapitated palm tree. Sliding to the ground, he took a seat. Panting like a dog, he raised a canteen in a victory toast. "I got off the beach," he mumbled. A few healthy gulps of warm water completed the celebration. *Now to raise some hell.* He chuckled.

"Lieutenant!" Gunny hollered from the security of a shell crater.

I knew that badass would make it inland, Roche delighted. Other helmets floated beneath the edge of the hole twenty yards to his right. Roche slowly peered around the tree trunk. The narrow gun port of a Japanese pillbox stared back. The one-eyed concrete bunker barely broke the ground's surface. A burst of machine-gun fire signified occupancy. Roche took a deep breath and tossed a smoke grenade in front of the pillbox. After a quick sprint he dove into Gunny's shelter.

"Mornin', Lieutenant," Gunny offered with his signature growl.

Roche looked up. Crouched down in the shallow pit were Gunnery Sergeant Duke, the altar boy PFC Doyle, and a barrel-chested, black-bearded brute. The bearded marine had a seventy-pound flamethrower strapped to his back.

"Good to see you, Gunny," Roche responded, noting an attempted smile on the sergeant's chiseled face. "Doyle, I'm glad to discover I'm not the only Catholic in the squad." Doyle's pimpled face glowed beet red. Grinning at his inclusion, the boy appeared terrified but in control. Squinting at the blowtorch marine, Roche asked, "What's your outfit?"

"Corporal Walker, Fifth Marines, sir," he answered.

"Fifth Marines?" Roche questioned. "You're not supposed to be here."

"Tell me about it." Walker shrugged.

"It's total chaos," Gunny interjected. "The only ones who know what they're doing are the fucking Japs." Closing an eye, he questioned, "The skipper?"

Shaking his head, Roche informed him, "He didn't make it off the beach."

A burst of machine-gun fire strafed the lip of the shell crater. Dislodged corral and sand tumbled into the hole. Gunny stuck the muzzle of his M1 Thompson over the edge and squeezed off a few quick answering rounds.

Roche peered out, stealing a glimpse of the concrete Cyclops. He grinned, recalling his moment of glory against North High. As time expired, he intercepted a tipped ball and ran it back sixty yards for the winning touchdown. It was his only score during his high school linebacker career. Many times, he delighted in visualizing every step across the field and every tackle he eluded. *If I can do that*, he reasoned, *I can run interference for the blowtorch.* Unclipping a smoke grenade, he spoke matter-of-factly, in a commanding tone. "Gunny, Doyle, you'll provide covering fire. I'll get the Japs' attention." Looking at Walker, he continued, "After that one-eyed slit blinks at me, get within range and light those bastards up."

The marines nodded. Roche pulled the grenade pin. Taking a deep breath, he tossed the canister. An expanding cloud of white smoke shrouded the playing field. Roche shot out of the pit. Gunny and Doyle fired into the haze. As he ran across the bunker's face, Roche's carbine spit rounds. The bullets joined the covering fire sparking off the fortification. The swirling smoke slowly dissipated. Roche's peripheral vision detected a machine-gun muzzle stalking him from the narrow slit. He grimaced. A wave of heat engulfed him as a gushing steam of fire bathed the concrete menace. Behind the high-velocity orange flames spewing out of a flamethrower nozzle, Walker advanced slowly. The inferno incinerated the brush concealing the pillbox, blackening the thick concrete roof. Walker halted his advance. In a wide stance, he sprayed the liquid fire into the Japanese gun port. Gunny, Doyle, and Roche charged. Walker released his trigger, extinguishing the flame. High-pitched wails of the enemy erupted out of the narrow slit. Munitions popped from within. Gunny poked his Thompson in the single embrasure and fired several bursts. Roche skirted the pillbox, followed by Doyle. A rusty metal rear door slammed open. Engulfed in flames, flailing his arms, an enemy soldier abandoned the post. Another ignited inhabitant followed. The duo stumbled and fell. Surrendering to their fate, they crumpled up into balls and burned. Doyle popped a few merciful rounds into the twitching, crackling heaps.

"Save your ammo," Gunny suggested as he approached with a cigarette attached to his lower lip.

There was calm in the storm. Small-arms fire still resonated. In the distance, the big stuff still fell. The immediate threat, however, lay sizzling on the ground before them.

"What now, Lieutenant?" Doyle inquired.

Roche snorted at the scorched human stench. "If that offer for a cigarette still stands, Gunny, I'm accepting."

With an I-told-you-so smirk, Gunny tapped out a Chesterfield. Roche accepted it and a light. Sucking the nicotine vapors deep within his lungs, he savored the distracting vice. After a refreshing exhale, he responded to Doyle, "We work our way inland to the airfield as planned and kill Japs."

CHAPTER SIX

The rural country road shook under the advancing metal treads of a Sherman tank. A dusty wake stalked the rumbling beast. Hitching a ride atop the armor bison sat a dozen Canadian soldiers of the North Nova Scotia Highlanders. Since the D-Day invasion a month and a half ago, the North Novies stature as a formidable force had increased significantly. Baptized by combat with the fanatic youths of the 12th SS Panzer Division, the Canadians had evolved into savvy battle-tested warriors.

Perched on the cupola of the tank, the commander, in a jaunty black beret, enjoyed a smoke in the crisp morning air. Unlike the hitchhiking troops, he was clean-shaven with the exception of a pencil-thin mustache. A gentle headwind caressed his confident pose. A low sun, over green pastures, blessed the scraggly passengers with warm rays. All were quiet as the vehicle ascended a slight grade into a French hamlet. The smoldering remains of a German halftrack drifted by. The dirt road narrowed into a cobblestoned main street. The noisy growl of the grinding tank treads escalated on the harder surface. Clusters of occupying Canadian troops tracked the passing new arrivals. A pile of dead Germans, shrouded by an olive-green oilskin tarp, occupied a sidewalk morgue in front of the hollow shell of a two-story inn.

The tank commander took one last satisfying drag off his smoke before flicking the glowing butt. Looking down into the turret, he shouted an inaudible order. The beast ground to a halt. "End of the line!" the commander hollered over the grumble of the idling heap to Lance Sergeant Archie Kerr.

Nodding gratitude for the lift, Kerr collected his gear. Nicknamed Badger by his troops, he was short and stocky. Even on limited rations, the pudgy Kerr still displayed a potbelly. Like his fierce moniker, overwhelming odds did not matter. The Scottish Canadian would tackle any objective that threatened him or his men.

"I hope you enjoyed your piggyback ride on my Ronson," the tank commander playfully added.

Kerr, slinging a heavy pack over a shoulder, tilted his head and questioned, "Ronson?"

Wiggling his thumb, the tank commander chuckled. "Ronson cigarette lighter…because just like the expensive smoking accessory, a Sherman tank is guaranteed to light up first time, every time."

Snickering, Kerr offered a friendly salute and joined his troops slowly peeling off the inferno-prone Sherman.

On the stone-paved thoroughfare, the disembarked passengers stretched. Snorting white smoke, the exiting tank rumbled into town. Exhaust fumes dissipated. The stench of a bloated horse carcass ambushed the North Novies. The dozen Canadians rapidly retreated upwind of death's decomposing fragrance. On the sidewalk in front of an imploded café, Sergeant Kerr retrieved a precious cigar from a breast pocket. After securing the fat tobacco log with his back teeth, he struck a match against his leather holster. Behind a shielding cupped hand, he ignited his vice. A satisfying exhale cleansed his senses of the aroma of dead horse. "All right, lads," he announced in his familiar gritty tone. "Stay out of trouble while I report in."

The weary men acknowledged the respite with slight grins. Puffing on his stogie, the short-legged Kerr waddled down the street in search of a command post. The Canadian troops slowly dispersed with the exception of Corporal Bruno Abbott and Private Jack Morton. The French Canadian Bruno was a small man at no more than five feet six in height. The broad-shouldered Morton, a Scottish Canadian, towered at well over six feet in height. He was known as Ox by his fighting companions. The inseparable Mutt and Jeff duo connected under heavy fire on Juno Beach during the D-day landing.

"Do you think this one-horse town has a brothel?" Ox teased, lighting up a cigarette.

"Nope," Bruno mumbled, glancing down the war-torn boulevard. Spotting the rotting mare harnessed to an overturned cart, he chuckled. "Besides the village's only horse is dead."

Ox laughed. Taking a long, deep toke off his smoke, he peered into the wreckage of the expired café. Stepping into the rubble, he picked a pristine dinner plate out of a debris mound. With a smoldering cigarette dangling from his lower lip, he admired the flawless dish.

"What is it?" Bruno inquired, joining his mate.

"Everything is broken but this," Ox answered, handing over the plate.

Bruno raised the dish and dropping it muttered, "All is right with the world once again." The plate shattered on impact.

Out of the rubble, a voice called out, "Aidez moi! Aidez moi!"

"Oh seigneur!" Bruno declared, leaping back from the talking debris mound. "Sounds like a Frenchman is trapped under there."

Sucking on a fresh cigarette, Ox shrugged his massive square shoulders.

Bruno chuckled as he started slinging bricks off the heap. "Give me a hand, Ox," he politely nudged.

Ox's face puckered. Groaning his displeasure, he flicked the precious smoke into the ground and joined the dig.

"Don't worry, monsieur; we'll dig you out!" Bruno shouted into the waste heap.

The Canadians paused. Bruno stepped back and placed his dirty hands on the small of his back. The remains of a German sergeant with a crushed skull lay atop a collapsed table. Bruno unholstered an Enfield Webley revolver. Ox grabbed the corpse's pea-and-dot camouflaged tunic and with a guttural grunt tossed the cadaver aside. Spouting sweat, Ox retrieved his bolt-action rifle. The tabletop slowly elevated before flipping open sideways.

"It's a fucking Heinie," Ox declared, targeting a hyperventilating blond, uniformed youth. "What's that smell?" he inquired, crinkling his face.

"The kid shit himself." Bruno chuckled.

"Schnell! Schnell!" Ox barked, jerking the barrel of his targeting rifle.

Max examined the massive Canadian through blinking sensitive eyes. "De l'eau, s'il vous plait," slowly rolled off his sandpaper tongue.

"The kid wants water," Bruno translated, holstering his sidearm and unleashing the canteen strapped across his torso.

"What are you doing?" Ox questioned.

Tossing the flask to the boy, Bruno chuckled. "What does it look like?... I'm hydrating a Hun."

Max caught the sloshing container and in a frenzy pulled out the cork stopper. Tilting his head back, he poured the lubricating freshness down his throat. Water ricocheted off his chapped lips and rolled down his neck. Opening his eyes, he gazed skyward. Sunlight penetrating what remained of the café roof graced his wet face. The moment of joy was brief. A massive paw grabbed the back of his shirt collar and pulled him out of the grave. His legs were like rubber. Jelly knees refused to engage.

Ox dropped the boy at his feet, grumbling, "All I wanted was a smoke and maybe a little sleep." Scowling at his captive, he added, "And now I have to act as a wet nurse for a Nazi with a full diaper."

Bruno pulled a tin of Canadian sardines out of his pack and tossed it at their panting prisoner. The metal container with key attached ricocheted off the young Nazi's thigh.

Max looked up slowly at the short Tommy. A puzzled squint emerged. "Merci," rolled out between breaths.

"Machts nichts." Bruno chuckled.

Peeling back the metal lid took effort. At the first glimpse of the compacted tiny fish, a dribble of saliva rolled out of Max's open mouth. An impatient dirty finger dug out globs of oily herring meat to feed a ravenous mouth at close range.

"The kid must have been planted for days," Ox commented, enjoying the gluttonous performance. Poking his captive with a gun barrel, he announced, "Mealtime is over."

Using his hands, Max crawled up the rubble into a wobbly stance. Staggering forward, he exited the café. Shadowed by the massive Canadian, he swayed on the sidewalk, scanning the hamlet occupied by invaders. A cigarette-smoking cluster across the street cast hostile scowls in his direction.

"Hands on your head, kid," Bruno politely requested in French. The prisoner complied. Turning his head away from the ripe boy, Bruno patted him down while Ox confiscated the boy's wristwatch.

"Ox snared a baby Nazi," a smoker from the troop hollered. Tossing his cigarette aside, he led a snickering audience to investigate.

The rabid pack encircled Max. Jeers and snide comments triggered raucous laughter. Max looked down. A grubby hand ripped the Nazi insignia off his uniform. The mob quieted and parted. Max raised his gaze. Before him, a fireplug of a man stood, chomping on a smoldering stogie. The chevrons on his sleeve identified a sergeant's rank.

Badger grinned. "Hey, McConnell, get your camera." The lanky McConnell nodded. Sergeant Kerr, alias Badger, looked the captive up and down and commented, "Not much of a trophy, Ox. Maybe we should give him a good spanking and send him home to his mum."

"He shit his pants, Sarge," Ox informed him.

McConnell arrived with a Zeiss Super Ikonta around his neck. Badger prematurely posed beside the prisoner. Ox and Bruno crowded into the photo opportunity. McConnell fidgeted with the finicky camera.

"Wait!" Badger hollered, flashing a flexed palm. "We need to toughen up our baby-faced prize." After a few quick puffs of his cigar, he shoved the moist end of the stogie into Max's mouth.

Max gazed upon his harsh audience and tapping the last of his inner strength stood erect, stuck out his chest, flexed his shoulders, and took a long, satisfying taste of his first cigar. The smoking experience turned bitter quickly. As he snorted the nauseating vapors, an uncontrollable cough erupted. The reaction evoked explosive laughter from the hostile audience.

Grinding a combat boot on the smoldering expelled cigar, Badger addressed Ox, "You caught the little soiled fish. You can deposit him at the command post down the street."

Bruno spoke up. "The kid speaks French, Sarge. I'll take him."

Slowly nodding, Badger signaled his acceptance.

"What's your name, Kid?" Bruno inquired in French.

"Max, Max Kohl."

"All right Max," Bruno said. "I dug you up, gave you water, and fed you. Now I'm warning you. Do not misinterpret my kindness as weakness, because if you show even the slightest hint of resistance, I'll blow your fucking head off." Gazing into the boy's deep-blue eyes, he nudged quietly, "Do we have an understanding?"

"Oui, monsieur," Max responded.

With his hands on his head, shadowed by the short Canadian, Max plodded down what remained of Main Street. The young German's passing stirred two local French farmers. In civilian attire, packing German rifles, they approached the young captive. Raising a waving fist, one shouted insults. The other's face puckered behind flared nostrils; emitting low grunting snorts, he conjured up and launched a mucus spitball. The gooey projectile smacked the side of Max's head.

Max didn't react. What could he do? He was hungry, tired, and weak. In a trance of despair, he tolerated the humiliating slime migrating down his cheek. His thoughts drifted. Visualizing a German counteroffensive turning the tables, he grinned. *The finicky French would then be spitting on the retreating Allies.*

"Buzz off," Bruno barked at the local pests. The snickering Frenchmen complied. "Your right hand," Bruno said to his captive. "Go ahead and wipe it off with your right hand."

"Danke," Max muttered as he swiped the side of his face.

A narrow, well-tread path led to a simple stone French farmhouse. A steep gray shingle roof capped the rusty stone facade. An oasis of large green canopy trees provided shade. Encircling flower beds displayed rich purple and candy-red flowers. Canadian troops milled around the designated command post. Soldiers reclined at the base of the towering trees. An open-mouthed driver snored behind the wheel of an idle jeep. The structure's chimney exhaled smoke seasoned with the salivating aroma of hot food. Bruno and his prisoner approached the open double-wide rough wood doors. The doorway framed officers seated around a bountiful breakfast table. Heaping platters emitted steam. Jars of various jams guarded a wicker basket overflowing with bread. Muffled laughter accented the smacking grunts of the piggish pack.

A guard with a rifle slung over a shoulder and a hot tin of coffee in hand appeared in the wide entrance. Fanning a crinkled nose, he exclaimed, "What's that smell?"

Peering around the captive, Bruno responded, "The kid messed his pants."

Taking a satisfying sip of hot coffee, the sentry examined the blue-eyed Kraut. "Around back," he mumbled, pointing with the misting tin cup.

"This way, Max," Bruno informed his prisoner, jerking his targeting rifle.

Fifty yards behind the farmhouse command post, a windowless white-washed barn-wood shed reflected the rising sun. An angled, warped roof capped the simple structure. A padlock secured a thick chain wrapped around wooden door handles. A sentry leaning against the shack enjoyed a smoke. Another guard reclined comfortably in an antique wheelbarrow. Both guards maintained their lazy reposes as Bruno approached with his prisoner.

With his legs dangling out of the wheelbarrow, the slouching sentry asked, "Did you pat him down?"

"The kid's clean," Bruno informed him.

The smoking guard flicked his cigarette. Slowly, he stood erect, and after fumbling with a key, he unlocked the clasp's pivoting loop. Reluctantly, the slouching guard rose from his wheelbarrow bed. Taking a deep breath, he elevated a carbine into firing position and targeted the closed door. A nod signaled his partner to remove the chain. Rusty hinges squealed as the planked door swung open. Stagnant air escaped. Invading sunlight illuminated a German officer, tending to a wounded comrade on a straw-covered floor.

With hands on his head, Max pivoted and offered a slight nod of gratitude to his Canadian rescuer.

"Adieu, Max," Bruno muttered before returning to the war.

Max stepped into the wood box cell. The door slammed shut behind him. He lowered his hands. Relief flowed across his shoulders and down his arms. A rattling chain secured the pen. Sunlight penetrating gaps in the blistered barn wood provided rows of illumination. The crouching officer rolled into a sitting position. Reaching into his mouth, he plucked a wedding ring from under his tongue and secured it on his finger. Leaning back on his elbows, he smiled in the soft light. An officer's black field cap, trimmed with golden-yellow soutache crowned his confident features. The shoulder straps of his black tunic displayed the rank of *Hauptmann*. The gapping tear over his right breast pocket indicated the confiscation of the national eagle emblem. "Welcome, *kamerad*," he said pleasantly. "I'm Captain Seigal." Lifting his chin, he proudly informed him, "A Panzer Lehr tank commander." After a moment of reflection, his shoulders dipped and he snickered, "That's *former* tank commander."

Max's reflexes trumped fatigue. His weary body stiffened. "Max Kohl, Twelfth Panzer SS," he barked, standing at full attention.

"Relax, Max," Seigal said. "Take a seat."

Max collapsed onto the straw floor.

"I'd introduce you to our roommate," Seigal offered, glancing at the bandaged prisoner beside him. "But unfortunately he is dead."

Max tossed a puzzled expression at the officer.

Seigal grinned. "Dead men have no appetite," he enlightened him. "When they feed us our meager meal, I don't think our deceased companion would mind if we ate his portion."

Max nodded slowly.

Seigal pointed to the darkest corner of the shack. "The wooden bucket over there entertaining flies is the latrine." Scratching the back of his neck, he closed an eye and asked, "You wouldn't happen to have any cigarettes?"

"No, sir," Max responded. "I don't smoke."

"I'm not surprised," the officer declared. "As a Hitler Youth, did you assist in the national antismoking campaign?"

"Yes, sir, I distributed information about the health risks of smoking to businesses in Nuremburg."

"Good for you," Seigal grumbled. Picking up a piece of straw from the floor, he stuck it in the corner of his disappointed mouth. Chomping on the dry blade, he asked, "Has Tommy interrogated you yet?"

"No, sir."

"They will," Seigal predicted. "And when they do, tell them anything they want to know." Falling back onto the grassy flooring, he gazed hopelessly into the dark, rotting wood ceiling. "Any tactical information you possess of our chaotic army in full retreat became invalid once it reached your ears." He sighed. "There is no chance of escape, at least not now. Our enemy has saturated the Normandy Coast with overwhelming power. Like a tidal wave, Tommy rolled in from the sea and with each passing day grows in strength and intensity." Propping himself up on an elbow, he studied his focused young audience and inquired, "How did you get captured, Max?"

"What day is it, sir?" Max replied.

Squinting, the puzzled officer mumbled, "Tuesday?"

Raising tired, enlightened brows, Max declared, "Two days...I spent the last two and a half days buried under the ruble of a French café. One moment, I was on the battlefield; the next, I lay beneath it. There was no explosion. A soft wind might have kissed the frail café or a passing flock of birds paused to rest on the teetering roof. Regardless, the structure collapsed, killing my sergeant and entombing me." Reflecting on his deceased mentor, he paused.

"Max, when was your last meal?" Seigal nudged.

"A French-speaking Tommy tossed me a tin of sardines this morning," Max answered.

"Probably couldn't resist your blue puppy-dog eyes." Seigal chuckled.

The chain on the wooden cage rattled. Seigal sat up and hastily pulled off his wedding ring. "Max," he whispered, "I want you to flash your baby blues and ask for a cigarette." As the creaking planked door swung open, he concealed the band of gold under his tongue.

Looking up, Max blinked in the invading light. A flat-helmeted silhouette stood in the doorway. The shadow tossed a sloshing canteen on the straw floor; three unmarked tin cans followed.

"Monsieur?" Max inquired, placing two extended fingers to his lips. Miming a smoking gesture, he raised his brows. The dark profile chuckled. From a breast pocket, the guard retrieved a crinkled pack. A gentle tap released a single unfiltered cigarette. Max delicately plucked the prize. In a well-rehearsed motion, the guard flicked open and ignited a hinged lid lighter. Leaning forward, Max accepting the flame and inhaled. Strong, acrid smoke tormented his virgin lungs. The lighter slammed shut. The guard retreated. The door closed with a bang. Coughing violently, Max relayed the foul vice to his cellmate.

Securing his wedding ring, Seigal nodded graciously and accepted the smoldering nicotine canister. "Well done, Max. Well done," he mumbled, admiring the luxury secured between his fingers. After a religious pause, he deeply inhaled the addictive vapors. A satisfying exhale followed. "I usually enjoy a good smoke after dinner," he declared. "But given the circumstances, I'll accept the deviation." Closing his eyes, he savored another toke. The cigarette's smoldering tip glowered red hot in the soft light. The passive smoke diluted the shed's foul odors.

Holding the metal canteen sheathed in a damp olive-drab wool cover, Max politely nudged, "Sir?"

Stirred out of his nicotine trance, Seigal flinched. "Go ahead, Max," he nonchalantly declared through billowing smoke. "We can forgo military formalities here in our wood box." Delicately holding the tiny smoldering butt between the tip of his thumb and forefinger, he sucked down another puff of pleasure.

Max popped the canteen's cork stopper. A quick swig evolved into gluttonous gulps. The water was surprisingly cold. Wiping his moist lips with the back of a hand, he surrendered the container.

The officer took a disciplined swig. Sitting cross-legged, he placed the three small unmarked food tins precisely between him and the boy. Interlacing his fingers, he stretched his arms, cracking his knuckles. Shaking his hands, he informed him, "I'll give you first pick. I'll choose second." Glancing over his shoulder at the corpse, he continued, "We then split the dead man's meal." As Max reached for the center can, Seigal teased, "Are you sure, Max? Choose wisely, my friend."

Max grinned and grabbed a tin. Seigal made his selection. Examining his mystery can, Max asked, "How do we open it?"

Seigal banged the tin against the iron heel of his boot. Yellowish putty oozed out of a narrow gash in the can. Seigal quickly sucked on the escaping nourishment. Smiling at Max, he declared, "Ham and eggs."

Max's hammering effort produced a small tear in the unmarked tin. Reaching under his collar, he unpinned the Hitler Youth shooting proficiency badge that had escaped the pat-down. Working the edge of his medallion in the fissure, he methodically produced a long enough crack to spread open the container. "Carrot and meat stew," he proudly informed Seigal, dipping two fingers into thick gravy.

"You chose wisely," Seigal mumbled. "Do you mind if I borrow your can opener?" he asked, extending an impatient palm. Max obliged. Examining the swastika medallion, Seigal counseled, "You really should lose this." Utilizing the tool, he continued, "Nothing invokes the wrath of our foreign custodians like the Nazi symbol."

"It means a lot to me, sir," Max replied. "If Tommy steals it, so be it. But I'm not going to lose it."

Returning the trophy, the officer respectfully nodded. Flexing his fingers, he admired his wedding ring and mumbled, "This means a lot to me. My wife's name is Inge. The photo of her was taken from me, as was my watch and wallet. The connection Inge and I had through the field mail service has been severed. The thought of her waiting for a letter that will never arrive tugs on my heart. It will be weeks, possibly months, before she will be informed of my fate."

"Sir?" Max quietly injected. "What is our fate?"

Seigal snickered. Picking up an empty ration tin, he held it up as an exhibit. "Feeding us is a good sign." Glancing over his shoulder at the locked door, he grinned at the passing shadow of a sentry. "Guarding us is another revealing indication of our capturer's intent. If execution was Tommy's desire, they would have done it immediately." Tossing the empty can onto the blanketing straw floor, he concluded. "A prisoner of war is nothing more than annoying ballast that requires food, vigilant policing, and transportation."

Max scratched at the inside hem of his field blouse with a blackened fingernail. The rough stitched thread surrendered. After creating a concealing pocket, he stowed his precious swastika medallion. Glancing at his curious cellmate, he said, "Hopefully my only possession will survive further pat-downs."

CHAPTER SEVEN

A cool, gray morning blanketed the wetlands. In the depths of ten-foot-tall elephant grass, a small Hmong hunting party advanced. Their flintlocks were cocked and ready. Teeb used his weapon's long barrel to part the razor-sharp reeds. Behind the seasoned huntsman, the Fackee Paul Claveau treaded with a heavy stride. The Frenchman's attempt at moving undetected was dismal.

The twenty-year-old Claveau hailed from Nice. His youthful good looks were marred by a truncated snout. Gapping nostrils centered his face. Self-conscious, he shrouded the disfigurement with a bandana. The most grateful of the Frenchmen rescued from a Japanese executioner's bullet, Claveau wanted to contribute to his room and board. Huffing and puffing, he adjusted the chaffing strap of a bolt-action Arisaka rifle.

"Quiet," Loc whispered to the Fackee.

Claveau, glancing over at the young translator, vigorously nodded. Moving forward, his large boots continued to pound the moist earth. Looking at his brothers, Loc snickered. Grinning, Leej and Vue shook their heads.

Teeb held up his hand, signaling a stop. Before him, a wide, trampled-grass pathway snaked through the tall growth. Gingerly, he stepped onto the recently blazed trail. Squatting down, he grinned at a two-foot high pile of dung. Next to the scat heap, a three-toed hoofprint confirmed the *phaw twy kum* sightings. Softly touching the fresh tracks, he knew the beast was close. "Let's hope it's a male," he muttered, rising. He signaled his sons to spread out. Cautiously, they crept forward, guns ready.

Concealing growth thinned. Behind the parting reed curtain, a dusty, slate-gray rhinoceros appeared. Its enormous lowered head displayed a single horn. Its thick-plated hide was caked with mud. Oblivious to the encompassing threat, the massive creature grazed on the banks of the marshland. As a swamp bird took flight, the beast looked up. Agitated, it stomped the moist ground. Grunting, it paced back and forth. Tiny eyes scanned the hunters. The mighty bull snorted in disgust.

Claveau took a step back. A branch crackled beneath his retreat. The rhino jogged forward, gaining momentum. Lowering its head, it broke into a full charge. For a large creature, it was fast, very fast. Heavy thumping hooves tossed chunks of sod into the air. The ground trembled under the galloping two tons of fury.

Flanking the Rhino, Leej fired at the moving target. The broadside hit seemed to accelerate the beast. Vue hit it from the other side. The bull flinched but continued its assault. Teeb stepped in front to intercept the stampeding animal. Calmly, he raised his musket and pulled back the hammer. Taking a soft breath, he sighted his target at the end of a long smoothbore gun barrel. In midstride, the rhino was airborne. A calculated trigger squeeze sent sparking flint into the weapon's flashpan. The tiny eruption ignited the main powder charge and ejected a pure lead musket ball. The projectile sphere ripped into the rhino's eye socket and expanded. Wincing, the bull turned its head to the side. Falling forward, it plowed a wide swath in the muddy soil. Implanted in weeds and muck, the prey gulped for life.

Watching his sons reloading, Teeb instructed the boys, "Kill it quickly. I don't want this noble animal to suffer."

Claveau, Leej, and Vue took aim. A volley of bullets terminated the *phaw twy kum*. A sulfur mist drifted over the large carcass. Utilizing a honed Hmong blade, Loc severed the nine-inch fibrous prize. Anticipating the Chinese opium merchant's addiction for acquiring rhino horns, he grinned. *I'll extract a high bounty for the trophy*, he thought, raising the bloody cone over his head.

"Loc, cut off a chunk of the hindquarter for dinner," Teeb instructed his youngest son.

"I'll do it, Father," Vue volunteered, twirling a machete.

Teeb nodded his approval.

Several well-placed blows penetrated the rough hide. Squatting down, Vue extracted large slabs of gamey meat. Placing the meal into a burlap sack, he rose as flies descended on the fresh kill.

"This is a good day," Teeb declared, balancing a flintlock across his shoulder. "Let's go home."

A rising sun burned off the cloud cover. The temperature rose. The tall grass of the savannah receded. A successful hunt produced a confident stride in the homeward-bound expedition. Even the Fackee strutted with a sense of accomplishment. As a soothing breeze flowed down the trail, Teeb broke into song. Proud of his voice, he belted out the Hmong standard. His sons joined in. To the rhythm of the catchy tune, Claveau injected meaningless lyrics.

Teeb stopped dead in his tracks. Placing his long rifle across a relaxed arm, he gazed into the sky. A large wooden box harnessed to a billowing white canopy slowly descended. It landed in waist-high grass with a crackling thud. An immense swathe of flittering white silk marked the location.

Loc pointed into the clear sky. The drone of an aircraft surfaced. Two more white parachutes appeared in the rich-blue heavens. The engine hum faded. The loads drifted toward earth at different speeds. The faster chute was tethered to another crate. The silhouette of a lone paratrooper slowly trailed the cargo.

"A Jap?" Claveau questioned unslinging his rifle.

Exiting the trail, Teeb waded into the brush. His sons and the Fackee followed. Spread out, they advanced on the fluttering silk shrouds. Ignoring the wooden crates planted in moist soil, they encircled a paratrooper struggling with his harness.

Startled, the helmeted trooper brandished an all-metal short-barreled firearm. He was short in stature, and his green uniform was new. Slowly, he exhibited a friendly white palm.

"He's French," rolled out of Claveau's open mouth. "*Copain!*" he hollered, vigorously waving.

Grinning wide, the paratrooper slung his weapon over a shoulder.

High-stepping in the tall grass, Claveau sprinted toward his countryman. With the national identity of the paratrooper solved, the Hmong hunters were more interested in collecting the flapping parachutes. Winded, Claveau bent forward in front of the new arrival. Resting his hands on his knees, he sucked down thin air. "Is the war over?" he questioned between breaths.

The paratrooper shook his head as he finished the task of unharnessing the chute rigging. "The war is not over," he responded with a deep voice. "But I'm happy to say Paris has been liberated, and the Nazi machine is in full retreat." Squinting at the panting, masked Claveau, he asked, "Who are you?"

"Pardon," Claveau uttered, standing erect. Offering a weak salute, he declared, "Private Paul Claveau." Tugging on the tail of the concealing bandanna, he exposed his truncated face and muttered, "A memento from les Japs."

Returning the salute, the paratrooper introduced himself as a member of the French Far East Expeditionary Corps, "Lieutenant Louis Guajac, Corps Expéditionnaire Français d'extrême Orient. My mission is to gather intelligence, harass the Japanese occupiers, and organize resistance fighters." Glancing around at the giddy Hmong salvaging parachutes, he asked, "What can you tell me about these tribesmen?"

"The father is Teeb, and those are his sons. Twenty years ago, a legionnaire named Henri DeSonier picked up more than a few bar bills for Teeb. To repay the favor, Teeb and his brother slit the throats of two Japs and rescued five Frenchmen from a firing squad." Taking an emotional swallow, he added, "I owe the man my life."

"Cigarette?" Guajac asked, reaching into a breast pocket.

"Thanks," Claveau responded, accepting a Chesterfield from a soft pack. Pulling down the bandit shroud, he placed the treat between his lips and accepted a light. A cupped smoking hand now shielded his disfigured face. "American cigarettes?" he questioned.

Chuckling, Guajac responded, "There are no limits to the Americans' wealth and contributions to the war effort." Lighting up a tab, he took a satisfying toke. After exhaling, he asked, "Have you learned any of their dialect?"

"Sadly no," Claveau responded. Glancing around, he spotted Loc standing on top of a crate. "We all rely on the kid. Teeb's youngest son, Loc, is our translator. The boy's French is actually improving. He spends a lot of time with the Corsican."

"Corsican?"

"Teeb saved four French soldiers and the Corsican businessman, Carlo Coty, from an early grave." Lowering his voice, Claveau shared, "Coty is an odd fellow. He is always trying to entice us with promises of wealth to escort him into China."

"What is Coty's business?"

"The opium trade."

Guajac snickered. "He's a *Unione Corse* gangster."

"I don't know." Claveau shrugged. "We are all just guests of a Black Meo clan. They are very generous hosts. Treat them with the respect they deserve."

Guajac dropped his spent cigarette onto the moist ground. Grinding the smoldering butt with a boot toe, he said, "I'm sure glad I ran into you, Private." Scanning the approaching tribesmen, he raised his brows. "Any advice?"

Covering his face with the scarf, Claveau offered, "Give them the parachutes." His eyes smiled as he added, "I hope you have a strong liver, Lieutenant. The Hmong love to drink."

Teeb and his sons encircled the Frenchmen, Vue and Loc each holding large bundles of white silk. The Hmong examined the paratrooper with blank expressions.

Guajac, looking down at Loc, smiled. "I understand you speak my language."

"Oui, monsieur," the boy responded.

"Please tell your father, I want to thank him for the French lives he saved." Looking at Teeb, he placed a hand on Claveau's shoulder and nodded.

Teeb understood.

Guajac continued, "To show my appreciation, please accept this fine silk as a gift."

Loc translated. Childish grins emerged.

CHAPTER EIGHT

Darkness engulfed the sliver of coral limestone smoldering in the Pacific. Seared by a tropical sun, the isle retained the long day's heat. The salty air was thick. Out of the black void, surf lapped at a rocky shoreline. Peleliu's nocturnal land crabs crackled in the brush. In a shallow foxhole, an exhausted, dehydrated Lieutenant Tom Roche sucked on a cigarette with a dry mouth. Slouched down in the jagged rock indentation, he watched Gunnery Sergeant Duke scanning the darkness. Cocking an automatic pistol hammer, Gunny extended a targeting arm into the black night.

"Lana Turner," a stale voice whispered from the surrounding brittle vegetation.

Bending an elbow, Gunny pointed his pistol skyward. "I was about to shoot you," he growled as skinny Private Bentley from New York slithered into the crowded shelter.

"Sir," Bentley addressed Roche. "I need water. I'm going crazy with thirst. I fear I won't last the night."

Roche nodded his understanding. "We are all parched, Bentley," he offered. "Even growing up in the heat and humidity of Louisiana, I find this muggy baked pile of rocks unbearable." Rubbing a hand across his bristly head, he grinned. Nudging his tired bones forward, he placed a helmet on his head. Securing the chin strap, he informed the other two pothole occupants, "Send the word down the line I'm going into the kill zone in search of aqua."

"I wouldn't recommend that, sir," Gunny interjected. "The Japs have perfected the art of infiltration. I've seen them calling out in English for a corpsman and then killing the approaching medic. Of the bodies blanketing the kill zone, I guarantee there are Japs playing dead."

Unsheathing a Ka-Bar knife, Roche replied, "No matter how devious our enemy is, they have difficulty pronouncing the letter L. So if you hear me articulating the actress Lana Turner's name with a slight southern drawl, don't shoot." Slithering into the darkness, he mumbled, "I shan't be gone long." Crawling on the sandy coral shale, he could hear whispers of his water quest being exchanged from foxhole to foxhole.

On his belly, Roche plunged into the hazardous abyss. *I'm living on borrowed time,* he realized, slowly advancing. *I should have died on the beach, like so many others. It's really not up to me if I'm destined to expire before the end of this campaign,* he concluded. Swabbing his cracked lips with a chalky tongue, he vowed that he wasn't going to die thirsty.

A shifting breeze slapped Roche's senses with a decaying stench. His blinking eyes adjusted to the darkness. Dead, decomposing bodies occupied the ground before him. No doubt these were Japanese casualties of the preinvasion bombardment. Annoying large land crabs scurried over and around the mangled corpses. A volley of small-arms fire suddenly popped in the distance. Roche hugged the warm earth as the echoing gunfire dissipated. Crawling forward, he grabbed the first carcass he came to. *Could be booby-trapped?* he questioned briefly before turning over the swollen body. A maggot-infested Japanese officer's face stared up into the night sky. The officer still had his samurai sword, pistol, and field glasses, and attached to a shoulder sling was an Imperial Japanese Army canteen. Roche cut the canteen free with his combat knife. Picking up the nearly full one-liter flask, he smiled. *That was easy.* Scanning death's harvest, he searched for more low-lying fruit. A facedown carcass ten yards away got his attention. It appeared fresh in a sea of rot. *It only takes a couple of hours in this Pacific frying pan to bloat a dead body,* he realized, tightening his grip on his blade's leather washer handle. His inner demon surfaced. Logic and rational thought retreated beneath an intense urge to kill. Wielding the combat knife high over his head, he charged. His prey lifted its head as Roche slammed a pinning knee into the hostile's lower back. Utilizing both hands, Roche plunged seven inches of carbon steel into his enemy's spine and twisted the knife's handle. Pulsing blood warmed his hands. The dying man emitted a low, guttural groan. Prying loose the honed blade lodged in bone, Roche felt exhilarated. Now was not the time to celebrate. Rolling onto the hard earth, he pulled out his forty-five-caliber pistol and fired at a charging shadow. The handgun's recoil was firm but manageable as he squeezed off a second shot. The silhouette, wielding a bayonet-spiked rifle, fell into the killing zone morgue. All was quiet as Roche scanned the dark night behind an extended pistol-clutching arm. With adrenaline pumping through his veins, he rapidly sucked down the rank air. *I'm one badass marine,* he declared, bathing in the euphoria of existence. *Why did I focus on the Jap playing dead?* he wondered. *How did I get the drop on the bayonet-lunging Nip? I need to trust not question my instincts,* he concluded, robbing the fresh kills of their canteens.

Precious water sloshed in the Japanese containers lashed across Roche's back. Resisting the urge to quench his thirst he crawled forward. Slowly, he worked his way back toward safety. He paused. Embracing coral shale, he realized he was not alone. The rustling noise in the dark void behind him went silent. He unhooked a hand grenade from his chest rigging and pulled the pin. A sweaty palm clutched the explosive as precious seconds ticked by. Finally, he threw it in a wide arc to his rear. At the zenith of its short journey, the tiny bomb detonated. Lethal shards rained down. In the wake of the echoing blast, the cries and screams of those caught in the downpour erupted. Roche tossed a second and third grenade in the direction of the Japanese choir. The multiple eruptions silenced the wailing glee club.

Roche's intuitive delay was brief. Slowly, he made his way to the outskirts of the marine foxholes. "Lana Turner," he whispered into the darkness.

"It's the lieutenant," a quiet voice responded, triggering a bevy of informative whispers down the line.

Roche crawled out of the abyss and sat on the edge of a gun pit. The old-breed gunny, patting the green lieutenant's shoulder, commented, "You're covered in blood."

Unscrewing a canteen cap, Roche took a long-anticipated drink of warm water. Glancing down at his plasma-soaked dungarees, he snorted, "The blood's not mine."

Gunny took a calculated gulp before handing the water flasks to impatient hands reaching into the shallow shelter. "You want to talk about it?" Gunny politely inquired.

"Nah," Roche responded. Rubbing his chin, he added, "It was kinda eerie how I sensed the threat of danger."

Gunny chuckled. "At Guadalcanal, I knew marines who could smell approaching Japs. Were you able to smell them?"

"Not in that maggot-infested cesspool," Roche answered, slouching down into the uncomfortable hole. Glancing down, he examined his sweaty, blood-stained hands. *I severed a man's spinal cord*, he reflected. Instinctively, he wiped the glistening palms across his soiled dungarees. Flexing his fingers, he paused to admire his wedding ring. With his right hand, he twirled the band of gold around his ring finger. Closing his eyes, he visualized his petite wife with her big blond curly locks piled high atop her head. *Debbie Higginbottom, the runner-up in the Miss Peach Blossom Pageant, was quite the catch. To sample the virtuous Miss Higginbottom's charms, I had to take the wedding plunge*, he reflected. *What she lacked in coupling experience, she more than made up for with enthusiasm*, he delightfully recalled.

The distant crackle of gunfire disrupted Roche's pleasant distraction. "What is it, Gunny?" he whispered to the vigilant sentry.

"Nothing, Lieutenant," Gunny grunted out the side of his mouth. "Try to get some shut-eye."

Folding his arms across his chest, Roche wondered if his fanatic letter-writing wife was destined to become a young widow. *The ten-thousand-dollar life insurance death benefit should help her cope with the loss of her only lover*, he concluded, rolling onto his side.

"Japs! Japs!" Gunny hollered, spraying the perimeter with his Thompson submachine gun.

Roche awoke, reaching for his carbine. A star shell from a marine mortar ignited the sky. Showering light illuminated enemy troops advancing across the dug-in marines' frail line. The Americans unleashed a firestorm on the exposed attacking Japanese. The false sunlight faded. The marines continued to feed the darkness with small-arms fire. Bursting flares relit a battlefield piled high with dead bodies and assailants in full retreat.

Gunny squeezed off a final routing blast, hollering, "Run, you bastards! Run!"

CHAPTER NINE

Exiting the wooden box, Max blinked. He looked down to avoid torment-ing sunlight. Attempting to focus, his weak eyes tolerated the discomfort. Beside him stood Captain Seigal; in front of him, an armed Canadian sentry sucked on a lazy cigarette.

"Hands in the air!" the sentry grumbled, flicking his expiring smoke.

Tracking the discarded smoldering butt, Seigal involuntarily sighed.

Lethargic hands patted down the prisoners. After the insincere inspection, the guard informed them in accented German, "Today is moving day; I trust the accommodations were satisfactory."

Shadowed by the guard, Max and Seigal, reaching for the sky, plodded past the Canadian command post. In front of the bustling farmhouse, an American truck, laden with defeated Germans, awaited. Behind the steering wheel sat a black driver, his nose and mouth shielded by a red bandana. Two burly American soldiers, armed with pistols and red-lacquered batons, conversed with a gaggle of their Canadian allies.

Spotting their new passengers, the Yanks flexed. Stepping forward, one grinned sadistically and beat an open palm with his candy-red nightstick. His inaudible comment evoked laughter from the victorious audience. Seigal climbed into the crowded transport. As Max attempted to follow, he received a swift kick in the ass. The blow sent him flying into the arms of a gruff German sergeant.

"Get off of me," the sergeant growled, rejecting the airborne Max.

Bouncing off another annoyed passenger, Max stumbled onto the splin-tered-wood truck bed. It smelled of urine.

"What is wrong with you, Sergeant?" Seigal snapped. The noncommis-sioned officer wilted under the weight of Siegal's rank.

"I don't know, sir?" the sergeant responded. Begrudgingly, he assisted Max from the rough wood platform. Sticking out his chin, he displayed a tennis-ball knot on his grimy forehead and added, "I'm having a bad day."

"Silence!" barked the ass-kicking guard as he and his companion climbed into the crowded truck. The Americans simultaneously pulled up drab-olive scarves tethered around their necks and secured the rough kerchiefs over their noses. The truck's cab door slammed shut. The Yanks latched onto the wooden stake used for the missing canvas cover. As the transport lunged forward, a jostling ripple rolled through the compacted German cargo.

A jeep occupied by four Americans set the pace through the French countryside. The overloaded truck of prisoners followed. It was a warm summer day. The rural road was quiet, the surrounding fields deserted. Behind highwayman masks, the two American guards engaged in casual conversation. As ordered, none of the captives spoke. Behind disconnected gazes, German soldiers gnawed on the bitter taste of incarceration. On tired legs, they swayed to the rhythm of the bumpy dirt road. The only seated passenger was a wounded POW, hugging his knees. Half of his face and the top of his head were wrapped in a crusty, bloodstained field dressing. A low, steady moan flowed out of his mouth as he rocked back and forth.

Max gazed out over the truck's cab. A dusty headwind caressed his youthful features. His empty belly growled. Swallowing with a dry mouth, he closed his eyes. Summer sunlight warmed his face. After two days planted in the ground, followed by three days in a windowless wooden box, he took a victorious breath of country air. A familiar stench nullified the simple pleasure. Max snorted and opened his eyes. A heavy sun hung high. Flocks of large black birds drifted across the blue sky. In the distance, smoke strings appeared. Man-made craters exhaling mist came into view. Like a polluted sea, smoldering, twisted metal debris contaminated the rolling terrain. Death's aroma intensified. Max shielded his nose with a bent arm. The maggot-ridden remains of men and livestock defiled the undulating hillsides. Flies disrespected the dead. Defecating birds plucked at decaying flesh and lifeless eye sockets. Random heaps of scrap metal, touting the bold black German cross, identified the vanquished. The reality of defeat tugged on Max's heavy heart. *How can this be?* he wondered.

The small caravan took a hard right turn north. Death's fragrance retreated. The charred carcass of a Tiger tank marked the battlefield exit. Empty fields drifted by. A lone cow, grazing in a meadow, seemed out of place. Snuggled in a cluster of tall, healthy trees, a rural village appeared. Inviting smoke escaped a tavern's stone chimney. Disinterested villagers strolled behind a split-wood fence. Fresh fruit decorated a small orchard. The peaceful hamlet taunted Max with images of a soft bed, hot food, cool water, and a lusty French maiden. An involuntary sigh erupted out of his dry mouth. *How long before the simple pleasures of a soldier's existence return?* he wondered. Max was not alone. Hopeless expressions tracked the passing picturesque setting as the oasis of freedom faded in a cloud of trailing dust.

A setting sun introduced long shadows. The jeep exited the main thoroughfare. The truck followed down a narrow dirt road. A ditch beset with weeds skirted the new course. Occasionally sunlight sparked off the water trickling down the canal. The parched cargo stirred. Dry mouths swallowed. Max licked his chapped lips.

The jeep skidded to a squealing termination in front of a log boom gate. The counterweighted barrier rose in a vertical arc. The convoy rolled into a barbwire compound. Razor-wire fences dissected the surrounding meadow into restraining pens. Thousands of sorted Germans sat idle within the sharp wire stockades. A large cadre of American soldiers, armed with crimson nightsticks, stood primed to greet the new arrivals. The truck passengers stirred. A breeze rustled the canopies of surrounding trees. The tinkle of water resonated from the ditch beside the road. The two escorting guards hopped out of the truck bed. As if rehearsed, they released the vehicle's tailgate and jumped aside. Thirsty prisoners spilled out of the transport. In a cloud of dust, the parched cargo stampeded toward the roadside canal. Like a thirsty herd of cattle, the POWs competed to hydrate themselves. Lying in a bed of weeds on the soft bank of the irrigation ditch, Max lapped at the clear water flowing by. As the initial refreshment flowed down his bone-dry throat, his gulps accelerated. Around him, sloppy swallows and sighs of relief reverberated. Water splashed. An American audience chuckled in the distance. The shrill blast of a pea whistle required investigation. Far from satisfying his thirst, Max looked up.

A pudgy American sergeant released a shiny metal whistle tied around his neck and politely nodded at a gangly German officer.

The German major stepped forward. In a crusty voice, he announced, "Comrades, the Americans require that you line up in three lines." With a stiff arm, he designated the alignment location and added, "Keep three steps' distance between each row."

"When will they feed us?" a private called out from the canal bank.

"Three lines," the major repeated.

"We need food," another irate captive hollered. "I'm done taking orders from the likes of you."

Seigal approached the major. They conversed in whispers. Seigal, the Panzer-Lehr commander, stood proud. Even in his torn and frayed uniform, he projected the prestige and distinction of Germany's elite armored division.

"Gentlemen," Seigal said in a commanding tone. "We are German soldiers," he declared. "So behave accordingly." Flexing his weathered frame, he barked, "Three lines."

Fatigued bodies reacted. The German POWs slowly fell into formation. Seigal nodded his approval and, with his head held high, strutted into line behind Max. Out of the cluster of red-truncheon-wielding guards, three American soldiers armed with clipboards approached the prisoner queues.

"Max!" Seigal whispered. "Don't look back," he instructed.

Max focused forward at the Americans questioning the men in the front of the lines.

"The Yanks are attempting to identify Nazis," Seigal quietly informed him. "Swallow your pride, Max," he counseled. "Respond to their questions with humble, appeasing answers."

Max acknowledged his understanding with a slight nod.

The POWs standing in line quietly shuffled forward. It became obvious. The fanatic wolves in the flock were being separated from the defeated sheep.

"Next," a thin American corporal called out. Beneath his steel bonnet resided a baby face. Looking up from his clipboard, he squinted at the blond, blue-eyed young Aryan. "Name and division," he inquired in perfect German.

"Max Kohl, Twelfth SS Panzer Hitlerjugend."

The corporal chuckled, "The baby division."

"Bauer!" the sergeant interrogating the prisoner in the next line over interrupted. The sergeant was heavy; actually, he was fat. His potbelly taxed his olive-drab uniform's buttons. A five-o'clock shadow infested plump jowls. His open mouth repetitively smacked on a large wad of gum. "Don't waste your time. The kid's a Nazi. And the Twelfth SS is not the baby division. It's the murder division." Chewing his cud, he scowled at Max and growled, "How many Canadian prisoners did you murder?"

Returning the American sergeant's scorn with a defiant squint, Max stood at attention and concluded, *If I'm to be convicted by this poor excuse for a soldier, I'll accept that. Regardless, I'm not going to plead my case to this lip-smacking heifer.* With his chest sticking out and shoulders back, he declared proudly, "Max Kohl, Twelfth SS Panzer Hitlerjugend."

"Get this Nazi punk out of my sight," the gruff sergeant snapped.

"Good luck, Max," Seigal whispered over the boy's shoulder.

CHAPTER TEN

The hillside village square bustled with activity on a warm afternoon. The warriors of the tribe converged around the stone communal well. Barefoot partisans were armed with crossbows, lances, and muskets. For the impending presentation, the short, stocky Guajac wore a jaunty red beret. In front of a focused audience, he loaded a virgin M2 carbine. Curious Hmong expressions bobbed in and out to catch a glimpse of the procedure.

Propped up on the stone lip of the waterhole, a disinterested Carlo Coty enjoyed a cigarette. In a wrinkled white linen suit coat, the silver-haired Corsican brought a smoldering tab to his mouth with a limp wrist. After an exquisite inhale, he tilted his head back and blew a smoky plume into the pure mountain air. Deep scars invested his prominent, bulbous nose. His pinkish aging features grimaced in afternoon sunlight. Snorting in disgust, he placed a hand on his shrinking belly. The growling stomach protested the meager Hmong cuisine. Civilization was what he craved. Beyond the mountains, a refined social order that pampered the privileged existed.

The four liberated French soldiers in torn and frayed uniforms entered the assembly, hauling the large lid of a supply crate. Alain was the tallest and widest of the quartet. Although he had lost weight, he still resembled a sumo wrestler. His injured snout appeared as just a blemish on a massive head. The oversized noggin was crowned with greasy black hair. Beside Alain, Luc, holding a corner of the panel, waddled forward. A fungal rash was the cause of his clumsy, swaying shuffle. The soft-spoken Luc was skinny before the drastic change in diet. His uniform still fit him well. The infestation of acne scars from his youth camouflaged his pierced beak. Grumpy Leon was the alpha of the pack. Like Claveau, the Japanese had torn off his nose. Above a scraggly black beard, he displayed exposed nasal passages with a perpetual scowl.

Leon was intimidating before the mutilation. A missing nose enhanced his bully demeanor. The self-conscious young Claveau concealed his absent appendage with a prosthetic fashioned out of a tin can. A leather lace, tied behind his head, held the tapered, folded metal replica in place. Above the artificial nose, rich blue eyes sparkled. It was rare that he made eye contact. Drooping shoulders and downward glances shielded his disfigured face from the world.

"Fifty yards!" Guajac hollered, pointing down the road leading out of town.

Roughly pacing off the distance, the French troops propped up the wooden crate lid with a bamboo pole. Across the grainy surface, Claveau, utilizing a charcoal stick, etched a human outline. On the silhouette's head, he drew a Japanese military cap with neck flaps. Stepping back, he admired the crude sketch.

The excitement escalated, as women in black cylindrical hats appeared on the elevated decks of the stilted hovels surrounding the square. Beneath the balcony seating, clusters of children stood in anticipation.

"This is the M2 carbine with a folding steel stock!" Guajac hollered, raising the weapon over his head. The crowd quieted. The paratrooper looked at Loc to translate as he slowly spun around.

Loc shrugged.

"It is lightweight," he continued.

Loc translated.

"And can be operated in both full and semiautomatic firing modes."

Once again, Loc shrugged. Teeb placed a reassuring hand on his son's shoulder.

"I'll show you," Guajac conceded, setting the selector to full automatic. With a sweeping hand, he urged the crowd to step back. Stepping forward, he faced the target in a wide stance. As he took aim, a skinny red dog wandered into the line of fire. The curious mutt meandered over to the propped-up wooden panel. After an investigative sniff, the canine raised a hind leg and marked the target with a healthy urine stream.

The audience broke out in laughter. The erupting levity startled the dog.

"That is one tough act to follow," Coty commented.

Surrounded by snickers and fading chuckles, Guajac raised the weapon waist high and squeezed the trigger. A tremendous cacophony of sound spewed a salvo of thirty-caliber rounds into the crate lid. Wood chips flew off the hard surface. Women screamed. Children cried. A panicked crowd took flight. The warrior class joined the terrified audience and hastily departed the stage.

Exiting dust swirled around the abandoned Frenchmen. A dumbfounded Guajac spun around. Hopping down from his uncomfortable perch, Coty stretched. "Didn't see that coming," he offered. "Now would be a good time to pack our bags and head to China."

Guajac eyed the Corsican with disdain. Spotting curious warriors returning, the lieutenant held out the automatic weapon and muttered, "Don't be afraid."

Teeb walked over to the target. The splintered scars of twenty rounds graced the wood panel. About ten bullet holes resided inside the lines of the charcoal silhouette. "A waste of ammunition," he commented to a returning audience. He walked over to the lieutenant. Politely, he coaxed Guajac to follow. At about two hundred yards from the target, he stopped. Raising his musket, he took aim and fired. A sulfur mist floated across the line of fire. Dissipating smoke revealed a musket ball ripped into the crate lid dead center of the outlined head.

"Amazing!" Guajac exclaimed. Slowly nodding, he commented, "You, my friend, are a world-class marksman."

Teeb rested the long barrel across a relaxed arm. He didn't understand French but realized Guajac had paid him a compliment. Graciously, he accepted the praise with a slight bow.

Guajac inserted a fresh clip into the carbine. Setting the selector to semi-automatic, he assumed a firing position. Taking aim, he squeezed the trigger. The gun popped. A bullet nailed the target figurine in the torso region. He fired again, registering another unimpressive hit. Lowering the weapon, he squinted down the firing range. Satisfied, he offered the automatic weapon to the tribal marksman. The target shooters exchanged rifles. Curious warriors crowded around.

Teeb took aim. The focused audience went silent. The short, lightweight rifle felt awkward. Teeb fidgeted in an uncomfortable stance and fired. A projectile bit off a corner of the panel but missed the crude Japanese soldier outline. Surprised, disappointed gasps rippled through the Hmong audience.

Teeb grinned, adjusted his aim, and squeezed the trigger. He fired again and again. Thirty-caliber rounds pulsed out the short gun barrel. Bullet after bullet chipped away at the target's head. The barking automatic weapon went silent. The echo of gunfire faded. Lowering the weapon, Teeb admired the precise, gaping hole he had created. His impressed neighbors cheered.

Patting Teeb on the back, Guajac muttered, "Remarkable." Surveying the enlightened expressions of the tribe, he realized this opportunity should not be squandered. "Loc!" he called out to the milling warriors. The young translator emerged out of the crowd. Guajac, winking at the boy, asked, "Can you translate for me?"

Loc nodded.

Guajac picked up the boy and placed him on the rim of the stone well. "I need warriors to take up arms against the Japanese invaders," the Frenchman declared to the assembly. Loc translated. "The Hmong and French fighting together eliminated the Black Flags from the highlands. Your enemies are our enemies." As Loc relayed the reference to the marauding Chinese bandits who terrorized the hill tribes, the crowd grunted in disgust. Holding an M2 carbine high in the air, Guajac proposed, "A rifle like this and ammunition will be given to all those who fight beside me."

The offer was well received by men whose most cherished possession was a homemade flintlock. Enthusiastic Hmong dialogue drifted through potential partisans.

An eager throng followed Guajac to the weapons cache. In front of a palm-frond lean-to, an orderly queue formed. Claveau and Leon used Japanese bayonets to pry open wood crates. Guajac exchanged a handshake and virgin automatic weapon with each volunteer. Luc and Alain handed out sparkling ammunition. Recipients squatted or stood in clusters, admiring their new firearms. Coty wandered over to the back of the shortening recruitment line.

Looking up at the Corsican, Guajac snapped, "What do you want?"

"An M2 carbine," Coty casually responded.

"What would you do with it?" the commando questioned.

"It may come as a surprise to you," Coty informed the lieutenant. "But I have experience with small arms. Although I prefer a pistol for close-quarters engagements, I'm not going to turn down the offer of a free rifle."

Guajac sighed and handed the gangster a carbine.

CHAPTER ELEVEN

Dusk approached. Flood lights awoke. A soft breeze cooled the summer air as it rolled down into an overpopulated meadow. Stilted guard towers secured the four corners of a massive razor-wire compound. From the tall perches, American machine gunners scanned the barbwire-embraced fields below. Across the enclosed valley, more than a division of captured Germans milled around or reclined. The populous all suffered, to various degrees, exhaustion, hunger, depression, and boredom. Captured officers, noncommissioned officers, soldiers, and evil Nazis were housed in segregated wire cages. Within the officer's pen, dark-green canvas tents acknowledged the summer wind.

Behind the log boom gate entrance, Max stood among a pack of condemned Nazis. Pinned to his breast pocket, a postcard label identified him as a "Prisoner of War." He watched as Seigal and a cadre of German officers were ushered off to their cage. *What is my fate?* he questioned, studying his fellow Nazis. Behind their obstinate expressions, rage simmered. They still believed unequivocally in a German victory. *At least my new cellmates possess a spine*, Max concluded.

Three Americans brandishing red nightsticks approach. Setting the pace, a wiry Yank walked bow-legged. It appeared he had just ridden into town on a horse. Strutting like a gamecock, he scrutinized the pack of Nazi wolves. His face puckered around a parrot snout.

"It appears this ass-licking cowboy is here to show us to our rooms," gruff Waffen SS Sergeant Stollhoof mumbled. Closed-cropped hair capped his big sooty noggin. A tennis-ball knot clung to the side of his forehead. A tattered uniform shrouded his broad shoulders and muscular frame.

The comment evoked snickers.

Educated in brute force, the hatchet-faced cowboy drew back his crimson baton and smacked Stollhoof across the back. It was a calculated blow to establish respect.

Stollhoof responded to the disciplinary whack with a chuckle.

The American returned the smile and rolled up the sleeve of his nightstick-wielding arm. A row of German wristwatches spanned from wrist to elbow. "This way," he growled, pointing the red-lacquered nightstick and timepiece display into the bowels of the barbwire maze.

Max followed toward the end of the Nazi column. The dirt path had been ground into moist, compact earth. Flanking spiked wire defined the outdoor corridor. Bearded German prisoners in shabby uniforms observed the passing of the new arrivals. In the corner of the immense camp, under an ominous stilted watchtower, the American escorts herded the captured wolves into the Nazi corral.

On tired legs, Max slowly pivoted. Disinterested inhabitants reclined on barren earth. There was a single gnarly tree reaching into the evening sky. The leaves were missing. Robbed of its bark, the trunk stood naked. Around the base, clawed holes had stolen shallow roots. *My god*, Max realized, *I'm going to starve to death.*

From the prisoners lounging at the base of the nude tree, a lieutenant rose. He was way too thin for his uniform. Beneath sharp cheekbones, a scraggly beard grew wild. Gnarled hair accented with dead grass crowned his narrow head. Taking a deep breath, he buttoned his oversized shirt. Muttering an inaudible comment, he solicited tired laughter from a reclining, lethargic audience. "Kamraden," he called out, approaching his curious new neighbors. "A hearty welcome to compound seven, Alencon, France. Lieutenant Krause is my name."

Max saluted the officer.

Casually returning the gesture, Krause chuckled. "I appreciate that, son. Although I am the officer responsible for this cage, we can forgo military protocol." Glancing around, he informed the new prisoners, "As you can see, there is no roof, beds, nor blankets in my hotel. But the summer weather has been kind. No need to point out the latrine; just follow your noses." Grinning, he concluded the introduction. "One important feature to note, if you wander closer than five yards toward our barbwire fence, you will be shot."

"Are they going to feed us?" Stollhoof growled.

"They did this morning," Krause answered.

"Water, sir?" Max inquired.

"I'm afraid you are in for a dry night," Krause said with regret. "Food and water comes at dawn. Now, along the wire at night, you can barter with our captors. Watches, rings, fountain pens, lighters, and medals are the currency." With a shrug, he confessed, "I purchased a can of beans with my iron cross last week."

"Those bastards!" Stollhoff snorted.

"Don't blame the Americans," Krause responded. "Our rapid retreat has stretched the Allies' supply lines. And we, my friends, are at the bottom of the food chain. Now if there are no more questions and if you don't get shot tonight, I'll see you in the morning at breakfast." His audience stood silent. "Good," he said, vigorously scratching his scraggly knotted hair. "One more thing," he added, walking away, "if you don't have lice…you will."

A wave of darkness spilled across the prisoners of compound seven. Hundreds of men lay on the moist ground. Stars sparkled above. Cautiously Max meandered through the reclining human labyrinth. His thirst trumped his empty belly. The bodies thinned as the stench of the latrine intensified. A septic trench, just outside of the kill zone, along the back of the wire pen, emitted the shithouse odor. Snorting, Max moved upwind and sat down in the quiet dark. Gazing through the sharp wire, he caught a whiff of rich tobacco smoke. From outside the cage, a smoldering cigar tip floated in the darkness. A helmeted GI, sucking on a fat stogie, appeared. Toting a canvas sack with a rifle slung over his shoulder, he squinted at Max. "What have you brought to barter with?" he asked in perfect German with a Bavarian twang. "I'm specifically in the market for German medals. An iron cross will buy you a fine meal."

Instinctively Max grabbed the hem of his field blouse and confirmed the concealed Hitler Youth shooting proficiency badge. *Am I that hungry? Am I that thirsty?* he wondered and realized, *The medal is what defines me.* "All I have is an empty belly and a dry throat," he informed the sentry. Studying the cigar-chomping German-American, he had to comment, "Your German is impeccable, spoken like a true Bavarian."

Exhaling a proud puff of smoke, the grinning Yank muttered, "Thank you, Jerry…Where are you from?"

"Nuremberg," Max responded. "My father was a bricklayer."

"No shit!" the Yank exclaimed. "My parents emigrated from Nuremberg, and my father was also a mason. The family name was Holtzman, but we shortened it to Holt in Wisconsin."

What a strange world this is, Max thought.

"What's your name?" Holt asked.

"Max, Max Kohl."

"Well, Max, my Bavarian kinsman, today is your lucky day." He reached into his canvas sack and pulled out a large tin can, which he tossed over the six-foot-high wire fence. It hit the moist ground beside Max with a thud.

"What is it?" Max asked, picking up the one-pound can.

"A free sample of corned beef hash." Holt chuckled. Throwing a smaller can into the cage, he added, "And here is some milk to wash it down with."

"Danke, Holtzman," Max mumbled, hastily snatching up the liquid prize.

"Now if you run across an iron cross in there, please let me know," Holt said, flicking his cigar through the razor wire. The red tip sparked as it hit the moist ground. Slowly fading into the dark freedom engulfing the cage, he disappeared.

Picking up the smoldering stogie, Max tucked the moist end into the corner of his dry mouth. A soothing toke brought the tobacco embers to life. Tilting his head back, he released a victorious plume of smoke into the sparkling sky. *Well, at least I'm not going to starve tonight.*

CHAPTER TWELVE

Ι t was raining. Low clouds concealed the peaks of the mountainous terrain. A golden tan deer leaped out of the dense forest. It stood on a narrow muddy roadway. It was a small animal, no more than two feet high. Its face was dark brown. Its antlers were one-inch nubs. Flexing, it gazed down the wet thoroughfare slicing through the jungle. The faint cough of a diesel engine escalated. Sensing a predator, the tiny buck lowered its head and emitted a barking warning. A herd of female deer scurried across the roadway behind their protector. Proudly, the male followed his harem back into the jungle.

An overburdened transport rounded the corner. Massive mud tires detonated soupy potholes. The Vietnamese driver downshifted as the grade steepened. In the passenger seat, Captain Ishibashi of the Imperial Japanese Army focused on a side-mounted mirror. The reflection of the trailing convoy slowly appeared in the glass pane. He counted as each truck came into view. Satisfied, he looked forward. Overworked wiper blades sloshed back and forth. Visibility was poor. Tall, embracing wet growth drifted by.

It had been a long travel day. The journey had started out at the port city of Haiphong. Traveling along colonial Route 7, the convoy had just entered Laos. The broken and battered arterial was the only option to feed the Japanese empire's occupation of the landlocked country. Japan's Indochina strategy had altered since the Allied liberation of Paris. The days of Vichy France supporting the Japanese war effort had ended. A free France stood poised to reclaim its valuable Southeast Asian colonies.

Ishibashi gazed out the passenger window. Small streams flowing out of the jungle fed the rushing torrent running alongside Route 7. He swallowed. The Ban Ban Bridge was the concern. *Once we cross, the threat of flash flooding will be eliminated*, he reasoned. He checked his watch and then the growing rushing water threat.

The rain softened. Ishibashi lit up a cigarette. Sucking down nicotine smoke, he grinned as the Ban Ban Valley appeared. Low clouds concealed the sky. A murky churning river cut through the basin. A stout wooden bridge spanned the racing muddy water. Small communities inhabited the opposing banks of the viaduct. *Crossing is no longer an issue*, Ishibashi thought, taking a comforting toke.

Mud-incrusted tires rolled onto the Ban Ban Bridge. The planked wood platform trembled under the passing transport's weight. Ejected chunks of muck ricocheted off wheel wells. Gazing across the rippling water, Captain Ishibashi flicked his smoldering butt over the side.

Lieutenant Louis Guajac of Corps Expéditionnaire Français d'extrême Orient viewed the Japanese convoy rolling across the viaduct with delight. Falling rain careened off his poncho. A smoldering American cigarette dangled from his lower lip. Crouched down in the weed forest along the riverbank, he placed a wet hand on an exploder handle. "One more," he muttered, eyeing a transport hesitating to cross. The lead vehicle dictated the assault. "Three it is," he mumbled turning the handle.

Just above the water line, under the first truck, a massive explosion splintered the bridge supports. A sequential series of blasts erupted beneath the spanning structure. Shredded timber flew into the cloudy sky. Twisting and turning, the collapsing bridge expelled three heavy-laden transports. The trucks plunged into the rushing river. Crated cargo and flailing troops surfaced in the rapids.

Standing on the muddy riverbank, five Frenchmen and thirty Hmong warriors observed the drifting carnage. On the opposing shoreline, Japanese troops milled around idle trucks. Their journey had reached a dead end.

"Kiss my ass!" Grumpy Leon hollered over the rumbling water.

"They can't hear you," Claveau commented.

"Maybe this one did," Leon responded looking down the embankment.

Crawling out of the river, a Japanese soldier collapsed in the shallows. A captain's insignia adorned his collar. Gasping for life, he rolled onto his back. The murky water surrounding him quickly turned a shade of red.

"He's a dead man," Guajac muttered. "Leave him."

Claveau frowned. Beneath his concealing metal beak, his breath accelerated. "*Tij Laug,*" he addressed Leej, using the term for *brother.* "I need your blade."

Leej obliged, unsheathing a fat-bellied Hmong knife. He handed the sharp tool to the Frenchman. The partisans all watched as Claveau shimmed down the slick embankment. He hopped into the crimson ankle-deep water engulfing the dying man. Grabbing a handful of the officer's uniform, he elevated the Japanese captain. A disconnected gaze attempted to focus on the Frenchman with a sharp, pointed tin snout. A sweeping blade severed the captain's nose.

Squatting down, Claveau cleaned the bloody blade on the officer's uniform. Making eye connect, he said, "Now you can die."

CHAPTER THIRTEEN

The sea was rough. The crowded transport vessel rocked and swayed in the harsh waters off the coast of Peleliu. The marines onboard, having served over forty days in hell, were being pulled out of the fray. No one spoke. Puffing on a fresh cigarette, Roche scanned the vacant expressions of his brothers. Spotting the wide-eyed Private Doyle, Roche grinned. The choirboy no longer looked like a kid. Rifle oil and coral dust tarnished the young leatherneck's scraggly beard. Doyle, mumbling under his breath, made the sign of the cross, kissed his finger, and pointed toward heaven in gratitude.

Doyle's guardian angel came through for him, Roche reasoned. *Good for him. Blind faith is as good as any compass to navigate the horrors of war. I relied on an inner demon to survive,* he realized. *My callous dark side's objective was to exterminate the enemy with extreme prejudice. I not only discovered my cruel persona; I relished the guilt-free sensation.*

The transport bobbed in the choppy waters beside a merchant troopship. The stoic marines methodically began climbing the cargo net to board. Exhausted, Roche rolled over the ship's gunwale. Ignoring the queues for hot coffee, citrus juice, and below-deck quarters assignments, he gazed across the blue Pacific at the hideous coral scab called Peleliu. The battle raged on. *How many more American lives will that hideous isle consume?* he wondered.

"Grapefruit juice, Lieutenant?" Gunny asked, offering a full paper cup.

"Thanks, Gunny," Roche mumbled, accepting the beverage. He tossed back the acidic treat in one gulp. The sharp, sour taste was invigorating. "Ah," he involuntarily sighed, crushing the paper cup. Tossing the trash wad overboard, he said, "Do you think there is any whisky on this barge?"

Leaning on the rail, the salty old marine looked longingly across the blue water. "I sure hope so, sir." Taking a composing breath, he added, "We need to raise a glass, to those we left behind."

Roche slowly nodded. "Let me see what I can muster up after a shower and shave."

After getting his quarters assignment, Roche waded into the quiet stream of battle-weary marines flowing below deck. Metal stair treads flexed beneath the descending troops. Foul body odors quickly polluted the warm atmosphere.

"I'm in the market for a war souvenir," hollered a large sailor at the base of the stairway. The rolled-up sleeves of his chambray work shirt revealed black-smith forearms. The white cotton Dixie-cup hat atop Li'l Abner's head leaned starboard. "Does anyone have a Jap flag or pistol they would like to sell?"

A few marines shook their heads. A couple stared at the solicitor with blank expressions. Most just shuffled by.

"I'm in the market for a war souvenir," repeated the corn-fed-looking swabbie.

"I'm in the market for whisky," Roche replied. "Is there any bourbon on this barnacle bucket?"

The sailor's farm boy good looks lit up. "You have a samurai sword?"

Slowly nodding, Roche asked, "You have bourbon?"

"Scotch," the crewman answered with an apologetic shrug. "A sealed bottle of Teacher's scotch."

Roche's nose crinkled. Realizing his reaction, he burst out laughing. *I risked my life for a sip of stagnant water*, he reflected, giggling. *And now I feel slighted having to sip scotch instead of bourbon.*

Startled by the cackling lieutenant, Li'l Abner took a cautious step back.

Chuckling, Roche flexed a reassuring palm and mumbled, "Inside joke." Dipping a shoulder, he dropped his combat backpack. Lashed to the side were four Japanese katana swords of various lengths. He retrieved the smallest one, which was just less than two feet in length. Offering the merchandise, he questioned, "Do we have a deal?"

Fixated on the remaining inventory, the sailor pointed at a prime blade and responded, "I like that one."

"And I like bourbon," Roche snapped. Focused on the sailor's name stenciled over a breast pocket, he added, "Do we have deal...Odenbach?"

"Yes, sir!'

"Good," Roche replied, relinquishing the small sword. "I'm going to stow my gear, shit, shower, and shave. After that, I'll expect to find the libation waiting for me in my quarters." Negotiation completed, he flowed back into the stream of ripe-smelling leathernecks.

In a relaxed trance, Roche headed back to his assigned rack. Cleansing himself of the stench of combat was a pleasurable experience. A canvas belt, cinched tight, secured his baggy fresh dungarees. He had lost weight. An investigating tongue continuously swabbed clean teeth. Below deck, the temperature was uncomfortably warm. Beads of sweat migrated down his back. Entering his stale quarters, he was delighted to see a bottle of Teacher's Highland Cream Whisky and a healthy bundle of mail on his bunk. Brown string wrapped the frayed compilation of letters from the home front. The balmy accommodations were vacant with the exception of a snoring second lieutenant on a top bunk two rows over.

Healing serenity soothed Roche's heart in anticipation of reading his dedicated wife's correspondence. Taking a deep breath of salty air void of war's stench, he retrieved the wax-wrapped photo of his loving bride from his knapsack. The elements of Peleliu had taken a toll on the five-by-seven black-and-white depiction. Regardless, he gazed lovingly at the image. A soft smiled graced her dark, painted lips. Golden-blond curls were pile high atop her head in a lush updo. Innocent dark eyes beckoned. "What a beauty," he mumbled. Cracking the seal on the bottle of booze, he took a well-deserved swig of bourbon's sophisticated cousin. Warm whisky flowed past his clean teeth and across a grateful tongue. *This definitely is not watered-down swill*, he concluded, wiping moist lips with the back of a hand. After resealing the precious fluid, he stowed it away. Climbing into the warm bunk, he placed the package of mail on his flat belly. Holding up his wife's picture, he mumbled, "So what's new in your world?"

For continuity, each envelope was numbered in the lower left-hand corner. Roche sequentially sorted the correspondence. An anxious fingernail sliced open number 152 in his wife's daily writing commitment.

August 13, 1944

My Dearest Darling,

I bought a car today. It's a 1932 Ford Coupe. The younger brother of the plant manager, Mr. Lewis, got drafted and had to sell. Marcy and I pooled our funds and paid seventy-five dollars for the black beauty. No more riding the bus to the factory. Marcy and I will be traveling in style to work. I know what you're thinking, but Mr. Lewis volunteered to teach us to drive. Our first lesson is tomorrow after work. I'm so excited. I can't believe that I bought a car with the money I earned.

Roche chuckled. *Marcy and Deb behind the steering wheel is an accident waiting to happen. I tried to teach the Higginbottom sisters to drive once*, he reflected. *That poor bastard Lewis has no idea what he got himself into. The clutch won't last the first lesson.* He continued to read, occasionally glancing at the image of the sultry Mrs. Roche.

I hate to write bad news, but Mass today was a sad affair. Father Mark informed us that Joey Albrighton was killed in action in France. Do you remember Joey? He was younger than us, the only boy in a family with six girls. As an altar boy, he got in hot water for getting drunk on sacramental wine. I knew his older sister Joyce but not well. All the Albrightons were there today. Father Mark asked us to pray for the family and all the men in uniform.

Please come home to me, Tom.

I miss you so much.

Your loving wife,

Deb

"I miss you too, sweetheart," Roche mumbled, tearing into letter 153. Around letter 162, Deb got a ten-dollar monthly raise, the coupe needed a new carburetor, and Mr. Lewis became Steve. The September 10 letter opened with an apology for breaking the daily writing streak, and apparently Steve wanted to enlist, but his migraine headaches and high blood pressure rendered him unqualified.

The dates between the correspondences widened as the text shrank. Roche opened the last envelope with a premonition.

October 15, 1944

Tom,

I'm sorry. There is no easy way to say it. But I want a divorce. It's not you. I'm not the same person you married. I've become very independent and found someone who loves the new me. I did love you very much and was proud to be Mrs. Tom Roche. However, the distance between us was too great for that relationship to grow. You will always have a special place in my heart, and I pray for your safe return.

Please forgive me.

Debbie

P.S. If you don't mind, I'd like to keep the wedding china.

"I'll be damned," Roche mumbled. "My virgin bride is fucking a four-fer." His heart rate accelerated. Snorting rage, his callous persona surfaced. A wicked grin emerged. "Good thing I didn't die on Peleliu. That bitch and her pantywaist boyfriend would be ten thousand dollars richer." He hopped out of his rack. Loose pages fluttered to the floor. Grabbing the bottle of scotch, he stormed out of the sweltering quarters. "I need to find my brothers," he muttered. "They are the only family I need."

CHAPTER FOURTEEN

Keying in a series of electronic dots and dashes, Lieutenant Guajac reached out across occupied Burma to an Allied airbase in Calcutta. It seemed ironic that he could communicate thousands of miles away, but if he needed to send a message to another hill tribe, it required a runner. The cheerful French-speaking Loc was his best errand boy. The cunning kid's linguistic talent and knowledge of the mountainous terrain was a valuable asset.

Having ordered a munitions drop to feed a growing Hmong resistance, Guajac stood up and stretched. Warm afternoon sunlight flowed through an open window. He turned off the obnoxiously large radio to preserve precious batteries. He smiled. Even headquarters was amazed at the clandestine operation's successes. *The Hmong are impressive warriors*, he reflected. *The speed and endurance with which they traverse the rugged landscape to strike have convinced the Japs that the French have returned in force. But my partisan army does not follow orders*, he realized. *The Hmong choose when and where they engage the enemy. If it doesn't suit them, they just walk away.*

Creaking stair treads preceded Coty's appearance in the doorway. A white linen suit coat hung on the shirtless Corsican. Wispy gray hair covered his exposed chest. Slung over his shoulder was his free carbine. "What's the news from France?" he asked.

"In Paris, German collaborators are being executed," Guajac mumbled to appease the inquiry. Conceding to the annoying Corsican's raised brows, he continued. "US and British troops have crossed the Rhine. And in the Pacific, the Yanks' island hopping toward Tokyo is succeeding with heavy losses. The fanatical Japs have resorted to suicide aircraft attacks."

Coty sighed. "It doesn't sound like I'll be going home anytime soon."

A disinterested Guajac shrugged.

Coty turned to investigate clopping horse hooves, barking dogs, and the jubilant cry of children.

"What is it?" Guajac mumbled, walking onto the bamboo terrace.

Six armed Chinamen led four packhorses into the town square. Curious local children and a pack of Hmong dogs escorted the merchants toward the town well. Three of the mountain ponies were transporting barter goods. The fourth horse was hauling wicker baskets full of opium balls.

"What do you think their agenda is?" Guajac questioned.

"Pure capitalism," Coty responded. "The Japanese occupation has disrupted France's opium monopoly. These enterprising bastards are filling the void. If the goods can't make it to market, you bring the market to the source."

The hierarchy of the caravan traders was apparent. Two coolies in conical hats placed their antique bolt-action rifles against the stone well and unloaded. A merchant in a brown fedora with Coke-bottle-thick spectacles lit up a cigarette. He was in his late twenties and short by Asian standards. With a watchful eye, he monitored the unpacking.

Ignoring the proceedings, three thugs strutted over to the shade of a stilted hovel. Leading the trio was a shotgun-toting ruffian. Long jet-black hair flowed out of a red bandana and down his shoulders. A frayed leather eye patch concealed a dead socket. Crisscrossing bandoliers of shotgun shells decorated his chest. Beside him, a massive brute of a man wiped the sweat off the top of his sparkling bald head. Fat jowls dominated his flabby face. A leather lariat around his short, thick neck was attached to the eyelet of a pistol grip. A dangling revolver swayed below his exposed barrel chest. Rounding out the security detail, wearing a red turban and complementary crimson sash, was a beady-eyed brigand. A slithering serpent tattoo adorned his face and neck. From the corners of his mouth, a slender, straight mustache extended down past his jaw. His chin anchored a third scraggly tendril. Tucked into his crimson cummerbund was a long-barreled Mauser machine pistol. The triad took a seat in the shade. The bald ogre sat Indian style. With a blank face, he stared into space. Laying a stubby double-barrel shotgun across his lap, the One-Eyed Jack pulled a cheroot out of his black tunic. Closing his good eye, he took a bite out of the small cigar and chewed. The snake-marked henchman, raising both hands over his head, yawned.

From his perch, Guajac examined the Chinese gangsters and commented to Coty, "They seem like pleasant fellows."

"That is my ticket out of town," Coty delightfully declared. "I just need to hitch a ride on the opium train headed toward civilization."

"Bad plan," Guajac interjected. "They will kill you for your carbine or turn you over to the Japs to gain favor. Regardless, once you leave this sanctuary, you are a dead man."

"Let me worry about the risk, Lieutenant," Coty replied.

In the town square, the opium road show set up shop. A tall goofy-looking lackey in a coolie hat tossed a ruff wool blanket on the dusty ground. His baggy trousers were cut short, exposing skinny calves and soiled feet. The gawky simpleton with a lemon-sized Adam's apple arranged merchandise on the cloth. Five-pound bags of salt, pots, bolts of cloth, sewing needles, and an assortment of cutlery were enticingly displayed.

The Chinese merchant, Wang Jishi, removed his fedora. With a shirt sleeve, he swept his moist forehead and took a seat at a commandeered table. An inkwell, pen, leather-bound ledger, and balancing scale occupied the tabletop. Wang dipped the pen in the well, opened the accounts book, and looked up at the first Hmong farmer standing in line.

In perfect penmanship, Wang recorded the weight of each ball of raw opium and barter goods exchanged. The process was orderly, haggling minimal. Wang conceded quickly on all negotiations by offering the fabric that nobody had an interest in. He was unaware that France provided parachute silk for free.

It had been a good day, he realized, closing the ledger. Behind him, the lackeys closed up shop. Wang lit up a cigarette, and leaning back, he exhaled. In his comfortable repose, he watched a middle-aged white man approaching.

Standing in front of the table, Coty asked, "Parlez-vous francais?"

After examining the Frenchman, Wang displayed a narrow gap between his thumb and forefinger. "I speak a little," he responded in guttural French.

"Good," Coty replied, dipping a shoulder and releasing the strap of his carbine. He placed the rifle on the table. "Take me to China with you, and this is yours."

Wang sat up. He appeared interested. "Lui!" he called over in the direction of the security detail. One-eyed Jack slowly rose. With a sawed-off shotgun balanced over his shoulder, he sauntered over to the negotiations. The Chinamen cackled in their native dialect. Lui picked up the automatic firearm with a lecherous grin. Slowly, he nodded his approval.

Coty grabbed the gun. Lui held tight before releasing his grip. Slinging the carbine over his shoulder, Coty addressed Wang, "When we get to China, I'll give you the gun."

CHAPTER FIFTEEN

It was a cool autumn morn. Six army-green transports awaited human cargo. In the shade of a large canopy tree, black drivers engaged in an animated dialogue. A cloud of cigarette smoke hovered over their boisterous exchange. In contrast, a grim, sluggish procession plodded out of the razor-wire internment camp. After two months in the wire-penned meadow, the elements and poor rations had sapped the incarcerated. Mighty German soldiers had been reduced to gaunt, lice-infested vagabonds. Scraggly beards and hermit hair fluttered under a soft wind. A fetid odor stained the chilled atmosphere. American handlers, protected by surgical gloves, assisted the weakest freight into the trucks.

In mud-encrusted boots, Max climbed into the lead vehicle. Gazing at the American barracks, he watched as the American flag was raised. The stars and bars waved victoriously. A bugle sounded reveille. *They are winning the war*, he conceded as the vehicle's engines stuttered before turning over.

The foremost transport launched forward. The caravan followed. The small convoy climbed out of the concertina-wire-shrouded meadow. The rising sun produced an unseasonably warm day. The pastel color palate of fall blessed the provincial terrain. The transport's mud tires stirred up fallen golden leaves. The lustrous yellow foliage twirled playfully in the disturbed air. Nature's colorful gift was lost on the solemn passengers. In a rippling field of lavender, a downed aircraft's vertical stabilizer tarnished the scenic vista. Like a metal tombstone, the implanted tailfin displayed the swastika and more than likely marked the pilot's grave.

Late in the afternoon, the air was crisp and clean. A barracks city rose out of the horizon. Smoke strings drifted above the hastily constructed facility. Fresh razor wire sparkled along the compound's perimeter. A German work crew toiled along the side of the road. They appeared healthy, well fed. Three armed Americans, lounging in a jeep, insincerely monitored the work detail's progress. The convoy rolled past the laborers into the gated community. Gravel crunched as the caravan glided to journey's end. The faint scent of hot food revived the hungry cargo.

"Line up in three rows!" a German staff officer shouted at the overloaded vehicles. His uniform was clean. His uncovered head displayed neatly sheared black hair. Sticking out a strong, clean-shaven chin, he repeated the order.

Spilling out of the transports, the frail rabble slowly fell into formation. All eyes focused on the flirtatious smoke of cooking fires. A squad of American blacks, in olive-green fatigues and matching caps, descended upon the assembly. With hand-pumped sprayers and sacks of white powder, they seasoned the prisoners with pesticides.

"Take off your shirts, and drop your trousers," the German staff officer instructed.

A shirtless Max closed his eyes. A short black man, stroking a hand-operated sprayer, shot misting blasts of DDT across his naked torso. "Kill them all," Max mumbled, relishing the death of the parasites that had tormented his scalp and crotch.

"A warm meal is in your future," the German officer informed them as he walked down a formation of white-powdered specters. "Pull up your pants."

The white-dust-covered captives marched to a narrow barracks elevated on cinder blocks. Flowing water resonated from within. Twenty men at a time pulsed through the bath wagon. Steam escaped with each shift change. Dreaming of a hot shower, Max fidgeted, calculating his turn. Finally, he climbed up the wooden bathhouse stoop. A massive black soldier, dripping with sweat, ordered Max's group to strip. The soiled party chuckled at the dark glistening attendant's German linguistic skill. Leaving piles of deloused clothing on wooden benches, the naked men retrieved a small bar of soap from a galvanized bucket. Like a synchronized unit, the bathers separated and selected one of the twenty dripping showerheads flanking the walls. Holding the soap to his nose, Max inhaled the cleansing scent. Wet slatted wood flooring supported his blackened feet. The burly bathhouse keeper turned a spigot. Hot water gushed from overhead. Max grinned as the hot, sanitizing water soothed his ragged body. Placing his hands on the wall, he sighed in the baptizing stream. A steady flow of grime flowed down his legs before draining into the slatted flooring. The comforting water terminated. Max joined his companions in shooting a perturbed scowl at the bathhouse master. Flashing a large-toothed smile, the brawny black American stuck out his pigeon chest and crowed the only other German phrase he knew, "Seife bis" (soap up).

Knowing his bathing experience would be brief, Max vigorously lathered. Warm water returned. As predicted, the stream abruptly ended.

The bathhouse keeper walked through the gantlet of naked Germans, tossing out olive-green towels. After accommodating the last bather, he turned and began shoving the wet men toward the exit. Still wet, Max grabbed his grimy uniform and stumbled bare assed out the door. The air was cool. A setting sun ignited the sky. In the pack of dressing captives, Max stood nude, admiring the crimson sunset. The crisp air caressed his exposed flesh. *I'm alive*, he realized.

"You trying to attract a French maiden with your shining baby ass?" the gruff sergeant Stollhoof commented.

Max chuckled. Regrettably, he pulled up the rough fabric of his dirty briefs. Stepping into the deloused pant leg of his grimy trousers diluted his cleansing euphoria.

"A French whore no longer tops my list of pleasures," Stollhoof declared, buttoning up his powdered field blouse. "After living in a pasture for two months like a cow, a warm meal and down mattress trump my desire for a buxom French filly." Tilting his head back, he inhaled the refreshing autumn atmosphere. Catching a whiff of hot food, he slapped Max on the back and said, "Well, Maximilian, let's see how well the Yanks plan on feeding us predatory Nazis."

The fumigated, bathed procession was escorted into the barracks city. Shabby boots plodded on fresh, clean asphalt. Wet, scraggly hair; rough beards; and tattered Waffen SS uniforms distinguished the new Nazi residents. Two helmeted guards swung open a spiked wire gate. Symmetric rows of vacant barracks reflected the setting sunlight. A wood placard labeled the subdivision number 11. Twirling a nightstick, one of the sentries scanned the passing prisoners with disgust. In the neighboring compound, fit Germans gazed compassionately on the malnourished captives. At the end of the asphalt pathway, three large stainless-steel stock pots awaited on a long table. Black Americans dressed in white, brandishing ladles, hovered over the misting containers. Neatly stacked metal serving trays sparkled. A ripple of anticipation flowed through the hungry parade, and the pace accelerated.

Intercepting the potential stampede, the clean-shaven German staff officer greeter hollered, "One line!" Holding up an outstretched arm and flexed palm, he added, "The sooner we demonstrate our famous discipline, the sooner we all eat."

Reluctantly, the starving rabble formed a fat queue.

Grabbing a metal tray and spoon, Max felt his breath accelerate. *It's been months since I had a warm meal*, he realized. The shiny platter was segregated into four recessed pockets. Slowly the metal dish slid down the long table. At the first station, a disinterested server, ignoring the platter's partitioned design, plopped a hearty mound of mash potatoes dead center. A side dish of spinach was dropped on top of the potatoes. The meat and gravy main course capped the summit of the warm food mound. A slice of bread appropriately found a recessed pocket on the tray. The metal platter was warm. Swallowing back secreting saliva, Max joined Stollhoof and the other famished diners on the hard blacktop. Kneeling over the steaming compilation, he rapidly shoveled the concoction into his salivating mouth. Chewing with open chops, he continued to feed his face. *Nothing ever tasted so good*, he thought, gnawing on large chunks of meat. He stopped to swallow—to catch his breath. Breaking out in a cold sweat, he dropped the spoon. Lightheaded, he scanned his gluttonous cellmates. The image blurred.

With a mouth stuffed full of potatoes, Stollhoof mumbled, "What's the matter, Max?"

Max's stomach cramped. Woozy, he leaned forward and vomited on the hard, dark surface. Across the blacktop dining room, other regurgitated meals erupted.

Rescuing his meal from the flying puke, Stollhoof stood quickly. Still feeding his cast-iron belly, he chuckled. "Nothing like enjoying a fine meal with friends."

CHAPTER SIXTEEN

The weather was generous for the opium caravan returning to China. The lanky coolie with the prominent lump in his throat led the processing. A bamboo conical hat fastened with a cloth strap shielded his tiny head. A leather belt across his shallow chest secured a bolt rifle against his back. Tugging on the lead of a pack animal, he coaxed two horses out of the forest. Before him, a grassy savannah unfolded beneath a late-afternoon sun. The wicker saddlebags of the mountain ponies were teaming with black balls of addictive product. Beside the beasts of burden, One-Eyed Jack scanned the changing terrain with his good eye, his shotgun at the ready. A warm breeze stirred the grassland and teased Jack's long black locks.

At a comfortable pace, the opium merchant, Wang, followed the first pair of horses. Exiting the tree line, he gazed skyward. Sunlight sparked off his thick glasses. Lowering his head, he adjusted the wide brim of his fedora. Protectively hovering behind the drug dealer was the bullnecked brute. Beads of sweat rolled off his happy-Buddha bald head. His massive chest was working overtime, sucking down thin air.

Another lackey, in a woven pointed straw hat, pulled along the last two horses. One of the ponies was hauling more opium, the other travel provisions. This laborer was old. A torn and patched black smock hung on his decrepit skeleton frame. A wispy gray beard flowed out his tired prune face. With sleepy eyes, he plodded forward.

A leash attached to the trailing supply horse was lashed around the wrist of a village girl. With not much of a choice, she kept pace with the nag. She was a young teen, not much of a looker, with a pancake face. Long, ratted black hair shielded her soiled flat features. She traveled not as a passenger but a commodity. At the last stop, Wang held a clearance sale of his remaining inventory of crap. A farmer with an addiction for his potent harvest had exchanged his mentally broken offspring for pots and pans.

Shadowing the female merchandise was the beady-eyed Fu Manchu with a painted reptile image crawling across his face. He constantly kept glancing over his shoulder at the Corsican. The focus of his quick peeks was an M2 carbine.

Carlo Coty smiled at the rubber-necked brigand. *I know you want it*, he realized, stroking the trigger with a patient finger. *Once we get to China, you can have it. Will they honor the agreement?* he wondered. *The further north we progress, the threat of being handed over to the Japanese fades. Maybe they are just keeping me around for an extra gun in case of an ambush. Once we are out of hostile territory, will they slit my throat?* Surveying the grassy plateau, he muttered, "Where the fuck am I?"

A long summer day of trekking concluded in a clearing beside the mountain trail. Trampled grass and a circular ash pit fashioned out of large rocks indicated prior usage. The old man watered the livestock and female cargo. The gangly coolie started a campfire. The security detail, sitting around crackling kindling, enjoyed a smoke and nips off a bottle of brand liquor. Reclining comfortably on an army-green tarp, Wang, with his hands behind his head, gazed skyward as dusk embraced night.

The Corsican steerage passenger kept his distance. On the edge of the fire's glow, Coty sat with his back against a tree. His muscles groaned. Seeking comfort, he leaned against the rough bark. It was going to be another long, sleepless night. From the shadows, he calculated a precautionary shooting sequence. One-Eyed Jack and Fu Manchu always topped the list. Happy Buddha's simpleton persona indicated a slow reaction time, hence a lower ranking. Wang was a questionable threat. Coty squinted at the opium merchant, staring into the starlight. *Is the accountant armed? Has he killed before?* Shooting a quick glance at the laboring coolies, he concluded they were no more than expendable extras.

The old man placed a kettle of rice over the popping fire. His beanstalk companion spread a gray wool blanket on the ground for the girl. She sat hunched forward. The nightly ritual was about to begin. One-Eyed Jack approached the broken flower. Instinctively, she lay down. The kettle's lid rattled. A cool breeze rustled through the forest. Grunts of an animal in heat surfaced. The comatose girl beneath the thrusting chief of security resembled a corpse.

The old man served a steamy bowl of rice to Wang. The drug dealer, utilizing chopsticks, ate slowly. Focused on the dining experience, he appeared disinterested in the fireside rape.

"Merci," Coty muttered as the fetid coolie handed him a meal. Lifting the wooden bowl to his mouth, he lapped up the sticky rice with an appreciative tongue. Gobbling down the sustenance quickly, he resumed his vigil.

A soft glow glimmered across the encompassing jungle. Around the campfire, Wang, One-Eyed Jack, and the coolies slept. Fu Manchu was finishing up his sloppy seconds. Happy Buddha sat patiently waiting his turn with the female merchandise.

It was midday. The sky was gray, the air muggy and warm. Coty staggered behind the girl lashed to a packhorse. His teetering head wobbled. Days on the road to China, lack of sleep, and the mental exertion of keeping his guard up had drained the middle-aged Corsican. *Is it all just a bad dream,* he wondered. *I need to sleep. I'll just give them the gun,* he thought, *and curl up in the shade on the side of the road. The dark comfort of deep slumber will be my reward.* His head jerked back. He slapped his face hard. *I've come too far to give up now,* he realized. A shrill train whistle pierced the humid air. The high-pitched sound of civilization rejuvenated the Corsican. "Oh yes," he mumbled, throwing his shoulders back. *It appears the opium merchant is going to honor our agreement after all,* he concluded. *Do they realize who I am?* "Les loups ne se mangent pas entre eux" (wolves do not eat each other), he mumbled.

The vista of a valley below stretched out before the opium caravan. The procession paused to admire the view. In the basin, a city of bricks, mortar, and glass pulsed with life. A meandering river fed the community. Boats of various sizes bobbed on the sparkling waterway. Puffs of smoke identified a locomotive heading north out of town.

Coty set his weapons firing selector to full automatic. The clustered-together Chinamen, gazing at the finish line, eliminated a shooting sequence calculation. "It's time to renegotiate," Coty mumbled under his breath. "Excusez-moi!" he hollered. As they turned, he opened fire. Thirty-caliber rounds ripped into flesh and bone. The bodies flinched violently. The emaciated collies and petite drug dealer toppled quickly. The fire-spitting carbine clicked silent. The corpses of the security detail wobbled upright. Lifeless, disconnected eyes relayed everlasting defiant expressions. The bald man-mountain keeled over first. He hit the ground with a thud. His companions folded over beside him.

Reflecting on Guajac's travel danger warnings, Coty chuckled. *I'm in the milieu, a gangster in Unione Corse.* Smiling at the bullet-riddled bodies, he snorted. *They were dead men the moment they agreed to take me to China.* Looking at the girl tied to a pack animal, he sighed. "What am I going to do about you?" Approaching her, he whispered, "Easy, sweetheart." Untying her bound hands, he winced. "Jesus, you smell bad." As she rubbed chaffed wrists, he separated the supply horse from the opium-hauling pony. Handing her the supply nag's leash, he declared, "Take this and go." She stood dumbfounded. "Shoo!" he hollered with sweeping arms. Through her ratted hair, she looked right through him. He shrugged.

Humming a victorious melody, Coty robbed the dead of their firearms and currency. Discovering an ankle holster and handgun on Wang did not surprise him. The opium merchant's ranking in a shooting sequence would not have changed. Placing Wang's pistol in the small of his back, he looked over at the girl. She had not moved. Her head was hung low. Scraggly hair shrouded her face. In a dangling arm, she loosely held the supply horse's controlling rope. "Someone else's problem," he muttered, securing the munitions plunder. "Adieu," he said in the girl's direction as he tugged on the lead pony's tack. A ripple flowed through the string of three opium-hauling horses. After the delay caused by the Corsican's renegotiations, the caravan was on the move again.

Having fulfilled his objective, Coty pondered a new agenda.

CHAPTER SEVENTEEN

In the shielding predawn gloom, men and boys prepared for battle. Their objective was the sleeping Khang Khay garrison, occupied by the trespassing Imperial Japanese Army. On the outskirts of the compound, the ranks of the assaulting forces swelled. It was an odd compilation of French army stragglers, Hmong warriors, French commandos, and an American pilot.

Proudly, Loc flexed, standing among his brothers, father, and uncle. He attempted to mask shivering in the cool predawn air. In a sweaty palm, he held a dated revolver. His young chest pulsed with a pounding beat.

The arrival of a rival Hmong clan evoked murmurs. The rift between the tribes predated their current populations. The chieftain of the Ly clan bowed respectfully as he passed Loc's father, Teeb. Loc beamed. Teeb's marksman talent and youthful heroics scouting for the Fackee were well known in the highlands. Squinting in the darkness, Loc spotted Guajac conversing in whispers with another commando. As a runner, Loc recognized a few of the other paratroopers. Standing to the side was the American. *The stocky pilot from the Texas tribe looks just like a Fackee*, Loc realized before concluding all white men looked the same.

"Something is not right," Teeb whispered to his family.

"What do you see, Brother?" Kaub asked.

Focused on the dark compound in the distance, Teeb answered, "Since we arrived I've seen nothing. No sentries, no signs of life, not even the flicker of candlelight. This is where the Japanese who attack defenseless Hmong villages reside. They could not have slipped through our net. Is this a trap? Have the cruel men outsmarted us?"

"Our Fackee shares your concern," Kaub whispered, nodding his head in the direction of the French commandos' murmuring conference.

Guajac and two commandos broke from the huddle. Crouched low to the ground, they headed in the direction of the garrison to investigate. Teeb grinned. *Our Fackee may not speak our language but he is a fearless Hmong warrior.*

The jagged horizon floated out of darkness. Rays of invading sunlight spilled over the sawtooth ridge line. The garrison's white plaster walls awoke. High on a pole, the war flag of the Japanese empire waved. Out of the compound, a single silhouette emerged. Waving a white kerchief over his head, Guajac hollered, "All clear."

The compound's embracing terrain came to life as partisans emerged from shadows, gullies, and brush. Those thirsting for blood were disappointed; those fearing death or a crippling wound were relieved.

Teeb, affectionately rubbing Loc's head, declared, "There will be no battle today." Glancing around at the warriors in his family, he took a deep breath. "Let's see what the fleeing cowards left behind."

Hmong troops entered the garrison with a looting and plundering agenda. Teeb and his sons pushed through the warriors milling around the gated entrance. They froze in disbelief. Random bodies of dead Japanese occupied the compound. Teeb and his family cautiously walked among the dead. They gave a wide birth to the ejected brains of an exit wound. The corpse lying face-down in the dirt held a pistol to the side of its head. Teeb slowly scanned the fallen. Seated beneath the flag pole, a dead soldier posed, gripping the handle of a bayonet lodged in his belly. Along a barracks wall, ten pairs of outstretched legs were connected to shredded torsos. Erupting blood splatter decorated the white plaster wall above the cadavers. "They blew themselves up," rolled out of Teeb's mouth.

"I don't understand," Kaub uttered. "They didn't kill each other; every man took his own life." Looking at Teeb, he asked, "Why would men do this?"

"Loc, ask our Fackee if he knows what happened here," Teeb ordered his youngest son.

After a quick nod, Loc ran off to find Guajac. Most of the Hmong lingered at the garrison's entrance, refusing to enter this heinous place. The French didn't seem to mind. The Fackee, mindful of booby traps, searched the garrison's numerous structures.

A burst of joy resonated from a small single white plaster building. The door and windows were open to the elements. A red tilled overhang shaded a wooden walkway. Over the doorframe, black Japanese font across a white board labeled the building's function. From within, French commandos engaged in happy, animated dialogue.

Jogging past a dead man sucking on a gun barrel, Loc leaped onto the stoop beneath the Japanese signage. He stood in the doorway. Against the wall, a large radio hissed static. The American pilot, Guajac, and two other French commandos cackled with wide grins. A large desk centered the room. Behind the desk sat the remains of a Japanese officer. Slouched back, the former commander gazed forward through lifeless eyes. A knotted face relayed an everlasting expression of intense pain. His dead hands grasped a dagger that traversed left to right across his abdomen. Glistening intestines cascaded out of the gaping gash.

"Monsieur," Loc politely interrupted the celebration.

Patting the American on the back, Guajac turned. "Loc!" he exclaimed. "What can I do for my carbine soldier?"

"What happened here?" the boy asked.

"I believe the term is *seppuku*. It is a ritual suicide. These fanatics would rather spill their guts, dying with honor, rather than be captured."

"They knew of our attack?" Loc questioned.

"Not at all," Guajac said, holding up a translated transmission. "It appears the Yanks dropped a big bomb, an atomic bomb, on Japan." Grinning wide, he declared, "The war is over."

"Merci," Loc responded, slowly turning. His stomach churned with the incomprehensible rationale for mass suicide. *If I survived a big bomb that fell on my village*, he thought, *I wouldn't kill myself. I'd hunt down those who dropped the bomb.*

CHAPTER EIGHTEEN

In the waning days of August 1945, high clouds concealed the blue Pacific sky over the island of Okinawa. Atop a freshly painted white pole, a lifeless American flag slept. Below the napping stars and bars, a massive US Marine Corps installation purred with military precision. On paved roads, MPs directed rush-hour traffic. Khaki-uniformed inhabitants wandered between row after row of Quonset huts and a bordering pyramid tent subdivision. Shirtless grunts dug drainage ditches. An array of growling service vehicles flowed into huge open-air lots. An adjacent landing strip emitted a steady thrum of incoming and departing aircraft.

Within the robust community, a plaque over the door of an arced corrugated tin structure read "Officers' Club." Salvaged wood tables and chairs furnished the elite drinking sanctuary. Artwork consisted of a torn and frayed Rising Sun flag nailed to the plywood back wall and a gallery of salivating Vargas pinup girls gracing the curved interior. A skinny baby-faced private, fresh off the boat, tended bar behind a counter fashioned out of shipping crates. The Nebraska native was lucky. The battle of Okinawa, the bloodiest battle in the Pacific, ended in June. On August 6, the *Enola Gay* dropped her atomic payload on the Japanese mainland. Nine days later, the war was over. The corn husker would never have to fire a shot.

Slouched back in a hardwood chair, the only patron, Captain Tom Roche, took a casual puff off a cigarette. A dwindling soft pack of Chesterfields, an overflowing coconut ashtray, and a whisky libation occupied the tabletop. Roche's dark tan face, defining him as a frontline veteran, contrasted with his crisp new uniform. A sip of Scotch crinkled his nose.

He hadn't mastered scotch's acquired taste. Good bourbon was in short supply. Kentucky distillers turned off the wartime spigot to produce alcohol for the synthetic tire industry. Across the pond, the bankrupt United Kingdom, in need of American dollars, increased Scotch exports. Bourbon men had to make allowances.

Exhaling a fresh plume, Roche, studying the ascending smoke, recalled Gunny's Peleliu prediction that he would pick up the cigarette habit by day's end. *The old salt was right*, he reflected. *I'm going to miss him*. Raising his glass, he mumbled, "To those we left behind." Flicking his wrist, he tossed back the sharp whisky in one gulp.

"Another snort, sir?" asked the drafted barkeep.

"Nah," Roche mumbled, sucking on his smoldering Chesterfield. "I'll take a beer."

The farm boy reached under the counter. The plywood door swung open. Harsh sunlight invaded the privileged enclave. A brass cadre and boisterous laughter flowed in with the bright light. The bartender flexed. In his comfortable repose, Roche squinted at a colonel, two captains, and a navy lieutenant.

"Vat 69!" The Lieutenant ordered, flashing four extended fingers.

"Yes, sir!" the barkeep snapped.

"Don't forget my beer," Roche muttered.

The officers acknowledged Roche with polite nods as they commandeered a vacant seating option. A slick captain in a pressed uniform took a second look and questioned, "Tom…Tom Roche?"

"You got that right," Roche responded, displaying a puzzled squint.

"It's me!" the captain exclaimed. "Chandler McConnell!"

A grin spread across Roche's weathered features. "I'll be damned."

"Excuse me, Gentlemen," McConnell said to his drinking companions. "I attended law school with this son of a bitch."

Joining Roche, he took a seat. Slapping the table hard, he declared, "It's good to see you, Roche…The last time we were together was…" He glanced into the curved ceiling, seeking an answer. His face lit up. Pointing a victorious finger at his former classmate, he continued, "At your wedding." Accepting a glass of scotch served neat, he took a calculated sip and chuckled. "As a Yankee Presbyterian at your Catholic ceremony, I got a little winded with the ritualistic standing, sitting, and kneeling calisthenics." Wagging his finger, he added, "But your backyard reception was something else. You southerners know how to celebrate with a spicy crawfish boil and cold beer."

Taking a nip of a longneck amber bottle, Roche flashed a naked ring finger.

"Oh, I'm sorry," McConnell offered, flinching. "Dear John letter?" he questioned.

"Yep," Roche mumbled. "It's really not that big of a loss. Island-hopping in the Pacific the last year has altered my perspective on what's important in life."

"You rotating Stateside?" McConnell asked, helping himself to a smoke.

"Nope," Roche replied. "Not enough points. Looks like I'll be serving out my time pulling occupation duty."

McConnell ignited the cigarette. Fanning a smoldering wood match, he grinned. "I have an idea."

"Captain McConnell!" the pudgy, graying colonel interrupted.

Snorting smoke, Captain McConnell turned to investigate. The scowling colonel displayed impatient palms.

"In a minute, Terry." McConnell sighed in disgust. "I'm catching up with an old friend." Turning his back on the senior officer, he shook his head mumbling, "Jesus."

"That took balls," Roche whispered. "Who's your rabbi?"

McConnell chuckled. "General William J. Donovan, head of the Office of Strategic Services," he proudly answered, taking a satisfying puff. "He was a good friend of my father's." Leaning in, he added quietly, "A good friend of Roosevelt as well."

"Office of Strategic Services?" Roche questioned.

"I can't go into details now," McConnell responded. "But I have a proposition for you. I'm assigned to an advanced team entering North China to arrange the surrender of the Japanese forces headquartered in Tiensen. I can pull some strings for you to join the mission. It is good duty, Tom, hotel accommodations, cocktail parties, and fine dining." Raising his brows, he added, "Did I mention women?"

"I appreciate it, Chandler." Roche nodded.

"It's just a New Yorker saying thank you for the invitation to a Cajun crawfish boil."

CHAPTER NINETEEN

On the outskirts of the border town, in front of a petite café, Carlo Coty sipped on strong coffee. Empty platters of local cuisine, two powder-blue packs of Gauloises cigarettes, a ceramic ashtray, and a Mauser machine pistol cluttered the dusty tabletop. A shake roof awning shaded the storefront. A gentle breeze stirred the three mountain ponies tethered to the establishment's hitching post. With his feet elevated on an empty chair, the Corsican sucked on the familiar acrid smoke of a Gauloises. *I'm fishing*, he realized, gazing at the wicker pack saddles teeming with black opium balls. *I hope this won't take too long*, he thought, downing his third cup of java. Scanning the quiet dirt road, he grinned. *My errand boy earned his fee*, he realized, watching a child of the streets leading a Catholic priest toward the coffee shop. The soiled, skinny kid tugged on the priest's arm with a sense of urgency. The clergyman, in his ankle-length black cassock and clerical collar, appeared confused. A square biretta cap, topped with tuft ball, rested atop the priest's gray hair. Stepping onto the café's wooden deck, the kid released his grasp and extended a dirty hand across Coty's table.

"Merci," Coty said, placing a virgin pack of cigarettes and a bank note on the impatient palm.

Flashing nicotine-stained teeth, the kid examined the fee before scurrying into the sunlight. The cleric stood dumbfounded, scanning the horses, the tabletop, and finally making eye contact with the seated Corsican. His breath accelerated. With a reddening face, he snapped, "I was told there was a Frenchman in distress!"

"Forgive me, Father, for I have sinned," Coty responded from his comfortable repose. "I have impure thoughts about young women, I kill those who oppose my agenda, and I lied to summon your presence." Motioning toward the opium-hauling beast of burden, he added, "I'm in need of a translator to assist with the negotiations of my cargo."

Surfacing rage erupted across the man of God's scarlet features. "Why!... Why would you ever think that I would be a party to the exchange of this evil product?"

Carlo took a final toke of his expiring Gauloises. Extinguishing the smoldering butt in the ceramic bowl, he looked up and answered, "Ten percent."

The priest stood silent.

All men have a price, Coty reflected. *The padre is quantifying the cost of morality, more than likely trying to justify the good he could do with the commission.*

"Twenty percent," the man of the cloth countered.

Coty chuckled before responding, "No, the fee for translating is ten percent. However, as a former altar boy, I'll tithe an additional ten percent to your parish."

"Acceptable," the priest quietly conceded.

Lowering his feet, Coty sat back, and offering the vacant seat, he asked, "Coffee?"

"Corsican?" the priest inquired sitting down.

"Oui," the gangster replied, extending his hand. "Carlo Coty."

Ignoring the greeting gesture, the priest said, "I don't need to know your name. I know what you are."

"Cigarette, padre?" Coty asked, flashing a pack.

The priest declined.

"I'm looking for a single expedited transaction, a bulk purchase of the cargo, pack animals, and an assortment of small arms that includes an automatic M2 carbine that was only fired once," Coty disclosed, lighting up a fresh dark tobacco tab. Tilting his head back, he exhaled a smoke plume. "My right to the chattel is possession. Wandering through the highlands, I came across these mountain ponies grazing in a meadow of lavender flowers."

Fidgeting uncomfortably in the wooden chair, the priest growled, "Don't insult me."

The Corsican shrugged. Glancing down the shaded wooden walkway, he grinned. "It looks like a fish is interested in the bait."

Four men strutted confidently. A silver-haired Chinaman, in a traditional long black robe accented with wide white cuffs, led the procession. A black satin skull cap restrained fluttering thin gray locks. His wrinkled face was small, his stoic gaze disconnected. Beside him, a twenty-something Asian in Western slacks and a short-sleeved white dress shirt kept pace. A cocky smirk dominated the young man's good looks. Bringing up the rear, dressed in laborers' rags, were two brutish henchmen.

"Do you know who that is?" Coty quietly asked the cleric.

"Sun Soon Eng," the priest answered. "He is a prominent citizen with several business interests, most notably his river barge company. The young Asian is his nephew Kwee."

"Do you know them personally?"

"I know of them."

The Chinese quartet encircled the table. Sun Soon Eng bowed respectfully at the seated clergyman. With some difficulty, he uttered, "Father Jac."

Father Jacque nodded.

"Apparently they know of you too," Coty muttered to the priest. "Please relay my desires."

Father Jacques cleared his throat. In cackling Mandarin, he defined the merchandise. Kwee, stepping into the sunlight, plucked a random opium ball from a wicker basket saddlebag and tasted it with the tip of his tongue. A greedy grin emerged. Sun Soon Eng sat down and tapped out a cigarette from the Corsican's supply. A shadowing goon ignited the vice. The priest and the potential buyer and seller sat quietly as Kwee, with a wagging index finger, counted black spheres. After relaying the tally to his uncle, he inspected the small arms. The automatic rifle evoked another satisfied smile. Over his shoulder, Sun Soon Eng barked an order. A henchman plopped a heavy satchel on the tabletop. Out of the bulky leather case, the Asian businessman pulled out a handful of twenty-franc gold coins. The bullion sparkled as he religiously stacked his offer into neat columns. His skeletal hand retrieved a few more coins to even out the stacks. There was something magical, almost hypnotic, as the mint-condition sovereigns clinked into formation. With a sweeping hand, Sun presented his bid.

Coty took a coin from atop a pile. With a twisting wrist, he examined the shiny disk, dated 1900. Looking across the table into Sun's sinister dark eyes, he smiled. Addressing Father Jacques out of the side of his mouth, he said, "What is he offering for the horses and weapons?"

The priest flinched. After taking a calming breath, he relayed the counteroffer.

Sucking on a cigarette, Sun Soon Eng cracked a smile. Smoke flowed out of his yellow teeth. Reaching into the money bag, he pulled out two gold coins and tossed them on the table. They landed with a clink and slow wobbled to rest.

"It was a pleasure doing business with you," the Corsican responded, reaching across the table.

The Chinaman offered his fragile, bony hand. A pale handshake sealed the transaction. Sun Soon Eng, assisted by his nephew, slowly rose. His bodyguards, brandishing pistols, took possession of the opium ponies. The henchmen, scanning their advance, strutted down the dusty road. Uncle and nephew exited down the shaded boardwalk.

"That was easy!" Coty exclaimed, scraping off 10 percent of the bullion consideration. "Your fee, padre," he said, playfully dropping the coins in front of the priest.

Father Jacques, frowning at his glistening pile of gold, asked, "What about your ten percent contribution?"

Coty rose. Stuffing the fortune into his coat and pants pockets, he responded, "I haven't forgotten about that." Tucking the Mauser pistol into his waistband, he added, "But first I'd like to see your church."

An enlightened Father Jacque declared, "You didn't need a translator. You used me as a human shield."

"I would have preferred an armed entourage but with a sense of urgency settled for the protective shroud of a Catholic priest. Even heathens detest killing a man of God." Securing his cigarettes in a breast pocket, he added, "Now that you figured out our employment relationship, I want you to escort me to the train station. I have pockets full of gold and a target on my back. The sooner I get out of town, the better."

The priest sat quietly. He appeared ill, disgusted at being used.

"Relax, Father," the gangster consoled. "You'll now be able to fix the orphanage roof, feed cripples and beggars, and spread the word of our savior."

Father Jacque conceded. The two Frenchmen strutted toward the train station. Coty's pants and suit coat jingled with each step. They set a brisk pace. Coty needed to exit town, and Father Jacque wanted to collect the contribution and sever the relationship.

"I always liked the fact that Jesus's first miracle was turning water into wine," Coty said, breaking the silence. "And not just any wine, but fine wine, the best anyone has ever tasted."

"It is never too late to change your ways," the priest replied.

"I'll think about it," Coty replied. "But right now with my small fortune, I'm focused on turning my impure thoughts about young women into reality."

CHAPTER TWENTY

A rush to fill the void created by the Japanese capitulation quickly snuffed out the flickering hope for peace in the Laotian highlands. It was September 2, 1945. The ink on the Japanese surrender was still wet. In Hanoi's Ba Dinh Square, thousands watched the raising of a red flag with a yellow star. Below the unfurling banner, a Vietnamese communist who had assumed the revolutionary name Ho Chi Minh declared independence from France. The Democratic Republic of Vietnam was born.

It was the dry season in Laos, harvesttime. Hmong women and children, with their noses and mouths covered, scraped the strong-smelling black sap off opium pods. The scarred green bulbs gently swayed. A hard sun beat down on the harvesters as they moved slowly through the poppy field. The distant clamor of men distracted the field hands. From the valley below, a hint of dust penetrated the blanketing foliage. All eyes focused on the mountain trail visible through a gap in the green canopy. An ascending column of uniformed troops appeared. A Hmong boy dropped his tiny blade and took flight. He ran full speed through the cultivated rows. Exiting the fields, he sprinted up the familiar rocky path to the hillside community. He scampered into the angled village square, and his bare feet skidded to a dusty termination. Taking a deep breath, he hollered, "Soldiers! Soldiers! Lots of soldiers are coming!" Lowering his head, he gulped at the thin air. Sweat rolled down his innocent face.

Within the stilted hovels, a bevy of small-arms clicked in preparation. Hmong warriors of all ages hastily heeded the call for battle. The combat-tested partisans quickly evacuated the village and disappeared into the embracing jungle.

The village chieftain, Va Meej, and four members of his war council stood in front of the communal well to greet the invaders. Va Meej was pushing eighty years of age. Balancing his arched spine on a bamboo cane emphasized the frailty of his years. His wrinkled complexion resembled cracked leather. With poor vision, he squinted down the trail leading into town.

Armed with the automatic weapons, Teeb and his eldest son, Leej, stood beside the tribal elder. Leej was a younger version of his father. Both men exuded a confident demeanor, Leej with fewer wrinkles and thick black hair. A green canvas cartridge belt crossed his bare torso. He was thin but all muscle.

Teeb stood definitely focused. A breeze stirred his thinning locks highlighted with a hint of gray. His silver necklaces sparkled. Below a ribbon pinned to his black smock dangled a square cross medal on two crossed swords. For heroism against the Japanese, France awarded Teeb the Croix de Guerre (Cross of War).

Two other battled-hardened warriors, brandishing M2 carbines, rounded out the reception committee. One, sporting a red beret, squatted on bare feet. A smoldering cigarette dangled from his lower lip. The other was the village blacksmith. He was short in stature with white hair and smelled of smoke. Next to his chief, the smithy stood tall.

A cloud of dust drifted into town. A bright-red flag decorated with a yellow star flapped above the brown haze. A Vietnamese officer in a black visor cap led a rabble of uniformed soldiers through the soil mist. The polished young officer had a flat face with sharp, jutting cheekbones. His brown-hued eyes scanned the advance with disdain. In baggy tan uniforms and wide-brimmed cotton boonie hats, his troops followed.

Teeb spotted a few Hmong and Japanese faces among the ranks of the mostly Vietnamese lowlanders. He always disliked the arrogant Vietnamese who inhabited the Lao river towns.

The arriving communists diverted their approach to trample a Hmong vegetable garden. They paused in the small furrow-rowed plot to stomp and kick sprouting produce. A barrel of rainwater was overturned. A loose chicken was snatched up, its neck broken. The vandal throng poured into the village square and encircled the Hmong war council. The Vietnamese officer walked past the greeters. In front of the well, he lowered his trousers and took a healthy piss down the watering hole's shaft. A snickering audience enjoyed the insolent gesture.

"We are the League for the Independence of Vietnam, the Viet Minh," the officer declared, shaking his manhood. Buttoning his pants, he turned and informed the Hmong chieftain, "We are here to confiscate all your firearms."

Teeb, looking at a Hmong in a communist uniform, said, "I know you. You are from the Lo clan. Why would you join these disrespectful lowlanders?"

Strutting into the conversation, the officer answered, "Our objective is to send the French back to Europe and neutralize the Hmong dogs who support them. Loyal Hmong clans have told us how you sheltered French soldiers and provided them intelligence and troops against the Japanese. To ensure peace in the highlands, we require you to turn over all your weapons."

On brittle bones, Va Meej hobbled over to the communist spokesman. He leaned in, almost touching noses. Staring deep into his adversary's eyes, he growled in a low, crackling voice, "You can't have our guns, but we'll gladly give you our bullets." Turning, he pointed his cane at the Lo clansman in uniform. A shot rang out. A bullet smacked the identified target's forehead. Spouting blood, the lifeless body crumbled to the ground. Fear rippled through the Viet Minh ranks. Pivoting communist heads scanned the surrounding jungle.

"Would you like another bullet?" Va Meej asked.

Snorting profusely, the officer turned red. After a hard gulp, he snapped, "You French-loving dogs will pay for this outrage!"

"Does that mean you would like another bullet?" Va Meej asked, waving his staff in the direction of the communist throng. The fickle cane slowly pondered the next target. Confusion and fear rippled through the assembly, as soldiers jostled to avoid selection.

The Vietnamese officer conceded. Pointing a swirling finger skyward, he signaled withdrawal. His apprehensive troops welcomed the order. Hastily, they retreated with jerking heads scanning the concealing terrain. The officer followed his men out of town. On the outskirts of the village, he turned and hollered, "We will be back!"

"You won't be coming back," Teeb muttered, raising his carbine. Taking aim, he fired. A bullet nailed the back of the officer's head. The communist flew forward. His troops panicked. Hmong sharpshooters opened fire. A Viet

Minh downhill stampede ensued. Random gunfire assaulted the fleeing Viet Minh.

To the fading crackle of small-arms fire, Va Meej hobbled over to the Lo clansman's carcass. He poked the corpse with his cane. "My sister married into the Lo clan," he informed the war council. "She was a beautiful girl," he added with a reflective grin. His tone hardened. "Her husband beat her. He beat her so bad she lost her soul." Deep within his throat, he conjured up a substantial wad of saliva. Snapping his neck, he spat on the dead body. Wiping his chin with a shriveled hand, he chuckled. "Choosing an example to demonstrate our resolve was easy."

"The Viet Minh will be back," Teeb commented.

A nodding council concurred.

"After the harvest, we will move the village further into the mountains," Va Meej declared. The harsh revelation produced a sobering pause. He continued, "Our Fackee weapons will need more ammunition." Looking at Teeb, he said, "Send Loc to the garrison to inform our Fackee that a new threat roams the highlands."

CHAPTER TWENTY-ONE

Roche awoke. He gazed up at the ornate lattice canopy of the oriental bed. *So this is China*, he reaffirmed, inhaling the fragrant cool air. Rolling onto his side, he scanned the posh Astor House Hotel suite. A ceiling fan churned the pleasant atmosphere. A floral arrangement on a rosewood entry table added color and a sweet scent. Oriental rugs blanketed the hardwood flooring. A glossy armoire housed his clean and pressed khaki uniforms. *Is this the dream, or was Peleliu and Okinawa just a nightmare?* he wondered. The Asian nymph sharing the bed stirred. He grinned, admiring the China doll's cascading jet-black locks. *Last night's sexual marathon was long overdue*, he realized. *Do I have time for one more entanglement?* he pondered, retrieving his watch from the nightstand. "Shit," he muttered. "I'm already cutting it close." Poking his bed companion, he informed her, "Sorry, sweetheart, your shift has ended."

With a petite fist, she rubbed a waking eye socket. Soft musical Chinese dialogue rolled out of her crimson-painted lips.

Roche hopped out of bed. Standing naked, he placed his hands together and bowed. "Thank you for a wonderful evening, but I gotta go." Leaving the tasty treat wrapped in cotton sheets, he flew into the adjoining bathroom. While shaving, he heard the click of the suite's door, confirming her exit. *That was a lot cheaper than a divorce.* He chuckled.

In polished shoes and starched khakis, Roche exited the hotel room. As he confidently strutted down the carpeted corridor, hotel employees dressed in traditional long black Chinese gowns bowed respectfully at his passing. Ascending a sweeping spiral staircase, he spotted an intercepting Asian in Western business attire, waiting at the base.

"Your breakfast is this way, sir," the hotel manager informed him, extending a directional arm.

"Thanks," Roche mumbled, accelerating across the lobby's polished marble flooring. A tuxedo-clad, white-gloved maître d' stood guard in front of a pair of French doors. As Roche approached, the host swung open the barriers. A dining room appeared. Provincial dining options encircled a stone water fountain, emitting a soothing trickle. The only diners were the thirty members of the American advanced team. Silverware clinked off fine China. General Norton's immediate staff ate on one side of the water feature. On the other side, the support personnel segregated themselves based on duties. The Chinese translators, Japanese translators, communication specialists, and flight crew ate quietly in small cliques.

"Over here, Tom," McConnell called out, waving a linen napkin.

"Sorry, I'm running a little late today," Roche apologized, taking a seat at the isolated table.

"No worries. The general's running late as well."

"Coffee, sir?" a waiter inquired, holding a silver carafe.

Turning over a porcelain cup, Roche nodded. The waiter served the rich black misting java. A soft blow preceded him taking a sip. "Ah!" He sighed. "I can get used to this."

"And for breakfast, sir?" the waiter asked.

"I recommend the omelet," McConnell commented, flicking a finger at his empty plate. "However, the flyboys were raving about the ham and eggs."

After ordering the omelet, a baffled Roche said, "I'm lost here. Who is paying for all this?"

McConnell chuckled. "The Empire of Japan." Raising his coffee cup, he added, "To the victors go the spoils." He took a proud sip. The attentive waiter topped off both cups. Leaning back, McConnell initiated a cigarette-lighting ritual punctuated with a satisfying exhale. "I couldn't go into details with you in Okinawa," he said, dabbing a tobacco flake off his tongue's tip. "You had to be vetted first. Now that you cleared the OSS security check, I can offer you a job."

"I enlisted for the duration of the war plus six months," Roche stated. "I won't be seeking employment until next summer."

"That doesn't matter," McConnell replied, blowing a second plume of smoke over his head. "Let me give you a little background. Before the war, the United States did not have a coordinated effort for gathering global intelligence.

The navy and army had code-breaking programs and piecemeal covert operations. Information sharing was nonexistent. The FBI handled domestic security. But beyond that, we relied on the Brits. Out of necessity, the Office of Security Services was created. The clandestine agency operates with unlimited funding and without congressional oversight. Its membership consists of academicians, journalists, inventors, linguists, and field agents. One thing the elite club members have in common is their patriotism."

"Why me?" Roche questioned.

McConnell paused as Roche's breakfast was served. As the waiter departed, he answered. "In college, your poker skills were legendary. You could read people." Pointing a finger across the table, he added, "And you speak French."

"Cajun French," Roche interjected.

"Whatever." McConnell shrugged.

"What would I do?" Roche probed.

"The global war has shuffled the deck. Enemies will become friends and allies adversaries. In this postwar world, information is the key to developing sound strategies to enhance the United States' role on the world stage. Our assignment in China is to handicap the horses left in the race, namely Mao Tse-Tung's communists and Chiang Kai Shek's nationalists. Information gathering has no restrictions; just don't get caught with your hand in the cookie jar."

"Salary?"

McConnell chuckled. "Your marine's captain salary will continue to flow." Glancing around at the lavish surroundings, he added, "Room and board will be provided by our Japanese hosts."

General Norton strutted through the double doors. Pushing fifty, he looked fit in his service uniform. The fruit salad on his chest relayed the accomplishments of a stellar career. The dining room occupants rose simultaneously.

"Gentlemen, please," Norton offered, saluting, "as you were." Glancing in the direction of the maître d', he said in a pleasant tone, "Coffee and toast." Pulling out a chair, he took a seat at the inner circle table. The rest of the room reseated themselves. Polite chatter slowly returned.

Roche dug into the folded fried-egg creation. "Good recommendation," he mumbled, chomping with a full mouth.

"Any questions about the job proposal?" McConnell asked.

"Nope," Roche replied. "As an untethered marine, the decision is easy… Fuck yeah I'm in."

"Welcome aboard," McConnell muttered.

Roche suddenly bristled. His shoulder muscles tensed. The discomfort flowed into a stiff neck. Slowly, he turned to confirm his premonition. Beneath the double-wide doorframe, a uniformed cadre of Imperial Japanese officers appeared. Flat-topped peaked caps covered their heads. A general sporting high brown leather boots and a matching long sword scabbard stood in front of the pack. The Chinese servers' cheerful demeanor soured with the arrival of the Japanese occupiers.

"I lost my appetite," Roche grumbled, pushing his meal aside.

"You OK?" McConnell asked.

Snorting in the direction of the enemy, Roche muttered, "A lot of good men are no longer with us because of those fucking fanatics."

"Their emperor ordered them to surrender," McConnell commented. "They are here to facilitate a smooth transition."

"Thank God for the atomic bomb," Roche mumbled, eyeing the passive Japanese delegation patiently waiting. The maître d' informed the American general of the Japanese's presence. Norton glanced over at the doorway and returned to his coffee and toast. Witnessing the snub, Roche grinned.

CHAPTER TWENTY-TWO

The winter night came quickly. A penetrating chill seeped into the cracks and crevices of the shanty prison barracks. The year was 1947. Christmas was less than a week away. A low, steady cough bounced off thin walls. A light bulb dangling from a frayed cord illuminated the quarters. In the shadows along the far wall, Max lay on a bed of straw. Puffing on a cigar butt, he stared into the exposed rafters, his young joints stiff from a long day of hauling broken bricks. Beside Max, the reclining Stollhoof coughed on cue. Sitting on the planked wood flooring, beneath the bright glass bulb, Dieter wrestled with the broad sheets of a stolen *Stars and Stripes* newspaper. Mumbling to himself, Dieter attempted to translate the week-old American publication. In the center of the Spartan accommodations, a rusty wood-burning stove produced soft heat. An anxious Gunter hovered over the stovetop. Five tin cans and three metal cups of coffee simmered on the hot, hard surface. The rationed remnants of the morning's java allotment produced an enticing aroma.

"Max!" the razor-thin Dieter exclaimed, peering over the newspaper. Spectacles clung to the tip of his beak nose. A crack traversed the length of a round right lens. "It says here that officers of your Hitlerjugend Division were sentenced to death by hanging for shooting Canadian prisoners of war."

Stollhoof sat up as if shot out of a cannon and growled, "War crimes, war crimes! I'm sick of hearing about war crimes."

Dieter retreated behind the newsprint.

From his comfortable repose, Max examined his irate cellmate. Somehow he and Waffen SS Staff Sergeant Stollhoof had eluded the Nazi hunters' atrocity net. *Was it just a bureaucratic gaff,* he wondered. *Regardless, the war ended two and a half years ago, and here we languish in a labor camp. Maybe this is our penance for association,* he surmised. *I was a soldier of the fatherland, not a criminal.* Reflecting on the execution of the Canadians, he shook his head. *It was a crime. I knew it then; I know it now. We were better than that. In the dissipating fog of war, righteous victors enforce justice on the immoral vanquished.*

The barracks door swung open. A rush of cold air and three POWs surged into the shanty. In heavy coats and upturned collars, Karl, Henri, and Rolph scurried to the stove. The huddling trio attempted to warm their gloved hands over the faint heat. The other occupants exchanged curious squints.

Coughing into a fisted hand, Stollhoof rose. Sliding into the stovetop huddle, he examined the mine-clearing volunteers' solemn expression. His stomach dropped. Although he knew the answer, he asked, "Forster?"

The cadre simultaneously shook downcast heads.

Stollhoof shrugged, picking up Forster's coffee tin. Divvying out the dead man's java into the remaining residents' warming receptacles, he probed, "What happened?"

Taking a composing breath, Karl responded, "All Forster talked about was earning his release by defusing the thirty-mine quota. Closing in on the milestone, he was giddy today. It was either number twenty-three or twenty-four that terminated his existence."

"Is it worth it?" Max questioned from the shadows. "It seems more of our kamraden are killed or maimed than actually earn freedom."

Rolph snickered. "If you have a wife and family, it is, my orphaned roommate. All I want to do is go home to my Greta."

"I don't want to leave," Stollhoof confessed. "Dresden was my home. An American release means handing me over into Soviet-controlled territory. A communist homecoming for a returning National Socialist would be less than hospitable."

The room went silent. Kindling crackled in the wood-burning stove. From the shadows, Max scanned the solemn expressions of his cellmates. Stollhoof existed in limbo, terrified of the Soviets and fearing an arrest for his Waffen SS affiliation. Karl, Henri, and Rolph risked life and limb for the promise of an early release. The camp cemetery was full of men who fell short of defusing thirty mines. *They must really love their families,* Max concluded. The tall, lanky Gunter suffered from a broken heart. After his wife informed him she had remarried, he drifted through each day in agony. The long, lean Roman Catholic's faith eliminated the suicide option. The spectacled Dieter was educated. His desire for release was no less than the mine sweepers'; Dieter just understood the odds. Max lay back down and sighed. Blindly, he reached down into the straw bedding and retrieved his Hitler Youth shooting proficiency medal. In the dim light, he admired the token. *Wearing of all emblems, insignia, and medals of the German National Socialist regime will be met with severe punishment;* he reflected on the May 1945 edict. The German Reich no longer existed. Rubbing the tarnished disc between thumb and forefinger, he realized he would always be a soldier, a soldier without a country.

The barracks door reverberated to a rapping fist. The echoing blows stirred the sleeping inhabitants. Under the rough fabric of an olive-green blanket, Max awoke in his work clothes. The room was dark, the atmosphere frigid. Taking a deep breath, he sat up and vigorously rubbed his shoulders. Beside him, Stollhoof rolled over on his side and drifted back into slumbering comfort. After putting on his boots, Max stood and yawned. With a twisting stretch, he victoriously cracked his back. Shuffling on the planked floor, he freed his scarf and overcoat from a wall peg and quietly exited. On the bowed stoop of the quarters, a cold wind slapped him hard. Wrapping his face in the shabby gray wool scarf, he wondered if it was worth it. Descending the creaking wood treads, he joined the other groggy volunteers, meandering to the back of the compound's latrine. *It's safer than defusing explosives.* He chuckled, retrieving two galvanized buckets full of shit. *It's not that bad in the winter,* he concluded. *The cold suppresses the stench.* The dark sky drifted in the direction of gray. The sewage brigade kept their distance from one another. Exhaling frosty plumes, the bucket-toting laborers gravitated toward the honey wagon parked at the main gate. Upwind, a disconnected armed guard stood watch. Leaning against the truck's cab, the tall, muscular black driver, Leon, puffed on a massive cigar. The flaps of a knit trapper's hat shielded his ears. A corporal's chevron adorned his sleeve. Between tokes, he sang a rhythmic work tune.

The seductive song caught Max's ear. Looking up from the asphalt pathway, Max spotted the familiar smoldering cigar tip and grinned. The black tenor could carry a tune. "Going back home to Mississippi," Max mumbled beneath his protective coarse muffler. *It was a shame Negermusik was banned by the Reich,* he reflected. *The German people were denied the enjoyment of the unique artistic expression.* Exchanging his full buckets for fresh pails, Max lingered beside the rancid vehicle to enjoy the a cappella performance.

Recognizing his Aryan fan, Leon nodded and terminated the repetitive lyrics.

"Morn'n, Leon!" Max exclaimed.

"*Guten morgen*, Max," Leon responded, offering his smoldering stogie.

Max accepted the tobacco treat. After taking a satisfying puff, he handed it back.

Leon waved off the exchange and muttered, "Keep it." Grinning wide, he announced, "I's heading home." Flicking a thumb at the honey wagon, he added, "This is my last load of German shit."

"Home?" Max questioned, not understanding the drawl-laced English.

Pointing westward, Leon responded louder, "US of A."

Nodding slowly, Max, in an exaggeratedly deep voice, sang, "Going home to Mississippi. Going to see Miz Eliza."

Leon broke out in a belly laugh. Shaking his head, he snickered. "I'm going to miss you, kid." Pulling a wrapped cigar from his breast pocket, he handed it to the Nazi youth and said, "Consider this my parting gift."

"Danke," Max responded.

Climbing into the truck cab, Leon turned over the ignition. The foul vehicle sputtered to life. Waving good-bye, the black man declared musically, "Well, I'm going to Mississippi. Mississippi, here I come."

Humming the black man's tune, Max strolled back into the cage. Puffing on the maduro cigar, he swung the galvanized buckets to the addictive beat. Sunlight appeared. Razor wire sparkled. Picturing Leon, he grinned. Nagging doubts about his National Socialist indoctrination surfaced. *Leon is a good man,* he concluded, *not the descendent of some inferior jungle tribe. Negermusik was not a plot by New York Jews to corrupt society. It's just good music.*

Behind the latrine, Max sucked hard on the stogie. In a cloud of smoke, he lifted up the stained hinged sideboard beneath the commodes and deposited the empty chamber pots. Dropping the lid, he took another stench-diluting puff. After meandering to the front of the facility, he shuffled to the back of the latrine orderlies' coffee queue. A hot tin of java was the payment for predawn septic services, Leon's cigars a bonus. Grasping his misting brew with both hands, Max lowered his head and inhaled.

The camp awoke. Barracks's stovepipes exhaled smoke into the gray sky. Active latrine doors swung open and slammed shut. With a tiny hammer and nails, a sentry tacked new edicts on the compound's information board. A particular notice attracted a prison audience. Murmurs flowed out of the inquisitive crowd.

With a belly full of warm coffee and caffeine stimulating his joints, Max sauntered over to investigate. Puffing on a cigar butt, he worked his way into the gathering. A broadsheet fluttered in the morning breeze. Large font declared, *"Legion Etrangere* is seeking qualified recruits for service in French Indochina." Max grinned wide. His heart accelerated. Beneath the subheading, "Conditions D'engagement," he scanned the fine print.

"What do you think, Max?" Stollhoof inquired.

Startled, Max looked over his shoulder at his cellmate. Returning his focus to the solicitation, he concealed his enthusiasm with a cough. Clearing his throat, he responded, "Decent food with wine, a warm bed, brothel privileges, and a monthly stipend reads like a dream." Shrugging, he defined the cost. "A five-year commitment, loyalty to France and the Legion, and the penalty for desertion is death by firing squad."

"The terms seem reasonable," Stollhoof mumbled. "Loyalty to France and French officers will be a bitter meal. But my options are limited. I wouldn't last long being released to Soviet-occupied East Germany." Placing his hand on Max's shoulder, he nudged, "You going to enlist?"

"I was a soldier," Max replied. "I now haul buckets of shit." Chuckling, he concluded, "I'd rather be a soldier." Glancing back, he asked, "You?"

"Of course," Stollhoof exclaimed. "The real selling point was the warm bed."

CHAPTER TWENTY-THREE

Night engulfed Saigon. The Imperial Hotel's lobby bar patrons thinned out on this Friday in the summer of 1954. Light bulbs dangling from dusty electric cords brightly illuminated the cantina. Insects of various denominations swooned around the addictive glow. Beneath the euphoric fluttering bugs, a Vietnamese harlot, wrapped tightly in blue satin, worked hard selling herself. The customer was one of Roche's colleagues. The broad-shouldered American, contemplating the arrangement, stroked his chin. Price seemed to be the sticking point in the arrangement.

"Good to see you mingling with the locals, Matthews," Roche muttered, strolling past the negotiations. In one hand, he grasped two long-necked beer bottles; in the other, he held a glass of water-diluted bourbon. Puffs of smoke escaped the cigarette dangling from his lower lip. At a corner table, he deposited the beverages.

"Danke," Max said, snatching up a cold brew. "You don't have to buy every round," he commented, taking a refreshing swig.

Taking a seat, Roche replied, "You terminate the Corsican, and we'll call it even."

"What if the Corsican kills us?" Max offered, glancing over at Loc.

"Shit!" Roche exclaimed. "I didn't think about that." Leaning back in his chair, he raised his libation. "I have confidence in you, Fritz. Hell, you are the man who walked out of Isabelle."

Max flinched. Grinning, he asked, "How do you know about that?"

"I told you. I'm in the information business, and I'm very good at what I do." After taking a sip of whisky, he justified the boast. "Of the approximately two thousand occupants fleeing the French garrison Isabelle, less than one hundred escaped to Laos. And out of that elite group of survivors, only a handful were European."

"I was lucky," Max uttered, taking a reflective toke of his stogie. Looking at Loc, he smiled. "I was lucky I had Loc as a travel companion."

"You pulled me out of mud," the shy tribesman injected.

"We took care of each other," Max stated, slowly nodding. "Stalked by the pale horseman, we stumbled into a friendly ridge-running Meo village."

"Is that where you met the French Jew?" Roche asked.

"His name is Jean Guillian," Max clarified. "One of the finest warriors I've ever known. For obvious reasons, we never discuss our past. But I found out he survived a Nazi labor camp; most of his family did not. I owe the noble paratrooper my life."

"Your commando friend sounds like a remarkable fellow," Roche commented. "As for me, I'm still carrying a Japanese grudge. I may never forgive the Land of the Rising Sun."

"My issue with the Corsican is also personal. It's not that he attempted to cheat me on an arms deal, nor that he wants me dead." Max shared, flicking his cigar's massive white ash. "Petru Rossi enjoys pummeling women. It's wrong to beat up a whore, especially if she is my whore."

Roche grinned. "When I encountered Rossi, he was sporting a pair of shiners." Raising a brow, he asked, "Was that your handiwork?"

Max chuckled. "I expressed my disdain for his deviant behavior. To emphasize the point, I broke the son of a bitch's nose."

Flashing a slight shrug, Roche questioned, "Why didn't you just kill him?"

"A weapons transaction was pending," Max replied. Chuckling, he added, "Business before pleasure."

"I like that," Roche muttered. "I'm curious; what's your agenda, after you finalize your Corsican issue?"

Max squinted, "Why would you ask?"

"My employer has substantial resources but very few employees. We like to operate on a contract basis with individuals who have local connections. The sudden withdrawal of the French from Northern Laos has created a void in the regional economy. Would you be interested in assisting with my assessment of France's abandoned opportunity?"

"Opium," Max muttered. "Like moths to a flame, the Corsicans, Chinese triads, and Vietnamese gangsters are drawn to the Plain of Jars to gobble up what France left behind. Even the pious communists crave the purchasing power of the black tar balls. On the undulating grassy hills speckled with boulders carved into jars two thousand years ago, powerful forces jostle for control of Hmong opium."

"Poppy fields near limestone outcroppings produce potent *ya-ying*," Loc contributed.

"The alkaline in the soil enhances the morphine content," Roche concurred. "How much opium…ya-ying…does your village produce."

"None," Loc replied. "My village is no more."

"I'm sorry, Loc. That was a stupid question." Downing his bourbon in one gulp, he shifted gears. "Gentlemen, it appears you have unique insights into the addictive commodity flowing out of Northern Laos. Are you interested in a job?"

Loc's cupped hand shielded a nervous grin sparked by the inclusion.

"Sure, Yank, we would be happy to contribute our expertise to your mission," Max replied. "After we finalize our outstanding obligation with Mr. Rossi, we will be flying back to Phong Savin. Eliminating life warrants a hasty Saigon exit."

"I understand. We can reconnect in Laos." Examining his empty glass, Roche said, "I need a refill." Looking across the table, he asked, "Are you ready for another round? We need to drink to our alliance."

Holding up a half-full amber bottle, Max replied, "I'm fine. Besides if I'm going to be working tonight, I need to maintain a sharp edge."

A faint telephone chime truncated the conversation. Roche turned. Max and Loc focused on the bartender. The pudgy, balding barkeep reached under the lacquered counter and terminated the clanging ringtone. Picking up a jet-black telephone receiver, he answered the call, shot a glance at Roche, flicked his glossy comb-over, and placed the receiver on the bar.

"It's for me," Roche mumbled as he stood. Looking over his shoulder, he added, "Let's see if my spotter located the objective."

As the American departed, Max asked Loc, "Do you want to get something to eat?"

"Let's see what the American found for us. I'm really not that hungry. Maybe after we kill the cruel man, we can get some vanilla ice cream before flying home."

"You and your vanilla," Max muttered, shaking his head.

Roche returned. Sliding into his seat, he leaned across the table and informed the assassins quietly, "The target was spotted entering the House of Butterflies. Are you familiar with the brothel?"

"Very," Max replied.

"The Binh Xuyen crime syndicate provides security for the Corsican-run whorehouse; the environment should be considered very hostile."

"It won't be my first time behind enemy lines," Max responded, extinguishing his cigar. He took a swig of beer, placed the bottle on the table, and looked at Loc. The partners simultaneously rose. "If all goes as planned, we can reconnect in Phong Savin at the King Cobra Lodge. If, by chance, tonight turns sour…thanks for the beers."

CHAPTER TWENTY-FOUR

It was a gloomy Paris afternoon in the summer of 1948. The remnants of a morning rain lingered on black, glossy asphalt. Active gutters flowed. Under dark, threatening clouds, pedestrians treaded with dormant umbrellas. The air was thick, the smell of impending rain heavy. In a French colonial infantry uniform, Jean Guillian strutted through the sluggish foot traffic. Honed edges defined sharp creases on his military ensemble. His khaki trousers were bloused smartly above sparkling black-laced boots. The chevrons of a *sergent-chef* adorned his sleeves. His red beret displayed an airborne insignia. The lanky paratrooper kept a brisk pace. The oncoming masses respectfully parted. With his shoulders back and head held high, his gaunt face sliced through the humid air. A fire burned in his dark eyes. His confident demeanor was justified. Recruited into the elite Groupement de Commandos Mixtes Aerortes (Composite Airborne Commando group), he passionately embraced the rigid training and graduated with the skills of a cunning killing machine. Rounding the street corner, he came upon a familiar outdoor café. A single customer sipped coffee beneath a scarlet-red awning. A tuxedo-clad waiter with a protective linen skirt apron stood watch on the sidewalk. Jean's heart sank, recalling his family's frequent visits to this restaurant. Visualizing a warm summer's eve dining with his brothers while his father held court, he paused.

"Table, monsieur?" questioned the waiter.

Jean shook his head.

"I know you!" the waiter exclaimed.

"You are mistaken," Jean growled, resuming his trek. *I once loved this city,* he reflected. *Paris did not betray my family,* he realized, *but she cowered under Nazi masters.*

On wet concrete, traces of falling raindrops appeared. Umbrellas sprouted to life. Jean strode amid scrambling Parisians. Ascending the stoop of an office complex, he entered the glass doors of the dated building. A musty smell dominated. Snorting, he jogged up a flight of wooden stairs. The treads creaked under his ascent. Exiting on the first floor, he gazed down scuffed linoleum flooring. On either side of the hallway, frosted-glass doors denoted tenant entrances. Strolling down the quiet corridor, he stopped in front of suite 111. Across the opaque glass door in bold font "Vogel, Masson, and Associes" identified the occupant. A typewriter chirped behind the glass barrier. Jean rubbed an extended finger across Masson. Shaking his head, he entered.

A secretary station stood watch in front of two executive offices. A corner pedestal fan churned the stale air. Wooden filing cabinets crowned with loose papers lined the walls. A skinny, long-necked secretary, sporting a hooked beak, banged away at a manual typewriter. The plunging neckline of her deep-purple floral dress exposed a bony, flat chest. Investigating the intrusion, she jumped, silencing the tweeting machine. Placing a hand on her washboard bosom, she exclaimed, "Monsieur Guillian!" Rising, she signaled louder, "Monsieur Guillian...Monsieur Hassan was not expecting you." Insincerely perusing a desk calendar, she glanced over her shoulder.

From a back office, a jostling ruckus preceded a coughing response. "It's all right, Simone...Monsieur Guillian does not need an appointment."

Jean interpreted the comment as an invitation and walked past the long-necked, fish-eyed Simone in search of Oliver Hassan. Framed by the counselor's doorway, Jean watched the plump attorney frantically patting down the coat pockets of a navy-blue pinstripe suit. Hassan's frumpy physique strained the limits of his attire. An oily sheen glazed his pinkish-fair skin. Gin blossoms decorated his bulbous nose. Hassan sighed, retrieving a black *kippa*. Placing the saucer-shaped Jewish cap on his balding head, he winced, discovering Jean's presence.

"You startled me," Hassan confessed, gulping air. Grabbing a linen napkin, he wiped off embarrassing globs of brown mustard staining his cheeks. "I was in the middle of a late lunch," he informed him, identifying a dark rye-bread pastrami sandwich and bowl of soupy coleslaw atop his cluttered desk. "Would you care to join me?"

"No, thank you," Jean replied, stepping into the office. Behind the desk, a large window caught falling rain. Cascading water distorted the view of an adjacent brick building. Rippling light reflected off tarnished plaster walls. A framed newspaper broadsheet decorated the room. The headlines of the French resistance newspaper *Combat* declared, "Les Troupes Francaises Entrent dans la Capitale Liberee" (French Troops Enter the Liberated Capital).

Hassan relocated his meal under a sleeping goose-necked desk lamp. "Although my attempts to dissuade your enlistment failed," he said, taking a seat in a swivel desk chair. Extending a hand across the desk at two aging red-leather chairs, he continued, "I must confess, you look dashing in uniform."

"Dashing?" Jean growled, sitting down. Leaning forward, he informed him, "I became a soldier...a commando with a single objective." Flexing, he emphasized, "I now possess the skills necessary to resist being loaded into a cattle car and forced to labor like a beast of burden."

"I understand, Jean," Hassan mumbled.

"Do you?" Guillian poked. "I see you haven't removed your Gentile alias from the door signage."

Hassan bristled. "I changed my name to Masson. I hid my Jewish heritage. I did what I had to do to survive." Softening, he leaned back. Interlocking his fingers over his chest, he said, "I have some promising news. I uncovered a very good lead on one of your father's Monet's."

"I appreciate your recovery efforts," Jean replied. "My mother's care is expensive. But that's not why I'm here."

"Jean, I know you resent my advice," Hassan conceded. "However, I was your father's council. He trusted me." Taking a deep breath, he offered, "You don't have to do this. Revenge will not heal your wounds."

"My father and brothers are dead," Jean stated. "My mother physically survived the Nazi labor camp. Mentally, she is broken." Slowly nodding, he conceded, "My father trusted you. And I trust that you will see to the care of my mother." Leaning forward, he squinted hard. His penetrating gaze examined the plump attorney. In a low growl, he inquired, "Now, Counselor, do you have the information I desire?"

Hassan nodded. Once again, he relocated his late-afternoon lunch. The soupy saucer of coleslaw left a moist ring on a manila envelope. Red buttons wrapped with twine secured the mailer flap. Hassan slowly unwound the locking string. Pulling out a mishmash of handwritten papers, typed documents, carbon-copied pages, and various black-and-white photos, he laid the documentation precisely on the crowded desk blotter. After securing a pair of reading glasses on his pineapple nose, he read from a typed cover page polluted with handwritten notations. "Hans Bachman fled to West Germany and attempted to register as a displaced person. The authorities were suspicious. He disappeared before he could be identified. He may have surfaced again in Offenburg in the French Zone under the alias Ernst Brack." Hassan gazed over his speckles at a focused audience. Swallowing with a dry mouth, he continued, "Ernst Brack, like many Nazi war criminals seeking sanctuary, enlisted in the French Foreign Legion. Brack is currently serving a five-year stint in Indochina with the Troisième Bataillon / Treizième Demi-Brigade de la Legion Etrangere." Shuffling through the documentation, Hassan pulled out a grainy black-and-white photo of a legionnaire. Handing it across the desk, he asked, "Is this Bachman?"

Accepting the image, Guillian snorted. Focused on the head shot of the ferret-faced Bachman in a French Foreign Legion kepi, Guillian's heartbeat accelerated. Although the pudgy gap-toothed rodent had lost weight, there was no doubt. This was Bachman, the camp guard who beat his father to death. Flicking his wrist, Guillian dealt the photo atop the pile of documentation. "It's him," he mumbled. Gazing at the rainwater rippling down the office window, he grinned, realizing the bastard was still alive.

"Jean, I'll bare the cost of the investigation and waive my fee," Hassan softly injected.

Guillian studied the attorney. Hassan appeared sincere. Graciously, he nodded, "Thank you, Counselor."

"I was planning on checking in on Celine…your mother, this evening, but don't want to intrude if you want to spend time with her," Hassan said. "I can postpone my visit."

"No need," Guillian responded. "I don't want to see her as a soldier. Uniforms frighten her."

CHAPTER TWENTY-FIVE

It was early morning as a young Loc closed in on the last few miles toward his destination. The air was crisp, dawn's first light comforting. Peasant farmers toiled in the terraced fields. It had been a long two days trekking. The urgency of the message and the looming Viet Minh threat to his village emphasized the passing of time.

Loc entered the frontier town that fed off the French garrison. Thatched-roof storefronts lined the short, dusty thoroughfare. The parasite community was still sleeping. A gentle breeze nudged a soiled mist down Main Street. On the sunny side of a two-story brothel, colorful silk garments danced on a clothesline.

The only visible inhabitant was a young Chinese merchant sweeping the covered walk in front of a provisioner store. Bin boxes of neatly stacked succulent oranges and peaches jumped out of the drab gunnysacks of rice and salt. The clerk, wearing a clean white bib apron, stopped sweeping as he spotted Loc. Leaning on the broom handle, he scrutinized the passing tribesman.

Loc ignored the curious Chinaman. Water was his objective. In the shadow of the shop, a concrete water trough beckoned. A rusty galvanized well pump fed the concrete crib. Dark-green algae lined the tub, which was filled with stagnant water. Stepping over a pile of horse dung teasing flies, Loc placed his hand on the pump handle. After a few strokes, cool, clean well water pulsed out a downturned spigot. Loc dowsed his tired head before opening a parched mouth below the gushing cascade. Rejuvenated, he stood, shaking wet locks.

"Shoo!" hollered the store clerk as he swatted the young Meo's head with the broom.

Stunned, Loc rubbed his face, stung by the dusty bristles.

The clerk stood waving a threatening broom.

With a reassuring touch, Loc confirmed the revolver in his satchel. He pondered his options before choosing diplomacy. "Monsieur?" he questioned. "I am a traveler quenching his thirst. Please do not deny me. I mean you no harm."

Throwing out a cocky hip, the clerk snorted. "An educated Meo is still a savage. This water is for livestock."

"Loc!" Guajac hollered, standing in the tavern doorway across the dirt road. "I thought that was you!" In a clean, pressed uniform, accented with a red beret, the decorated commando stepped off the raised walkway into the sunlight. Wearing a big grin, he strutted toward the watering trough. As he gazed at the clerk, a scowl replaced his joy. "What's your issue?" he snapped.

Lowering the menacing broom, the clerk, shaking his head, muttered timidly, "I have no issue, sir."

"Good," the commando barked. "Now fuck off." As the retreating clerk turned, a size-ten combat boot kicked the grocer's exiting ass. "La chatte," (pussy) Guajac muttered at the accelerating, fleeing racist. Patting Loc on the back, the Fakee's pleasant demeanor resurfaced. "It's good to see a brother-in-arms. How's your family?"

"I have an urgent message," Loc responded.

"Let's discuss it over breakfast," Guajac offered, flicking his head in the direction of the tavern. "It looks like you could use a hot meal."

Loc gazed at the local café. He had never eaten in a restaurant before. Nodding slowly, he accepted the invitation. Anticipation swelled as he crossed the street on tired legs. As he stepped on the establishment's planked wooden walkway, the aroma of fried bacon tempted his senses. Standing in the tavern doorway beside the Fackee, he flexed his young frame.

Dining options consisted of square wooden tables and hardwood straight-back chairs. The occupancy teetered around 50 percent and was exclusively French military personnel. Coffee drinkers puffed on cigarettes. Gluttonous servicemen, employing barrack's etiquette, gobbled down grub. The clang of cheap metal utensils striking ceramic dishes accompanied boisterous dialogue. A scurrying Laotian boy, toting a blue galvanized pot, topped off impatient coffee mugs. A local waitress in a white blouse and short black baggy pants flew out of the kitchen with a misting tray over her head. Her younger sister followed with a basket of bread.

Sitting at an idle table sorting receipts, the proprietor rose as he spotted the lieutenant and Hmong youth. For a low-land Laotian, he was tall, his flat face void of emotion. He flicked his stone expression at the arriving patrons.

"Steak and eggs with breads, butter, and jam for my friend and me," Guajac hollered in a friendly tone. "Coffee for me…" Glancing at Loc, he added, "And a large glass of milk for my Hmong brother."

The owner nodded and pointed at a vacant table against a wall decorated with the tricolor flag of France.

"This way, Loc," Guajac muttered, placing a hand on the uneasy Hmong's shoulder.

"Who's your friend, Lieutenant?" hollered a bullnecked sergeant.

The room went silent. Slowly turning in the middle of the seated audience, Guajac informed the inquisitive soldier, "This is Moua Teeb's son Loc. His father was awarded the Croix de Guerre for killing Japs and rescuing French soldiers from a Japanese firing squad."

"I've heard of the sharpshooting Teeb!" exclaimed a fair-skinned private. "The Hmong apparently never misses." Turning to his table companions, he spoke quietly of the famous Hmong warrior.

"Forgive my curiosity, sir," the sergeant offered. "No disrespected intended."

Guajac nodded his acceptance as he pulled out a hardwood chair. "Take a seat, Loc," he said, motioning to an empty chair.

Loc sat down. The younger waitress plopped a tall glass of milk and a steaming mug of java on the chipped and splintering tabletop. Grasping the cool tumbler with both hands, Loc chugged the nourishing protein. "Ah," he involuntarily sighed, sporting a milk mustache.

Leaning back with warm mug in hand, Guajac asked, "What can I do for you?"

With a flexed finger, Loc erased the milk residue clinging to his upper lip. After a shallow breath, he began, "Viet Minh soldiers came to our village. They demanded we turn over all of our firearms. Our clan was sought out because of our friendship with the Fackee. They said they would drive the Fackee back to

France and punish the Hmong dogs that serve them." After pausing to swallow, he added, "We killed five communist that day and wounded many more. We are in need of ammunition."

Initiating a cigarette-lighting procedure, Guajac pondered a solution. Blowing a puff of smoke over his head, he verbalized his thoughts in a muttering ramble, "The Yanks funded our last munitions drops in the war against the Japs. However, now that that war is over, the Americans oppose France's return to Indochina. France is still recovering from the Nazi occupation and has limited resources. There is no shortage of munitions, due to the accelerated demise of Japan." After taking a long toke, he exhaled, grinning. "I know of a flight crew that enjoys turning a blind eye toward regulations. The pilot, Rene Begot, owes me a big favor. I think I can muster up a supply drop."

"I don't understand," Loc said.

"It's simple." Guajac chuckled. "Soldiers take care of soldiers, while governments fuck those who served with honor and distinction. That's the way it is, and that's the way it will always be."

Two heaping platters slid onto the scarred tabletop. A basket of assorted breads and a saucer of peach marmalade were placed between the hearty servings. Although famished, Loc studied the Fackee, flicking a napkin and placing it on his lap. Methodically Guajac sliced up the slab of beef flanked by fried eggs. With an observant eye, Loc mimicked the Frenchman's etiquette. Chomping on a juicy chunk of meat, Loc surveyed the fine-dining establishment. Visualizing telling his family of the unique experience, he grinned. *I delivered the message and got a positive response*, he realized. *After this fine meal, I'll get some sleep and head home.*

Smearing jam on a fresh roll, Guajac broke the feasting silence. "I can't vouch for the quality and quantity of munitions. But tell your father to expect a present from the sky above our last drop zone." Grinning, he added, "As for you, my carbine soldier, after breakfast, I'll fix you up with a bed to get some shut-eye before driving you to the trail."

"Merci," Loc muttered with a very full belly.

CHAPTER TWENTY-SIX

It was a warm Saigon summer day in 1948, the year of the rat, according to the Vietnamese zodiac. The port city pulsed to a feverish tempo. The cruel Japanese occupiers had been evicted. The French had returned to reassert their colonial economic interest; abundant resources of rubber, tin, coffee, and tea were the prize. Beneath France's colonial facade, brothels, gambling halls, and opium dens flourished.

Under a cloudless blue sky, the humidity registered uncomfortable. Down a tree-lined boulevard flowed automobiles, bicycles, motor scooters, and an ox-drawn cart teeming with timber. Horns beeped. Scooters tooted. Food vendors encroached on the crowded sidewalk. Sharp, pungent cooking odors competed with exhaust fumes. The pedestrian traffic cast consisted of soiled peasant farmers, dapper local businessmen, clusters of uniformed schoolchildren, Buddhist monks, and slender Asian women in white, long-paneled *áo dài* dresses with conical hats.

The migrating herd parted for four legionnaires. In white linen uniforms and the signature flat circular kepi, the conscripts kept a brisk pace. Glossy combat boots pounded the cracked and uneven pavement. Max trailed the pack. The baby-faced Aryan's deep-blue eyes absorbed the exotic orient with awe. The weight he had gained since his POW ordeal was all muscle. Honed by rigorous training, he strutted confidently in an athletic frame. It was good to be a soldier again. Concealed beneath his shirt collar was the Hitlerjugend shooting medallion. The medal was the only memento of a past life swept clean by the Legion Etrangere's absolution policy.

The massive Muller set the tempo. He claimed to be Swiss, but there was no mistaking his Bavarian accent. Beneath his legionnaire kepi, a shiny shaved head capped the summit. A wide neck secured his slick noggin to broad shoulders.

The stocky Stollhoof hailed from Dresden. A slight paunch defined his post-POW weight gain. The opportunity to avoid a Soviet East Germany added a spring to his step. Absolved of past sins, he had a second chance in life. Killing Asian communists was a bonus.

The hatchet-faced, gapped-tooth Brack was a mystery beyond the Heidelberg dialect that signified his southwest German origin. His perpetually crinkled nose and flared nostrils were annoying. As he arrogantly strutted along, his beady eyes scanned the locals with disdain.

Glancing at the focused Muller, Max grinned. His Bavarian kinsman pretending to be Swiss was likable. *Stollhoof and I have history*, he realized. *But that rat-faced Brack is an asshole*, Max concluded. *A slacker, not much of a soldier. My three companions have one thing in common*, he reflected. *They all have a distinctive scar under their left arm. I saw Stollhoof burn off the gothic letter denoting blood type with cigarettes. Muller and Brack must have cut off their incriminating Waffen-SS tattoos.*

An overburdened coolie in a cone hat rounded the corner. A wooden yoke across his back balanced bulging gunnysacks. A shabby singlet hung over his scrawny torso. Sandaled feet took short, heavy, measured steps. Muller drifted out of the frail hauler's path. Brack accelerated a collision course and with a straight arm nailed the emaciated obstacle in the chest. Dropping his load, the gaunt target fell backward.

"What is wrong with you?" Max snapped. Offering an assisting hand to the fallen laborer, he scowled at Brack and scolded, "Act correct!"

Brack bristled. Clenching his fist, he growled, "Don't rebuke me, boy, concerning this *untermenschen*…this yellow monkey."

Muller floated into the fray. Frowning, he informed the ferret-faced Brack, "I'm on a mission to drink and fuck. So act correct! Or I'm going to add backhanding a Heidelberg ass to the agenda."

Brack lowered his head.

Looking over at Max, Muller winked.

"I can take care of myself," Max declared.

"I know," Muller muttered, resuming their bordello quest. Under his breath, he reiterated, "But our mission is to get drunk and fornicate."

As they entered the Chinese district of Saigon, establishments that trafficked in vice appeared. It was late afternoon. The warm air was thick. Mostly vacant bars flanked the sunny side of the thoroughfare. Across the street in the shade, saloons bristled with commerce. Colorful lanterns strung overhead idly awaited dusk. Soldiers and sailors replaced civilian pedestrians. Like roaches, street children scurried about. From second-story balconies, painted working girls purred at passing potential customers.

"Not much further," a focused Muller informed the cadre. Midblock, he stopped at the courtyard entrance of a two-story French colonial manor. Under the summer sky, utilizing various seating options, an assortment of French military personnel and barmaids fraternized in the cobblestone atrium. The working girls far outnumbered the servicemen. A red-tiled roof canopy shaded a long outdoor bamboo bar. In a jaunty red beret, a lone paratrooper, leaning against the counter, surveyed the festivities. An inebriated sailor, assisted by a girl of pleasure, staggered up the stone stoop into the house. Escaping drapes and lecherous grunts fluttered out of second-story windows.

Perched on a bar stool just inside the entry, an overweight mama-san stirred the air with a black lacquered fan. Relinquishing her elevated seat, the pudgy madam adjusted the snug yellow silk gown taxing her girth. Through wrinkled candy-red lips, she greeted the new customers in guttural French. "Welcome, gentlemen, to the House of Butterflies. We have many clean young girls to choose from." Raising a painted brow, she asked, "What is your pleasure?"

Addressing Max in German, Muller said, "Tell her we would like to lubricate our desires before partaking in the merchandise."

"What?'" Max shot back.

With an exasperated shrug, Muller rephrased, "Tell her we want to drink before we fuck."

Max nodded and relayed the message. The madam led the way toward a vacant round table and four empty hardwood dining room chairs. Boisterous conversations dominated. The sharp, fragrant aroma of cheap perfume lingered in a hovering cloud of cigarette smoke. A high-pitched scream of passion from the second floor quieted the crowd. Murmurs and snickers restarted the barroom clamor.

Weaving through the rabble, Muller slapped Max on the back and questioned, "First time, kid?"

"Hardly," Max replied, taking a seat.

"Tugging on your manhood doesn't count," Muller teased as he and Stollhoof sat down.

A transfixed Brack stood. With a crinkled nose and flared nostrils, he glared at the French paratrooper leaning against the bar. The French jumper smiled back and acknowledged the rude gawk by politely raising a fluted lacquer glass.

"What now?" Muller sighed.

Maintaining his focused gaze, Brack uttered, "That French commando… there is something…I don't know." Conceding, he shook his head and sat down.

A slender barmaid with long, sparkling jet-black hair placed a full serving tray on the wobbly tabletop. On the metal platter, four perspiring amber bottles of cold brew, shot glasses, and a tall bottle of local liquor awaited. The thick glass of the whisky magnum distorted a pickled cobra. The preserved snake's head and expanded hood was poised to strike. The reptile's tail was coiled smartly at the base of the bottle. The bar maiden expertly poured and served four jiggers of the potent *rượu rắn*.

Max held up and examined his tiny serving of the murky, venomous moonshine. A cautious sniff stung.

Muller shrugged, raised his glass, and toasted, "Constantly enjoy life… You're longer dead than alive." With that being said, he led his companions in tossing back the intoxicating aphrodisiac. Wiping his lips with the back of a hand, he declared, "That'll stimulate your loins."

The Asian hostess offered an innocent, angelic smile. Muller delicately grabbed her petite wrist and spun her onto his lap. Instinctively, she latched onto his wide neck.

Lighting up a cigar, Max flinched as a round-faced local beauty began kneading his stone shoulders. "I can get used to this," he exclaimed, relishing the massage.

Scanning his options, Stollhoof made eye contact with the cackling covey of Vietnamese quail at the end of the bar and flicked a finger invitation. A flatnosed whore flew out of the flock. With a slight shrug, he muttered, "Not my first choice." Standing beside him, she draped a naked arm across his shoulder. Reaching up, he stroked the smooth young limb.

A disengaged Brack helped himself to another snort of snake juice. Craning his neck for the umpteenth time, he stared in the direction of the French commando.

After frowning at the sour Brack, Muller took a healthy swig of the chilled local pilsner and, smiling wide, nudged, "So, young Max, do you think you can handle a Siamese hellcat?"

Taking a contemplating puff off his stogie, Max exhaled through a grin and responded, "Don't you worry about me, old man."

"Do you want to share with us your vast experience with the opposite sex?" Stollhoof teased. Sucking on a cold bottle, he raised inquisitive brows.

"Never question a legionnaire's past," Max scolded with a wagging finger. Leaning back into the comforting grasping harlot's fingers, he volunteered, "But if you must know, my journey into manhood was initiated by the buxom butcher's daughter."

"Why is it always the butcher's daughter?" Muller injected.

"I have no knowledge about the daughters of Swiss meat vendors, but my local butcher's daughter in Dresden knew how to handle sausage," Stollhoof joked.

The young vixen working Max's shoulders leaned down and, after kissing his ear, purred a sultry proposition in Vietnamese. No translation was necessary. Reaching under the table, Max subtly adjusted the reaction in his pants and rose. Interlacing her dainty fingers with his callused hand, she smiled up at him with inviting dark sapphire star eyes. She was short, at a little over five feet tall. A snug-fitting glossy red silk dress exposed her shoulders; the plunging neckline revealed a flat chest. Max's heart rate accelerated. A swarm of butterflies flirted in his belly. He took a calming toke off his stogie. Tugging on his arm, she flicked her head in the direction of the bordello.

"Well, are you going to fuck her, Max?" Brack spat. "Or just stand there like a love-sick schoolboy."

Max shot a puzzled expression at the obnoxious rodent-faced legionnaire. A grin evolved. After taking an exiting puff off his cigar, he dropped the smoldering butt in Brack's whisky jigger. Looking down at the exotic flower, he surrendered to her jerking arm.

In tow, he followed her through the outdoor saloon and up the stoop into the House of Butterflies. Standing in the foyer, on frayed red carpet, he scanned the brothel. Scantily clad women in various seductive poses lounged on weathered French colonial furniture. Bare shoulders and short skirts stirred his desire. Inviting smiles reeled him in. The butterflies in his belly once again took flight. Staking her claim, the grasping lotus flower jerked him over to the cashier at the base of the stairs.

The toll taker was a skinny, middle-aged Chinaman in a tattered black suit. Beneath a dog-eared white collar, a tiny knot secured a narrow black tie. Thick, oily hair was plastered across his scalp. At the tip of his sharp nose, wire-framed bifocal glasses defied gravity. A lazy cigarette dangled from a blistered lower lip. Glancing up at the legionnaire, he pointed at a one-price menu that calculated the fee in terms of French francs, Indochina piastres, British pounds, and US dollars. Max paid the fare. The gatekeeper handed his petite employee a room key attached to a lacquered bamboo stalk and labeled twenty-two. Her flirtatious demeanor faded. With a sense of urgency, she raced up the wooden staircase. Max followed. At the top of the stairway, the air was warm. Long corridors flowed in both directions. Halfway down the hallway to Max's right, his date unlocked bedding chamber number twenty-two and entered. Lagging behind, he plodded down the passage. Behind the passing closed doors, metal headboards rapped against thin walls. Active bedsprings creaked. Standing in the open doorway of room twenty-two, he gazed at his purchase. She lay naked on the white sheets of a metal frame bed. Staring up at an idle ceiling fan, she impatiently patted the bedding beside her.

Focused on the Asian nymph, he appreciated her sense of urgency. She was a professional, and this was a volume business. For a few piastres, what did he expect? Undressing quickly, he placed his folded uniform on the room's only chair. Demonstrating the virility of youth, he achieved his goal. Her enjoyment of the coupling was monetary. Lying on the tired bed, he watched her dress and exit. *Not bad*, he concluded, *not great, but not bad*. A satisfying grin spread across his face. *At these prices*, he realized, *I will be able to pluck another flower before night's end*.

CHAPTER TWENTY-SEVEN

The passing terrain grew more familiar with each step. Loc knew he would soon be home. *Before long, I'll be informing the war council of the Fackee's munitions commitment*, he realized. Detecting the aroma of smoke, he scanned the sky. A few puffy clouds graced the blue canvas. Sniffing the clean air, he concluded it was nothing. *Over the next rise, I'll gaze upon the village's poppy fields*, he thought. The grade steepened. The growth thinned. His anticipation of lush, green cultivated terraces faded. Before him, a blanketing ash shrouded the hillside fields. *Were the crops torched because of the community's impending relocation?* he wondered. Deep angst gnawed at his gut as he approached the scorched earth. Discovering the ash mounds contaminating the blackened farmland were charred human remains, he froze. Lightheaded, he stood gawking at a toasted skeletal corpse. The skull's open mouth memorialized a terrible demise. Sweating profusely, Loc staggered past the ghastly display. Powdery ash detonated with each step. The ground was still warm, the stench of coal oil strong. Exiting the seared landscape, he drifted in a trance toward home. A bullet-riddled Hmong carcass lay facedown on the trail. "My family," he mumbled, stumbling past his dead neighbor. "Where is my family?"

Entering what remained of the town square, defined by a stone communal well, Loc wobbled on jelly knees. His breath rapidly accelerated. The cremated remains of the hillside community unfolded before him. Swirling soot danced over the fire-consumed residences. It reeked of death. The village pathways were littered with dead inhabitants, dogs, and livestock. Scavenging long-beaked crows disrespected the fallen. In front of the stone well, a ten-foot bamboo pole, crowned with a human head, swayed softly. Terrified, Loc slowly looked up at the spiked communist message. Atop the pole, a peaceful expression graced Teeb's decapitated remains. Emotions swelled in Loc's dry throat. Melting to the ground, he wept.

Feasting crows took flight. Fluttering black wings stained the blue sky. Loc looked up. An old Hmong woman in a cylindrical stovepipe hat waved a threatening stick at the escaping feathered parasites. She was rail thin, with a shriveled prune face. Her indigo-dyed skirt and smock top were elaborately embroidered with red, yellow, and green. Spotting Loc, she winced.

Loc recognized the old mother. She was not right in the head. To battle the discomfort of old age, she inhaled the dragon's breath. The opium addiction only enhanced her descent into madness.

"Are you a ghost?" she questioned, pointing the stick.

"No, Grandmother," Loc responded, rising. "I'm Teeb's son Loc."

Immediately, she glanced up at the spiked head and grinned. "Your father and brothers killed many of the invaders."

"What happened?" Loc asked.

"There were more communists than we had bullets."

"No," Loc scolded. "How did all this happen?" he repeated, motioning with a sweeping arm.

She leaned in close. After glancing over her shoulder, she whispered, "It was early morning when a swarm of evil descended upon the village. Hmong warriors fought back the initial onslaught. Their wives and children fled. Those, like your mother, who hid in the poppy fields made a poor choice." Stepping back, she grinned, flashing gnarled, rusty teeth. "As an old woman, I sought sanctuary by lighting up a dream stick. I floated through the morning untouched. Our guns slowly went silent save one. I discovered it was the legendary warrior Teeb." Squinting at Loc, she asked, "Are you aware Teeb never misses?"

Loc nodded proudly as tears rolled down his soiled cheeks.

"He had been shot and was bleeding. But still he continued to collect death's harvest. After firing his last shot, he laid down his rifle and expired. The encircling rabid pack was so enraged by the magnitude of their losses they took his head and placed it on that pole." With a twitching skeletal hand, she pointed up at the communist trophy.

"Are there many survivors?" Loc asked, tweaking a sniveling nose.

"Not here in the village of the dead. Those who escaped into the jungle vanished with the wind." Shaking her head, she added, "They killed my dogs." Looking at Loc, she raised scraggly silver brows and asked, "Will you help me bury my dogs?"

"After…" Loc snorted. "After I bury my family."

The sky was gray over the deserted village square. Loc placed a bulging gunnysack beside the stone well. A late-afternoon breeze soothed his tired bones. Surveying the ghost town, he halfheartedly looked for the crazy old opium smoker. *She probably is lost in the depths of a dream session*, he reasoned, flexing raw hands. Grave-digging blisters and abscessed sores tormented his tender palms. He kicked over the burlap bag. Two communist heads rolled out. *Somehow, the receding Viet Minh swarm abandoned half a dozen of their deceased comrades*, he concluded. *Separating the bodies with a shovel blade was enjoyable. Burying my brothers, my father's head and torso, and the charcoal remnants of my mother and sisters will live with me forever.* The pain in his gut swelled. Rubbing his empty belly, he visualized the disemboweled Japanese officer. The troops of the Rising Sun reacted to the news of a devastated homeland by killing themselves. *What a waste*, he thought, plopping a communist head on the lip of the stone well. "Spiking my father's head was your message," he growled, symmetrically arranging the other severed Viet Minh heads around the well's rim. He stepped back and informed the captive body-less audience, "I am Moua Loc, son of Teeb. I vow to make communist mothers weep and their children orphans." Slinging a satchel over his shoulder, he took the first steps in a very long journey toward the Xieng Khouang province and enlistment in the Fackee Territorial Army.

Before entering the jungle pathway, Loc took one last look back. A flock of flesh-eating crows descended on the meal lining the brim of the well. The long-beaked black birds merrily pecked away at dead eye sockets.

CHAPTER TWENTY-EIGHT

The French Commando Jean Guillian was a loner. There was sadness in his focused gaze. Robbed of family and a life of privilege by the invading Germans, the Jewish holocaust survivor existed to complete a single task. The quest led him to Indochina. *Would tonight be the night?* he wondered, strutting down the foul streets of Cholon. The Chinese district of Saigon reeked of fresh garbage. Plate-glass storefronts reflected the late-afternoon sun. The air was moist. It was painfully hot. Disconnected from reality, Guillian disregarded the street hawkers, hookers, and beggars soliciting favor. *Patience is the virtue of a successful predator*, he surmised, entering the House of Butterflies's courtyard. Pausing at the entrance, he scanned the watering hole, looking for specific prey. Below his red beret, which displayed the airborne insignia, beads of sweat clung to a shiny forehead. Under his arms and at the small of his back, a khaki uniform soaked up migrating perspiration. Perched on a greeting stool, the mama-san acknowledged the quiet returning patron with a nod. Knowing the paratrooper would park himself at the bar all night, there was no need to peddle her stable of flesh.

Guillian made his way to the long bamboo bar beneath a red-tiled canopy. A welcoming breeze flowed down the shaded counter. Spotting the stoic Guillian, the barkeep, Quan, served up a glass of murky yellow *pastis* and a jug of diluting water. The boyish Quan looked much younger than his twenty-two years. A scraggly part meandered through his ruffled jet-black hair. A gap-toothed smile accented his pleasant demeanor. A child of the port city, he could offer shallow conversations in several languages.

Putting a splash of water into the licorice-flavored spirit, Guillian mumbled, "Thank you, Quan." After wetting his lips with a calculated sip, he turned and, resting his elbows on the glossy surface, initiated the nightly vigil.

Four legionnaires in white linen uniforms lingered at the courtyard entrance. Guillian's spine stiffened. As the mama-san greeted the new arrivals, a slight smile broke on Guillian's chiseled features. "Tonight is the night," he muttered, grinning at the rat, Hans Bachmann. Flexing confidently, he raised his aperitif at the gawking rodent. *Does he see me as the frail Jew he tormented? Or does he sense the closeness of death?* Guillian wondered. Realizing he could easily walk over there and snap the Nazi's neck, he grinned. *Since exterminating the vermin is my life's quest, why act in haste?* he reasoned.

While the German legionnaires enjoyed women and drink, Guillian reflected on the nightmare that extinguished his family. Each day of forced labor began and ended with the *appell* (roll call). Standing in silence, in prison rags, the incarcerated endured the elements and SS officer Hans Bachmann, "the Rat." The tedious task could take hours. Wielding a nightstick, Bachmann delighted in cracking skulls. If you fell from the blow, you were punished. Punishment meant death. The Rat's favorite victim was Guillian's father, Etienne. The tall, once-proud patriarch of the Guillian clan eventually vanished behind the shell of a disengaged mute. On a cold winter's night, he expired in his sleep with a fractured cranium. The next morning, Guillian and his brothers carried their father's corpse into the snow for the morning *appell.* An accurate count was imperative. As the Allied forces closed in, Guillian's brothers were transported to a death camp.

As the only male heir of the clan, Jean Guillian took a sip off his aperitif. A healthy dose of family vengeance was about to be served.

Bachmann's companions had all made their way into the bordello. At the empty round table, the Rat drank alone. Dusk surrendered to night. Overhead, red paper lanterns came to life. Customers flowed into the courtyard. Fueled by alcohol, the rabble's clamor escalated. Stroking his chin, Guillian realized it was time to flush out the rodent.

"Quan," Guillian muttered over his shoulder, "do you still have that nightstick under the counter?"

"Yes, sir," the bartender replied. Reaching under the counter, he retrieved a fat black police baton.

Turning to examine the weapon, Guillian asked, "Do you want to sell it?"

Revealing his signature gap-toothed smile, the enterprising server answered, "Everything is for sale at the House of Butterflies."

Pulling out a rolled-up wad of colorful local currency, Guillian fanned a generous offer across the countertop. Detecting Quan's salivating delight, he added to the negotiations, "I also want you to shout out a name after my departure."

Rapidly bobbing his head, Quan accepted the terms.

"Repeat quietly after me," Guillian said with a negotiating palm on the banknotes, "Hans."

"Han," Quan replied.

Shaking his head, Guillian emphasized, "Hansss."

"Hans," the bartender snapped.

Nodding his approval, Guillian said, "Bachman."

"Boc man," Quan answered.

"Close enough," Guillian conceded, sliding the graft across the counter. "Five minutes after my departure, shout out that name."

"Hans Bocmun," Quan muttered, placing the folded fee in a shirt breast pocket.

Guillian downed the balance of libation with a single gulp. Nodding farewell to Quan, he picked up his purchase. Holding the truncheon in the palm of his hand, he concealed the weapon under his arm and exited.

After clearing the counter, Quan checked his watch. Wiping the glossy surface with a moist rag, he mumbled, "Hans Boc-man." Under his breath, he repeated the name over and over. Approaching the five-minute mark, he cleared his throat. Standing tall, he threw his shoulders back and hollered, "Hans Bachman!"

Like a dog responding to a shrill whistle, the war criminal flinched. Seeking the source, his stiff neck jerked back and forth.

Looking down, Quan shielded a snicker with a cupped hand. As the Rat's inquisitive scan rotated, Quan shouted, "Hans Bachman," at the back of the curious noggin.

The Rat jumped to his feet. Dropping a crinkled wad of money on the table, he took flight. Running into the street, he glanced back and stumbled over an idle bicycle. Tumbling hard onto rough asphalt, he winced in pain. Scrambling to his feet, he ignored a torn pant leg and bleeding scraped knee. At a brisk pace, he tried to put as much distance as he could between himself and the utterance of his given name. Exiting the main drag, he shot down a side street. Sweating profusely, he stopped and looked back. A lone cyclist rolled by. Realizing he wasn't being followed, he took a deep breath. A sharp sting of pain proceeded an engulfing sea of darkness.

"A truncheon blow to the head hurts, don't it?" Guillian commented, slapping the Rat back into consciousness.

The alley was narrow. Moist moss clung to the brick walls lining the passage. The ground was wet, the stale air putrid. Sizable roaches scurried about. The scamper of larger vermin inhabited the dark shadows.

Seated in a stagnant puddle of filth with outstretched legs, Bachman tried to focus on the squatting commando before him. "Monsieur?" rolled out with a pleading groan.

"Here let me help you up for the appell," Guillian offered, grabbing the Nazi's shirt collar. Pulling the disoriented rodent to his feet, he leaned him against the wall.

Wobbling on fragile knees, Bachman implored, "Monsieur, you've mistaken me for someone else."

Drawing back the billy club, Guillian unleashed a sharp blow. The rodent's face exploded. "Silence…Don't you remember, there is no talking permitted during roll call?" Guillian said, casually reaching for the back of Bachman's head. The Rat threw out a lazy arm in resistance. Brushing it aside, Guillian moved in close and grabbed the back of his adversary's head; his other hand secured the man's jaw. "My father's name was Etienne Guillian," he whispered to the condemned as he twisted the head to one side. "This is for you, Papa," he uttered with a deft, violent reversing jerk. A muffled crack signaled the rupture of the axis vertebra. A lifeless bundle of evil collapsed at Guillian's feet. Looking down, he felt surfacing emotion erupt. Bursting into tears, Guillian tilted his head back and hollered. The pent-up rage of one man's suffering echoed off the walls of the tight enclosure. The cry aroused the human scavengers of the urban jungle. Lost in reflection, Guillian quietly walked away as street children stripped the carcass of valuables.

CHAPTER TWENTY-NINE

A desk lamp in the corner illuminated the active work station. The light faded as it spilled out across the large, dark room. A manual typewriter randomly clicked. The sound of a torrential downpour flowed through open second-floor windows. With flexed index fingers, Tom Roche scanned the keyboard, hunting and pecking. A porcelain cup of cold tea rippled with each frustrated pounding stroke. On the rim of a crystal ashtray, a smoldering cigarette methodically discarded a whisper of white ash.

"How's the report coming?" McConnell asked, stepping out of the shadows.

"Jesus Christ!" Roche exclaimed, catching his breath. "Clear your throat... shuffle your feet...but for Christ-sake, announce your presence." Swiveling in a desk chair, he snatched up the cigarette and took a calming toot. Glancing back at the progress displayed on the machine's roller, he shook his head. "I'm afraid it's not good news. Storm clouds of an impending civil war are gathering, and the Chinese communists are likely to prevail."

"You spent two weeks in Yan'an with the communist elite and came to that conclusion?" McConnell questioned sweeping his wet hair with a moist palm. At the edge of the soft light, he took a seat on the edge of a vacant desktop.

"I met with the communist hierarchy through army intelligence and the Office of War Information. The sessions were useless. The food was good, the wine terrible. My summation is based on field interviews with the common folk. Through that annoying translator, I spoke to teachers, shopkeepers, villagers, and low-level communist officials. After enduring the Japanese invasion, the populous is optimistic. Communism has taken root and is flourishing. Education is mandatory. Everyone I interviewed was articulate. They believe a higher standard of living is achievable in the short term."

Shaking his head, McConnell challenged, "After a steady diet of Marxist propaganda, I'm not surprised. Could the test subjects in your Chinese opera have been communist plants?"

"I know what you're saying," Roche replied. "But I eluded my communist escort more than once. The results were always the same. I went to the local library. The librarian spoke Russian and passable English and had devoured most of the Russian literature and classics lining the shelves. This is a savvy, motivated population."

"Have you read any of the Russian classics?" McConnell questioned.

"I saw *Anna Karenina*, starring Greta Garbo. Does that count?"

"I don't see why not."

Extinguishing the smoldering butt, Roche continued, "The real tell to the communist might is their military. During a countryside excursion, we yielded to marching troops of the communist revolutionary army singing. They sang of unity for all. Our communist escorts joined in the a cappella performance of the catchy tune. Did I mention morale was high? A couple of days later, I witnessed soldiers toiling in fields alongside peasant farmers. That is a far cry from the pillaging nationalist troops."

"Did you share your findings with army intelligence and the Office of War Information?"

"Yeah…right. They were as friendly as polio," Roche replied sarcastically. "They didn't want to show me theirs, so I wasn't going to show them mine." Leaning back, he reflected. "I realize there has always been rancor between the service branches, reflected in the labels 'gyrenes,' 'dogfaces,' and 'swabbies,' but we respected one another. But the rivalry between the information-gathering agencies caught me off guard."

"It's called politics, my friend," McConnell offered, rising from his desktop perch. "Let's get a drink. Your report predicting a communist China can wait till Friday. Dour forecasts are easier to swallow at week's end. Besides, the hotel manager, to make up for his last matchmaking fiasco, has procured us two high-class girlfriends for tonight."

Roche shook his head, mumbling, "Matchmaking fiasco." Frowning at his friend, he reminded him, "The last two girls were city buses."

"Buses? They were young and thin!" McConnell snapped.

"Like city buses, many men have enjoyed short, quick rides on syphilis Sue and Claudia clap."

"Mr. Tang emphasized high-class in his description. These may be courtesans skilled in the art of sexual intimacy."

"Why not?" Roche conceded, rising from the swivel chair. "I always wanted to be an agent in the orient seduced by a dragon lady."

"Dragon lady." McConnell snickered. "Were you a fan of the comic strip *Terry and the Pirates?*"

"Who wasn't?" Roche replied, turning off the desk lamp.

The rain had stopped. City lights reflected off drenched pavement. The scent of fresh rain briefly cleansed Tientsen of its urban stench. McConnell and Roche paused at the stairway leading down to the Crescent Moon supper club. A yellow lantern over the arched oak door illuminated the stairwell with a golden hue. Wet stair treads sparkled. Soft, melodic music reverberated behind the hardwood entrance.

Straightening the lapels of his blue blazer, Roche asked, "Looks kinda classy. Are we dressed appropriately?"

"Who gives a shit?" McConnell responded. "We're Americans."

"Don't you think Tang is a bit of an odd duck?"

"Our host is a sissy but a well-connected sissy. Just enjoy his attempts to buy our favor," McConnell replied, descending into the English basement.

The door swung open as they approached. Soothing music escaped. A slick Asian in a tuxedo bowed politely. Behind the greeter, a posh dining hall unfolded. Red-tasseled lanterns symmetrically hanging across the ceiling dimly lit the room. Individual table candles added ambience. The mostly male patrons, dressed in Western suits and ties, were exclusively Chinese. It smelled of fresh flowers. On a tiny stage, four Asian women in matching tight-fitting black silk gowns plucked on traditional instruments. On a small wooden dance floor in front of the string quartet, two embracing local beauties danced. The swaying girls, dressed in glamorous lotus-printed red satin cheongsam gowns, appeared to levitate over the lacquered surface. Their angelic expressions were exhibited above stiff mandarin collars. The high slits in the form-fitting skirts exposed an abundance of seductive young flesh.

"I feel like I'm on a movie set," Roche muttered out of the side of his mouth.

"I'm feeling underdressed," McConnell conceded.

"This way, gentlemen," the doorman announced in fairly good English. "Mr. Tang is expecting you."

The Americans followed the greeter to a booth along the wall. There sat the giddy Mr. Tang in a navy-blue pinstripe suit. Fidgeting on the red leather upholstery, he could hardly contain himself. The skinny businessman flailed effeminate arms with delight. "My American friends have arrived. I am so delighted!" he declared with his signature shrill tone that annoyingly extended the last syllable of each sentence. "Bring us champagne!" he ordered the lingering maître d'.

"Where are the girls?" McConnell rudely questioned, sliding into the cubicle.

"You will be very pleased. I pick very pretty girlfriends for you tonight. But first I want to propose business opportunity," Tang informed his captive audience.

Roche rolled his eyes.

"Even at a soup kitchen, you have to listen to the preacher." McConnell chuckled. "Go ahead, Tang. Let's hear your proposition."

"Now that war is over, I looking for American partners for import/export venture. I send you inexpensive Chinese products that you market in United States. You arrange for materials to be shipped back to China." Leaning back, Tang smiled widely and asked, "What you think?"

"We're flattered, Tang," Roche responded. "But to set up a marketing infrastructure in the United States would require excessive capital, and honestly, I don't have the funds to contribute to a venture of that magnitude."

Tang's grin widened. "I like the way my new partner thinks. I will bear the cost of setting up the businesses on both sides of the ocean. You will be responsible for coordinating activities in America."

Roche shot a curios glance at McConnell as a waiter set up a stainless-steel bucket of ice and a magnum of champagne beside the table. Scooting across squealing red leather, Tang announced, "That is enough business. You gentlemen think about it." Standing beside the booth, he added. "I go get you your girlfriends now."

Roche pulled a pack of cigarettes and a Zippo lighter out of his blazer's side pocket. He placed the tobacco cargo on the table as a waiter filled broad-bowled stemmed glasses with sparkling wine.

Cradling a champagne glass in his palm, McConnell nudged, "What do you think?"

Lighting a cigarette, Roche shrugged. "His proposal is a ruse to gain favor. Tang is a businessman attempting to buy an exiting insurance policy for when the shit hits the fan. The waiting room for wealthy Chinese seeking sanctuary will exceed capacity." Taking a puff, he continued, "It's kinda sad. Capitalism is inherent in the Chinese culture. Communism is going to extinguish that competitive spark. Uncle Sam can sway nationalist policies with foreign aid." Raising a brow, he clarified, "Foreign aid is code for bribe, and the communists cannot be bought."

"I feel sorry for Tang and his elite class," McConnell offered, taking a sip of champagne. "Regardless of their wealth, they are still Chinese, and the Chinese are nonmigratory people. Fleeing communism eliminates the inbred desire to be buried with your ancestors."

"Tang is a clever man. He'll survive."

"Would you offer your assistance if he asked?" McConnell questioned.

"It depends." Roche chuckled. "It depends what my girlfriend looks like."

"Something like that," McConnell offered, flicking his head in the direction of the dance floor.

The cheery Mr. Tang stood on the parquet surface, conversing with the dancers. The stunning beauties flashed flirtatious smiles in the Americans' direction. Form-fitting gowns emphasized elegance, grace, and shapely figures. Their thick jet-black hair was pulled back into a swirling bun at the nape of their necks. Jewel studded hairpins and jasmine flowers adorned the chignon hairstyle. Makeup accented the desirability of youth. Tang offered each girl an escorting elbow. They accepted the invitation. With a focused audience, Tang ushered the girls to the Americans' table.

"Your mouth is open," McConnell mumbled in Roche's direction.

"You're drooling," Roche replied.

"Does this mean we are in Tang's debt?" McConnell asked, rising.

"Most definitely," Roche said, standing up to meet his girlfriend.

"Ladies," McConnell said with a slight bow.

"This in Lin, and this is Jin," Tang informed the Yanks. "They will be your beloved girlfriends tonight."

"Beloved?" McConnell questioned.

Leaning forward to huddle with the Americans, Tang delightfully explained quietly, "Lin and Jin are *changsan* in the hierarchy of courtesans. They service three types of customers—dry, wet, and beloved. Dry is a pleasant evening with no sex. Wet includes the bedchamber. Beloved she will be offering herself both physically and emotionally."

"Thanks for the clarification," Roche responded, focused on his *beloved* acquisition.

CHAPTER THIRTY

From the sandbag maze capping hill number 117, Max studied the wet countryside. It was monsoon season. The air was thick. It smelled of rain. Large, billowing clouds floated across a darkening vista. A red-dirt road snaked through tropical terrain before skimming along the base of the protected mound. Max glanced down. Row after row of swirling concertina wire enveloped the descending grade. "That's a hell of an obstacle course," he mumbled, taking a toke of a short stogie. The setting sun peeked through the clouds. Penetrating rays identified small groups of men moving behind the tree line of the surrounding hills. "Hey, Muller, you know how the Viet Minh suddenly appear and eliminate French outposts?" he asked the lip-smacking legionnaire sitting at his feet. Hunched over a can of cold beans with a metal spoon, Muller nodded his big, bald head. "I think we are next on the target list," Max declared.

"Shit," Muller muttered, dropping his spoon in the tin can. Placing a steel bonnet on his head, he resumed the dining experience. Probing the bottom of the can, he scooped out another mouthful.

As night fell, the approximately one hundred defenders of hill 117 prepared for the inevitable. More than half the men were German. Poles, Romanians, Hungarians, and French rounded out the hilltop inhabitants. They were legionnaires now, a collection of criminals and mercenaries no longer with a country. Their loyalty was to the legion. No one spoke. The command post's radio crackled in the night air. Weapons clicked. They knew what they had to do. They knew many, if not all, would die before it was over. French Lieutenant Emile LeBlanc was the officer in charge. The stocky Frenchman with an explosive temper calmly walked around, observing the preparations.

In a prone firing position, Max arranged several rows of five-round stripper clips. Looking through the iron sights of a bolt-action rifle, he blindly reached over and practiced reloading. After several rehearsals, he perfected the simple maneuver. He took a deep breath. It was going to be a long night. *Most of the legionnaires are German, Wehrmacht veterans*, he reflected. *Taking the hill is going to be expensive. My tenure in the Twelfth SS Panzers was terminated by a collapsing café, and here I am again on a battlefield. Once again, the food is terrible, the pay lousy, and I'm considered expendable. But this is what I do.* He grinned. *It should be interesting to see how those devious yellow bastards plan on breaching the meadow of swirling razor wire.* A chill rolled in. The night darkened. Realizing it was *crachin*, the seasonal dense, soupy jungle fog, he sighed. *The shrouding mist will linger until late tomorrow morning, provide cover for the illusive Viet Minh, and eliminate our air-support advantage.* "Son of a bitch," he mumbled.

Max drifted in and out of shallow slumber. He spent his waking moments gazing into the dark void. Beside him, Muller snored through a flared snout. On the other side, a restless Stollhoof tossed and turned, seeking comfort. Dawn's first light was tardy. A milky haze embraced the fortified hilltop. In the depths of the opaque mist, rustling foliage identified the enemy's presence. The metallic snip of active wire cutters resonated.

"Guten Morgen," rolled out of Stollhoof's yawning mouth.

Max nodded.

"Should we wake Muller?" Stollhoof questioned. "We wouldn't want him to miss the party."

Focused on the shadows darting in the haze, Max ignored the question. A trigger-happy legionnaire discharged a round. The echoing pop stirred the tense defenders and woke Muller. "Hold your fire!" snapped Lieutenant LeBlanc. "Ammunition is precious!"

"Has the show started?" Muller wondered, rolling into a prone firing position.

Fog fluttered in and out of the barbwire obstacle course. A flat-helmeted silhouette emerged approximately three-hundred yards out. Max squeezed off a shot. A crimson plume stained the white mist. The shadow folded over as the echoing kill shot faded.

"That bullet wasn't wasted," Max muttered. In anticipation of a close-quarters finale, he tucked a handgun into his belt at the small of his back. Targeting the void, he waited patiently.

Dressed in black and wrapped in explosives, Viet Minh Volunteers of Death threw themselves into the razor-wire barrier. Randomly, they detonated. Out of the swirling smoke and fog of rippling explosions, breaches in the wire barrier strewn with severed body parts appeared. "Tien-len! Tien-len!" (forward) hollered an attacking communist wave, racing through the fractured obstacle.

The defenders of hill 117 opened fire. The uphill-charging horde seemed endless. Machine gunners unleashed short bursts into the People's Army to conserve ammunition. Bodies began piling up. But like a rising tide, the determined Viet Minh slowly gained ground.

Ignoring the long odds of survival, Max did his job. *Every bullet must count*, he realized, squeezing the trigger. He fell into a rhythm. Mumbling a shot count under his breath, he plugged torso after torso. "Five," he grunted, nailing another hostile dead center. Reloading, he resumed the count, whispering, "One." Another wave rolled in over the fallen. The kill zone was shrinking. Max accelerated the tempo and altered his targeting strategy to head shots. His precision fire briefly diverted the onslaught. The fog began to dissipate as he fed his hungry rifle a fresh clip. Communist bullets zipped through the air. Incoming rounds ripped into the sandbag shelter. Cascading granules rained down.

"Augh!" Stollhoof groaned as a projectile tore off a chunk of his shoulder. Rolling on his back, he grabbed the pulsing wound.

"Ammunition!" Max hollered at his impaired comrade.

Stollhoof refocused, replenishing Max's diminishing supply with his last twenty rounds.

Draining another five-round clip, from his peripheral vision, Max detected the invaders cresting the Romanians' position. Dropping his empty rifle, he rose. Standing exposed, he reached for the small of his back. Grasping the comforting power of a fully loaded sidearm, he proudly flexed. Sharp reflexes spun the automatic pistol into firing position. His muscular arm locked. A sensitive trigger finger launched eight precision rounds into four hostiles.

"Max," Stollhoof hollered, offering a primed rifle.

Dropping the pistol, Max took the long gun. Standing tall, he felt invincible. Patches of blue appeared in the gray sky. Sunlight bathed the hillside blanketed with dead and dying Viet Minh. Behind a targeting rifle, Max scanned for immediate threats. Satisfied, he selected targets out of a receding Asian tide. The defenders' sporadic gunfire decelerated. Cries of pain surfaced. The vanishing misting veil revealed hundreds of communist troops surrounding hill number 117.

"Shit," Muller exclaimed. "We cannot repel another assault."

"They don't know that," Max commented, taking a knee.

Compressing a plasma-saturated wad of gauze over his clipped shoulder, Stollhoof, referring to his wound, grunted, "It looks worse than it is."

Surveying the overwhelming might of the Red rebel forces, Max mumbled, "It doesn't look good from my perspective."

Warmth accompanied the invading sunlight. The life left in the mangled bodies on the sloping battlefield stirred uncomfortably. "Long live Ho Chi Minh!" a voice cried out from the bloody heap.

"Death to the French!" shouted another dying rebel.

"You have to admire their resolve," Max commented.

The shrill blast of a metal pea-whistle pierced the muggy air. The battered, exhausted defenders slowly turned to investigate. Standing in front of the sandbag mound command post, an anxious LeBlanc spit out the attention getter and hollered, "Take cover!" His attempt to repeat the simple order was drowned out by the drone of low-flying aircraft. Metallic birds of prey swooped in over the undulating terrain. The communists initiated a hasty withdrawal. Viet Minh scampered into the concealing jungle. The deadly flock ejected large egg-shaped containers over the fleeing communist troops. The napalm droppings ignited on impact. Massive fireballs tumbled skyward, the crackling inferno consuming the jungle and hostile inhabitants encircling hill 117.

Rippling heat rolled over the hunkered-down legionnaires. The devil's exhale carried the sweet stench of charred flesh. Exhausted defenders slowly rose. A scorched and burning panorama greeted them. They exchanged bewildered expressions. The reality of victory was difficult to comprehend. Breaking the silence, a gruff Romanian lifted his rifle in the air and shouted, "Vive la Legion!" Grins spread across the faces of hard men.

"Vive la Legion!" a cluster of Germans hollered.

"Vive la Legion!" a victorious hilltop chorus sang out.

"Legion Notre Patrie," (Legion our Fatherland) Max muttered under his breath before taking a swig off his canteen. The gulp escalated. After chugging most of his water, he tossed his metal bonnet to the ground and emptied the refreshing coolness on his head. Shaking his wet bleach-blond locks, he sighed, "It's good to be alive."

"Smecker!" (sly dog) a burly Romanian sporting a Rasputin beard shouted to get Max's attention. Bowing to show respect, he added, "Danke."

"Es machts nichts," (It's nothing) Max graciously responded.

CHAPTER THIRTY-ONE

Raspy twin engines of a C-47 transport groaned with an occasional stutter. Above, the sky was blue; below, a dense rain forest carpeted a harsh mountainous terrain. Jagged pinnacles penetrated the undulating sea of green. Sharp chasms and deep ravines appeared as gaping wounds in churning foliage.

The sputtering drone of the ageing aircraft reverberated through the cargo hold. It was cool. The flight crew resided behind a closed cabin door. In the cavernous fuselage, three French airborne commandos sat isolated from one another. Crated weapons and supplies provided the aroma of fresh wood. To amuse himself during the long flight, Lieutenant Jacques Torcy tossed his combat knife at close range into the side of a wooden box. Leaning forward, he plucked the stuck blade, sat back, and tossed it again. Close-cropped prematurely gray hair, resembling worn brush bristles, capped his head. Numerous breaks to his nose had left him with a scraggly snout. A disfigured left ear was a memento from a close-quarters engagement; the Nazi adversary fared far worse. A veteran of World War II, he served in the multiallied Number Ten Commandos. After parachuting into Nazi-occupied France, he gained notoriety for his many successful covert missions. Uncomfortable with the celebrity status of war hero, he volunteered for this assignment.

Holding on to a cargo net for balance, nineteen-year-old corporal Marcel LaLande stared into the ribbed ceiling with a blank expression. An open mouth displayed a slight overbite. Ripe acne blemished his narrow face. Disciplinary action for raucous behavior bought the wiry-thin blond a ticket on this flight. Somewhere, a group commander was happy to exile the troublemaker.

Sitting forward with his elbows on his knees, Sergeant Jean Guillian rocked softly. Wanting to get as far away from his past as possible, he was heading two hundred miles behind enemy lines. This was a one-way ticket. Parachuting in was easy, returning to civilization improbable. The mission's exit strategy was a crippling wound, death, or an end to communist hostilities.

The cabin door swung open. Two adolescent-looking French Air Force lackeys in baggy khaki jumpsuits staggered into the cargo hold. "We are getting close," one casually informed the knife-flicking Torcy.

Torcy sheathed his blade and stood. Methodically, he suited up for the jump. In silence, Guillian and LaLande followed his lead. The crewmembers opened the cargo door. A sobering blast of cold air flooded the fuselage. The commandos checked each other's riggings. Satisfied with the inspections, Torcy led the way to the howling exit. A flashing red light behind the isolated cabin signified arrival. The crewmembers began shoving the crated payload into the sky. Torcy, Guillian, and LaLande followed the last of the cargo.

Drifting back to earth, Guillian scanned the magnificent vista. Below him, cargo tethered to billowing white canopies descended aimlessly toward the rain forest. A sawtoothed ridgeline defined the summit of a lush mountain range. Smoke trails rising from the undulating sea of green signified life. A bed of cultivated white flowers blanketed a slopping butte. Field hands dressed in black appeared in the blossoming opium crop. Above the flowering meadow, a hillside community clung to the steep grade. Stilted structures peeked out of gaps in the forest. Scrambling inhabitants obviously detected the arriving paratroopers. A greeting party appeared and disappeared as it scurried down the switchbacks of a jungle path.

Plunging through a challenging obstacle course of tall trees, Guillian expertly glided into a small clearing. Torcy was collecting his chute as Guillian's combat boots softly kissed the moist rain forest basin. A scraggly tree reached out and snagged the trailing LaLande's fluttering chute.

"Shit," LaLande hollered, dangling five feet off the ground.

Sunlight provided warmth. Pockets of cool air resided in the shade. The air was thin. Decomposing foliage produced a tart odor. Shedding his rigging, Guillian approached the snared paratrooper.

"I got this," LaLande declared, sliding out of the harness to complete his fall to earth.

"Sergeant!" Torcy hollered at Guillian. "The time has come to test your linguistic talent."

Ten heavily armed Hmong warriors approached in a half circle. Moist foliage crinkled under sandaled feet. In soiled black tunics and short baggy trousers, they brandished an impressive collection of vintage weaponry. The flintlocks, crossbows, and Japanese bolt-action rifles seemed out of place among the cheerful greeters.

In a blue turban, a short, round-faced partisan broke ranks. An antique French revolver dangled from a leather lace around his neck. Approaching the paratroopers, he couldn't restrain a budding missing-tooth smile. "I'm Chue," he informed the Frenchmen. And as was the custom of his tribe, he volunteered, "I'm twenty-two years of age and of the Fang clan."

Stepping forward, Guillian, in the local dialect, responded, "I'm Jean, also twenty-two years old, from the Guillian clan." As the rehearsed introduction rolled off his tongue, he realized he was the only member of the Guillian clan. The long and proud lineage would end with him.

In contrast to Guillian's solemn realization, Chue lit up. Placing a welcoming hand on the commando's shoulder, he said, "You speak very well for a Fackee." Patting Guillian's shoulder, he shouted, "*Nam lu!*" The phrase delightfully rippled through the Hmong warriors.

Guillian chuckled, nodding his acceptance.

"Translation, Sergeant?" Lieutenant Torcy muttered over Guillian's shoulder.

"They are welcoming us to their village," he informed Torcy. "The universal greeting loosely translates as…let's get drunk."

"I'm all for that," Torcy chimed in.

The forest was thick, the steep mountain trail narrow. Single file, the Hmong greeting party and their French guests plodded uphill. Bringing up the rear and falling off the pace, munitions porters hauled the arduous cargo. Sweating in the cool atmosphere, Guillian glutinously gulped down thin air. *I'm in the best shape of my life*, he realized, *and I am no match for the montagnards'* (mountain people's) *stamina.* A sharp, sweet floral fragrance taunted his sense of smell. Pinching his nose, he exited the foliage tunnel. Across a slopping butte, women in bright-red turbans and blue long-sleeve blouses waded waist deep in a white flowering meadow of opium poppies. The feminine field hands waved enthusiastically at the passing men. *Flowers of evil*, Guillian thought, returning the greeting. *While French politicians denounce the illicit narcotics trade, France encourages the montagnards to grow opium. Immense profits are addicting. Opium pays the bills of war.*

On the forgiving grade beside the fragrant crops, Guillian caught his breath. Massive tropical mountains dominated the skyline. Intense sunlight warmed the air. A soft breeze teased the blossoming harvest. The colorfully costumed farmhands sang a happy tune as they scored bulbous seedpods with sharp blades. Gazing across the field of snow-white petals, Guillian began to hum the simple melody. *Joy is like a flickering flame,* he concluded, *a reminder of what life could be.* A young girl in a red-and-blue bandana smiled at the murmuring commando. Large silver looped earrings dangled from pierced lobs. Elaborate yellow-and-green embroidery accented the trim of her indigo blouse and skirt. For her appreciative fan, she sang louder. Her taut, radiant complexion glowed during the angelic performance.

"I wouldn't mind taking a ride on that Meo mountain pony," LaLande commented, grabbing his crotch for emphasis.

An irate Guillian stopped dead in his tracks. Turning, he scowled at his gruff companion and cursed, "May you grow like an onion with your head in the ground."

Shrugging with a puzzled expression, LaLande responded, "What the fuck is that supposed to mean?"

"It means behave yourself," Torcy interjected, passing the dumbfounded LaLande on the trail.

Before resuming the trek, Guillian nodded his appreciation to the gifted singer. Blushing, she looked down and innocently giggled.

Exiting the snow-white meadow, the procession slid through the tight opening in the dense growth. The grade steepened. A tight green corridor spiraled uphill. Rays of sunshine occasionally pierced the foliage canopy. Cold air lingered in the darker switchbacks. The Hmong guides politely provided a forgiving pace for the huffing and puffing French commandos. The protective shroud thinned. The incline softened. Stray Hmong conversations floated in the thin atmosphere. Barking dogs quickly drowned out the local dialogues as the column entered the sloping red-clay town square of a mountainside community.

Guillian snorted. It smelled like a rural French dairy farm. Whiffs of smoke diluted the stench. Stout poles elevated pitched thatch-roofed hovels. Chickens and dogs roamed freely. A foul waste wood sty, infested with excrement, restrained a massive pig and squealing piglets. Beneath a stilted house, a circle of women in black pillbox hats embroidered elaborate, colorful designs into dark cloth. The cackling sewing circle went silent to study the Frenchmen. Reclining on a raised porch, a skinny gray-haired old man, sucking on an opium pipe, showed no interest. Neither did a raisin-faced old woman toting firewood. The grandma with a healthy load of kindling strapped to her arched back plodded past the commandos. The shrill joy of children accompanied a gaggle of half-naked kids running into the square. Happy, soiled faces stared up at the Fackee who fell from the sky.

"This way," Chue instructed his guests, pointing to the communal longhouse up the road. The raised structure rumbled with commotion.

The commandos waded through their young fans toward Chue. Passing the perched opium smoker, Guillian snorted at the sweet smell of slow death. A disgusted Torcy shot the sergeant a sour expression.

"Chue!" Guillian called out.

Raising accommodating brows, the guide paused.

"Are there many *ya-ying* smokers in the tribe?" Guillian inquired, flicking his head in the direction of the old man lost in the devil's trance.

Chue chuckled and responded, "No, it is a benefit we allow the elderly to soften the pain of growing old. Warriors are prohibited from inhaling the demon smoke."

Nodding his understanding, Guillian translated the response to Torcy.

"That's a relief," Torcy muttered as the Frenchmen followed Chue up the creaking stair treads of the assembly hall.

A steep pitched thatch roof crowned the open-air structure. A capacity crowd of armed men sat across a ribbed bamboo-stalk floor. The attendees' ages ranged from baby-faced teens to shriveled, silver-haired seniors. It smelled of cigarette smoke and fetid occupants. Wicker-encased bottles of hooch circulated through the boisterous assembly. The moonshine-fueled clamor subsided as the Frenchmen entered. A heckler's slurred comment broke the silence. Laughter followed. A corked bottle of murky liquor was tossed at the standing commandos. Torcy plucked it out of the air. Utilizing his back teeth, he removed the cork stopper and took a healthy swig. After grabbing the bottle, Guillian raised it high. Slowly rotating, he nodded gratitude to his hosts. Tilting his head back, he poured the sharp spirit down his throat. Respectful murmurs resonated as Guillian passed the white whisky to LaLande.

The skinny corporal took an investigative sniff. His faced puckered.

"Drink up," Torcy growled through gritted teeth.

LaLande shrugged, took a gulp, and exclaimed, "Jesus Christ!"

Random snickers surfaced from the focused audience. A high-pitched whistle silenced the erupting levity. Blowing hard with two fingers in his mouth, the village chieftain called the meeting to order. The town hall fell silent as the shrill sound faded. Out of a cross-legged seated position, the chieftain rose. He was a short man, probably in his midforties. Silver necklaces adorned his neck. Ratty black locks flowed out of a black tribal cap. A deep scar traversed diagonally across his face, slicing through a flat nose. Slung over his shoulder appeared to be a Soviet or possibly Chinese submachine gun.

"Behave," Torcy ordered over his shoulder at LaLande. Flicking his head, he instructed Guillian to follow. The two commandos waded through the seated audience toward the chieftain. "Tell the chief we have come to eliminate our common enemy," Torcy instructed quietly.

Before Guillian could translate, the chief dipped his shoulder, freeing his weapon. Catching the falling burp gun, he held it high overhead and declared, "I am Vue Keej of the Vue clan." A cheering audience erupted. Addressing the Frenchmen but playing to the crowd, he continued, "If you are looking for communists to kill, you are late." Rubbing his chin, he grinned. "The Viet Minh sent troops to our village with the task of confiscating our weapons." After pausing for effect, he bellowed, "Our guns answered no!" The primed crowd cheered. Pivoting, Keej nodded his appreciation. As the ruckus subsided, he continued, "Those who escaped the initial assault were tracked down and eliminated. The trespassers bodies were thrown into a deep grotto. Missing soldiers cannot speak."

Guillian quietly translated for Torcy's benefit.

Nodding, Torcy mumbled, "Dead men tell no tales." Grinning at Vue, he asked Guillian, "See if our host knows anything about the communist Chinese supply lines flowing south through his mountains."

"Are you aware the Chinese communists are feeding the Viet Minh dogs through your lands?" Guillian inquired.

Vue chuckled. Displaying his Chinese burp gun, he corrected, "They are attempting to feed their Vietnamese dogs. Like ant trails, the never-ending columns of coolies hauling munitions south appear and disappear on mountain passes and in the dense jungle."

"You understand," Guillian respectfully responded.

"I understand that a starving dog is not a threat." Looking at the lieutenant, Vue asked, "What gifts have my Fackee brothers brought me to eradicate this festering intrusion?"

After translating for Torcy's benefit, Guillian answered, "Bolt-action rifles, ammunition, and...land mines."

CHAPTER THIRTY-TWO

Plodding up the sweeping cobblestone driveway, Loc was exhausted. A warm breeze flowing across the manicured grounds stirred his baggy fatigues and floppy bush hat. Mud, dust, and the salt residue of sweat stained the shabby uniform. A desire to sleep eliminated the apprehension of speaking to the commanding officer. Beside the tribesman, Sergeant Garlard, in a crisp, clean military ensemble, kept pace. His portly frame challenged the sharply pressed creases. A Bigeard cap crowned his large head, the two-pronged swallowtail design shielding his face and neck from the tropical sun.

"I'm sorry about this, Loc," Garlard offered. "How long were you in the field?"

"Fifteen days," Loc softy replied.

"Shit," the sergeant uttered. "Hopefully this won't take too long. Then I'll make sure you get a cold beer, hot shower, and soft bed."

"Merci," Loc mumbled.

The circular driveway swept through a grand covered portico marking the entrance to the two-story officers' club. Symmetrical arched windows graced the first and second stories. Even though moss blemishes tarnished the white plaster facade, the tired French colonial architecture, surrounded by a lush landscape, still emitted a sophisticated eloquence.

The shade of the covered driveway enticed an involuntary sigh out of Garlard. He and Loc paused briefly, looking up the few stairs leading to the impressive, high-ceilinged foyer. Two uniformed guards stationed in front of classic columns flexed as the tribesman and sergeant entered the officers' sanctuary. Potted palm trees decorated the lobby, which featured checkerboard flooring. A wooden desk, dwarfed by the massive hall, was occupied by an adolescent-looking corporal. Distant laughter flowed through the facility.

"Good afternoon, Corporal," Garlard said with a lazy salute. Offering a folded page, he informed the receptionist, "My lieutenant wants this scout to personally relay the intelligence gathered from his last mission to the lieutenant colonel."

Examining Loc, the corporal's young face soured. Raising a questioning brow, he scanned the document.

Snatching the paper back, Garlard barked, "He speaks fluent French, has spent the last three weeks in the jungle, and has killed more communists than you will ever see from behind that fucking desk."

The receptionist wilted. "The lieutenant colonel is playing tennis," he offered sheepishly. "You will find the tennis court on the grounds accessible at the end of that corridor."

"Merci, branleur," (wanker) Garlard grunted.

Loc's and the sergeant's combat boots squealed crossing the polished black and white ceramic tiles. The hallway was wide. High overhead, ceiling fans churned the humid air. Sunlight and the fragrant scent of the adjacent land-scaped courtyard flowed through arched windows.

"You familiar with tennis, Loc?" the sergeant inquired.

"No," Loc answered, exiting the facility. He and the sergeant stopped.

On an elevated deck, French officers enjoyed cool beverages. Barefoot Laotian houseboys in high-buttoned starched white dress shirts served the privileged class. Below the porch was a flat red-clay surface. On opposite sides of a taut net, white chalk lines designated identical boundaries. Two Fackee in bleached white shorts, shirts, socks, and shoes hit a small ball back and forth with webbed paddles. *The sweating, silver-haired white man must be the important chieftain,* Loc concluded. The other competitor's jet-black hair sparkled in the bright sunlight; he was younger, more agile, less winded. Sitting courtside around a small table, under a canvas umbrella, two Frenchwomen sipped cocktails. The age difference of the men was reflected in their female companions. A short, pleated tennis skirt accented a youthful brunette's shapely gams; a modest white smock tennis dress concealed the seasoned frame of her middle-aged counterpart. Emitting a low grunt, the commanding officer smacked the ball. His opponent hit it back. To rhythmic pops of the struck ball, the women's heads continually pivoted back and forth. Loc grinned. *The Fackee are a strange tribe.*

The small ball hit the net. The women politely clapped. A few of the officers on the deck applauded. "This is not your day, Calvin," the beaming lieutenant colonel declared.

"You are just too quick for me, sir," Calvin replied.

Loc tugged on the sergeant's sleeve and whispered, "What is the objective of this activity?"

Out of the side of his mouth, Garlard replied, "Apparently making sure the lieutenant colonel wins."

The tennis players exited the clay court and joined the women. Laughter punctuated the two couples' lighthearted dialogue. Standing under the protective lee of the canvas canopy, the sweaty men wiped themselves with white towels.

Garlard and Loc approached the courtside festivities. "Excuse me, sir!" Garlard said with a stiff spine and a rigid, flat-palm salute. Offering the folded page, he continued, "Orders from Lieutenant LeRouge. This Hmong scout has urgent information concerning communist troop activities along the border."

Taking a deep breath, the commanding officer exaggerated an exhausted sigh. Halfheartedly, he returned the sergeant's salute and accepted the document. Rolling his eyes for the women's benefit, he placed the folded paper on the tabletop. Securing the document beneath a perspiring glass of gin and tonic, he responded, "The war and you can wait, Sergeant. I'm in the middle of a tennis match." Grinning at his opponent, he commented, "The way I'm playing, I doubt the match will go to a fifth set."

"Charles," the older woman chimed in, pinching her pug nose. Her face soured. "Could you ask your soldiers to wait over there?"

"But of course, sweetheart," the commanding officer answered. "Sergeant, you and the Meo can wait over there in the shade," he instructed, pointing in the direction of the attentive servants watching the match.

"Yes, sir!" Garlard snapped at full attention. He and Loc proceeded as instructed. "I'm sorry about this, Loc," the sergeant mumbled under his breath.

Loc shrugged and pulled a soft pack of Lucky Strikes from a breast pocket. Falling in beside the impeccably dressed houseboys, he lit up. "Your chieftain is also a *branleu*," he commented, taking a satisfying toke.

Garlard snorted a laugh and counseled, "I don't think you are allowed to smoke."

Loc looked up at the sergeant and placed the nicotine treat between his lips. He took a long, healthy toke. Exhaling the exhaust out of the side of his mouth, he said in a matter-of-fact tone, "Two days ago, I killed three men. Two were unsuspecting targets…easy terminations. The third took flight. I ran him down and slit his throat." Displaying a bloodstain on his tattered shirt sleeve, he declared, "This is his blood." After taking another relaxing puff, he continued, "I didn't ask permission to sever a communist windpipe, nor am I seeking authorization from a Fackee who hits a tiny ball back and forth in his underwear to enjoy a cigarette."

Garlard nodded his understanding. A sinister grin surfaced. "Can I borrow a fag?"

Retrieving his pack, Loc tapped out a Lucky and offered flame.

"Thanks," Garlard muttered, taking a defiant puff. Looking over at an idle houseboy watching the tennis match, he asked, "Could you get us two iced teas while we wait?"

The request startled the baby-faced Laotian. "Sir?" he sheepishly replied, pointing to the chevrons adorning the noncommissioned officer's sleeve.

"Is there a problem, boy?" the sergeant growled.

The timid server shook his head slowly, retreating to fulfill the request.

Loc dropped his smoldering butt on the orange-clay surface. The twisting toe of his scuffed jungle boot extinguished the tiny ember. Glancing up at the Fackee hitting the small ball back and forth, he shook his head. The plop-plop of the tennis match was grating. *Was it a mistake to join the Fackee army?* he wondered. *With all of their resources, their leaders lack a sense of urgency. Maybe it is that they have the option of going home. I don't,* he sadly reflected with a heavy heart.

A burst of good cheer erupting across the officers' observation deck interrupted the action on the court. The sweat-glistening silver-haired lieutenant colonel, scowling at the revelry, hollered, "What's going on?"

Approaching the porch railing, a grinning officer, looking down, answered, "Captain Louis Guajac dropped in to say his farewells."

"I'll be damned," the lieutenant colonel declared. "Please send him down; I would like to meet the legend."

Standing in the shade with the servants, Garlard took a refreshing sip of cold tea and asked Loc, "Are you familiar with Louis Guajac, the decorated commando?"

"I know him well," Loc responded with a reflective grin.

"You know Guajac?" the surprised sergeant asked.

"I fought beside him," Loc quietly replied.

"You must have been a kid."

"I was."

Surrounded by well-wishers, Guajac strutted onto the deck in civilian attire. The sleeves of a white-cotton dress shirt were rolled up to his elbows. Baggy pleated tan slacks terminated in cuffs over polished leather shoes. His hair was longer and slicked back. The gaunt jungle fighter had put on a slight bit of weight, mostly in his face. Even out of uniform, he still maintained his signature confident stride. Descending the few steps to the clay court, he gave a playful salute, and extending his hand over the net, he said, "Welcome to Indochina, sir! I'm Louis Guajac, formerly of the Corps Expéditionnaire Français d'extrême Orient."

"Lieutenant Colonel Charles Rolland," Rolland declared, shaking his hand. "It is a pleasure to meet the famous commando Guajac."

Leaning into Rolland, Guajac confided, "Even I was impressed after reading what the French press made up about me."

Rolland snickered at the comment and offered, "Best of luck with civilian life."

"Thank you, sir," Guajac responded, adding, "To capitalize on my experience in delivering cargo, I'm heading to Saigon to establish a freight company."

"Splendid!" Rolland exclaimed. Motioning to the women, he said, "I'd like you to meet—"

"Our Fackee!" Loc hollered across the tennis court.

Rolland flinched before scowling in the direction of the tribesman. The startled women appeared perplexed, Calvin confused.

Guajac's face lit as he muttered, "Oh seigneur!" After catching his breath, he yelled back, "Carbine Soldier!" Blindly, he mumbled, "Excuse me," to the tennis quartet. "It's good to see you, Loc," he declared, approaching the tribesman. After recognizing Sergeant Garlard with a nod, he smiled at his old friend and stuttered, "I thought…I thought…you were dead. I heard—"

"My people are no more," Loc interjected. "They disappeared with the wind."

"I was so sad when I got the news. Your father was one of the finest men I've ever known."

"The Viet Minh spiked his head," Loc quietly commented.

"I should have done more," Guajac uttered, shaking his head.

"You delivered the munitions, as you promised. I thank you for that. There was nothing more you could have done." Loc responded. "After I buried my family, I enlisted in the Lao Territorial Army to kill communists. That is what I do. I go into the jungle and kill Viet Minh."

Guajac nodded respectfully. "You know, Loc," he commented in a positive tone, "thanks to the Paris newspapers' embellishment of my Indochina service, I still have some influence in French military circles. If you are interested, I can get you into an officer training program."

Loc, slowly shaking his head, answered, "No, thank you. I'm just a soldier." Pointing a finger at the former commando, he added, "You have a warrior's heart." Glancing around at the elite Frenchmen basking in the lavish, privileged sanctuary, he concluded, "I don't think many of these officers do."

CHAPTER THIRTY-THREE

Roche awoke to the steady thrum of the military transport. Beams of sunlight pouring through the portside portholes lit the cabin. The aircraft had seen better days. It smelled like stale cigarettes. The half-dozen servicemen hitching a ride from Hawaii had spread out during the long flight. Each passenger staked a claim in the abundant torn and frayed vinyl seats. Roche checked his watch. *Less than hour to go*, he surmised. Craning his neck, he felt a painful jolt shoot down his spine. Yawning, he rose. Standing in the aisle, he twisted and turned. The crackle of his backbone signaled realignment. *It will be good to get back to work*, he thought, sitting back down. Shaking his head, he contemplated the overwhelming task at hand. *The world sure turned to shit quickly after the defeat of Germany and Japan. Our Soviet allies became adversaries and successfully tested their own atomic bomb. The communist cancer seized power in China. The objective of the People's Republic is to spread the infectious disease throughout Asia.* Roche took a deep breath. *Communism can and will be contained*, he vowed, reflecting on his DC briefings. *It was good to put faces to names. Not many Catholics among the Protestant ranks of the CIA.* He chuckled. *It must be a holdover from the OSS recruitment policy. It makes sense, in an agency where trust and loyalty are imperatives; there is comfort in associating with members of your own tribe.* He grinned. *I also can cross visiting my mother off the to-do list for a while.* Recalling her weeklong badgering concerning him getting married and producing grandchildren, he shook his head. *The agency should adopt her effective interrogation technique.* Slumping down in the seat, he sighed, realizing you could never go home. *Has everything changed, or have I?* he wondered. *Stateside was too orderly, predictable. It lacked the exotic charm of the orient.* Focused on the duct-taped patch of the seatback in front of him, he reflected on his brief homecoming.

Holding a six-pack of Jax beer, Roche stood in an empty aisle at the A&P. It was Tuesday morning. The grocery store was quiet. Symmetrically arranged cans, bottles, and boxes lined the parallel shelves. The colorful merchandise's prices were prominently displayed. Unlike the bustle of Asian commerce, it seemed sterile, the abundance sinful. There was no haggling, no interaction with a shopkeeper, no service. "Progress," he muttered before migrating toward the check-out station. He paused behind the only other customer. A mother in an unflattering black-and-white polka dot smock dress held a screaming bundle of joy. A simple powder-blue scarf concealed the curlers rearranging her hair. Seeking freedom, the wailing baby arched its back like a fish on the line.

"Hush, Stevie," the woman scolded as she dug into a large purse with her free hand. "This is so embarrassing," she mumbled to an audience consisting of Roche and a teenage store clerk. "I was sure I had a five-dollar bill in here somewhere." Conceding defeat, she pulled out a coin purse and sighed. "Let's see what I can afford today."

Her voice, Roche realized. Beneath that homemaker costume is a former Miss Peach Blossom contestant...my Debbie. "I got this, sweetheart," he offered, placing a crisp twenty-dollar bill on the counter. As "sweetheart" rolled off his tongue, he winced, wishing to retrieve the affectionate moniker.

"Tom!" she exclaimed. "I heard you were back in town. I was hoping to run into you." Looking down, she touched the bulging scarf encapsulating her head and confessed, "But not looking like this." Her son's tiny hand latched onto a concealed curler. "Let go," she growled, tugging on the baby's arm.

"And who might this be?" Roche asked, looking at the snot-nosed, sniffling infant.

Adjusting the fidgeting burden, she sighed. "This is Steve Junior. He is quite the handful."

Roche collected his change from purchasing the Lewis family groceries and plopped his beer in front of the clerk. "I'm only in town a few more days," he informed his ex-wife. "I wanted to check in on my mother." Displaying his purchased six-pack, he added, "I'll need this to get me through the night."

She chuckled. "I just love your mother."

He picked up her brown bag of groceries and his beer. They exited the A&P together. He followed her the short distance to the black 1932 Ford

Coupe parked in the shade of the storefront. A long crack traversed across a grimy windshield; the left fender was snarled. She opened a creaking passenger door and said, "Just place the bag on the seat."

"It was good seeing you," he offered, obliging her instructions.

"You know, Tom," she injected. "I can get my sister to watch this little terror. We can catch up over a cocktail."

"What about Mr. Lewis?" he asked.

Tears welled up in her brown eyes. "I made a mistake, Tom…a big mistake."

"The war created casualties on a lot of fronts," he consoled. Reaching out, he touched her cheek. She melted beneath the familiar caress. "I don't think getting together is a good idea. I wish you all the best."

Dejected, she looked down. With a baby in her arms, she waddled around to the driver's side. Child birth had not been kind to the Miss Peach Blossom contestant's hips. Roche offered a friendly wave as she fired up the jalopy. As she was backing out of the parking space, the baby began to wail.

"Will you shut up?" she hollered at the kid as she drove off.

Roche grinned. *Nothing like dodging a bullet. She hated my mother*, he recalled. *And boy did she have a large ass.*

Turbulence jostled the transport. *Was her bottom really that big?* Roche tried to comprehend. *Or did my steady diet of slender Chinese cuisine inflate the visual. Regardless, reflections of Debbie helped me cope with some long nights on Peleliu. As far as Asian dishes go, the courtesan Lin was the best meal I ever had. Probably the most fulfilling sexual encounter I ever will experience.* He closed his eyes and grinned. *The professional temptress, after deciphering my desires for an innocent wanton woman, played her role with perfection.* Squinting, he wondered what Lin and Jin's services for that night cost the giddy Mr. Tang? Visualizing the flamboyant Chinese businessman, he snickered. *Nevertheless, it paid dividends*, he concluded. *McConnell and I settled the debt by pulling a few strings to establish Tang and five of his sissy friends out of communist reach in Taipei.*

The aircraft touched down with a jolt. As it decelerated down the runway, the handful of passengers prepared to disembark. Roche swallowed with a dry mouth. Methodically he put on a pair of dark-green aviator shades. Standing, he brushed his wrinkled ocean-blue Hawaiian shirt with the back of a hand.

Slinging a garment bag full of aloha wear over his shoulder, he shuffled in low gear through the emptying cabin.

"Welcome to the Philippines, Major," a flight crew member called out from the cockpit.

"Yeah," rolled out of Roche's cotton mouth. Exiting the airplane, he stopped at the top of the gangway. A blast of intolerable tropical heat slapped him hard. The hot, sticky air smelled of burned garbage polluted with the stench of raw sewage. The foul, humid air induced images of Peleliu. Beneath the sparkling dark-green sunglasses, a wicked grin emerged. The comforting power of Roche's dark side surfaced. Gazing across the horizon, he realized there was a malignant communist tumor that needed to be extracted.

CHAPTER THIRTY-FOUR

It was the dark of the moon. Chilled air engulfed two hundred Hmong partisans loading and cocking small arms. The random click-click of metal on metal competed with the crackle of nocturnal creatures scurrying in the surrounding brush. Away from his concealed troops, Vue scanned the darkness with Torcy's field glasses. The French commando's gesture to use the binoculars a week ago was interpreted as a gift by the tribal chieftain. The small man stood tall, his magnified gaze focused on the campfires flittering in the shallow valley below.

A grueling one-hundred-mile forced march had brought the war party to this hilltop. Along the journey, Hmong villages provided food, shelter, and additional warriors. That was four days ago. Upon arriving, the guerilla brigade strategically mined the area. The locations of the antipersonnel explosives were mapped. The trap was set.

Through the confiscated binoculars, Vue surveyed the dancing light illuminating a former French outpost. Licking light lapped at the tarnished walls of three single-story white plaster buildings. A raised wooden deck and awning accented the facade of the largest structure. A harsh environment had inflicted its presence on the isolated complex. Satellite wooden premises had been reduced to piles of collapsed timber. Invading vegetation occupied the grounds. Around a vacant flagpole, life rippled in the form of exhausted Chinese laborers. On moist soil, the overworked coolies slept. A shabby pile of bamboo carrying poles lay at the base of stacked wooden crates. Two uniformed communist guards in flat helmets stood watch over the munitions cargo. The naive sentries casually puffed away on cigarettes. On the rooftops, Viet Minh gunners manned fifty-caliber machine guns. The parapet sentinels emitted wisps of light conversation punctuated by laughter. Communist troop attendance appeared light, but based on scouting reports, Vue knew the Hmong were outnumbered. The bulk of the unsuspecting intruders were riding out the cold night within the complex's aging buildings. Lowering the field glasses, he grinned. Turning, he lowered his head and slid into dense growth.

Rustling brush signaled Vue's return. He acknowledged the three French commandos with a side glance. In camouflage battle fatigues, steel helmets, and rubber jungle boots, the Frenchmen appeared overdressed.

Utilizing a camo stick, Guillian painted his face black. The usually obnoxious LaLande stood silent.

Nodding at Guillian, Torcy whispered, "Do you have confidence in our allies?"

"We are about to find out," Guillian muttered, swiping dark, greased fingers across a breast pocket.

Vue flicked his head. Ten warriors in dark tribal clothes, armed with knives, flowed downhill. A contingent of fifty warriors with virgin bolt-action rifles followed.

"He's dividing his forces?" Torcy quietly questioned.

"Vue seems to know what he's doing," Guillian muttered.

With a beckoning finger, the chieftain summoned the three Frenchmen. The commandos followed the chieftain through the brush to the observation deck. Under a dark sky, the four men, standing atop the hillock, gazed upon the trespassing communist bivouac.

A breeze swept the basin encampment. Freed embers twinkled above expiring campfires. The encompassing jungle exhaled. Riding the wind, ten Hmong assassins floated into the complex. Black silhouettes silenced the cargo sentries. Dark shadows spilled onto the rooftops. Honed blades terminated the Viet Minh gunners without a sound. Removing the breechblocks, the raiders rendered the machine guns useless. The dark specters flowed down from the weathered buildings. After lighting a short fuse on the communist munitions cache, the cadre of death receded back into the jungle. A coolie raised his head to investigate a sparkling hiss.

My God, Guillian gasped. *Did that actually happen? How can men move so flawlessly, so quietly?*

174

A massive explosion erupted. An ascending ball of fire lit up the dark night. Ignited ammunition popped. Terrified coolies scrambled. Fire and smoldering kindling rained down. Viet Minh troops burst out of the compound's structures. The communists fired blindly into the commotion. Random bullets tore into emaciated bodies. Unlucky coolies wailed. Fire crackled. The smoldering mound of cargo rumbled. Cries of dying lackeys punctuated the chaos.

A Viet Minh officer, with pistol in hand, peered out of a doorway. Stepping over a dead laborer, he walked into the carnage. Looking up at the vacant rooftops, he hollered. Soldiers scurried onto the buildings. Reports of dead comrades and useless machine guns filtered down. In the diminishing firelight, the officer slowly turned. Gunfire from the surrounding forest sparked. Precision rounds ignored the stampeding labors. Exposed Viet Minh collapsed where they stood. An investigating soldier fell from the roof. The white-plaster sanctuaries released a torrent of returning fire. The assaulting gunfire terminated. Communist bullets continued spraying the dark forest.

From his observation perch, Vue took a deep breath. Assisted by binoculars, he scanned the disoriented sucker-punched communists. "The hook is set," he mumbled out of the side of his mouth. "Let's see if they take the bait."

"The plan is to draw the Viet Minh into the jungle," Guillian summarized for Torcy's and LaLande's benefit.

"Neeb!" Vue hollered over his shoulder.

A thirteen- or maybe fourteen-year-old boy scurried out of the brush. The short, enthusiastic teen stood beaming. A black headband knotted on the side of his head restrained shoulder-length jet-black hair. An antique double-barrel shotgun was strapped across his skinny back. With accommodating innocence, he stared up at the chieftain.

Vue acknowledged the boy with a nod and informed Guillian, "This is Neeb; he will lead you to the rendezvous."

Guillian's painted face puckered. "We are battle-tested warriors. No disrespect, but we do not need an escort."

Vue chuckled. "At the rendezvous, you can demonstrate your talent. But to get there, you have to pass through mined terrain." Placing his hand on the boy's shoulder, he continued, "Neeb will guide you safely."

Guillian nodded and translated the order. The commandos shouldered their weapons and joined the Hmong troops retreating into the concealing Sherwood rain forest. Dark silhouettes drifted uphill into dense brush. The pace was brisk. Foliage crackled underfoot. Grasping brittle branches snapped. With Torcy and LaLande on his tail, Guillian religiously followed the nimble kid through the explosive-laden darkness.

In the fleeing Hmong's enticing wake, sporadic gunfire popped. Pursuing Viet Minh had taken the bait. A distant erupting landmine singled one possibly two fewer communist predators. The luring trek turned into a slow climb as the guerillas crawled up a boulder-strewn bluff.

Gulping on thin air, Guillian stayed on the agile boy's heels. The other panting Frenchmen brought up the rear. Ascending partisans began taking shelter in the rocky hillside. Behind a massive eroded slab of rock, Neeb terminated his assignment. In a wide stance, the boy offered an inviting hand to take a seat.

"Merci," Torcy offered, dipping his shoulder and releasing his pack.

"What now, little brother?" Guillian inquired.

Attempting to suppress a nervous smile, the shy boy answered, "We wait for the invaders and then kill them."

"What did he say?" LaLande asked, taking a seat on hard shale.

"Nothing significant," Guillian informed his colleagues.

The horizon glowed in anticipation of dawn. Escalating light distinguished the Hmong warriors blanketing the rocky bluff as old men and boys.

"It appears we have been pulled out of the battle and assigned to the reserves," Torcy commented, scrutinizing the troops.

"After witnessing the Hmong in action, I'm not going to question the chief's strategy," Guillian replied. "I suspect he views us as his supply line. There is no shortage of skilled jungle fighters in these mountains. But air drops of French munitions are a precious commodity."

"What the fuck is that?" LaLande interrupted.

Following the corporal's downhill gaze, Torcy and Guillian squinted in the limited light. At the base of the bluff, just above the mountain trail, three gray-haired tribesmen toiled with a large log. The six-foot stump banded with iron appeared hollow. The old men elevated the tree trunk with cradling rocks. A brief debate preceded the agreed placement targeting a bend in the road.

Bracing the butt in the ground, they loaded the jungle cannon with gunpowder. From a rough cloth sack, they fed the wooden howitzer old knives, rusty nails, and chain lengths. The artillery unit paused briefly to admire their accomplishment. After congratulatory pats on the back, they vanished.

"I'll be damned," Torcy mumbled.

Sunlight peeked over the horizon. Invading rays spilled over the steep, serrated landscape. The hillside reserves retreated into the long shadows of the boulder bluff. In the depths of the jungle below, small arms crackled. The firefight soundtrack escalated. A Hmong warrior with a wounded companion across his back jogged into view. Two partisans flew out of concealing rock to assist. Three other Hmong casualties plodded up the trail. Their pace accelerated before they slid into the shale sanctuary.

Intensified gunfire preceded the appearance of thirty retreating partisans. Laying down suppressing fire, the baiting Hmong troops performed a classic peel and reload tactic. The calculated withdrawal drifted past the occupied bluff. Locked and loaded hillside reserves focused on the bend in the trail. Cautious pursuing Viet Minh in olive-green fatigues and leather sandals advanced slowly behind bursts of covering fire. Woven bamboo helmets decorated with a red star adorned their heads. Short-barreled Chinese submachine guns, spitting out quick bursts, dictated the progress. More communists rounded the switchback. A salvo of automatic weapons to the Viet Minh's rear sparked confusion. The uniformed pursuers froze. Heads jerked back and forth as the communist predators realized they had become prey. Old men, boys, and three French commandos opened fire. A hailstorm of lead rained down on the congested jungle path. Bewildered Viet Minh fell. A fuse was lit. A log cannon vomited scrap metal into the confused trespassers. The junkyard blast cut a wide, consuming bloody swath through the communist ranks.

Vue and his elite forces charged around the bend into the fray. Encircling tribesman herded their quarry toward the only exit availed. The communist spilled over the narrow road into the jungle. A detonated landmine launched a uniformed torso skyward. Another mine discharged. The erupting booby-trapped forest expelled earth, timber, and chunks of the invaders.

Waving his arm, Vue signaled a cease fire. Partisan guns fell silent. The rumbling blasts of the active minefield faded. A sulfur-laced mist floated over the kill zone. The low moan of dying men echoed. Across the slopping mined forest, petrified communist survivors stood waving white handkerchiefs.

Vue took a deep breath. The rocky hillside came to life as the ambushing reserves emerged from the shadows. Partisans exchanged triumphant glances. Smiles appeared. The three black-faced Frenchmen maintained a respectful distance. They were outsiders, and this was a Hmong victory. The short tribal chieftain, Vue, pivoted. At his feet, the bodies of his enemies littered the jungle trail. He acknowledged his baiting troops with a bow. Rotating, he grinned up at the bushwhacking seniors and boys. A special wink recognized the silver-haired artillery unit. Under his breath, he mumbled, "Well done, my brothers. Well done." Focusing on his elite warriors, he barked, "Round up the prisoners; the spoils are too be shared by all."

Brandishing seasoned automatic weapons, ten hardened Hmong youths strutted to the edge of the explosive-consuming landscape. With a waving arm, the tooth-missing Chue summoned the kerchief-waving communists. Able-bodied Viet Minh assisted their maimed and wounded comrades. The first soldier to exit was patted down. His cigarettes, watch, and revolver were confiscated. Chue helped himself to a smoke before tossing the spoils to start a communal pile. An orderly captive queue formed. Taking a satisfying puff, Chue shoved the routed communist onto the hard road. The soldier took a seat.

In the cool shade beside the detonated log cannon, the artillery unit tended to wounded tribesmen. Other partisans robbed the dead. Merciful bullets hastened dying communists into the afterlife. Enemy carcasses were tossed into a growing morbid mound.

In the buzzing aftermath, the French commandos lingered like wallflowers. Tapping a soft baby-blue pack of Gauloises cigarettes, Torcy pulled out an exposed tab with a moist lip. Turning his wrist, he offered nicotine treats to his companions. They accepted. The dancing flame of a Zippo lighter ignited the smokes. After a satisfying toke, the lieutenant's soiled fingers plucked the cigarette from his lips. Following a healthy exhale, he mumbled, "Somewhat of a humbling experience."

"I don't understand," LaLande said.

"We came here to teach," Guillian injected, "but realized there is much to learn."

Escalating Hmong dialogue distracted the Frenchmen. A tall, thin tribesman appeared to challenge the short, confident Vue. The scar-faced chieftain simmered as the wiry warrior ranted. The lanky partisan barked as he pointed at the tight compilation of thirty, possibly forty, prisoners sitting on the dusty path. The wounded bled, and the terrified rocked with hands in the prayer position. A few mediated with closed eyes. A lone communist officer sat erect, studying his arguing captors with a defiant scowl.

"Rival clans?" Torcy questioned, squinting at the animated quarrel.

"Possibly," Guillian mumbled. Tilting an eavesdropping ear in the direction of the impassioned debate, he summarized, "It appears String Bean is opposed to leniency for the prisoners." As the tall tribesman's rhetoric softened, Guillian translated, "Last summer, Viet Minh entered String Bean's village and seized his opium harvest...his livestock...and daughter...make that two of his daughters."

"You can't blame him for being pissed," LaLande interjected.

"He is demanding the execution of the prisoners," Guillian translated.

Towering in front of Vue, String Bean placed fisted hands on his narrow frame. A harsh scowl solicited a response.

Vue nodded his understanding. Unholstering his revolver, he wet his lips. Twirling the pistol, he offered the gun's butt to the distraught father.

The lanky instigator took a step back. Studying the offered weapon, he took a deep breath. Sticking out his shallow chest, he snatched the pistol. Breathing heavily, he waded into the subdued, condemned flock. Prisoners cowered at his feet, with one exception. The Viet Minh officer stuck out his chin, his dark eyes burning with disdain. The tribesman locked his elbow and extended a pistol-wielding arm. The gun popped. A bullet smacked the communist commander's forehead. His head snapped back. Lifeless eyes gazed skyward. Desperate pleas rippled through the seated prisoners. The grinning executioner informed the terrified men, "Nkauj and Paaj were good girls."

Guillian reflected on his termination of Bachman. It didn't bring back his father and brothers, but it felt good. He watched as the executioner returned Vue's revolver and bowed. Apparently the penalty for loss of opium, livestock, and daughters was a Viet Minh officer's life. All sins between men have consequences.

Brandishing his pistol, Vue, looking across the downcast heads of prisoners, shouted, "Go...You are free...Take your wounded and never return." The captives slowly rose. Vue discharged an expediting round skyward. Scrambling communists got the message. Carrying and assisting wounded comrades, the reprieved departed in haste.

"Sergeant," Vue hollered in the direction of the French trio, "inform the lieutenant we will need more land mines."

CHAPTER THIRTY-FIVE

Max awoke. It was hot. He was swimming in sweat. Seeking comfort, he rolled over into a retreating sliver of shade. Conceding to the late-afternoon sun perched over hill 117, he sat up. Beside him, along the sandbag barrier, exhausted defenders attempted sleep. Lightheaded, Max stood, sweeping fingers through his moist scalp. Taking a deep breath, he stretched tired bones and stood up. The fog of slumber slowly receded. Taking off his saturated field blouse, he felt a warm wind caress his sweaty torso. Slinging the wet garment over a bare shoulder, he gingerly stepped over his reclining comrades. With a full bladder, he plodded through the sandbag maze.

On the hill's summit, the tricolor flag of France flapped victoriously. Legionnaires pulling guard duty scrutinized the surrounding scorched terrain. Under the shade of a parachute canopy, twenty wounded men reclined on army cots. A dog-tired medic in bloodstained fatigues waded through the symmetrically arranged portable beds. The infirmary was quiet. Critical casualties floated in morphine-induced euphoria. Behind the open-air field hospital, olive-green tarps shrouded the fifteen fallen defenders of the isolated post.

Passing the hospital, Max accelerated. He was on a mission. Sucking in his breath, he entered the foul environment of the latrine. The structure had three barn-wood walls and a sloping corrugated tin roof. Sunlight flowed through the gaps in the blistered timber. Oval holes cut into a wood-plank bench could accommodate ten patrons. An active wasp mud nest overhead competed with the flies buzzing in the pit below. Eyeing the ominous hornets, Max hastily emptied his bladder. Exiting, he exhaled. *I should check on Stollhoof,* he thought meandering toward large canvas bags of water suspended by a bamboo pole. Avoiding the mud puddles beneath the camp's water supply, he opened a spigot and greedily doused his naked frame. Cupped hands splashed his face. After rubbing his teeth with a moist index finger, he spat.

The encampment slowly came to life. Groggy soldiers shuffled toward the privy shanty. The aroma of coffee blessed the warm air. Inaudible light conversations surfaced. An informal changing of the guards transpired.

Dripping from the field shower, Max entered the open-air hospital. Overhead, the silk shroud fluttered. A sleepy-eyed medic shot him a curious squint. Max, pointing to Stollhoof reclining in the corner, received a consenting nod. It was religiously quiet as Max walked past reclining damaged men. Lying flat on his back, Stollhoof stared skyward. His left arm was tucked into a sling covering his bare chest. A budging wad of white gauze covered his shoulder.

"Max!" a surprised Stollhoof exclaimed.

"What did the doctor say?" Max asked quietly.

Lifting his head in search of the medic, Stollhoof grimaced. "He's not a doctor." Returning to a comfortable repose, he added, "The medic doesn't know shit about the lack of feeling in my arm." Looking up at Max, he confessed, "I fear my limb may be dead."

Max chuckled. "You are not getting any sympathy from me, *kamerad*. You're heading to the land of clean sheets, hot food, sponge baths, and French nurses. If I recall, after our open-air incarceration, a down mattress and warm meal topped your list of desires. A buxom French filly barely made the agenda. Now you can have all three. As for me, I'm staying put on hill 117 earning the same twenty piastres a day with the fear of becoming dead."

A grin spread across Stollhoof's somber expression. "We've been traveling together for a while, Max. It's been a rough journey, but I enjoyed the company."

"The ride isn't over with yet, my friend. You'll be back." Smirking, Max teased, "Don't fret; if your arm is dead, you still have your right hand to keep you company."

Stollhoof laughed.

"I'm in need of coffee," Max said. "Can I get you a cup?"

"Nein," Stollhoof answered. "I'm in need of sleep."

"I'll check in on you later," Max offered, retreating.

Stepping into the sunlight, Max blinked. Shielding his eyes, he scanned the blackened countryside. In the distance, a cloud of red dust barreled down the twisting dirt road. An army convoy appeared beneath the soiled haze. Diminished supplies would be replenished. The wounded would be evacuated. Hill 117 sprang to life. Cigarettes and liquor dominated the inhabitants' wish lists.

Lowering his field glasses, a sentry hollered, "The BMC is in the convoy! I can't believe it. The BMC is coming to hill 117." Reference to the hallowed French military institution Bordel Mobile de Campagne sent the legionnaires into a feeding frenzy. Like a pack of dogs locked on the scent of a bitch in heat, the soldiers scurried toward the compound's entry gate. Lieutenant LeBlanc lingered behind the ravenous hounds. A satisfied grin graced his face as he mumbled, "Who needs a morale officer when you can summon the BMC?"

A twelve-foot-high razor-wire barrier swung open. All eyes focused on the approaching cloud of orange-red dust. Most of the mercenaries in the audience were shirtless. Sweat glistened off bare flesh. The salivating crowd parted as the convoy rolled into the outpost. The troops immediately converged around the two-and-half-ton BMC trailer truck. A French army sergeant hopped out of the passenger cab to address the troops. He was a tall, well-built mulatto with thick black hair. His impeccable pearly whites sparkled as he flashed a big smile to the lustful gathering. "Legionnaires, I am Sergeant Nouri," he hollered over the focused mob. "You can thank Lieutenant LeBlanc for the arrival of the BMC. He felt, regardless of the remoteness of your location, his troops deserved the services enjoyed by all the colonial forces in Indochina. The ladies you are about to meet volunteered for this assignment in enemy-occupied territory. These are special ladies indeed. They hail from the Ouled Nail tribe that inhabits the Atlas Mountains of Algeria. The women are called Nailiyat and have a long history in the erotic arts. For centuries, mothers have passed down the skill of giving pleasure to their daughters." Surveying the anxious crowd, he grinned. "Let's meet the ladies." Placing a wooden stool beneath the trailer's door, he gently rapped on the metal barrier.

The door swung open. A cloud of cannabis smoke escaped. A giddy naked mocha-skinned harlot in a crown headdress of gold coins cascaded out of the truck. Her exposed breasts were small but shapely. Her large dark eyes conveyed a seductive innocence. Multiple coin necklaces and innumerable bracelets of silver and gold jangled as she pranced for an appreciative audience. Riding low on her shapely hips, a chain-fringed belt partially concealed her sex. A rehearsed twirl presented a plump derriere.

A second tall, dark, sultry young beauty appeared in the metal doorframe. A shear powder-blue shawl rested atop her bullion-decorated headdress. The transparent fabric flowed down her bare backside. An ornate necklace highlighted a perky bosom. Posing, she exhibited an enticing example of a long, lean, ripe female form. Wrapping the thin garment around her taut caramel skin, she stepped into the sunlight and hugged her naked companion from behind. "Bonjour, messieurs," she cooed, embracing her associate.

"Bonjour!" simultaneously erupted out of an open-mouthed crowd.

Sergeant Nouri, holding an upturned helmet in his hand, joined the ladies. "The fee for a single coupling is one hundred piastres." The reaction to the price of five days wages was always the same. There was none. From a white bag, he poured numbered poker chips into the steel bonnet. "For those who are interested, we will draw lots to determine an order." He wandered through the crowd. It was a seller's market.

"What did you get?" Muller asked Max.

Displaying the number thirty-seven on a poker chip, Max shrugged. "Looks like I'll be in the back of the line."

"Don't ride her too hard, Max," Muller said, flashing chip number fifty-two. "Save some for those bringing up the rear."

"Number thirty-seven!" hollered the procuring Sergeant Nouri. Seated behind a folding table next the mobile bordello, he scanned the milling troops. Max stepped forward with money in hand. Tossing the numbered poker chip on the table, he paid the fare. "Fifteen minutes," Nouri instructed, cranking the dial of a kitchen timer. Max nodded his acceptance of terms.

Stepping on the portable stoop, he entered the trailer and removed his field blouse. The transport rocked slightly. It smelled of sweat. Bare chested, he walked into an inviting open boudoir. Hoping for the tall drink of chocolate, he felt a twinge of disappointment seeing the plump harlot. Sitting hunched over on the edge of the bed, she was breathing heavily. Utilizing a damp washcloth, she wiped her face and rubbed the back of her neck. Looking up at her next customer, she inhaled deeply and tossed the moist cloth in a bowl of water on the nightstand. Rolling back into the bed naked, she offered herself.

"Long day?" Max questioned.

She nodded.

"Catch your breath, sweetheart," Max offered, walking over to the nightstand. Ringing out the cloth, he sat beside her and began sponging off taut mocha flesh. Closing her eyes, she sighed.

Startled, she opened her eyes and cautioned, "You are wasting your session's time."

"Consider it professional courtesy," Max commented, admiring the female form.

"What?" she muttered, savoring the bath.

"We are both professionals plying our trade in a foreign land. A brief reprieve from our harsh tasks is always appreciated."

"What is your name, soldier?" she asked.

"Max."

"I'm going to remember you Max," she cooed. Reaching up, she grasped the back of his neck. Pulling his head down, she offered an amorous kiss. He melted into the embrace of a well-schooled professional of the erotic arts.

CHAPTER THIRTY-SIX

A steady rain fell from a charcoal sky. A spark of light flashed behind intimidating black clouds. After a relaxed pause, faint thunder crackled. It was going to be a wet afternoon in Saigon. On crowded sidewalks, clear sheets of plastic sheltered shopkeepers' exposed merchandise. Murky water, burdened with rubbish, gushed down open gutters. Motorbikes zigzagging through sluggish traffic spat up oil-based spray.

Under the protection of a green oilpaper umbrella, businessman Louis Guajac navigated the congested walkway. A tailor-made gray suit fit his short frame like a glove. He detested his new wardrobe, longing for the comfort of baggy combat fatigues. The downpour accelerated. Exiting the pedestrian stream, he entered the drenched courtyard of the House of Butterflies. Overturned chairs rested on hardwood tables. Rain gutters fed growing puddles across the cobblestone plaza. The brothel's two-story facade appeared to be napping in preparation for the nocturnal trade. Avoiding the water hazards, Guajac ascended the concrete stoop. Vigorously opening and shutting the Asian umbrella, he expelled remnants of the storm before entering through the thick speakeasy door. A clanging bell overhead announced his entrance. Like Pavlov's dogs, young Asian females responded to the chime, dipping bare shoulders, hiking up skirts, and flashing seductive smiles. The merchandise was on display. Guajac waved off any potential advances with an apologetic hand and mumbled, "Thank you, but I'm not interested."

A hefty mama-san entered the parlor through a beaded curtain. Her silk floral-printed gown was wrinkled, the back of her bouffant hairstyle matted. A teetering false eyelash confirmed the fact she had just woken up. "What is your pleasure?" she inquired with a slight yawn.

"I have a meeting with the proprietor," Guajac announced. Checking his watch, he added, "I'm slightly late because of the rain."

"Maybe girl later?" she prodded.

Guajac laughed. *The industrious Vietnamese view everyone as a customer, every opportunity a sale. You have to admire their determination.* "Maybe," he politely responded.

"This way," she said, retreating through the beaded barrier.

He followed. Facing the wall, an accountant pulled back on the handle of a manual adding machine. Puffing away on a cigarette, the bookkeeper stayed focused on his task. The steady click of the calculator dominated the back of the property. There was a tired sofa leaking stuffing. Seated at the end of the dying couch, a bullyboy, utilizing chopsticks, shoveled noodles into his open mouth at close range. He was a large man with a massive head. A bulging belly jiggled beneath a taut white singlet. The sleeveless garment displayed intimidating limbs. Lacking any sense of dining etiquette, he raised his scruffy noggin to investigate the guest. Escaping noodles dangled down his chin. Grunting approval, he buried his face back into the steaming bowl.

"Is that Lieutenant Guajac?" a familiar voice called out from a back room.

Nodding at the mama-san, Guajac dismissed her of her charge and entered the corner office. Open windows secured with decorative bars allowed the sound of rainfall and moist cool air to flow through the enclosure. A tiger skin decorated a wall. Brand liquor bottles and a crystal serving set complemented a teak liquor cabinet. A redwood mother-of-pearl inlay desk defined the room. Framed by the doorway, Guajac, looking across the ornate workstation, said, "Hello, Coty."

The Corsican beamed as he leaped out of a swivel chair. He had put on weight. A fat face diluted his scarred bulbous nose. His white hair had thinned considerably. In a blue-striped seersucker suit, he still projected a dapper quality. Extending a welcoming hand across the desk, he proclaimed, "Always good to see an old friend." A firm shake confirmed the sentiment. Wandering toward the liquor cabinet, he questioned over his shoulder, "What are you drinking?"

"It's a little early for me," Guajac graciously declined.

Pouring a shot of scotch into a crystal glass, Coty commented, "You know, I actually have a craving for that Hmong moonshine. I just hope our Hmong hosts are weathering the communist storm."

"You don't know?"

"Don't know what?"

"They're all gone, erased by the Viet Minh. The lone survivor was Loc. The industrious lad is now a soldier in the French colonial forces."

Coty took a sobering breath. His shoulders sagged. He poured a second scotch. Offering the libation, he said, "Please join me in drinking to the memory of our Hmong benefactors."

Guajac nodded, accepting the sparkling whisky. The Frenchmen touched glasses. To the clink of heavy crystal, they muttered, "*Nam lu*," the universal greeting of the hill tribes.

"Looks like you've done well for yourself," Guajac said, glancing around and taking a seat in a red leather chair.

Clearing his throat of lingering emotions, Coty responded, "Yes, yes, I have. I parlayed your gift of an M2 carbine…or should I clarify, the *bullets* of the automatic rifle into the seed capital to acquire this establishment." Grinning widely, he declared, "There is a lot of money to be made in selling *la chatte*."

Guajac chuckled. "You summoned me. What can a struggling freight business owner do for a *la chatte* trafficker?"

Snickering at the label, Coty asked, "How is business?"

"Insurance premiums escalate with the increase in communist hostilities. My lucrative military contracts are not so lucrative," Guajac answered. A gulp of scotch cleansed his palate of the bitter admission.

"You still maintain your military contacts?"

Guajac nodded.

"That's why I summoned you," Coty informed the war hero. "One of the occupational hazards of my establishment is the sickness of Venus. Contaminating your customers is bad for business. And the disease drastically shortens the peak earning years of my employees. Since my customer base is almost exclusively French military personnel, I'd like you to reach out to your military contacts. My objective is to have army medical give the House of Butterflies a certificate of cleanliness. I'll compensate you for brokering a relationship and pay the medical staff for whatever inspections they deem necessary."

"I'll see what I can do," Guajac responded. Raising the last of his whisky, he added, "Bravo, my sly friend. In a country with an escalating conflict, this certification would likely direct an incoming army through your front door."

The mama-san appeared in the doorway. Coty frowned. Guajac turned to investigate.

"What is it?" Coty snapped.

"Mr. Rossi," she replied.

Coty shook his head in disgust. Addressing Guajac, he said, "In addition to checking my employees for the diseases of their profession, have army medical include treatment for fatigue and hospital care for the occasional beating." Looking at the concerned handler, he asked, "How bad was Mr. Rossi this time?"

"I'm not sure," she answered, catching a breath. "It sounded pretty bad."

Exhaling, Coty rose. "I'm sorry to cut our reunion short, but I need to handle this."

"I understand," Guajac offered, placing his empty whisky glass on the ornate desktop. Standing, he added, "I'll get back with you in a couple of days with the ranking military's response."

After a quick handshake, Coty abandoned his guest and followed the anxious mama-san out of the office. She burst through the beaded curtain. He followed in her wake. In the parlor, concerned, terrified lambs stared up the red-carpeted stairway. The mother hen waved off her chicks as she raced up to the second floor. Utilizing the dark wood railing, Coty kept pace. The top of the stairs intersected with a long corridor. In both directions, closed doors defined tiny bedding chambers. In front of unit 216, Coty waved off his manager. *My Unione Corse associate is a sadist*, Coty realized. *We all have our fetishes*, he reasoned, politely knocking and entering.

A broken, naked dove whimpered in the corner. Blood splatter stained the white sheets of an unmade bed. In front of a washbasin, beneath an oval mirror, a barefoot Petru Rossi, in white slacks and an undershirt, splashed his face. "Hello, Carlo," he muttered. Looking up, he raked his thick, greasy black hair with moist fingers. Admiring his reflection through piercing dark eyes, he mustered up a satisfied grin. Turning, he smiled at his Corsican kinsman and added, "Always good to see you, Coty."

190

Coty nodded. The mama-san rushed in to examine the damaged merchandise. Petru took a seat in the room's only chair and shook a sock before putting it on.

Focused on the whimpering bundle of flesh in the corner, Coty asked, "How is she?"

The mama-san, glancing at Rossi, appeared nervous. "I can't tell," she answered before offering, "Possibly missing a tooth."

"Two teeth," Rossi volunteered, putting on another sock. "And her nose is broken."

As the mama-san was assisting the battered girl out of the room, Coty announced, "I'm going to have to charge you extra."

"Put it on my tab," Rossi calmly replied, lacing a shoe. Rising, he slipped on a dress shirt. Fidgeting with the buttons, he asked, "Do you have time for drink, Carlo? I'd like to discuss smuggling black market piastres into France and cashing them into francs at a more favorable rate. The reconversion could produce substantial profits."

"Sounds like a promising opportunity."

CHAPTER THIRTY-SEVEN

A peaceful afternoon graced the remote Hmong village. A sprinkling of puffy white clouds blessed a rich blue sky. A bright sun produced lazy warmth. The static atmosphere held the rank aroma of the hillside community in check. Muffled tribal conversations faded in and out. A happy dog barked in the distance.

On the deck of a stilted hovel, sitting beside a bottle of white lightning, Torcy stared at the cover of a dated *Cinemonde* magazine. The hypnotic image of Marlene Dietrich adorned the torn and frayed periodical. The wrinkled monthly still captured the movie star's exotic bedroom eyes. Lost in a fantasy, the lieutenant stroked the seductive portrait. Crackling static within the raised shack interrupted the daydream. He sighed.

A faint voice from the civilized world reached out of the annoying hiss.

"Requesting a munitions drop," Guillian hollered.

Turning, Torcy glanced through the open doorway. The Jewish sergeant, sporting a scruffy beard, shouted out a laundry list of killing stores into a hand-held black microphone. "Have them throw some magazines and newspapers into the weapons cache," Torcy suggested from the porch.

Guillian nodded at the eavesdropping lieutenant. Leaning into the transmitter, he said, "Please add reading periodicals to the list."

The transmission terminated. Guillian rose. The shanty creaked under his weight. Plodding out of the frail one-room hovel, he stood on the porch and stretched.

Looking up with a one-eyed squint, Torcy asked, "What did they say?"

"Expect the weapons drop in two days," Guillian answered. "Based on the radio operator's tone, I suspect the war is not going well."

Torcy's crooked-nosed face puckered. "No!" he snapped. "What did they say about the magazines?"

Guillian shrugged. "I don't know if that request was received."

The lieutenant's shoulders deflated. Gazing out across the stilted shacks clinging to the bluff, he confessed quietly, "I fear this isolation is driving me mad."

"It's only been six months," Guillian countered.

Torcy exaggerated an exhale.

"Relax, Lieutenant, only madmen proclaim their sanity." Squatting down like a tribesman, Guillian counseled, "Work on your language skills. Try to assimilate; these are gentle and generous people. Hell, LaLande has embraced the culture."

"Corporal LaLande le con!" (the idiot) Torcy popped. "The only thing that bucktoothed baguette has adapted to is getting drunk with the locals and fucking their daughters."

"The Hmong girls are promiscuous," Guillian quietly agreed.

"God help us if he gets a tribal flower pregnant," Torcy muttered, shaking his head. "Or worse, what if he contaminates the garden with the sickness of Venus?"

"LaLande is a putz." Guillian chuckled. "But you can't fault a French soldier for partaking in earthy joys."

"Every fool has a hobby," the lieutenant muttered, taking a swig of moonshine. Wiping his moist lips, he gazed at the starlet's image on his lap.

"Well, now that that is settled," Guillian concluded, "what is the cause of your displeasure, Jacque?"

Backhanding the magazine, Torcy blurted, "This...this is churning my intestines. A world exists beyond the endless mountain ridges of the Indochina highlands. A planet occupied by Marlene Dietrich motion pictures. A place with automobiles, flat roads, electricity, and water closets that flush. Cities inhabited by tall, slender white women in silk gowns." Closing his eyes, he tilted his head back and mumbled, "Stoic, long-legged blondes."

"We are GCMA commandos on assignment," Guillian interjected.

Torcy's spine stiffened. "An unappreciated assignment with no end! We have successfully slapped the communist supply lines hard and diverted the

Viet Minh weapons flow. Does anyone in Hanoi, Saigon, Paris, or in Marlene Dietrich's world have an inkling of our victories, losses, and sacrifices?"

"A lack of recognition is the source of your melancholy?" Guillian questioned, standing up. Grasping the rough wood deck railing, he scanned the napping village. "This is our world now, Lieutenant. The Hmong celebrate victories. The Viet Minh retaliate for defeats. No quarter is offered. Celebrity does not exist. Our *montagnard* allies don't know or care about the civilized universe you and LaLande may one day return to. Total victory is the only option for their survival."

"Don't you think about going home, Jean?" a surprised Torcy questioned.

An enlightened smile appeared on the Jewish commando's face. "I have no home."

Laughter distracted the Frenchmen. A successful Hmong hunting party paraded out of the jungle. The silver-haired Zoov, with a crossbow balanced over his shoulder, led the procession. Behind the chuckling middle-aged hunter, his sons hauled the carcass of a strange-looking bison. Lashed to a bamboo pole, the dangling two-hundred-pound mammal's unique parallel horns skimmed the moist ground.

"Zoov!" Guillian shouted from his elevated perch. "What did you kill?"

Halting the procession, Zoov puffed out his shallow chest and proclaimed proudly, "A saht-supahp" (polite animal). With the bowed pole challenging his sons' shoulders, Zoov walked back, reached down, grabbed a two-foot-long horn, and lifted up the animal's head. "The skull will decorate my house, and the juicy meat will fill my belly."

"It looks like an African oryx," Torcy muttered from a seated repose.

"It is an impressive kill," Guillian complimented the beaming hunter.

"Join us, Fackee," Zoov offered, releasing the long, sharp horn. "Tonight we will feast on a hindquarter and drink to our good fortune."

"He's invited us to dinner," Guillian translated over his shoulder.

Torcy rose. Mustering up a smile, he nodded his acceptance.

"Let's find the corporal," Torcy mumbled, strolling through the village. "LaLande can listen to static while we feast on that strange venison."

"A swordsman is easy to locate," Guillian commented, setting the pace toward the community love nest.

A rickety ladder led to an elevated, windowless shack. A burlap drape concealed the entrance. Premarital sex was not only permitted within the tribe, but the community provided this shrine for coupling. Behind the rough cloth curtain, LaLande sang a simple French tune.

"Corporal!" Torcy hollered up at the blanketed doorway.

The hatchet-faced LaLande stuck his head out of the curtain and coughed. "Yes, sir?"

"Get dressed," Torcy barked. "I need you to man the radio."

LaLande's head receded. Muffled female-laced dialogue preceded his narrow noggin's reappearance. "Five minutes, sir?" he humbly requested.

"I'll give you three," the lieutenant conceded.

A wide grin signaled LaLande's acceptance as he vanished behind the curtain.

Looking at Guillian, Torcy shrugged. Grunts escalated within the love nest. High-pitched female delight answered.

"A soldier's earthly joys." Guillian chuckled beneath the amorous duet.

Glistening in sweat, a bare-assed LaLande flew down the ladder. Dropping his boots and uniform on the moist ground, he stood at attention. Buck-naked, displaying his *veuve et les orphelines* (widow and two orphans), he saluted, "Corporal LaLande reporting for duty, sir."

Guillian laughed.

Suppressing a snicker, Torcy responded with a halfhearted salute. "Cover your *service trois pièces*, Corporal, and proceed as instructed."

LaLande dressed on the fly. Slipping into a pant leg, he snared a foot and tumbled onto the dirt road.

Observing the corporal's clumsy departure, Torcy mumbled, "The man's a moron."

"We need to hold our liquor," Guillian commented. "Or we will be stumbling back to the shack."

Resuming the stroll, Torcy asked Guillian, "Have you acquired a taste for the local hooch?"

"The Hmong love to drink, and we wouldn't want to offend our host. But the rice whisky would go down smoother with a little ice and a shot of seltzer."

"Every libation is softened by ice and soda," Torcy muttered. Squinting, he inquired, "What is our host's name?"

"Zoov!" Guillian exclaimed. "The skilled hunter is one of the tribe's best communist trackers. He's a good man, a seasoned warrior. I heard he lost his brother fighting the Japanese. As is their custom, he married his widowed sister-in-law and adopted his nieces and nephews."

"How many children does he have?"

Guillian shrugged. "I have no idea. I'm still trying to comprehend the fact he has two wives."

Both Frenchmen simultaneously took a deep breath. The aroma of grilled meat teased their senses. Torcy swallowed. Guillian licked his lips.

At the end of a well-tread pathway sat Zoov's humble residence. Raucous laughter resonated from within. In front of the grass shack, a pack of scurrying small children stirred up dust around the spiked head of the spindle-horned saola. Surrounding a smoldering fire pit, a pack of teenage boys held court. A squatting youth turned thick slabs of red meat decorating a rectangular metal grill. A bamboo frame suspended the grating a foot over white-hot coals. Blue flames randomly appeared. Dripping fat splattered.

As the Frenchmen approached, the fireside audience rotated to avoid shifting smoke. The teenage boys acknowledged the foreign guests with raised brows. Encompassing children halted the commandos' advance. Surrounded by gawking, soiled faces, Guillian smiled at his admirers. A four-year-old latched on to Torcy's hand and dragged him through the assembly. At the low open doorway, the young escort released his grasp. Bowing his head, Guillian entered the mud-floored hut. Torcy followed.

It was a large one-room shelter. Smoke lingered under a pitched palm-frond ceiling. Bedding lined the perimeter. An array of garments dangled from various clotheslines. Jars, pots, and wicker bottles filled planked shelving across the far wall. Beneath an open window in the corner, Zoov's two wives and three teenage daughters squatted around a small cooking fire. Suspended over coals, a large black kettle's lid battled escaping steam. In the center of the room, seven tribesmen, sitting on grass matting, encircled a low square table. Wooden bowls, brimming with vegetables, bamboo shoots, and steaming rice, cluttered the tabletop. Orbiting the buffet, a whicker-encased flagon of murky white whisky replenished bamboo stock beakers.

Zoov's eldest son, clutching a bamboo flask, took a gulp. The jet-black-haired twenty-something Tuam appeared out of place among the other male diners, who were all graying. A wide, drunken grin dominated his youthful features. Apparently, this was his first feast at the adult table.

"The Fackee are here!" Zoov declared.

Wobbly heads and sleepy eyes gazed up at the white guests.

Intercepting the circulating jug, Zoov slowly rose. In a teetering stance, he balanced the jug on his shoulder and took a nip. "Let's get drunk," he proclaimed, extending a strait moonshine-wielding arm at the Frenchmen.

Accepting the libation, Guillian toasted his host, "To a fine kill, my friend." Taking a calculated swig, he felt the harsh disinfectant tormenting his tongue before the scorching journey down his throat. Instinctively, he coughed.

The tribesmen erupted in laughter.

"Probably would have gone down smoother with a splash of seltzer," Torcy joked before taking his turn. After miming a toast, he took a gulp. "Whoa," he exclaimed. "That'll defiantly clean out my plumbing." After stealing another healthy belt, he leaned into Guillian and muttered, "Maybe getting rotten drunk is the cure for my melancholy."

Guillian's face puckered. *Is Torcy a happy, quiet drunkard?* he wondered. *Or will the disciplined lieutenant be transformed into an angry, inebriated fool? I guess we will all find out.*

"Sit…sit, my friends," Zoov insisted, motioning for his relatives to make some room. "H'Liana!" he called out to his eldest daughter. "Get bowls and bamboo stocks for the Fackee."

Taking a seat on the hard surface, Guillian pivoted to get a glimpse of H'Liana. *The gifted singing angel from the poppy fields,* he realized. She smiled at him as she approached. This time, the local beauty in a red-and-blue headscarf did not shield her expression. Perfect white teeth resided behind supple lips. A seductive innocence resonated from the depths of her dark gemstone eyes. The symmetry of her fair-skinned face defined elegance. An awestruck gasp escaped Guillian's open mouth. *My God, she is special,* he thought, attempting to catch his breath. "Merci," he mumbled as she squatted down and filled a bamboo mug with hooch. Focused on her widening smile, he detected a pinkish hue blessing her soft cheeks.

"You're smitten," Torcy mumbled, tossing back his jungle mug.

Guillian took a composing breath and a sip of white whisky. The firewater calmed his racing heart. He stole another glance at the Hmong vision as she returned to the women's corner.

A teenage boy with a steel platter of sizzling meat entered. Salivating anticipation rippled through the men as the youth placed charred steaks on the table. Ravenous hands snatched up the meat. Wooden spoons ladled out side dishes. Smacking lips accompanied gluttonous groans. Fingers fed bowed heads.

Lancing a juicy slab of meat with a table knife, Guillian inspected the delicacy. Black grill marks branded the venison steak. He bit off a mouthful. It was surprisingly tender. Spicy seasoning diluted a gamy quality. "What did you call this?" he questioned before ripping off another chunk.

Zoov looked up, his jowls glistening with grease. "A polite animal," he grunted with a full mouth. After swallowing, he added, "It is a gentle creature that moves through the forest in silence. I've heard it called a spindlehorn, because its parallel horns resemble the posts of a spinning wheel." Biting into the meat brick in his hand, he concluded with a chopping mouth, "Right now, I'm calling it very good."

"It is a very rare creature," an old man in a blue turban quietly chimed in. He was short and rail thin. The weather-beaten wrinkles of his rawhide face suggested a tough life.

What is his name? Guillian wondered. *He lost a son in the outpost raid. His son's name was Dang. His name is…Pao. That's it, the fabled warrior Pao.* "Pao!" Guillian exclaimed. "How many polite animals have you feasted on?"

The old warrior beamed at the recognition. A nervous hill-tribe smile appeared. After a composing cough, Pao answered, "Many seasons have passed since my last taste. Even as a boy, I knew killing a polite animal was special."

"How do the Fackee celebrate good fortune?" Zoov asked. Pressing his full belly, he launched a tremendous belch.

After mustering up a burp, Guillian replied, "Drink, fine food, and camaraderie are universal, my friend." The image of his father toasting at a family gathering in the back room of a Parisian café surfaced. Fine wine flowed. The cuisine was always exceptional. Tuxedo-clad waiters scurried about. Standing tall, Etienne Guillian delivered a humorous monologue. Raucous laughter was always the response to Papa's amusing observations of life. *Did that life ever exit?* Guillian wondered. *Or was it just a dream that preceded the Nazi nightmare?*

Returning to the Hmong feast, Guillian watched Zoov embellishing a hunting yarn. *There are constants that are inherent in all cultures*, he surmised. Infectious laughter followed the well-spun yarn.

"I need a refill," Torcy slurred, pounding the spent table with an empty flask.

No translation was necessary. Ever the attentive host, Zoov clapped his hands. H'Liana hastily pulled a whicker jug from the wall. As she approached, Guillian relieved her of the heavy decanter with a smile. She showed her appreciation with a slight bow and whispered, "Merci."

"You speak French?" Guillian exclaimed.

Shaking her head, she retreated into the women's circle.

Guillian filled up Torcy's consistently empty beaker. A crooked smile highlighted the lieutenant's glassy-eyed expression. *My superior officer is a quiet, happy drunkard*, Guillian concluded.

After dinner, cigarettes sparked to life. Torcy's head bobbed as he casually tapped on a soft powder-blue pack of Gauloises smokes. Inadvertently, he launched three cigarettes onto the cluttered tabletop. Responding to the mishap with a dumbfounded flinch, he methodically picked up an escaping tobacco canister. After studying the tab, he sighed and attempted to insert the cigarette back into the package. Even at close range, his hand and eye coordination were out of sync.

"Let me help you, Lieutenant," Guillian offered, relieving Torcy of the simple task. Displaying the stubborn cigarette between his thumb and forefinger, he said, "Open."

Attempting to focus, Torcy presented an inviting mouth. Guillian delicately placed the nicotine treat on the lieutenant's moist lower lip. Torcy grinned. A dangling cigarette accented the victory. Striking a match, Guillian ignited the after-dinner treat.

Torcy took one puff. His eyes ascended beneath heavy lids. A lazy neck conceded beneath his teetering head. Slowly rolling backward, he collapsed on the earthen floor. Secured between his lips, a smoldering cigarette pointed into the pitched ceiling.

The old Hmong beside the comatose Fackee snickered. Reaching down, he plucked the lit cigarette. Tilting his head back, he took a long, satisfying toke.

"It is always better to be the first to pass out," Zoov interjected.

"How so?" Guillian questioned.

"Because the burden of getting you to bed falls upon your friends," the skilled hunter replied.

CHAPTER THIRTY-EIGHT

Beneath a dark, starless sky, the ominous rain forest vibrated with life. Two Filipino commandos, armed with automatic weapons, stood guard over a clearing in the Luzon jungle. In the tiny pocket void of growth, an additional dozen commandos squatted in a casual circle on the moist ground. The glowing red dots of active cigarettes pierced the darkness.

Sitting on a decomposing log, CIA operative Major Tom Roche enjoyed a smoke. Sweat migrated beneath his army-green fatigues. Hoping to dissuade the mosquito buzzing his head, he snorted secondhand smoke. *The oppressed peasants always seem to gravitate toward that communist bullshit,* he reflected. *A lot of American blood was spilled evicting the Japanese from these islands. The communist cancerous tumor must be eradicated before it spreads across the Philippines. The Huk fought the Japanese, and now the communist Huk want to overthrow the pro-American government.* "Allies become adversaries," he mumbled, standing to stretch.

The commandos standing guard bristled. Their comrades rose, tossing cigarettes aside. Firearms clicked into operation. Roche stared down the ink-black entry path. Two commandos escorted a blindfolded, gagged, bound Huk captive into view. The disoriented hostage's head twitched from side to side. An unbuttoned plaid shirt revealed the taut skin of youth.

"Why are they always so young?" Roche mumbled. Answering his own question, he realized, *Because their life expectancy is so short.* "Let's get this over with, Flores," Roche said to the officer in charge.

Captain Flores had a dark-brown complexion, round face, and small nose. His size and quiet nature added a boyish charm to the polite local. After a quick nod in the American's direction, he poured chloroform onto a fraying white hand towel. A strong chemical scent tainted the muggy atmosphere. Flanking soldiers held the prisoner firmly. Flores jammed the saturated rag into the rebel's unsuspecting face. The teen's head jerked violently; his gagged mouth emitted muffled groans. Resistance was brief. The Huk guerilla collapsed.

Wielding a pair of ice picks taped together, Flores crouched over the crumbled body. In the darkness, his extender fingers searched for the communist's jugular vein. Locating the pulsing blood vessel, he plunged the twin prongs into the boy's neck. Blood erupted. The body twitched. Dracula would have been proud. As if rehearsed, a commando bound the victim's feet together. Tossing an end of the rope over a tree limb, he hoisted the upended carcass into the air. The bough creaked as life slowly drained into a growing crimson puddle.

Roche took a calming toke of his expiring cigarette. Recalling the Stalin quote, he mumbled, "One death is a tragedy, one million a statistic." *We can't be dropping atomic bombs on all our enemies,* he reasoned. *The cost of inoculating this region from the Huk rebellion is this single life. Exploiting the local superstitions is a powerful weapon.* Tossing his cigarette aside, he asked the executioner, "Do you believe in vampires, Flores?"

Focused on the pale upturned body, Flores replied, "Many Filipinos fear the *aswang*. An *aswang* is a shape-shifting ghoul that walks among townspeople during the day and transforms into an animal to feed on strangers at night." Glancing in Roche's direction, he confessed, "I'm Catholic. I believe in the Bible." Pulling out the gold cross displayed on his necklace, he added, "Jesus protects me from the aswang."

Roche checked his watch. Daylight was three hours away. "It's time to plant the evidence on the trail," he informed Flores.

The amicable officer relayed the message in Filipino. Two commandos cut down the bloodless cadaver and disappeared into the surrounding darkness.

Roche lit up another smoke. Picturing the Huk troops discovering their fallen comrade and fleeing the region in fear of the dreaded aswang, he grinned. *It works every time.*

In a white linen untucked Filipino dress shirt and chinos, Roche strutted down Field Avenue, Angeles City, Philippines. His salt-and-pepper hair was cropped smartly into a short, bristled flattop. It was late afternoon; high clouds shielded him from the harsh tropical sun. Bars and brothels flourished along the asphalt arterial feeding Clark Air Base. The establishments that trafficked in the vices of servicemen slowly awoke. Roche's penny loafers confidently pounded the cracked and buckling sidewalk. A front pants' pocket full of loose change added a jingle to his stride. The coins were a necessity for the less fortunate toll takers who plagued the seedy route.

A flock of colorfully packaged working girls stood beneath the dormant neon signage of High Rollers. In bright-red, yellow, and green dresses, the three fallen doves posed to enhance their charms. Youth was the common denominator. "You want sucky sucky?" the one in the snug yellow garment called out to Roche.

Roche responded with a curious side glance. The tall beauty in the bright-red dress perked his interest. Yellow and green not so much. "Thank you, but no," he politely responded in passing. *Liquor and women always seem to blossom around armed encampments*, he reflected. "Hookers," he snorted, recalling the tale of *Fighting Joe Hooker* the Union general. *The women who followed his army during the Civil War were dubbed hookers. The moniker stuck. It's a much more forgiving label than LBFM*, he concluded. *At least the acronym disguises the derogatory little brown fucking machine reference for Filipino sex workers.*

As he caught a whiff of a fetid blind beggar sitting on the sidewalk, Roche's face puckered. After dropping a handful of coins into the poor soul's wooden bowl, he jogged across the street into the Red Rooster Lounge. A clacking cluster of barmaids went silent as he entered. Recognizing Roche, they politely smiled before returning to the rapid high-pitched dialogue. The bartender wiped his hands on an apron and slapped a fat bottle of San Miguel beer on the counter.

"Thanks, Marco," Roche said, snatching up the cold amber glass container. Surveying the empty tables and chairs, he figured he was the first to arrive for the meeting. The only other patron was a young airman wrapped in the clutches of a seductive barmaid. She was a petite beauty with big dark eyes. *Definitely the pick of the litter*, Roche concluded, taking a refreshing swig.

At the end of a counter, a middle-aged mama-san, utilizing reading glasses, sorted receipts. Pancake makeup filled the creases of her seasoned existence in the sex trade. Looking over the perched spectacles, she informed Roche, "Your friends are waiting for you in the back."

"Gracious," Roche muttered, flowing past the proprietor. His sweeping hand parted a velvet-draped barrier concealing a corridor. The passage was narrow. Stacked crates of empty bottles blanketed one wall. After taking a swig of cold brew, he rapped on the hollow wood door at the end of the hallway and entered.

The windowless backroom was small. A single dangling light bulb illuminated the tiny enclosure. The stagnant air was warm but tolerable. The stained white plaster walls were barren with the exception of a San Miguel beer calendar, displaying January of last year. A cloud of cigarette smoke hovered over a round wooden table occupied by McConnell, Matthews, and a Poindexter-looking stenographer. A slouching McConnell raised a pausing finger at Roche as he dictated the details of an anticommunist propaganda film currently in production. The focused Poindexter feverously scribbled in shorthand on a steno pad, occasionally stopping to push up the thick black-framed glasses sliding down his short, pointed beak.

I'm going to miss McConnell, Roche realized. *He brought me into the company, and now he is departing to pursue a political career. With his family connections and expertise with dirty tricks, he will make a fine politician.* Pulling out a chair, Roche took a seat across from Matthews.

Looking at Roche, Matthews rolled his eyes in response to their associate's long-winded rant. In one hand, Matthews clutched a bottle of brew; the other hand navigated a smoldering cigarette to and from his lips. A starched white dress shirt highlighted broad shoulders. Chiseled good looks resided on his square head, highlighted by a massive forehead. A dab of Brylcreem gave his thick black hair a smooth, shiny aesthetic.

Matthews is likeable, Roche surmised. *But his self-promoted reputation as a ladies' man gets old real quick. And in a city inhabited by LBFMs, his repetitive tales of sexual conquest impress no one. You have to know your audience. As for Matthews's anecdotes involving Red Cross volunteers, navy nurses, and USO showgirls, they would play very well in a high school locker room.*

McConnell finished his summation and, slapping the table, exclaimed, "Well, if it isn't Bela Lugosi. I thought you only came out at night."

Raising his bottle, Roche replied, "It's good to see you as well, Senator." Glancing at Matthews, he nodded. "Casanova."

Matthews chuckled.

"This is Wellington Keagley," McConnell said, introducing the stenographer. "He is here to chronicle the dirty tricks that are squelching the Huk uprising."

Reaching across the table, Keagley offered a dead-fish handshake and said, "Please to meet you, Major Roche. I'm tasked with developing a strategic blueprint of your successful unconventional tactics." Glancing at McConnell, he clarified. "Actually, it's Wellington Keagley III, and I prefer the term 'psychological warfare' instead of 'dirty tricks.'"

"OK, Professor." Roche chuckled. "I always find it amusing that the academicians in the company rely on semantics to dilute the atrocities necessary to achieve the goals of Western democracy. Our strategy is not unprecedented. Instilling fear in the enemy and rallying support for your agenda were utilized during prehistoric conflicts." Leaning back in the wooden chair, he wet his palate with carbonated pilsner and added, "The communists embedded in the peasant population control the masses with fear and false promises. Our task is to promote greater fear for embracing that bullshit ideology and enticing the ignorant populous with incentives."

"Winning hearts and minds," Matthews interjected.

"Driving through a rural community with a truckload of dead Huks is very effective," Roche said. "In this particular exercise, body placement is important. A truck bed overflowing with dangling and swaying arms and legs and expressions of terror frozen forever sends a convincing message along the parade route. Presentation is everything."

"Defining your target market is very important," McConnell chimed in. "Filipinos are very superstitious. Suspected communists living among the locals would awake to discover an *all-seeing eye of providence* painted on a wall facing their residence. The mysterious appearance of an accusing eye was followed up with the offer of amnesty for a confession."

"At the pinnacle of the uprising, we poisoned the communist well," Matthews contributed.

"Literally?" Keagley questioned.

"Nah, metaphorically," Matthews replied. "We fed the Huks munitions through what they thought was corrupt military personnel. The ammunition was designed to explode when fired. Reports followed of attacking guerillas... literally...blowing themselves up."

The scribbling stenographer paused to wipe the sweat collecting on the tip of his sharp nose. He appeared uncomfortable.

"When it comes to waging a successful counterinsurgency campaign, there are no rules," McConnell contributed with a smirk.

Looking across the table at his smug colleague, Roche asked, "Are you going to miss this, Senator?"

McConnell chuckled. "No doubt dirty tricks play a role in American politics. But unfortunately there are rules. I won't be able to drug my opponent."

Roche and Matthews laughed at an apparent inside joke.

"Did I miss something?" Keagley politely prodded.

After the field agents exchanged glances, McConnell took the floor. "Uncle Sam picked a horse in the Filipino democratic process. A carefully crafted and financed political campaign established an inside lane, but drugging the opposition's candidate along the campaign trail ensured victory. A lethargic demeanor highlighted with slurred speech does not instill confidence among voters."

"You mentioned enticing incentives?" Keagley politely poked.

Roche, slowly nodding, replied, "Plots of land...homesteads were offered to the guerillas in exchange for them laying down their arms. Those who signed up early received the real estate bribe; word of the generous gratuity spread. The line waiting to cash in grew rapidly. Those in the back of the queue were introduced to fine print. Only a couple of hundred benefited from the program, but thousands surrendered."

"Is there a tactic behind the Bela Lugosi reference?" Keagley nudged.

"Just another variation of capitalizing on the superstitious locals," Roche answered. Casually flashing a lit cigarette, he continued, "We snatch a Huk, puncture his jugular with a two-pronged ice pick, drain a gallon and a half of his blood, and plant the dry corpse as a vampire victim."

Keagly took a deep, composing breath and placed his pen on the table. Removing his spectacles, he mopped a sweaty brow with the back of a hand and muttered, "Please forgive me, gentlemen."

"Looks like you could use drink, Professor," Roche offered to the shaken scribe.

A pale Keagley slowly nodded.

"I'll take another beer," Matthews interjected, examining his empty bottle.

Displaying a flexed index finger, McConnell chimed in, "Make that two."

"Beer, Professor?" Roche questioned, rising.

"I'm going to need something stronger," Keagly responded. "A scotch, neat, please, preferably single malt, Glenlivet would be fine."

"Four beers it is then," Roche declared, exiting the tiny room to place the order.

CHAPTER THIRTY-NINE

The large mud tires of a troop transport locked; high-pitched wailing brakes accompanied a jostling termination. Exhausted legionnaires in battle fatigues slowly rose. The truck's tailgate dropped with a crash. The conscripts disembarked slowly. Max tossed his pack on the dry soil and followed it with a calculated leap. Placing his hands on the small of his back, he stretched. Dormant muscles slowly awoke. Yawning through a wide-open mouth, he surveyed the collection point.

An old, abandoned Catholic church marked a once prosperous village reduced to a refugee shantytown. Rich green vegetation clung to the house of worship's thick stone walls. The shattered remnants of the steeple lay partially submerged in a field of encroaching weeds. Looking up, Max blinked in the bright sunlight. A shielding hand allowed a glimpse of the decapitated belfry occupied by a machine-gun emplacement. A whiff of foul air distracted his gaze in the direction of the surrounding shantytown. The harsh sunlight beat down on a compilation of corrugated-tin, palm-frond, and plywood rooftops. Plastic tarps flapped in the wind. Smoke strings rose out of the hastily constructed hovels and shacks. The squalid community pulsed at full capacity with a transient population.

Max grinned. The refugees ebbed and flowed like the tide. This high-water mark signaled a communist assault was not on the horizon. Days before an actual attack, the locals catering to the French quickly dissipated. *A few days of rest are long overdue*, he realized, slinging his rucksack over a shoulder. "I'm on a quest for a beer," he informed the German clique.

Muller nodded his inclusion. The quiet Helmut shook his head to decline. The fair-skinned Gregor, stroking the chin of a perpetually sunburned face, answered, "I'll join you later. I need to take a shit."

"Don't rush on our account," Muller replied.

Max and Muller emerged from the milling multinational troops. On tired legs, they plunged into the refugee ghetto. With each step, the red dirt at their feet exhaled crimson dust. Through open windows and doorways, emotionless expressions observed the passing legionnaires. Hungry children cried. Harsh odors drifted in the hot, moist atmosphere.

In the middle of the narrow road, a grinning ten-year-old boy greeted the Germans with an inviting wave. Clad only in a pair of shorts, the skinny kid's bird legs held his ground. Pointing to his left, he exclaimed, "Fresh, cold *biere!*"

Approaching, Muller, rubbing a thumb across his fingers, asked, "How much?"

Flashing flexed fingers, the young barker declared, "Ten piastres."

"Jesus," Muller muttered, "that's twice the price of a Saigon beer."

"But we are not in Saigon," Max enlightened him. "Merci, garcon," he said to the kid. Adjusting the strap of his load, he licked his lips in anticipation and entered the open-air saloon.

A gentle breeze flowed beneath the low, planked-wood ceiling and above an earthen floor. Sunlight penetrated knots and gaps in the flawed timber roof. Red dust swirled in the invading rays. There were four empty tables; one of them was round. A collection of mismatched chairs and stools encircled the tabletop drinking options. It appeared to be a family-owned business. A petite Vietnamese couple bowed at their first two customers. In the center of the cantina, two gawking young girls stood guard over a large galvanized tub, teeming with ice and large amber bottles of brew.

Max dropped his pack on the moist ground beside the round table. Flashing two fingers, he took a seat. Muller followed suit. Sheepishly, the proprietor held out his hand.

"Looks like we pay in advance," Max concluded, pulling a wad of colorful currency from a breast pocket. "I'll by the first round," he added, carefully peeling off a purplish twenty-piastre bank note and paying the fare.

Examining the currency in his soiled palm, the proprietor beamed. Over his shoulders, he placed the order. His young daughters retrieved, opened, and raced over with two perspiring bottles of brew. A shy young girl in a frayed white dress that was too large for her small body handed Max the chilled glass container.

"Danke," Max mumbled, grasping the bottle. It chilled his callused hand. Closing his eyes, he raised it to his lips and tilted his head back. The carbonated cold refreshment flowed past parched lips, across a dry tongue, and down a dusty throat. The familiar taste invoked celebratory memories. *I'm still alive enjoying cold beer*, he realized, guzzling the luxury. Emptying the bottle, he smiled. Opening his eyes, he came face to face with the inquisitive innocence of his young server. The girl stared deep into his blue eyes with a sense of wonder.

"Apparently you have a very young admirer, Max," Muller teased, taking a swig off his bottle.

Retrieving his daughter, the owner apologized. "It your..." He pointed at Max's face. "Eye...eyes," he corrected. "Blue eyes, she never see such blue eye."

"Merci," Max responded, raising his empty bottle. "It's your turn to buy," he informed his drinking partner. Looking at the girl, he winked. She giggled.

While Muller searched for his elusive currency, the boy barker directed three Romanian legionnaires into his family's cantina. The full-bearded, Rasputin-looking legionnaire known as Cezar offered an acknowledging wave in Max's direction. Max responded with a friendly nod.

"So when did you become chummy with the gypsies?" Muller teased, sorting his crumpled bank notes.

"We are all brothers-in-arms," Max responded.

"Does that hold true for the Corsicans?" Muller asked, flicking his head at the entering legionnaire quartet.

The one they called Borgo was the alpha of the pack of former criminals. He was a wide brute with a perpetual five-o'clock shadow. Deep-set dark eyes scanned his waking moments with sinister intent. His henchmen were no more than lapdogs. They endured Borgo's sadistic persona out of fear and for inclusion in a protected crew.

"I heard the locals view large men as inherently evil," Max commented as Muller paid for another round. Watching the Corsicans commandeering a table, he took a refreshing swig. "Borgo enhances the theory."

"He is not much of a soldier," Muller commented. "I suspect he joined the legion to avoid the guillotine." Squinting in the direction of the topic, he added,

"The Corsican gangsters have this fanatic sense about family honor. A bloody vendetta is their solution to the slightest insult." Shrugging, he concluded, "I avoid them not out of fear, but because while killing communists, I don't have time to keep looking over my shoulder."

Around the galvanized tub, smiles dominated the enterprising family. Their jungle beer hall was bearing fruit. More legionnaires were snared by the skinny boy's solicitations. Alcohol-fueled clamor escalated. The barefoot giddy girls scurried about the pub full of large men, filling prepaid orders. A growing cloud of cigarette smoke hovered beneath the low ceiling. A one-sided debate between the tiny owner and the bullnecked Borgo quieted the rabble. The Corsican thug latched on to the petite arm of the youngest girl and pulled her onto his lap to end the discussion.

Max rose.

"What are you doing?" Muller questioned.

"Sparking a Corsican vendetta," Max replied.

"Oh *scheisse*," Muller mumbled, standing up.

"Hey, butter fingers!" Max hollered at the wide brute. "Let go of the girl like you did with your weapons when the Wehrmacht rolled over France."

Borgo released his hostage. She ran into the protective embrace of her mother. Standing tall, the Corsican stuck out his massive chest. A wicked grin emerged on his large face. "Does the Teuton bastard want to polka?"

A standoff unfolded. The family retreated around the iced tub. Most of the soldiers stood as neutral observers. Max and Muller faced the four Corsicans. Surprisingly, the Romanians joined the two Germans.

"You and me, pretty boy," Borgo growled at Max. To disclose he was weaponless, he displayed open hands. "When I'm finished with you, you won't be pretty anymore."

Max exhibited open palms. Pivoting slightly to the left, he cocked his hip, clenched a fist, and fired a lightning-fast left hook into the Corsican's temple. The full force of his rotating body's weight was behind the potent blow. Borgo's hammered noggin released a painful grunt. On jelly knees, the Corsican's wide torso teetered before keeling over. The glassy-eyed head's earthbound journey was altered after it slammed into the edge of a square hardwood tabletop.

Borgo and an upturned table came crashing down onto the earthen floor. Face up, the Corsican's large chest pulsed as he snored.

Shaking his swelling hand, Max informed the stunned audience, "Shooting him would have been easier." Addressing the hesitating Corsican crew, he said, "Can you children clean this up? My beer is getting warm."

"Smecker," the burly, bearded Romanian said playfully to Max. "I was hoping to return a favor." Glancing down at the Corsicans attempting to revive their boss, he continued, "You sure didn't need any assistance."

"I appreciate the gesture, Cezar," Max replied with a nod.

"You throw a hell of a punch, Max," Muller commented as they returned to their table.

Sitting down, Max flexed his damaged paw. A grimace accompanied his inspection. "Before Schmeling knocked out Joe Louis in '36, he studied films of the Brown Bomber's prior fights. He discovered Louis would lower his left when throwing a jab. Schmeling took advantage of this fault, knocking Louis down in the fourth round and out in the twelfth." Leaning back with his beer, he took a gulp and said, "To defeat an opponent, you just find and exploit his weakness."

"What was Borgo's weakness?" Muller seriously questioned.

"He has a big fucking head," Max casually replied. "My strategy was to hit it fast and hard, hoping he'd fall down."

Muller chuckled. Watching the Corsicans assisting a wobbly Borgo into the sunlight, his levity faded. "You know, Max, we have just declared war with those fanatic gangsters."

Max shrugged. "What are a few more adversaries in a land infested with hostiles?"

CHAPTER FORTY

The morning air was cool. It had rained during the night. In comfortable bedding, the lanky Jewish commando Jean Guillian stared up into the pitched palm-frond ceiling. A satisfied smile graced his lips. A deep sleep had embraced him during the night. The Nazi ordeal that typically tormented his slumber did not arrive. Beside him, a naked flower stirred. Propping up on an elbow, he examined the innocent H'Liana. *Not so innocent.* He chuckled. His admiring gaze lingered across her bare shoulders before stalling at the nape of her neck. *Her kisses were playful bites,* he delightfully recalled. *I know I'm not her first,* he realized, *but I prefer an experienced cat over a naive lamb. Definitely her first circumcised lover.* He snickered.

Slowly, he rolled out of the creaking frontier bed. Quietly, he slid into a pair of baggy army-green trousers. On the balls of his bare feet, he delicately exited the single-room bungalow. On the raised deck, he closed his eyes and inhaled chilled mountain air. Scanning the hillside community, the reality of war tugged on his heart. *The world is occupied by cruel inhabitants,* he reflected. *The cost of extinguishing evil is expensive.*

Neighboring stilted shacks began exhaling cooking smoke. Morning sunlight reflected off the drenched shelters. Steam rose. Orange-colored puddles dominated the village's red-clay pathways. Three dogs prancing in the carroty mud paused for a communal sniff. One of the mutts saw fit to mark the discovery.

I need to pay the lieutenant a visit today, Guillian concluded. Realizing he hadn't seen Torcy since the last sortie, he grimaced. *I found H'Liana over a month ago, and the lieutenant found the cure for his melancholy at the bottom of a liquor bottle. It should come as no surprise Torcy discovered the crutch of alcoholism. The pressures of combat, the lieutenant's self-imposed celibacy, an abundance of free liquor, and a society that promotes heavy drinking are milestones on the path to addiction. I'll check in on him this morning,* he decided, knowing the homesick officer would be drunk by early afternoon. *I might as well drop in on the newlywed LaLande,* he snorted. *The highland satyr fertilized the wrong tropical flower. What are the odds? Of all the village girls LaLande poked, the swordsman impregnated one of the chieftain's daughters. Now Vue has a grandchild on the way and a French son-in-law. I'll take H'Liana with me to see the LaLandes,* he decided. *That's what French couples do.*

The rising sun bathed Guillian's naked frame. Stretching in the warm rays, he paused. A magnificent rainbow spread across the tropical vista. The reflex phrase from his youth, "God's reminder," rolled off his tongue. The flimsy flooring creaked. He turned. An open doorway framed his Hmong lover. Wrapped in a colorful embroidered blanket, she smiled.

"What is your word for *rainbow*?" he questioned, pointing at the arched spectrum gracing the view.

"Don't point!" she exclaimed. "Zaj sawv (Rising Dragon) will snatch your finger."

"Your word for rainbow is dragon?" He chuckled, playfully shaking his hand.

Nodding seriously, she answered, "One end is Zaj (dragon) tail; the other is its head drinking water, very bad."

"In my tribe, we were taught that a rainbow…a zaj sawv, is a reminder from God that never again will a great flood destroy the earth."

"We also believe a massive flood covered the mountains," she replied. "The only survivors were a brother and sister who floated on the rising waters in a large funeral drum. The drum rose so high that it hit the top of the sky."

It's amazing how many cultures have myths and legends concerning a global flood, he reflected, following the cloaked feline back into the shelter. "My people believe a six-hundred-year-old man named Noah built a big boat. On it, he and his family and two of every animal drifted until the waters receded."

H'Laina chuckled. "Your stories are silly."

Taking a seat on the rickety bed, he laughed. Surveying the planked flooring, he retrieved a ripe sock and shook it.

Crawling back into bed, she asked, "Did the cruel men appear in your dreams?"

"Not last night," he answered, searching for the second sock.

Placing her hands behind her head, she said, "I'm glad."

"You've filled my head with happiness," he responded, slipping into his jungle boots. "There is no room for the evil Nazis." Rising, he put on a shirt. "I need to visit the lieutenant this morning."

"That is good." She nodded. "The sad lieutenant needs someone to fill his head with happiness."

Leaning down, he kissed her forehead, realizing she was special.

Shimmying down the shack's ladder, he paused on the last rung. His combat boot tested the density of the orange mud surrounding the hovel. Satisfied, he stepped down. The air was heavy. The scent of the passing storm lingered. Focused on the glistening pathway, he calculated each step. His boots grew heavy. "Fuck it," he mumbled, conceding to the clinging mud.

Passing the home of the old warrior Pao, Guillian slowed. The residence was in mourning. On the elevated porch, the tiny Pao sat staring into space. A black tribal cap encased his long silver locks. Gray stubble sullied his cheeks and chin. Across his lap lay a yellow dog. Two other junkyard mutts reclined on the deck. The usually rambunctious canines seemed to share in the family loss. The yellow mutt observed the passing Fackee with a raised ear. Lost in thought, the old man methodically stroked his grieving companion.

Guillian bowed his head in respect. *Fathers should never have to bury their sons*, he thought. *And sons shouldn't have to avenge their fathers*, he surmised, reflecting on his own tragic tenure. *Snapping Bachman's neck didn't terminate my nightmares*, he realized. *H'Liana did.*

On the bowed stoop of the lieutenant's shack, Guillian attempted to scrape off his mud-caked boots.

Torcy in a pair of boxer shorts appeared in the doorway. His tan face, neck, and arms were a stark contrast to his pinkish-white trunk. Battle scars decorated the pale torso. At the end of a lazy arm dangled a clear bottle of local hooch. "To what do I owe the pleasure of your company?" he questioned.

"Good morning, Lieutenant," Guillian exclaimed. Flicking a finger in the direction of the potent liquor, he added, "It appears you started early today."

Torcy's expression crinkled. Holding up the half-full bottle, he examined it at close range. "We all have our vices. Personally I prefer a fine cognac. However, given our current incarceration, I've been forced to make allowances."

"We are not prisoners, Jacque," Guillian commented.

Stomping onto the deck, Torcy held out and swung the bottle across the horizon. "This is our cell," he snapped. "Two hundred miles behind enemy lines marks the boundaries of the cage. The rising communist tide has sealed all exits. We can talk to the world. Aircraft can drop in supplies. But there is no escape."

"Apparently, we won't be abandoning our post," Guillian mumbled as he untied his boot laces. In stocking feet, he ascended the stairs. Walking past the lieutenant, he entered the tiny room. Tussled dirty bedding lay on the floor. Cockroaches meandered in and out of open ration tins strewn about. Looking down, Guillian stepped on a fat, amber antenna-waving roach. It terminated with a crunch.

"Housekeeping has been lax," Torcy commented.

Wiping the insect remains off the bottom of his sock, Guillian scrutinized the silent short-wave radio in the corner.

Anticipating a question, Torcy volunteered, "The batteries are running low."

Guillian nodded.

"Just as well," Torcy added. "The news hasn't been good. Viet Minh reprisals against the hill tribes have been devastating. Entire villages have been extinguished. Savvy Hmong communities are declaring neutrality." He took a palate-cleansing pull off the bottle. His tone softened. "Two days ago, on the wire, I heard a GCMA commando pleading for his evacuation. The paratrooper feared his Hmong hosts would turn him over to the communists to gain favor. The transmission terminated."

"I have confidence in our tribal allies," Guillian stated. Snickering he added, "Besides, LaLande's marriage to the chieftain's daughter has ensured their loyalty."

A wide grin appeared on the lieutenant's face. "Pauvre connard," (poor bastard) he chuckled. "The corporal's bride is no prize." Raising the bottle, he added, "Now, Sergeant, your delicate Meo orchid is definitely the crème de la crème."

"Her name is H'Liana," Guillian replied.

CHAPTER FORTY-ONE

Encompassing growth grasped, scratched, and clawed at passing partisans. It was a small patrol, seven tribesmen and three French commandos. Foliage crackled. Overhead, dense growth imprisoned late-afternoon heat. Tropical bird calls randomly accented insect clamor. At point, the likable warrior Chue nimbly sliced through the rain forest. In leather sandals and loose-fitting black attire, Chue's Hmong brothers followed single file. Blue bandanas adorned the tribesmen's heads. On their backs, surplus World War II haversacks contained food and ammo.

Bringing up the rear in camo fatigues and floppy bush hats, Torcy, LaLande, and Guillian trekked in canvas rubber-soled boots. OF 37 hand grenades dangled from their chest riggings. Nicknamed "little brown jugs," the one-pound deadly pomegranates produced a healthy fragmentation payload. French troops had always had a fondness for the tiny bombs.

The entire hunting party was armed with MAT-49 submachine guns. The Manufacture d'Armes de Tulle produced the eighteen-inch-long, nine-pound automatic firearm. The weapon was revered by the French forces for its size, durability, and overwhelming firepower. On full automatic, it only took seconds to empty a thirty-two-round magazine.

Drifting off the Hmong's blistering pace, Torcy grumbled, "Jesus." Perspiration freely flowed down his face. Huffing and puffing, he accelerated. His battle garb was saturated with sweat. Sporadic grunts emphasized his aggravation.

Once again, the lieutenant's foul temperament surfaces, Guillian thought. *It's the local hooch. The war hero has been reduced to an angry alcoholic. I can handle a grumpy drunkard,* he reasoned. *Now, dealing with LaLande's eroding sanity is a dilemma. The homesick corporal can't walk out on his flat-nosed, wide-hipped Hmong bride.* Glancing around, he surveyed LaLande's and Torcy's tropical prison. *One man's cage is another man's domain. I no longer fight for France,* he realized. *The struggle for the survival of my adopted community is the objective.* Visualizing H'Liana, he smiled.

The Hmong warriors stood in a cluster.

"What is it?" Guillian questioned as the Frenchmen closed in.

Extending an arm, Chue pointed into the rugged growth. Guillian squinted in the direction of the targeting finger. A ghostly white specter stood waist deep in foliage. Scabs, insect bites, sweat, and clotted blood defined the poor soul's face. Through sunken tombstone eyes, the vagabond in a shredded commando uniform scrutinized the patrol.

"My God!" Torcy exclaimed.

A shallow breath launched the apparition forward. Stumbling onto the narrow trail, the poor bastard wobbled in a teetering stance. Blistered lips produced a painful smile. Torcy approached. The walking corpse raised a blackened hand to a pockmarked forehead and saluted, "Warrant Officer Paul Rochelle."

Torcy returned the respectful gesture. Rochelle's knees faltered. His eyes rolled up as he keeled over. Torcy hastily handed his weapon to a Hmong warrior, unsheathed his metal canteen, and took a knee beside the crumpled mound of flesh and bone. Elevating Rochelle's scab-covered head, he informed the group, "The son of a bitch is burning up with fever." Slowly, he poured a trickle of precious water onto festered lips. A swollen tongue appeared.

Rochelle coughed. "Tell me I made it out."

Torcy reached down and pulled back the warrant officer's unbuttoned shirt. The left side resisted. Carefully, he peeled back the bloodstained fabric. The rotting stench of infection escaped. The huddled audience reacted with snorts. The left side of Rochelle's abdomen had died. Maggots now feasted on what remained. Looking up over his shoulder at Guillian, Torcy slowly shook his head.

Guillian nodded his concurrence and reached into the medical kit slung over his shoulder.

"Yes, you made it out of this fucking jungle, Rochelle," Torcy declared. "The French garrison is right behind those trees. Rest easy; stretcher bearers will be here shortly."

Rochelle's eyes remained shut. A faint sigh floated out of his mouth.

Torcy blindly extended an open hand. Guillian placed a morphine syringe ampoule in the lieutenant's palm. "A hot shower, clean sheets, and a juicy steak are just minutes away," Torcy said as he injected the dying man. A peaceful wave flowed through the warrant officer. Torcy reached back. Guillian handed him another vial. The second dose produced shallow breaths. The third needle poke sent Warrant Officer Paul Rochelle into the afterlife.

After carefully placing the dead man's head on the jungle floor, Torcy rose. Saluting the carcass, he said, "You made it out." Taking his weapon back, he nodded at Chue.

The war party was on the move again. The undergrowth thinned. Tall trees provided a high ceiling. The vanguard spread out, moving quietly through the forest. The grade gently sloped downhill. The escalating trickle of cascading water teased the parched partisans. Dry tongues swept thirsty lips. A meandering stream feeding an embankment of tall weeds produced smiles. After wading through the invading growth, the warriors knelt in soft mud. Cupped hands hydrated dry mouths.

So refreshing, Guillian thought, gulping down mountain water. Utilizing both hands, he wet his face. Reflecting on Rochelle's euthanasia, he realized he was wrong about the lieutenant. Torcy's bedside manner showed the war hero was in control, not the alcoholic. Dipping his parachute-silk neck scarf into the flowing water, he gazed downstream. Penetrating sunlight randomly sparked off the surface. A breeze teased the encroaching growth. *What is that fluttering in the wind?* he wondered, squinting fifty yards down the far bank. Holding his breath, he got the attention of his water-drinking companions and pointed downstream at a flapping clothesline of communist uniforms.

Concealed by weeds, the scouting party hugged the moist earth. Perched atop the trees, a blackbird cawed and took flight. The tumbling stream mumbled. On their bellies, the partisans slowly retreated. They froze. Whistling a simple tune, a communist soldier plodded down to the strung-out laundry. Dropping a collection of pots and pans at the water's edge, he felt a flapping uniform. After a shrug, he squatted down on his haunches and began washing the cookware.

Humming a happy song, the naive dishwasher toiled. The guerrilla fighters observed patiently. Upon completing the chore, the cheery commie neatly stacked the metal cookware, picked up the load, and disappeared behind the camouflage underwear and clothing waving on the line.

Chue pointed at the twenty-something Tuam. The baby-faced Tuam nodded and slithered forward. At the water's edge, he rose into a crouch. Holding his automatic weapon over his head, he duck-walked through the shallow stream. In the purple-flowering growth of the opposing bank, he disappeared. The partisans remained motionless. The tranquil cascading creak trickled. A swarm of large, colorful dragonflies played in the shallows. The moist ground twitched with investigating insects. A snake, rat, or possibly just a lizard scurried through the tall grass.

Across the sparkling stream, Tuam's head poked out of blossoming weeds. A sinister grin dominated his innocent features. Showing his palms, he flashed extended fingers. He repeated the gesture five times, indicating fifty hostiles.

"We are outnumbered five to one," LaLande whispered.

"Adding surprise to the equation diminishes their advantage," Torcy mumbled in response.

Tuam's head receded into the violet tropical flowerbed. Chue forged the stream first. One at a time, the war party made the crossing. Wet, focused, and guns ready, they headed inland. Blanketing brush thinned. Tall trees dominated the rising grade. The raiders quietly darted from tree to tree. Tuam, at point, stopped abruptly and pointed to his left downhill.

Torcy whispered to the lead-footed LaLande, "Watch our backs."

LaLande nodded.

The warriors spread out. Creeping forward slowly, they headed downhill in the direction of the communist creek side bivouac. Comforted by his training and combat experience, Guillian breathed easily. The sound of flowing water returned. Faint Vietnamese dialogue drifted in the thick air. A burst of laughter pierced the communist conversations. The falling grade accelerated.

Through a foliage curtain, an enemy encampment slowly emerged. The attackers paused. Well-concealed palm-frond lean-tos lined the shoreline. Movement within the angled hovels confirmed occupancy. Toting water from the creek, a soldier passed a squatting cluster of Viet Minh enjoying a smoke. The water bearer disappeared in a hootch constructed out of underbrush.

These are the troops harassing Hmong communities, Guillian realized. *These bastards have forced the hill tribes to relocate higher up into the mountains. Here we stand undetected, ready to pounce. How can that be? Are they that clueless?* Comprehending the rarity of the opportunity, he felt his pulse accelerate. *Even with the element of surprise, this assault is ambitious,* he realized, glancing around. Ten yards on his left, Torcy stood, simmering with anticipation. On his right, an anxious warrior salivated. In the surrounding brush, the rest of the small patrol awaited Chue's signal. In front of them, fifty hostiles casually tended to camp duties.

A Viet Minh officer crawled out of his hootch. Dusting off his hands, he gazed into the thick brush. The silhouette of a Hmong warrior took his breath away. Time stopped. All was quiet. The flash of a MAT-49 gun barrel terminated the communist's life journey.

The war party followed Chue's lead. A steady burst of automatic-weapons fire sprayed the campsite inhabitants. Disoriented, Viet Minh, scrambling for cover, died in flight. The arced trajectory of hand grenades cluttered the blue sky. Erupting little brown jugs spit out lethal shards. One of the tiny tossed bombs fell through the roof of a communist hootch. A massive explosion launched the stick-and-branch structure skyward. Smoldering scrub brush burst into flames. Smoke drifted across the kill zone. Agile Hmong warriors appeared in the haze. Running through the carnage, they tossed grenades into earthen structures.

Guillian jogged through the sulfur-laced mist. Torcy and a Hmong partisan flanked his advance. The trio fired short bursts into fleeing hostiles. Wounded, disorientated prey made for easy targets. Engulfing haze limited visibility. In front of them, the flash of gunfire toppled the Meo warrior. Simultaneously, the Frenchmen fell to the jungle floor. Communist bullets zipped overhead. Hugging the moist earth, they saw a trench of Viet Minh preparing a defensive stand.

"They're dug in!" Torcy hollered, rolling onto his back. Slamming in a fresh magazine, he flashed a wicked grin and declared, "I feel like dancing."

"What?" Guillian questioned.

Torcy unsheathed his pistol. Ricocheting projectiles tenderized the surrounding soil. Taking a deep breath, he unhooked a hand grenade from his web gear. Pulling the pin, he smiled at Guillian and tossed the one-pound oval. "Adieu, brother," he muttered. The tiny bomb exploded. The lieutenant leaped to his feet. With a pistol in one hand and a howling submachine gun in the other, he charged. Smoke swirled around the sprinting commando. Catching a round, he stumbled. Standing at the edge of the occupied ditch, he emptied his machine gun. Tossing the expired weapon aside, he extended his arm and fired the pistol into the trough. The handgun went silent. "Putain de merde!" (fucking hell) Torcy hollered, throwing the empty gun. A volley of Chinese bullets tore into the lieutenant's torso. He collapsed.

Standing behind the trench, Chue squeezed his trigger hard. The MAT-49 submachine cycled fresh rounds into the chamber and spat out spent cartridges. At close range, a deluge of bullets rained down. Uniformed hostiles twitched violently. Guillian appeared and unleashed his automatic weapon. Chue reloaded and fired short, calculated bursts. The deafening salvo faded. All was quiet. Gun smoke floated over the low guttural moans of dying men.

Slinging a submachine gun over his shoulder, Guillian reached down. Latching onto the lieutenant's chest rigging, he dragged the officer off the battlefield. Behind a shale outcropping, he ripped open the lieutenant's battle fatigues. Three bullet holes across Torcy's pale chest oozed thick blood.

Torcy coughed. A trickle of blood rolled out of the corner of his mouth. "I'm finally going to exit this *bordel de patelin*" (god-forsaken place).

"You're not dead yet, Jacque," Guillian offered, compressing a wad of gauze on the crimson-leaking torso.

Conjuring up a cocky grin, Torcy muttered, "It was a good day."

CHAPTER FORTY-TWO

Loc gazed across the rich green valley. The sluggish Nam Yum River dissected this remote fertile scar of the Vietnamese highlands. The moist air smelled of smoke. A blazing sun sparkled high overhead. In the valley's basin, large brushfires crackled. The controlled burns peeled back thick vegetation from formulated fields of fire. Thousands of shirtless soldiers toiled with picks and shovels. Along the perimeter of the blossoming garrison, French paratroopers in camouflaged fatigues strung razor wire. In the middle of this industrious commotion, combat engineers finalized the assembly of a steel-plated runway. The skeletal remains of villages pillaged for building materials fringed the riverbank. A series of active intersecting trails, paths, and dirt roads exhaled reddish dust. Above, aircraft performed a symmetrical ballet. Flying Boxcars gave birth to more paratroopers. Tethered to billowing silk canopies, sky soldiers drifted toward earth. South of the deposited human cargo, lumbering transport planes spit out tons of airfreight. The parade of circling aircraft seemed endless.

Behind Loc, a twig snapped. He casually glanced over his shoulder. It was Xiong in the green military dungarees of a T'ai soldier. "Where is the patrol?" Loc questioned.

A smile emerged on Xiong's boyish Hmong features as he answered, "Breathing heavy a few clicks down the trail."

Lagging Fackee always elicited an impromptu cigarette. The tribesmen squatted comfortably on their haunches. From a breast pocket, Loc pulled out a moist pack of Lucky Strikes and tapped out two moldy tabs. The crouching Xiong ignited the vice with a hinged lid lighter.

Inhaling deeply, Xiong, surveying the chaotic vista, asked, "What are the names again of the garrison's strong points?"

Loc pointed at the nearly completed airstrip and explained, "The headquarters is centrally located around the runway with positions Huguette to the west, Claudine to the south, Dominique to the Northeast, and Elaine to the east." Swinging his targeting finger further up the valley, he continued, "That's Anne-Marie taking shape in the northwest, Gabrielle to the far north, and Beatrice to the northeast." Pivoting to the far south, he targeted a busy dirt road and concluded, "A few miles south is Isabelle, and the second runway."

Xiong, scratching his sweaty scalp under his bush hat, declared, "Those names are so difficult to remember let alone pronounce."

"They are female names and refer to the French commander's women," Loc replied, taking a toke.

"His wives?" Xiong exclaimed. "I thought a white man could only have one wife. Are they his whores?"

"Not wives or whores," Loc answered. Squinting, he tried to conjure up a Hmong term for an acceptable adultery relationship. "The Fackee term is *mistress*...They are his...secret lovers."

"Does the colonel have a wife?" Xiong probed.

"I suppose."

Xiong's face crinkled with confusion. "The colonel has a wife and secret relations with eight women, and nobody knows each other," he pondered. Nodding his head, he reasoned, "He must live in a very large village."

"When I was in Lai-Chau," Loc reflected, "the French army would show us these short black-and-white films. There was one about a village in America called Chic-ago. Watching it, you felt like you were drifting above a migrating herd of white men and women. They all were in a hurry, not running, but walking briskly, their eyes focused straight ahead. The Chic-ago inhabitants wore fine clothes and flowed in both directions. Shops of stone, brick, and glass flanked one side of the concrete path. Idle vehicles, lined up end to end, separated the walkway from a wide paved road. There were so many unused automobiles. On the roadway, large cars flew by in the blink of the eye." Taking a puff off his Lucky, he summarized, "In a place like Chic-ago, it would be possible to have eight secret lovers and a wife." Grinning at his transfixed companion, he added, "The most amazing thing about the film was at the end, it showed a view of Chic-ago from a long distance away. Tall buildings rose up to touch the sky, but across the surrounding horizon, there were no mountains."

"No mountains!" Xiong gasped.

"None," Loc emphasized. "The roads are long and straight, and the land was flat as far as the eye could see."

The tribesmen jumped to their feet. Out of the sky, decorated with billowing silk plumes, a rapidly accelerating massive piece of equipment fell to earth. Loc got a glimpse of a bulldozer chased by the shredded remnants of a failed parachute. In the valley below, the troops retrieving freight scurried for cover. On impact, the six-ton tractor plunged deep into the moist soil with an unimpressive thud. The evacuating audience slowly returned to investigate the implanted bulldozer. To show their appreciation for the brief but spectacular distraction, the troops applauded.

"What is it?" Sergeant Palu growled in his unique baritone voice. Twisting a shoulder, he parted the brittle brush encroaching on the narrow trail and joined the tribesmen overlooking the valley. Behind him plodded twenty exhausted paratroopers under his charge. Palu was a quiet, hard man. A perpetual scowl dominated his furrowed face. After three days of searching the countryside for the elusive People's Army, he appeared more perplexed than frustrated. The sortie produced more questions and no clues. *Where are they hiding? What are those hit-and-run communists planning? How can they just melt into the terrain?* Shaking his head, he peered into the canyon.

"A large vehicle broke free and fell out of the sky," Loc, pointing down at the embedded tractor, informed the sergeant.

A very rare and brief smile flirted with the corners of Palu's parched lips. After a quick nod to acknowledge Loc's response, he initiated his descent into the valley of Dien Bien Phu. Another paratrooper emerged from the foliage-veiled pathway and proceeded downhill. Loc and Xiong tossed their expiring cigarettes aside and fell into the staggering procession. Like stable horses with the barn in sight, the patrol accelerated. In a scraggly single-file line, they passed terraced rice paddy fields before entering a tree-lined thoroughfare of a recently abandoned farm villages. A bridge constructed out of vacated residences spanned the murky Num Yum River. The terrain flattened. Weaving through a labyrinth of barbwire hindered progress. The soldiers stringing the snaring obstacle course reluctantly offered directional assistance.

On the outskirts of the Base Aero-Terrestre, a pup-tent community blanketed the valley floor. The olive-green oilskin pitched tarps were seasoned with red dust. Random smoke rose from cooking fires. The multinational inhabitants consisted of French, Foreign Legion, Moroccan, Algerian, and Vietnamese troops. The clamor of idle soldiers filled the stale air.

Silently, Sergeant Palu's patrol drifted into the international bivouac. Loc and Xiong paused. Under the healthy foliage of a mango tree, a troupe of Hmong partisans rested. The tree's green crown was tainted a shade of yellow by soiling red mist. Squatting in a tight circle, the tribesmen smoked and conversed in whispers.

As Loc and Xiong approached, a spokesman rose from the huddle. "I am Kub of the Pha clan."

"I am Loc of the Laotian Moua, and this is Xiong."

"You are far from home, Loc," Kub commented. Grinning, he added, "My father once visited your people to compete in a shooting competition." Looking down at his companions, he continued, "My father was a skilled marksman. Rumors of a legendary rifleman of the Moua clan drifted through the highlands of my youth. My father had never been bested. He and my uncles traveled to Laos to challenge the Moua shooter. The stakes were high; the wager was our sorrel horse. The target was a bronze coin at two hundred yards. The Moua clansman never missed. Although my father regretted the loss, he cherished retelling the story of competing with the famous sharpshooter Teeb." Addressing Loc, he said, "You must be familiar with the legendary warrior of your clan."

Shielding a grin with a cupped hand, Loc nodded. Swallowing a surfacing stone in his throat, he responded, "Teeb was my father." To the rustling of a surprised audience, he said to Kub, "I was at that completion. Your father was indeed a very skilled marksman."

Stroking his chin, Kub questioned, "What is the son of a famous Hmong warrior doing in a Fackee uniform?"

"Killing the communist dogs that spiked my father's head," Loc answered solemnly.

Nodding in approval, Kub said, "When I was a child, my village, in search of fertile soil, relocated. The site we chose happened to be the hunting grounds for a streak of tigers. The large striped cats did not fear us. They raided our community and carried away the young and old. To eliminate the predators, we set up traps. Flintlocks rigged with trip wires targeted live bait. Pigs and goats were used. The strategy appeared to terminate the threat. However, one large, cunning feline eluded the deadly snares. There was no easy solution to end his reign of terror other than to track down the beast and kill him in the jungle." After glancing around at the embracing valley, he continued, "The Fackee set up these garrisons in hostile terrain to entice the communist tiger. Don't be the bait. Our enemy is more devious than a cunning feline. Join us in the highlands where we can hunt and kill the Viet Minh like Hmong warriors."

As Loc pondered the invitation, a Dakota cargo plane roared over the lip of the valley. The deafening growl of twin 1,200 horsepower engines escalated. Rapidly descending, the Douglas Skytrain buzzed the tent city. Prop wash churned up crimson soil and blew a swath of flapping oilskin shelters in its wake. Irate soldiers hollered and shook their fists at the passing airplane.

Fanning the aroused dust with his hand, Loc scanned the Hmong partisans. "We have chosen different routes to the same destination. I look forward to when our paths may cross again. Until then, happy hunting brothers."

The Dakota aircraft deposited its cargo of secondhand American howitzers. As the dust churned up by its landing slowly settled, it prepared for take-off. The workhorse's twin engines, snorting white exhaust, sputtered to a fever pitch. Rotating propellers evolved into a circular blur. The prop wash provoked napping red sand. At full throttle, the pilot shot down the steel-plated runway. Aided by a thermal in the thin air, he navigated the Skytrain out of the river valley. At four thousand feet, the isolation of the French garrison was punctuated. Harsh, undulating terrain of dense growth spread out in all directions. Climbing to a cruising altitude, the pilot took one last look down. A grassy savannah of yellow dry brush swayed in a gentle breeze.

As the homeward bound Dakota became a fading speck on the horizon, the parched, grassy plain came to life. Division 308 of the People's Army, cloaked in concealing straw, rose from the ground. The Viet Minh, whose extensive training included repeated rehearsals of attacking fortified French outposts, resumed their march.

CHAPTER FORTY-THREE

So this is Isabelle, Max thought, scanning the darkness embroidered with razor wire. A few stars sparkled through the clouds drifting overhead. The moist ground at his feet flirted with being called mud. A damp chill permeated through his jungle boots on its journey to harass stiff joints. He turned his helmeted head to the side. A soft wind carried the faint sound of active picks and shovels. *We fill their trenches in each day; the communists dig them out and encroach closer every night.*

"Evening, Max," Muller offered quietly as he approached.

"Muller." Max nodded, adjusting his rifle sling.

"No cigar tonight, Max?"

"Like all our dwindling supplies, I'm rationing my puffs of pleasure."

Squinting in the direction of the distant communist excavation activities, Muller commented, "The industrious monkeys are really getting close. It sounds like they are just outside our wire."

"Tomorrow may be the day," Max muttered.

"You have to appreciate the yellow bastards' resolve." Muller snickered. "When we attack, they retreat. When we retreat, they attack. Our sorties to determine their strength produce legionnaire casualties and nothing else. They vanish with their dead and wounded like specters dissipating into the never-ending sea of growth."

"Like roaches," Max corrected. "Cockroaches…Listen to them out there. You cannot see them but hear them scurrying about. Every patrol discovers freshly dug trenches creeping ever closer, like a tightening noose."

"I hope tomorrow is the day," Muller declared. "I'd like to get this over with. No more of this hit-and-run bullshit. That peasant army does not stand a chance in a pitched battle with battle-hardened veterans like us."

"I hope you are right, my friend," Max replied.

Gazing in the direction of industrious digging, Muller pondered, "What time tomorrow would you wager?"

"Five in the afternoon," Max confidently replied. "Do you want to bet?"

"Nah," Muller answered, stroking his chin, "Why five?"

"The Viet Minh are as predictable as they are elusive. Dusk provides daylight to coordinate an assault. Approaching darkness neutralizes aerial retaliation."

"It's nice being on the side with air superiority for a change," Muller commented.

"I thought you were Swiss," Max teased.

It was a gloomy, overcast day. An attack was imminent. A four-man listening post on Isabelle's periphery had vanished during the night. A few mortar bombs fell into the compound at dawn. Sightings of Viet Minh spotters in freshly dug trenches circulated. The surrounding terrain appeared to pulse. Tension was high. Officers barked orders with a sense of urgency. Radio links were checked and rechecked. On the steel-plated runway, a welding team repaired damaged panels. Mechanics swarmed around a grounded transport, frantically trying to heal the broken bird.

Sitting on an ammo box, in a sandbagged trench, Max dropped his spoon in an empty ration tin. A probing tongue dislodged a clump of the meat-and-potato concoction wedged between molars. Grinning, he decided to light up a precious cigar. Gregor handed him a smoldering cigarette to ignite the fresh stogie. Max nodded his gratitude. Taking a jubilant toke, he tilted his head back and blew a smoke ring into the gray sky. Overhead, a chorus of deadly whistles escalated. Recalling the Allied artillery barrage during the battle of Caen, his heart sank. Spitting out the cigar, he lowered his head and hugged his knees. A deafening blast shook the earth. It continued to tremble as death's payload rained down. A pressure wave towing a blast of wind sucked the oxygen out of the narrow trench. Gulping for air, Max braced himself as dirt, stones, and splintered wood poured into the shelter. *I'm going to be buried alive for a second time*, he feared. Blinking in the uncomfortable haze, he spotted a severed finger sticking out of his empty ration tin. *Is it mine?* he questioned as the man-made thunderstorm intensified.

236

Precision rounds marched down the steel tarmac. Metal plates were tossed skyward, along with particles of surprised welders. The hard, compact vertebrae of their spinal columns were the only evidence that they ever existed. The idle aircraft erupted. Fountains of earth and stone shot up into the charcoal sky. Shell fragments swirled through out Isabelle. Shards of various sizes and speeds dismembered and disemboweled exposed defenders. Shock waves ruptured eardrums and internal organs. Legion machine-gun posts and mortar pits evaporated under the deluge. Incoming rounds sought out the headquarters bunker with its telltale aerial. Surgical accuracy methodically extracted Isabelle's artillery emplacements. Detonated munitions popped.

The soiled mist around Max slowly settled. Flexing his fingers, he confirmed all of his digits were intact. Dangling over the lip of the trench, an arm grasped for hope. Latching on to the muscular limb, Max tugged on the desperate, groaning legionnaire. The large soldier with shredded legs tumbled into the ditch. It was the Corsican Borgo. His face was covered with soot. Blood flowed out of his ears. A terrified child's expression dominated his wide-eyed gaze. Max gave his former sparring partner a reassuring nod. Muller handed Max a morphine ampoule. Max injected the Corsican in the thigh as Muller and Gregor applied tourniquets to Borgo's leaking legs.

"Pourquio?" Borgo questioned.

The three Germans exchanged glances. Grinning, Max answered, "Honneur et fidelite" (honor and fidelity).

A soft smile surfaced on the hard Corsican as he peacefully drifted toward drug-induced oblivion. Covered in dust, Muller pinched his nose. It smelled of shit. Muller pointed down at their patient.

"I won't fault a soldier for loss of muscular control after that hell storm," Max said. "I came very close to pissing my pants."

Borgo was not the only unhinged trench occupant with bowel and bladder issues. Down the narrow sandbagged ditch, shell-shocked soldiers twitched and trembled. Unable to comprehend the dire reality, they sat disconnected in their feces and urine. The calloused professionals in the herd slowly rose to peer out of the rancid sanctuary.

The runway is dead, Max surmised, scanning the damage. Mortar bombs randomly fell. He ignored the bloody carnage. Now was not the time to decipher whose misting rib cage lay before him. The sucker-punched headquarters bunker showed signs of life. Out of a battered artillery pit, four defiant howitzers returned fire.

"You have to admire the gesture," Muller commented.

"Kamraden," Gregor nudged.

Enemy infantry spilled over the mountain crest. In dish-shaped helmets and light-green uniforms, the People's Army flowed down the hillside, seeping into a network of virgin trenches.

"They will attempt to breach at the terminated machine-gun posts," Max declared, dipping down. At his feet, he picked up his fractured cigar. Breaking it in half, he lit up the jagged end. Securing the smoldering stogie with back teeth, he confiscated the munitions from a disoriented broken legionnaire.

"I underestimated the little yellow monkeys," a dejected Muller confessed, shaking his head. Observing his industrious companion, he asked, "What are you doing?"

Laden with ammunition and puffing on a cigar, Max crawled out of the shelter. Looking back, he answered, "I'm going to show those commie bastards they underestimated us."

CHAPTER FORTY-FOUR

In the sweltering backseat of a cheap taxi, Roche gazed out an open window as the squalor of the Philippines drifted by. A warm breeze caressed his throbbing head. The aftertaste of coffee and cigarettes lingered in a gritty mouth. Thick green aviator sunglasses shielded tender eyes. *It was supposed to be my day off*, he grumbled. Taking a deep breath, he envisioned sleeping in, nursing a hangover, and the potential of a late-afternoon massage. *A happy ending wasn't meant to be*, he conceded as the taxi pulled up to a Clark Air Force Base checkpoint. Glancing into his billfold, stuffed with colorful pesos, he grinned. "I can't use this where I'm going." Handing the wad to the wild-eyed Filipino cabbie produced a yellow-toothed smile. Exiting the rust bucket, he slung a duffel bag stuffed with dirty clothes over a shoulder. Returning the crisp sentry's salute, he plodded into the facility with a downcast head.

"Over here, Major Roche!" a voice hollered out above the distant drone of aircraft.

Roche raised his heavy head. Behind the wheel of a military jeep sat the nerdish Wellington Keagley. The academic, sporting thick glasses, sat erect with a cheery grin. "Jesus," Roche mumbled under his foul breath as he sauntered toward the utility vehicle. After tossing his hastily packed wardrobe into the backseat, he climbed aboard.

Keagley popped the clutch. The jeep launched forward, snapping Roche's frail neck. "Sorry for the short notice, Major," Keagley offered while driving erratically through the installation. "You'll be hitching a ride with the Thirty-First Air-Sea Rescue Squadron; it was the first flight available. I prepared a classified summary of the crisis for your review on the long flight." Taking his hand off the steering wheel, he patted a sealed red-brown accordion folder. Driving onto the tarmac, he accelerated toward a bloated-belly amphibious aircraft. The twin props came to life. Slamming on the brakes beside the howling seabird, Keagley offered, "I feel bad your Stateside trip was cancelled."

"No, you don't," Roche muttered, retrieving his luggage and classified reading material.

"Major!" Keagley hollered over the growling aircraft. Presenting a paperback book, he added, "I got you a farewell gift that may come in handy."

Roche adjusted his duffel bag strap and accepted the gesture. Looking down, he chuckled at the title, *Welcome to Vietnam, a Tourist Guide.* "Thanks, Keagley, but I would have preferred a bottle of booze."

Blowback blasted Roche as he tossed his duffel bag into the hatch on the left side of the fuselage. A welcoming arm reached out to assist with the short climb up a ladder into the flying boat. "Morning, Major," a twenty-something in a flight suit said while retrieving the ladder and securing the hatch. "This way, sir," he instructed toting Roche's luggage past the bunks used by the crew on long flights. He dropped the duffel bag in one of four empty seats just outside the cockpit's open hatch. A curious flight crew glanced back to examine the mysterious passenger dressed in baggy chinos and a loud aloha shirt. "Once we are airborne, would you care for a cup of joe?"

"That'd be great," Roche replied, buckling in. Leaning back in the uncomfortable bucket seat, he closed his eyes. The familiar acceleration of an aircraft taking flight lulled him toward sleep. Thoughts of the successful Philippines anticommunist psywar produced a smile.

"Your coffee, sir," nudged a friendly voice accompanied by the rich aroma of hot coffee.

Roche took a sobering breath and accepted a misting white ceramic mug, sporting the squadron's "Vigilance and Honor" logo.

"I hope you take it black."

"Is there any other way?" Roche joked. After taking a soft sip, he placed the hot mug on the seat beside him and plopped the accordion folder on his lap. Opening the document pouch, he found, filed in different slots, bundles of Vietnamese piastres, Laotian kip, and US greenbacks. From a side slot, he retrieved a forty-page memorandum titled "An Analysis of the Indochina Predicament—May 2, 1954." The CIA logo and "Top Secret" were prominently displayed on the cover page along with the warning, "This document contains classified information affecting the national security of the United States within the meaning of espionage laws, US Code Title 18, Sections 793, 794, and 798. It is to be seen only by US personnel especially indoctrinated and authorized to review such information."

Roche flipped over to the "Summary Discussion."

The desired goal was to have a military solution to the Vietnam problem. Excessive US military, economic, and technical aid was channeled to the French. France, seeking an honorable exit to the war, planned to strengthen a negotiating position with a major military victory. The strategy was to draw the Viet Minh into a set-piece battle where superior French artillery and airpower would decimate the communists.

The valley of Dien Bien Phu was garrisoned. Two airfields were installed to supply and reinforce the airhead if necessary. On March 13, 1954, the battle of Dien Bien Phu began. Communist capabilities were miscalculated. The Viet Minh had superior numbers, weapons and an ingenious battle plan. In the first five days, strong points Anne-Marie, Gabrielle, and Beatrice were overrun by superior forces. The airfields were rendered useless. A tightening communist siege ring has all but eliminated airdrops of reinforcements, munitions, food, and medical stores. It should be noted that the Agency's covert Civil Air Transport Airline and twenty-four CIA pilots are currently engaged in the airdrops of the encircled French garrison. As of this date, there are no American casualties.

Conditions at Dien Bien Phu are grim. A French defeat and Viet Minh victory is imminent within the next couple of days. Although discussed and debated at length, US military intervention is no longer considered an option. The battle of Dien Bien Phu will become an enormous morale and symbolic victory for the communists. France will abandon its military efforts in Indochina. To halt the communist advance in Southeast Asia, the United States will have to go it alone.

"Miscalculation?" Roche mumbled under his breath. *Is there no cure for this communist cancer?* he wondered. Looking up, he saw the pilot climbing out of the cockpit hatch. The naval aviator was tall; thick gray hair conflicted with his youthful features. With the swagger of a confident flyboy, he approached, holding a red-tartan thermos.

"Can I top off your coffee, Major?" he asked, standing in front of the mystery passenger.

"Nah, Captain," Roche responded. "But I'm up for a highball if you're buying."

The pilot chuckled. "Call me Goose," he offered, extending his free hand.

"Tom Roche. Thanks for the lift," Roche replied with a firm shake.

"First trip to Saigon?" Goose asked, glancing down at the Vietnam tourist manual.

"Yep," Roche answered, casually filing the classified document. "Any advice for a first timer?"

"Ask for lots of ice when ordering a drink," Goose advised. "And make sure you sheath your blade before sampling the fine local cuisine. The French disease is running rampant in the colonial port city."

"Thanks, Goose."

Exiting with the coffee jug, the pilot, looking back, informed his passenger, "We won't be heading to Saigon until after we complete our patrol of the South China Sea. Feel free to use one of the bunks. It is going to be a long flight."

Roche nodded as Goose climbed into the cockpit hatch. His thoughts drifted back to the dour memorandum. *Did someone draft a memo like this concerning the battle of Peleliu? The results of a miscalculation of the Japanese defenses and the strategic importance of that sliver of coral were ten thousand American casualties.* Miscalculation *is a kind word when generals and admirals really fuck up. The First Marine Division paid the price.* Recalling the lack of water during his Peleliu tenure, Roche swallowed. His breath accelerated. Disdain for Japan surfaced. *I'll never forgive the Empire of the Sun,* he vowed, retrieving the classified document. Flipping over the cover sheet, he realized the French high command really fucked up in Vietnam. Thinking of the common soldier, he paused. "God have mercy on the defenders of Dien Bien Phu," he muttered, returning to the text.

CHAPTER FORTY-FIVE

Isolated on the southern tip of the main French forces of Dien Bien Phu was Isabelle. The strongpoint was no more than a one-acre plot of swampland along the banks of the Nam Yum River. There were neither trees nor any other vegetation. A charred aircraft skeleton occupied a crater-pockmarked runway. In a gun pit ravaged by enemy artillery, only two of eleven fieldpieces were capable of firing. Ammunition was scarce. One out of three tanks was operational. A hospital bunker far exceeded capacity with over a hundred dying men. Evacuation was not an option. In shallow dugouts, the eighteen hundred defenders existing on minimal rations endured constant communist bombardment. Monsoon rains had filled the trenches with knee-deep mud. The daily shelling rearranged the muck, destroyed exposed ordinances, and launched rotting body parts on the morass's surface. It smelled of death and decay.

It was Friday night, May 7, 1954. Isabelle's sisters to the north slowly folded beneath the communist onslaught. Claudine radioed, "I'm afraid it is over. Isabelle is free to attempt a *percee de sang* (blood breakout) on her own."

Peering out of a dugout, Sergeant Palu's heartbeat accelerated. His grasp on a heavy gunnysack of canned food tightened. Mud geysers percolated across Isabelle. Motivating his departure with a silent countdown, he leaped out of the shelter. In a low crouch, he scampered through the kill zone. Orange sludge rained down. The pummeled ground shook. His boots grew heavier with each successful step. Seeing the crippled bridge spanning the Nam Yum, he realized he might actually deliver the message.

Flashes of light revealed the stoic faces of the dug-in T'ai Partisans of the 432nd Mobile Auxiliary Company observing Palu's river crossing. The solemn audience parted as the French sergeant dove into the shelter. The fortification was no more than a network of four-foot-deep trenches filled with a foot and a half of soupy swill. Squatting on an empty ammo box, a tribesman assisted Palu to his feet.

"Merci," Palu muttered, handing over the satchel of meager rations. There was a sense of order as the canned goods were passed down the line, opened, and consumed. Standing in the shallow mire, Palu shook the muck from his hands. After wiping a wet hand across his chest, he pulled a virgin pack of Chesterfields from a breast pocket. His audience stirred. "Unfortunately, we will have to share," he announced, delicately breaking a cigarette in half. The tiny stubs were handed out. Smoke soon diluted the stench. "Take pride in the fact that Isabelle was the only strong point not to be breached," Palu announced.

"Sergeant?" Loc questioned. "What are you saying?"

"It's over," Palu informed the troops. Several partisans immediately slithered out of the ditch. "Now is the time to flee," the Frenchman concurred. "Heading southeast, you may have a better chance of linking up with GMCA tribal commandos."

"What about you, Sergeant?" Loc asked, greedily sucking on the tiny nicotine tab.

"If I make it back to the hospital," Palu answered, "I'll tend to the wounded."

"Good luck, Paul," Loc offered, flicking the smoldering butt.

Loc felt a sense of relief as he crawled out of the ditch. He was free to go. The concealing comfort of the highland rain forest was his objective. A sizzling flare illuminated the night sky. He froze, squatting on his haunches. On the banks of the Nam Yum, fleeing partisans drifted south. In the main compound, Legionnaires flowed through a barbwire obstacle course in the same direction. Calculating an escape plan, Loc realized the devious communists would easily terminate the obvious route. *I have a better chance of slipping through the assaulting Viet Minh as a loner,* he reasoned. *They will be focused on the prize,* he concluded, taking off his steel bonnet. After smearing mud on his pale complexion, he headed west. Low to the ground, he utilized his talent as a silent, stalking Hmong hunter.

Ominous shadows drifted across the muddy battlefield. Sporadic gunfire popped in the distance. The air was rancid. Progress was slow. A fading star shell somewhere in the north captured glimpses of the trenches, swirling barbwire, and dead men. Artillery rounds whistled through the dark sky. *How quickly the French confidence faded when the unrelenting bombardment began*, Loc reflected. He glanced at the smoldering remnants of the Isabelle garrison. *The People's Army paid a heavy price for that plot of mud; they will show no mercy. Surrender was not an option. The long odds of escape are more appealing than having my head spiked. I just need to make it to the tree line*, he thought, jogging in the warm air. *Once in the jungle, I'll find a friendly clan and shed my uniform. Hopefully one day, I'll return to hunting down the communists on my terms.*

A massive explosion shook the earth. A fireball tumbled skyward above Isabelle. *The ammunition dumps*, Loc realized, embracing the battlefield. The artificial sun limned occupants fleeing south out of the dying garrison. Advancing Viet Minh patrols opened fire on the exposed fugitives. Seeking cover, Loc rolled into an open trench. Tumbling down the slimy embankment, he plunged into engulfing mud. Chest deep in the mire, he listened quietly as the one-sided firefight dwindled. Catching his breath, he tried to free himself. The muck held firm. *My God, I'm stuck*, he realized, clawing at the slick walls. Twisting from side to side, he sank deeper into the pit. Gasping on rank stench, his heart accelerated. *Is this my grave?* he wondered.

A massive white forearm reached down out of the darkness. Loc flinched. The arm shook impatiently. Loc latched onto the muscular lifeline. His benefactor emitted grunts extracting him from the grasping bog. Covered in mud, Loc crawled back onto the battlefield and mumbled, "Merci."

A stocky legionnaire, looking over his shoulder, nodded briefly before continuing his slithering escape. Loc latched onto the soldier's leg. The perturbed legionnaire responded with a scowl. Loc shook his head, pointed up, and hugging the earth, played dead. The white man followed suit. The escalating sound of sandaled feet preceded a wave of Viet Minh flowing downhill. "Tien-len! Tien-len!" the communist surge sang out, rippling past the lifeless bodies cluttering the hillside. The stampeding choir seemed endless. The rhythmic pounding of the Viet Minh assault slowly abated. Listening to the random stomp of straggling communists, Loc held his breath. Eventually his racing heartbeat was all he could hear. Opening a cautious eye, he scanned the quiet darkness.

"Parlez-vous Francais?" the Legionnaire whispered, sitting on the moist ground.

"Oui," Loc replied, rolling onto his side.

"Do you know how to navigate through the jungle?"

"I am Moua Loc of the Moua clan. Yes, I know the jungle beyond this valley."

"Please to meet you, Loc. I am Max Kohl. Let's go find that fucking jungle."

CHAPTER FORTY-SIX

N ews of the massive communist victory at Dien Bien Phu drifted far into the depths of the Vietnamese highlands. Standing in the middle of a Hmong hillside cemetery, Sergeant Jean Guillian realized the empowered Viet Minh would threaten his self-imposed exile. Dressed in the black tunic and trousers of his adopted community, he scanned the sloping grade of the grave-yard. Long black hair cascaded out of a blue headband knotted on the side. A full beard complemented his tan gaunt gaze. Mounds covered with stones marked graves. Small fences around each plot protected the entombed from the harm of evil spirits. Two simple white crosses stood out. Lieutenant Jacque Torcy was buried over a year ago. Corporal Marcel LaLande's funeral was six months after that. Squinting at LaLande's Christian marker, Guillian shook his head. The cause of LaLande's illness and rapid demise remained a mystery. Even the local shaman was perplexed. *Was it an insect bite, a rare tropical disease, or the corporal terminating his mission by entering the spirit world? It doesn't matter*, Guillian concluded. *Dead is dead.*

It isn't if the Viet Minh retaliate against France's Hmong allies, but when, Guillian realized. A munitions drop was desperately needed. Unfortunately the radio expired shortly after LaLande. The option of fleeing deeper into the rain forest produced angst. H'Liana was with child. Knowing he would soon be a father, Guillian smiled. *We will exist one day at a time*, he concluded. *Why should today be any different than yesterday?* Bidding adieu to his fallen comrades, he offered a respectful salute.

The sun hung high overhead as he meandered respectfully through the graveyard. A narrow dirt path snaked its way down to the mountainside com-munity. On the outskirts of town, an animated crowd of his neighbors gath-ered beneath the shade of a stilted residence. Guillian accelerated. "What is it,

Grandmother?" he asked, approaching an old woman standing at the back of the assembly.

"White men cheating death," she answered.

Guillian's heart skipped as he plunged into the gathering. The audience parted as he advanced. Lying on the ground were five soldiers in French uniforms. One appeared to be Hmong. Chue, squatting over the outstretched legs of a barefoot survivor, used a lit cigarette to extract feasting leeches. The man's pant legs were shredded. His swollen, black-and-blue feet were only identifiable by their anatomical location. Bloodsuckers covered his calves. Looking up at Guillian, Chue took a long, satisfying puff, preparing the glowing-red tip for the next sizzling termination.

Grinding the smoldering butt into a plumb dark-purple worm, Chue said, "This poor bastard is burning up with fever." Flicking his head in the direction of the four passed-out fugitives, he added, "The Hmong and the yellow-haired soldier staggered in first. The three other Fackee trickled in later. After we gave them water and cigarettes, they all fell into a deep sleep. The Hmong is Loc of the Moau clan. He informed me there were only five."

"Where did they come from?" Guillian asked.

"Dien Bien Phu."

"Oh seigneur," Guillian gasped. Nodding slowly, he mumbled, "Impressive." Standing over the snoring blond, he said, "Let's get them off the ground, wash out their wounds, launder their clothes. Once they awake, we'll feed them."

Chue instructed a covey of village girls in the bathing and laundry task.

Reaching down with both hands, Guillian grabbed the blond's shirt. The collar flipped over, revealing a swastika-embossed disk. Guillian flinched. Stepping back, rage simmered beneath a solemn expression.

"What is it?" Chue asked, squinting at the hooked cross medallion. "Is he from the tribe that killed your family?"

"He is not a Nazi today," a composed Guillian replied, reaching back down. Lifting the heavy German, he added, "Today he is a brother-in-arms." Elevating Max over his shoulder, he grinned. Even though he had not spoken French in months, the phrase "Encore un que la Grosse Bertha n'aura pas" rolled off his tongue.

"What does that mean?" Chue asked, picking up the groaning, feverish Frenchman.

"Yet another one that Big Bertha won't get," Guillian answered, hauling the dead weight toward the communal well. Depositing his load on a table next to a girl heating bathwater, he caught Chue's puzzled reaction to the translation. "In the First World War, a large German canon named Bertha was positioned far from Paris. The big gun pounded the city. The expression refers to enjoying moments in time without German intervention."

It was a crisp, clean highland morning. Pockets of cold air floated through the hillside community. Cooking fires sparked to life. In the distance, a cock crowed. Guillian stealthy ascended the stair treads of the survivor's stilted residence. He stood in the doorway undetected. The fever-stricken Felix lay in a comatose state. The tank crew driver's face was covered with beads of twinkling sweat. On the cot next to the grave Frenchman, Augustin, in a fetal position, mumbled incoherently. In low gear, Loc, the German, and Jean Paul slowly dressed. Guillian focused on the thirty-something Jean Paul. *J.P. seems likeable enough*, he reasoned. *Can I solicit his favor?* Stepping into the hovel, he said, "Good morning, gentlemen. How are we doing today?"

Slipping on a clean shirt, Max smiled and responded, "Good morning, Sergeant. I slept very well high above the ground with a full belly. Thank you again for your hospitality."

Guillian responded with an insincere nod. Addressing Jean Paul, he asked, "J. P., if you are up to the task, can you join me for a morning stroll? I have something I'd like to show you."

"Sure," Jean Paul responded, lacing up his boots. Looking at his able-bodied roommates, he asked, "Max, Loc, would you care to join us?"

Frowning at the inclusion, Guillian exited. At the base of the stairs, he waited for Jean Paul. As J. P. descended, he started to walk.

Catching up to his host, Jean Paul asked, "I hope you don't mind me inviting Max and Loc to join us?"

Glancing over his shoulder at the trailing German, Guillian quietly informed his guest, "I'm a Jew. If I am not cordial to your German companion, it's because my mother and me are the only members of my family who survived Nazi incarceration. My mother survived physically. Mentally, she is dead."

"Max is a good mate," Jean Paul responded. "On our jungle ordeal, he and Loc did all the heavy lifting. I owe him my life."

Guillian accelerated as the grade steepened. On high ground, he stopped in front of an elevated A-frame bamboo shed. Palm thatch leaves covered the steep pitched roof. A large open doorframe exposed stacked bundles of raw opium. Guillian addressed the approaching Jean Paul. "This is last year's harvest. The Chinese caravan that barters for the drug was absent this fall."

Max and Loc lingered into the presentation.

"I fear France will abandon their Hmong allies," Guillian continued. "The Viet Minh will give no quarter. We require munitions." Focused on Jean Paul, his tone stiffened. "I need a broker to negotiate an arms deal." Acknowledging the tightly packed jungle warehouse with a slow waving hand, he added, "This is our currency."

Jean Paul stood dumbfounded. Breaking the awkward silence, he asked, "What do you want?"

Guillian's expression soured. "I'm soliciting your services. I'm asking you to find a party interested in exchanging guns for opium."

"Me!" Jean Paul exclaimed. "Why me? I wouldn't know what do. Why can't you do it?"

"Because this is my home now," Guillian snapped. "I can't leave my pregnant wife in the middle of looming communist reprisals."

"I'm sorry, Sergeant," Jean Paul said sheepishly. "I'm just a common soldier, a tank crew radio operator. I just want to go home."

"I have no home," Max declared, injecting himself into the conversation. "I'll do it." He looked at Loc. The tribesman nodded his inclusion. "We will do it," he clarified.

A skeptical Guillian studied the blue-eyed Aryan with concern.

"Sergeant," Max offered, "when I was at death's doorstep, you took me in. I will be eternally in your debt. The favor you ask is a simple task. When we depart, give Loc and me a sample of your product for bait. Fishing in the pond of Corsican drug dealers, we will snare you an arms deal."

"I misread you, Max," Guillian confessed.

"No apology necessary, my friend," Max responded.

CHAPTER FORTY-SEVEN

The setting sun sparked long shadows of thousands of megalithic pots sprinkled across the green rolling hills of central Laos. The lipped urn boulders varied in height and diameter from three to ten feet. The rocks were chiseled out more than two thousand years ago. In random clusters, ranging from a few to several hundred, the jars of the Plain de Jars basked in the fading sunlight. A sputtering single-engine airplane disrupted the scenic panorama.

Descending quickly, the Cessna's silhouette floated across the decorated fertile plateau. After buzzing the archaeological landscape, the prop airplane kissed the red-clay tarmac of the Phong Savin airport. Trailed by crimson dust, the aircraft taxied over to one of the many corrugated tin hangars. The pilot abruptly cut the engines and disembarked. Displaying discomfort, he briskly walked to the side of the large tin shed and relieved himself. Exhibiting a confident pilot's stride, Rene Bergot, buttoning his fly, returned to his plane.

The tall, lanky Bergot, a French Air Force veteran, was an agreeable chap with a quick wit who kept his drinking in check. As an independent contractor, he never questioned the payloads he flew out of this blossoming frontier town. Like the other hard-core opportunists flocking to Phong Savin, he was becoming wealthy. Opening the baggage hatch, he hollered, "Kale!"

The Laotian mechanic Kale, wiping greasy hands with a red rag, peered out of the hangar. A perpetual cigarette dangled from his lower lip. Scratching matted hair with slick black fingers, he snorted smoke and sluggishly answered the call.

Anticipating a one-sided conversation with Kale, Begot chuckled. "Good evening, Kale. If you unload and secure the smokes and liquor, you can have a carton of Camels and a bottle of Johnny Walker."

Kale tossed his soiled red rag aside and reached into the cargo hold. Pulling out a cardboard box, he plodded toward the hangar beneath a puffing cloud of cigarette smoke.

"Merci, Kale," Bergot offered.

Evening approached as Bergot entered the remote town of Phong Savin. In a community dominated by steep Laotian pitched roofs, the King Cobra Lodge stood out as an architectural misfit more suited for the African veldt. The Cobra was the preferred watering hole for drug dealers seeking to fill the void of France's abandoned opium monopoly. Kerosene lanterns illuminated the elevated porch that encircled the large single-story inn. Bergot jogged up the tavern's bowed entrance stairs. The structure vibrated with raucous clamor. The small lobby consisted of a bamboo front desk manned by a local teen in a skinny black necktie. Ratty, stained cushions highlighted a rattan sofa set. A mounted deer's head and a sign that read, "No Smoking Opium in Lobby," adorned the wood-paneled walls.

Acknowledging the young clerk with a half salute, Bergot plunged into the adjoining rowdy saloon. "Excusez-moi," he muttered, slicing through a suit-and-tie cluster of Vietnamese gangsters. In a well-lit corner, he took pause beside a round table occupied by a stable of young Asian flesh. A sign over the working girls questioned, "You want a girlfriend? See bartender." After scanning the fillies, Bergot squinted hard into the smoke-filled cantina. The babble was deafening. Shattered glass punctuated the racket. A compilation of cheap perfume, smoke, stale beer, and sweat filled the warm air. Light faded as it reached across a maze of tables and chairs inhabited by seated and standing patrons. A long bar ran the length of the back wall. There were no vacancies between the mobsters and French war veterans bellied up to the watering trough. Behind the counter, in the eye of the storm, the plump, happy, Buddha-looking Jimmy and two bar-backs toiled at a feverish pace. Large drops of sweat clung to Jimmy's polished crown as he fulfilled the drink order of a large black man. At well over six feet, the Moroccan Rifle Regiment veteran stood out. An open shirt exposed a muscular chest garnished with a patch of gray. A closely cropped silver ring crowned his large round head. Spotting *le Gorille Gris,* Bergot grinned, shimmying forward. Weaving through the crowd, he passed a Yank in a loud floral shirt and aviator sunglasses, ordering bourbon with lots of ice. Squeezing up to the counter alongside the Gray Gorilla, Bergot hollered, "Good evening Hakeem!"

"Rene!" Hakeem exclaimed heartily, patting the French pilot's back. "How was Saigon?"

"It's crazy," Bergot answered, trying to get the barkeep's attention. "France's military structure is hastily being dismantled for the next war in Algeria. A US wind is initiating a changing of the guard."

Flicking his large noggin in the direction of the Hawaiian-shirted American, Hakeem injected, "Looks like the CIA is staking a claim on the Deuxieme Bureau's vacated opium business."

Stealing a quick glance of the Yank, Bergot shrugged. "You can't blame the Americans, trafficking in jam pays the bills." Getting Jimmy's attention, he asked Hakeem, "Is our German friend here tonight?"

"Oui," Hakeem responded, motioning with a massive paw holding a petite lacquer jigger. "Max and Loc are somewhere over there."

Wiping his moist head with a bar towel, Jimmy asked, "What can I get you, Rene?"

"Three beers," Bergot responded. Pointing at Hakeem's empty glass, he added, "And a pastis for le Grille Gris."

"Merci," Hakeem mumbled.

"Put it on my tab, Jimmy," Bergot directed, snatching up three chilled amber bottles. "Excusez-moi…Excusez-moi," he muttered, blazing an erratic path through the crowd.

Through a smoky haze, Max and Loc, seated in the corner, emerged. The German's bleach-blond locks complemented tan features. A snug exposed shoulder holster emphasized a muscular torso. As he was engaged in an animated conversation, the maduro stogie lodged in the corner of Max's mouth emitted random puffs. Leaning back, a focused Loc, in a short-sleeve white dress shirt, sucked hard on a cigarette. The Hmong warrior had adopted a taste for Western fashion.

"Gentlemen," Bergot exclaimed, plopping three fresh bottles on the blistered tabletop.

"Good timing, Rene!" Max responded, grabbing a cold brew. Raising the bottle, he added, "Danke."

Pulling out a chair, Bergot took a seat and a swig of beer. "Ah," he sighed. "It's been a long day."

"Did our jam sample arouse any Saigon buyers?" Max asked.

Bergot slowly nodded. Bending forward, he informed the Isabelle survivors, "The kilo had an exceptionally high morphine content and sparked the interest of a retiring French intelligence officer. A weapons for jam exchange is doable. The Deuxieme Bureau captain's agent is a Corsican, Petru Rossi." Taking a breath, he cautioned, "Petru Rossi is a Unione Corse assassin. He has a reputation for rubbing garlic on the barrel of his pistol before a kill to enhance the bullet's sting."

Loc snickered.

Chuckling, Max asked, "Does he rub starch on his snake before coupling to enhance the stiffness?"

Bergot, mustering up a grin, sighed. "Don't take the gangster lightly, Max. There is a high degree of risk when dealing with Corsican fanatics."

"Set up a parlay," Max instructed the pilot. "I'd deal with the devil if I had to for our commando friend."

Bergot nodded his acceptance. Focused on the German, he asked, "Are the rumors true, that your mystery commando is a Jew?"

Max's spine stiffened. Puffing hard on the cigar, he studied the pilot. "Our commando brother desires anonymity. Let's just leave it at that."

"Fair enough, Max," Bergot conceded downing his beer. Placing the empty bottle on the tabletop, he confirmed, "I'll set up a meeting with Rossi." Pushing back, he rose. "Now if you'll excuse me, I need to see Jimmy about purchasing a girlfriend for the night."

"Good job, Rene," Max muttered to the departing pilot. As Bergot disappeared into the crowd, he snorted. "Why ask if Guillian was a Jew? What difference does it make?"

"I don't understand," Loc interjected. "Are the Jews a rival clan of your people?"

"I'm afraid it's more complicated than that, partner," Max confessed. "It's a deep wound that may never heal." Taking a sobering breath, he paused. "As a POW, reports of the German concentration camps surfaced. The gassing and extermination of the Jewish people by the Third Reich was a mystery to all the

German prisoners in France. The Americans required us to watch a half-hour film about German atrocities committed against the Jews. Reactions varied. Disbelief, shock, doubt—some even convinced themselves it was a Hollywood propaganda production. As for me, the reality of being associated with extreme inhumane hatred cut deep into my sense of being."

"But, Max, you said it was a mystery to you. You didn't know about it," Loc offered.

"Didn't I?" Max questioned. "I was taught that Jews were vermin, less than human. That they were to blame for all the woes of the world. As a boy, I not only believed it; I was an active participant in the Hitler Youth. We vandalized Jewish businesses, tormenting and humiliating the shopkeepers. Those who spoke out against Hitler as well as the Jews needed to be removed, incarcerated. I had no idea where the Gestapo was taking them, nor did I care, until I saw the thirty-minute film."

"We hated the Laotian low-land merchants," Loc interjected. "I was taught that they were nothing but cheats and thieves. I know they despised the Hmong. I don't dwell on it." Flicking an ash, he looked at Max and grinned. "We are both orphans of war, men without a tribe. You pulled me out of mud. You didn't have to, but you did. Guillian brought us back from the dead. He didn't have to, but he did. He asked us to secure him weapons. We don't have to, but we will. There is nothing complicated about that."

"Thanks, partner," Max muttered.

CHAPTER FORTY-EIGHT

It was the summer of 1954 in Saigon. The city pulsed with an erratic beat of uncertainty. Vietnam was temporally being divided into north and south. In the seedy Cholon district, the bars, brothels, opium dens, and gambling halls flourished under capitalistic exploitation. It was business as usual. It had rained earlier in the evening. Wet roadways reflected the colorful neon signage soliciting sinners. The air was thick. It smelled of wet garbage. On the slick sidewalk, Max and Loc walked side by side.

"You know," Max commented, reflecting on their mission. "I killed many men as a soldier. The first was a Canadian sergeant during the battle of Caen. We surprised each other. For a brief second, we looked into each other's eyes. Time froze. The image of his apprehensive expression still haunts me to this day. I was quicker. I shot him in the face. Just like that, he no longer existed. After that, I didn't see humans when I shot. They were just targets. In the Red River Delta, I fired into the surging tide of attacking Viet Minh with a calculated survival instinct. I was indifferent to the lives I terminated. In the wake of the communist assault, dying Viet Minh shouted insults at the defenders of hill one-seventeen. At that moment, they became human again."

"Unlike you, Max, I take pleasure in terminating the communist militants who exterminated my clan. I view the Viet Minh as fanatics, brutally punishing and killing those who oppose a philosophy that they don't even comprehend," Loc explained.

"I can appreciate that, partner. That is how I feel about tonight's agenda," Max responded. "I'm looking forward to it. It's not just that the Corsican tried to swindle us on the arms deal, beat my favorite whore, and placed a bounty on our heads. Petru Rossi is shit. The world would be a better place without him breathing its air."

"What is our plan?" Loc asked.

"I've sampled the pleasures at the House of Butterflies on several occasions," Max disclosed. "It is a two-story labyrinth of boudoirs. Most of the patrons are French military personnel so not a concern. A couple of large Asian bullyboys are the visible security. The brutes rely on size to intimidate rowdy customers. A targeting pistol should neutralize them." Pausing, Max took several puffs off his expiring cigar. Satisfied with an examination of the glowing red tip, he continued, "Everything is available for a price at the brothel. We walk in the front door, buy the location of Mr. Rossi, and you secure our exit while I seek out and terminate the hostile. After that, we calmly blend in with the exiting masses and fly to Laos." Taking a satisfying toke of his stogie, he concluded, "In the next couple of days, another unsolved murder will appear on page 3 of *Le Journal de Saigon*."

Standing in the courtyard of the brothel, Max and Loc paused. Red lanterns strung overhead produced a seductive crimson glow. Moths fluttered in the tempting light. Beneath a sparkling night sky, the wet tables and chairs were vacant with the exception of a passed-out sailor. A disinterested bartender wiped down the outdoor bamboo bar with a dishrag. In stark contrast, the facade of the House of Butterflies was alive. The structure emitted the sounds of seedy passion. Drapes waved out of open windows. Silhouettes drifted across the portholes of softly lit bedding chambers.

"You ready to do this, partner?" Max asked.

Loc confirmed the pistol concealed in the small of his back and nodded.

"Let's go see how good the American's information is," Max muttered, stepping forward. Ascending the stoop, he took a deep breath and opened the thick wooden door.

The foyer was dim. In the shadows, young girls occupying an array of colonial furniture stirred. As Max's and Loc's eyes adjusted to the dark atmosphere, a beaded curtain parted. The house madam made her entrance. Max grinned. She had put on weight since his youthful visits. A flabby midriff burdened the floral motif of her yellow silk gown. Behind a liberal application of makeup, she attempted to conceal the years. Utilizing a black lacquered cigarette holder, she took a prenegotiating puff. Exhaling exposed nicotine-stained dentures.

"What is your pleasure, gentlemen?" she inquired with a raspy drawl.

Flashing a five-hundred-piastre note, Max answered, "We are here for the Corsican Rossi."

Loc focused on her painted features. Concern sparked in her dark eyes. He reached back for his pistol.

"We don't want any trouble," she signaled loudly, snatching the offered currency.

As anticipated, two large goons emerged from behind the beaded veil. Taut white singlets exposed intimidating limbs. Greasy scowls indicated an interrupted meal. One snorted like a bull. The other growled like a junkyard dog.

Ignoring the bullyboys, Max produced another powder-blue bank note and reiterated, "Where is Petru Rossi?"

Brothel security latched onto the German. Loc drew his pistol and flexed a targeting arm. The gun barrel kissed a thug's glistening forehead. The henchmen wilted, taking a retreating step back. The pimp mama, crossing her arms, stood defiantly. All was quiet. Scrutinizing the madam, Max pondered his options. A shrill scream from upstairs neutralized the stalemate.

"You good, partner?" Max questioned, drawing his pistol.

Focused on the goons, Loc nodded.

The German took flight in search of the whore-beating sadist. The thump of his heavy stride faded as he ascended the staircase. The furious madam, sucking hard on a lacquered smoking stick, snorted smoke. A bullyboy took calming breaths through an open mouth. His associate used the back of a hand to wipe his sweat-leaking forehead. Loc eyed the trio as a patient hunter. His sensitive ears focused on the hostile environment. As a child of war, he could distinguish the distinctive sounds of various small-arms fire. From upstairs, Max's Tokarev pistol rang out. A heavy thud followed. The second-story creak of brothel production paused. In the foyer, the flock of lambs gasped. The panting bullyboy started to hyperventilate.

"You and the German will pay dearly for this," the madam delightfully informed Loc.

Loc responded by cocking back his weapon's hammer. A second familiar gunshot popped, followed by a third. A rapid clip-clop descended the staircase.

Max, sporting a large knot on his forehead, appeared. Handing the mama-san a wad of colorful currency, he muttered, "For your troubles."

Cautiously, the Isabelle survivors exited. In the courtyard, they accelerated into a brisk stride. Behind them, the House of Butterflies erupted like a violated hornets' nest.

"Did you terminate the threat?" Loc questioned.

"To savor the kill, I hesitated," Max confessed. "Like a fucking amateur...I hesitated."

"Is Rossi dead?" Loc reiterated.

"Some goon burst in. I killed him as that Corsican shit threw an elbow," Max answered as he instinctively touched the tender bump. "I shot Rossi in the back as he leaped out the window but can't confirm the kill." Beneath the wail of a distant police siren, he muttered, "Never hesitate."

CHAPTER FORTY-NINE

A light rain hindered a wakening Saigon. Beneath the protection of an Imperial Hotel awning, Tom Roche enjoyed a curbside cup of Vietnamese coffee. Introduced to coffee during French colonization, the Vietnamese transformed the caffeinated beverage into a potent, rich roasted delicacy. The morning drizzle and a Camel cigarette augmented the soothing comfort of the unique cup of joe. A continuous cyclist brigade, sprouting umbrellas, peddled past the outdoor café. In search of fares, a pod of blue-and-white Renault taxis trolled the hotel's facade. On the sidewalk, all classes were represented. Flicking an ash, Roche singled out the women strolling by. Female laborers in conical hats, baggy trousers, and white blouses maintained a brisk stride. In a traditional *Ao Dai* dress, consisting of a long-paneled blouse over loose-fitting slacks, a local beauty strutted eloquently in high-heeled sandals. The pointed hat strap under her chin emphasized an oriental innocence. Two clerical workers in Western skirts, blouses, and heels held hands and giggled like schoolchildren. Roche grinned. There were definitely no heifers in this herd. Glancing over his shoulder, he spotted Matthews and his blue-satin-clad harlot in front of the hotel's doublewide entry door. Roche shook his head. Matthews appeared refreshed, satisfied. Daylight had erased the rented female's Asian charm. The whore gave him a quick peck on the cheek before merging into foot traffic.

"Wow!" Matthews exclaimed, pulling out the bamboo chair across from Roche. "That Vietnamese thoroughbred just took me for one hell of a ride."

"Spare me the details, Don Juan," Roche grumbled. "We are here for a purpose."

"Lighten up, Tom," Matthews replied, summoning the lone waiter. After securing a misting java cup, he took pause to inhale the seductive aroma. "Hmmm," he hummed, closing his eyes. Leaning back, he raised the hot brew and toasted, "To the Saigon Military Mission and the expeditious solution to the Viet Minh."

"I wish I shared your optimism," Roche snorted. "The French underestimated Ho Chi Minh, and it cost them Indochina." Taking a toke off his Camel, he grinned. "When I was in China after the war, I had a couple of beers with a fellow OSS agent who actually knew Ho Chi Minh. I didn't give it much thought until my classified Vietnam briefing. Ho really impressed the shit out of this agent. He referred to the fifty-something revolutionary, who rescued downed American pilots, as 'Old Man Ho.' At the time, Ho had an affinity to the United States. Apparently, in Ho's youth, he worked in the galley of a French freighter that landed in Hoboken. The young Ho took a ferry to Manhattan and the subway to Chinatown. Ho admired the acceptance of the Chinese in the New York melting pot."

"He's a communist," Matthews injected. "The Soviets and Filipino Huks were also once our allies."

"Have you read the reports? Ho reached out to the United States after the war, seeking support for an independent Vietnam. We backed the French instead, forcing Ho to turn to the Soviets and Chinese as willing sponsors. With communist backing, he transformed a guerilla movement into a formidable conventional army. The Viet Minh victory at Dien Bien Phu will embolden communist uprisings throughout Southeast Asia. A reunited Vietnam is a communist Vietnam."

"That's your problem, Tom," Matthews said, stealing a cigarette. "You're thinking like a military man. I, on the other hand, have a marketing background. The solution is simple. We create a product and then sell it to the world. The product is the Republic of Vietnam. Packaged in liberty, freedom, and democracy, it's an easy sell. A negative ad campaign against our communist competitors to the north will enhance our product's value." Exhaling a nicotine plume, he concluded, "It's all smoke and mirrors."

Roche nodded his concurrence.

Scooting back in his chair, Matthews crossed a leg. In the comfortable repose, he took a refreshing toke. Exhaling, he asked, "How did the Aryan poster boy do with the Corsican assignment?"

"His name is Max...Max Kohl," Roche corrected. "The German and the Hmong are really quite likable. My contacts informed me they caught a flight to Phong Savin early this morning. The body of a Binh Xuyen thug was found at the crime scene. The Corsican's corpse hasn't surfaced. I'm having the hospitals and morgue checked for a confirmation."

"Are you planning to use the German again?"

"Most definitely." Roche nodded. "Like I said, he's personable. He has an aura about him. You know the type, the players in our cast who are impervious to death."

CHAPTER FIFTY

S tomping through the House of Butterflies bedding chamber maze, Carlo Coty exaggerated each pounding step. "Everybody has a hand out," he growled through gritted teeth. *One little shooting incident and the police and press expect a bonus.* Grasping a doorknob, he swung open the barrier. Three working girls sitting Indian style on the wooden floor were playing cards. They jumped at the intrusion. "Where is he?" Coty mumbled, slamming the door shut and resuming his quest. *How much will this eventually cost me?* he wondered, peering into the adjacent bedroom. Standing in the doorway, he took a composing breath.

The French medical officer Henri Tillie stood gazing out the open second-floor window. Urban noise and a warm breeze caressed his stoic expression. The epaulets of his crisp khaki uniform denoted the rank of lieutenant. A soft, satisfied smile slowly graced his lips. Kneeling in front of the Frenchman, a naked dove demonstrated her oral talents. Her long raven-black hair swayed back and forth across a bare back as she enthusiastically serviced the brothel's medical examiner.

"Stow your *cigare*, Lieutenant!" Coty declared. "I'm not paying you to sample the merchandise."

Henri placed his hands on the young courtesan's oscillating head. Closing his eyes, he pleaded softly, "Five more minutes."

"No!" Coty snapped. "I have a medical emergency. You'll have to postpone having my talented employee inhaling your smoke."

Henri begrudgingly stepped back. "What is it, Coty?" he asked uncomfortably securing his fly.

"Gunshot victim," Coty replied, abruptly turning to exit.

The Corsican set a fast pace. Henri, adjusting his crotch, lingered behind. They proceeded down the wooden stairway. A house amah was mopping the lobby floor. She never looked up as the owner and doctor gingerly walked across the sleek surface. On the tired carpet lining a long corridor, they accelerated. At the end of the hallway, Coty unlocked a door and entered. The medical examiner followed.

The windowless room was small. A slow, rotating ceiling fan emitted a pulsating squeal. A nightstand lamp, sans shade, brightly illuminated the chamber. On a metal-framed bed, a gangly naked man lay facedown. Large blood splotches stained the white linen bedding. Wadded up on the victim's lower back was a blood-saturated terry cloth towel.

Coty locked the door. Walking over to the beaming nightstand, he snatched up a half-full bottle of Johnny Walker scotch. After taking a swig, he asked, "Can you save him?"

Henri delicately removed the wet, concealing towel. A single blood-clotted entry wound appeared. He motioned for the electric lamp. Coty obliged. "Is this the man who was shot last night?" Henri inquired, examining the ballistic puncture with a cautious finger.

"My name is Petru Rossi," the patient growled into the pillow, his body jostling for comfort.

Henri winced. Catching his breath, he handed Coty the lamp and informed the victim, "Well, Mr. Rossi, we need to get you to a hospital."

"No!" Petru grimaced. "If the men who did this think I'm dead, my vengeance will taste sweeter."

"Who did this?" Coty casually inquired, taking a nip off the bottle.

"That Boche bastard Max and his savage sidekick, Loc," Petru declared, wiggling uncomfortably facedown.

"Max Kohl?" Henri questioned.

"Max Kohl is a dead man." Petru snorted as his breathing accelerated.

Henri motioned for Coty to exit. "We'll be right back," he informed Petru. "I'll get you something for the pain."

Outside the sealed room, the doctor gave his diagnosis. "He lost a lot of blood and requires a transfusion. I can administer that here. The bullet appears to be lodged next to his spine. For it to be extracted, he will have to go to a hospital. If the projectile is not removed, and he survives, there will certainly be long-term painful consequences."

"Who is this Max Kohl?" Coty asked, lighting up a cigarette.

"The man who walked out of Isabelle." Henri snickered. "The German and a Hmong named Moua Loc gained some notoriety from breaking out of the siege at Dien Bien Phu."

"Moua Loc?"

"Oui," Henri replied. "His father was some famous Meo marksman."

Taking a reflective puff of his cigarette, Coty grinned.

"What do you want me to do about Rossi?" Henri asked.

"Give him the transfusion," Coty answered, walking away. Halfway down the corridor, he added, "Leave the bullet in his back."

***

49074212R00155

Made in the USA
San Bernardino, CA
12 May 2017